KU-355-073

THE WORD FOR LOVE

Also by
ALAN BURGESS

★

NO RISKS—NO ROMANCE
COME LIVE WITH ME
THE SMALL WOMAN
SEVEN MEN AT DAYBREAK
THE LOVELY SERGEANT

THE WORD FOR LOVE

*

ALAN BURGESS

THE
COMPANION BOOK CLUB
LONDON

This edition is published by
The Hamlyn Publishing Group Ltd. and is
issued by arrangement with
Michael Joseph Ltd.

*Made and printed in Great Britain
for the Companion Book Club
by Odhams (Watford) Ltd.*

S.4.569 U/C

PART I

CHAPTER ONE

In the storeroom, the flurry of passion over, the madness blurred into a physical peace, reality crept back like a slow return from sleep, and with it the inescapable sense of guilt.

His universe, which for the past few seconds had been contracted into a grappling of flesh, a fierce probing for fulfilment, now widened and expanded to familiar peripheries: he was aware of his own body again, his heavy breathing, an arm cramped under the body of the African girl. He pulled it free and rolled over on to his back.

Motes of dust rose from the sacks of maize on which they sprawled, and he watched them float upwards and disappear into the haze of sunlight sifting between the top of the clay walls and the heavy thatch. Other sounds intruded: a fly gyrating in frenzied spurts against the clouded window pane, someone whistling tunelessly in the police compound outside.

He looked down at the face of the girl, tranquil again after the recent struggle. The thick, black lashes curved down lightly upon the smooth, pale-coffee cheeks. Her small nose was straight, the nostrils only slightly flared; her lips were full but without the pouting thickness of the Bantu. Somewhere back in her ancestry, no doubt, a light-skinned, thin-lipped Arab trader had taken his pleasure, and long since departed, dhow-bound for Paradise.

'Lupin,' he said quietly. And then louder, 'Lupin!'

She did not answer and he did not move. His mind was clear again, but now uneasy, almost as if a vaco-litre was feeding a slow drip of disquiet into his bloodstream. What he had done was stark staring madness. Lunacy in the hot sun! Sarah? Yes, he could understand that. But this African girl? He had watched her in the kitchen, or as she'd served the meal, noted only subconsciously, he would have sworn, the way her bosom pressed against her dress, how the old print dress of Milly's flared against her hips. But never with awareness, never sensuously, never desiringly. Or was he deceiving himself?

The sun! It must be the sun! 'My lord, as mitigation of this man's guilt one must accept the fact that in certain parts of Rhodesia the temperature can rise to as high as one hundred degrees in the shade.' Thirteen years in the police force and a man's mind responded to certain stimulae with courtroom oratory or flippant forensic logic, 'Oh yes, my lord, in the Sabi valley the sun burns down from a brazen sky and you fry in your own sweat!'

But here it was like lying on the bottom of a deep dark pool. From the cool pebbles a great fish exhausted after the frenzy and milt over the deposit of eggs would stare up with bright, unwinking eye through the clear water to the pale green ceiling high above. Did he know the massive soporific peace which Field now felt lying against the warm, motionless body of the girl?

He should, he knew, move himself, conceal the evidence of his action, hurry Lupin out of the storeroom, warn her not to talk. The door was unlocked. A dozen African convicts were working around the lawn outside. At any moment someone might pass and peer through the grimy window. It was, after all, scarcely the position expected of a B.S.A. Inspector of Police in the middle of a fine and sunny working morning.

Yet he did not move. Some wilful perversity beyond rationalization kept him there, extracting the last illogical seconds of sensual pleasure from his inertia.

The months of European food, or at least the remnants from Milly's kitchen, had curved Lupin's body. Her skin was really quite pale. It was quite obvious why they had made her the rain goddess. The legend of the golden stranger, the white god descending from the clouds, was deep-rooted in man's primitive subconsciousness. No longer was she the girl who had stood naked, skinny and immature, under the falling screen of silver water above the Sabi river; now, with the thin nylon blouse rumpled up so that a light band of skin showed above her waistband, her skirt above her knees, she was provocative and shapely.

In South Africa, of course, she would be classed as 'non-white', unable to marry a white man, forced to carry an identity pass, permitted only to live in a designated area. Here in Southern Rhodesia, she was 'African', but then all the white Rhodesians called themselves 'African', so the whole issue was confused. According to your emotional flash-points, the anomalies of the great continent were enough to make you laugh or cry. In Addis Ababa in the north, comely Ethiopian girls waved from the main street brothels offering predictable delights, and yet, at the southern end of the continent, merely to be found within the arms of a girl with Bantu blood in her veins was an offence punishable by flogging and gaol.

In Paris or London with the right impresario and television appearances, Lupin might emerge as a new Lena Horne or Eartha Kitt. Field had often heard her singing as she dusted and tidied up, and her voice wasn't bad. In New York, as a 'high yaller', she would be able to sing sad songs of Negro persecution, probably marry some white American implicated beyond recall by the sensuous abrasiveness of sex and racialism; but here, almost inevitably, she was condemned within a year or two to marry a houseboy back from the big city with his accumulated wages and new wisdom. He would delight her with his stetson-size hat, pointed shoes and light coloured jacket, and in ten years' time, blowzy and unattractive, she would squat on the verandah of some shack in the Tribal Trust Lands, her body bloated with incessant child bearing, a few summers removed from the other skinny, bag-breasted grannies sucking cheroots through toothless gums. Leave life to the natural wastage of the African social system, and, by God, it was cruel.

His eyes, suddenly curiously alert and perceptive, turning from the girl, scanned instinctively a sheet of paper pinned to the shelving. Perched behind it were the orderly bottles of linseed oil, turpentine, and brushes, the tin of soft soap, and the new, neatly-folded Union Jack and written across the top in the round schoolboy hand of Patrol Officer

Potterson, and underlined, was 'Prisoners' Rations'. Underneath the list: '1 lb. 8 ozs. mealie meal, 6 ozs. beans, ½ lb. fresh meat, 1 oz. fat, ¾ oz. salt, 1 oz. suger; soap, one bar per week.' Sadly Field realized that Potterson had spelt sugar with an 'e'.

The sudden stiffening of the girl's body startled him out of his day-dream. She made a choking noise in her throat, the fingernails of her hand lying limply against his forearm digging fiercely into his skin. He swung his head to look at her, saw that her frightened eyes were staring at the window and glanced across in time to catch a blur of shadow moving away. Left behind as proof that the shadow had been no cloud moving across the sun, was a small, cleaned circle of glass made by the peeper's forefinger.

She sat up, dragging her skirt down over her knees, struggling to get off the mealie sacks, clicking and clucking indignantly in her Sabi Shangaan dialect like a young hen chased from its nest.

'Lupin!' Field said sharply, but she ignored him. 'Wait,' he said and put out a hand to stop her but she brushed it off, and jerking away scurried across the hut. A blinding oblong of yellow light struck his eyes as she swung open the door. It closed behind her and she had gone.

'Bloody idiot!' he said angrily. Twenty pairs of eyes would see her racing out into the compound and wonder what the hell was the matter.

'Bloody idiot girl!' he repeated, taking his time as he lifted himself off the sacks, brushed his shorts and shirt and did up his buttons. He picked up his cap and dusted it off. He made to move towards the door, remembered his sunglasses and stopped to pick them off the floor where they had fallen. What the devil had he come to the storeroom for in the first place? The storeroom entry book, that was it. He found it on the shelf next to the kerosene can and tucked it under his arm. At the doorway he hesitated and took a deep breath. He opened the door and stepped through, turning the key in the lock behind him. The sun was very hot. Even with the protection of his sunglasses he could feel the glare in his eyes and its heat across his shoulders through the thin uniform shirt.

Fifteen yards away, five prisoners wearing the regulation issue of faded red shirts and khaki shorts, sliced vaguely at the coarse grass with machetes and turned their heads to stare. One muttered something, and they all sniggered.

Field snapped, 'Constable, keep these men at work, this is a prison rota, not a picnic.'

The African constable, grey-shirted, with green-banded khaki topee and rifle slung over his shoulder jumped to attention. 'Yes, sah,' he said, and shouted at the convicts but still grinning they continued to slash at the grass with complete disinterest, and, walking away, Field reflected that there was no way known to civilized man which would alter their demeanour. 'Dumb insolence,' they called it in the army. The B.S.A. police had words to define it. 'Conduct to the prejudice of good order and discipline,' they said. But try and enforce *that* as statutory law!

Instinctively Field headed for the house. She would run back there. He hadn't the faintest idea what he would say to her but the impulse which he recognized as one compounded of anxiety and a peculiar sort of exaltation impelled him in that direction.

The police post at Chapanda stood on a hillside, an escarpment really, looking down over the tiny, tree-shaded settlement of single-storey bungalows, shops and houses and the one large tourist hotel. Ten miles away, dark blue against a light blue sky you could see the jagged mountains which separated Southern Rhodesia from Portuguese East Africa. It was, by police standards, the smallest sort of unit: one European inspector, two European patrol officers, Potterson in the office and Longman, who was on leave at that moment, one African sergeant, twelve African constables. At the back were the African lines, sealed off by barbed wire, which held the round, thatched, pole and dagga huts where the African constables lived with their wives and families. The bachelor quarters of the two patrol officers stood to the right of the low, four-roomed concrete police station, the mandatory Union Jack hanging from a tall, white flag pole in front. Field's old-fashioned, rambling wooden bungalow built when the police post was first established in 1901 stood a further fifty feet along the hillside.

He strode along the concrete path flanked with flower beds where Milly had spent so much of her time planting and weeding, climbed the three creaky wooden steps to the verandah, side-stepped the flower-patterned chiffon-covered settee (police issue) in the lounge and walked through into the kitchen at the back.

Abdul's pockmarked, suede-coloured face was screwed in concentration over a pot of simmering rice. He was small and muscular, his round head covered with half an inch of iron-grey wool. 'Hallo, Boss,' he said amiably.

'Where's Lupin?' asked Field.

Abdul looked at him disinterestedly, the dark brown pupils of his eyes, in which it was impossible to recognize an iris, swivelling slowly against the reddish whites, his thick, grape-blue lips pursed in concentration. Field let him take his time. Abdul had been his cook boy ever since he had passed out of training depot, following him to every part of the colony in which Field had served. Field had spent more time with Abdul, knew him better and sometimes thought he liked him more than any other man on earth. His infuriating slowness, impenetrable stupidities, gigantic loyalty and bubbling mirth still constantly exasperated or amused him. He also realized that Abdul probably knew just as much about Inspector William Field of the B.S.A. Police as he did himself.

'Matshilobe, that bloody bastard, take her,' he said at last. He smiled at Field, knowing he had interpreted his mood exactly. 'Matshilobe come in and say she go along with him. So she go along with him.' He turned back to his rice pot.

The precise simplicity of his announcement sent a small cold shock boring into Field's brain. 'What for?' he said.

Abdul stirred his rice with a wooden spoon.

'I don't know, Boss. I not understand.' He turned back to his pot. 'This very good rice.'

'Curry?' said Field.

'Very good curry, Boss.'

Field walked back into the lounge, making a mental note that he had to do something about Abdul and curry. Now that Milly had gone, Abdul cooked curry every day. It was his favourite dish.

He went out on to the verandah and stood for a moment looking out at the great sweep of green valley which rose to the distant mountains. Usually it never failed to lighten his spirit but now he stared up with a sense of deep foreboding.

So that 'bloody little bastard'—as Abdul had so succinctly put it—had her. He knew with a keen and experienced policeman's 'nose' that the scene in the storeroom and Matshilobe's intervention were linked in some way. How else would you expect a minor agitator to react. At this very minute, almost certainly, Ali Hassim Khan was listening avidly with a keen appreciative look in his dark eyes. Field had left himself wide open for a counter punch; no doubt the return right cross was on its way.

He forced his eyes to focus on the distant wall of mountains. He remembered the first time he had climbed to the ridge, a young sunburned trooper, fresh from England, just out of training depot, attached to a station for the first time. He had taken the day off, and borrowed the Land Rover, and spent most of the morning scrambling up the steep granite rocks. Panting, he had stared out across the blue-green immensity of high plateau which stretched eastwards for five hundred miles before it fell into the blue haze of the Indian Ocean. The sun had burned down. Two Batteleur's eagles had swung on an aerial trapeze against the blue tent top of sky and he had been filled with an immense sense of exaltation at the realization that this great continent was now his homeland.

He knew that Zinganthropus man, short, strong, hairy with a flat, brutish face, the earliest human link with man's slimy past, had stared long ago from this ridge. Up north Professor Leakey had dug what was left of him out of the fourth rocky strata of the Oldavai Gorge where his body had been pressed into the warm mud some million and three-quarter years before. He wondered if those small eyes, recessed under beetling brows, stared up at this same sky in bewilderment or fear, or perhaps felt a similar exaltation?

Strange how the idle thoughts of that random but explicit moment should have stayed in his head—what must it be—thirteen, nearly fourteen years ago! When he first arrived in the Eastern Highlands of Southern Rhodesia he had not expected such country. He had anticipated deep thick forest, endless Zambesi bush with primitive African tribes like the Batonkas or open veld studded with little trees and rocky kopjes rolling on for hundreds of miles like the country between Salisbury and Umtali. But these immense grass-lands rolling up from five thousand feet to the ten thousand foot peaks of the Chimanimani mountains were unexpected; they could feed ten million sheep, immense herds of cattle; already they were growing acres of wattle, forests of conifers. And over these wide grasslands, sublimely ignoring any man-made boundary between Rhodesia and Portuguese East, wandered the lion and the leopard, the baboon and the elephant; the fat and deadly Gaboon viper mottled in a dozen iridescent colours, bred amongst the hot, grey ledges of rock. A thousand species of insect and beast hummed, roared or bleated here, living precariously, insolently or timidly in this great terrain of high mountains and slow black rivers.

He left the verandah and walked slowly back along the path in the shade of the trees towards the station, the sense of imminent disaster still with him.

An old African sat dejectedly on the verandah outside the charge office with Strongbow, the senior African sergeant, poised above him. Six foot four in height, muscular, ebony black, a small bristle of waxed moustache smeared across his upper lip, small eyes screwed up behind horn-rimmed spec-tacles, lips severely compressed, Sergeant Strongbow came to rigid attention as Field approached, crashing his right foot to the verandah. Field knew that one day the damned fool would put his foot right through the floorboards. He never could quite reconcile the horn-rimmed spectacles with what he knew of the rest of Sergeant Strongbow's character, but he knew he was as blind as an old buffalo without them.

'Stand at ease, Sergeant,' he said irritably and went into his office. He crossed to his desk backed by the shelves of files whose titles annotated in a neat summary the reason for his existence: *'Grass Fires and Game Laws', 'Brands', 'Masters and Servants', 'Native Slaughter Methods'. 'Lost and Found Property', 'Cordons and Special African Con-stables', 'Outbreaks of Foot and Mouth Disease', 'Rations',*

'Licences', 'Native Beer and Harmful Liquids', 'Native Inns and Eating Houses', 'Legal Opinions of High Court Cases'.

Patrol Officer Potterson, a tall, thin young man with the apostolic face of a martyred St. Anthony and the intelligence of a prefect in the lower fourth, was seated at his own desk writing diligently. He was also depressed; Field knew that immediately. He knew Potterson pretty well. With habitual courtesy Potterson said, 'Anything up, Skipper?'

'No,' said Field shortly.

This verbal residue of dated R.A.F. slang also irritated him. Six months ago when P.O. Potterson arrived long-faced, well-scrubbed, impeccably creased, direct from training depot, he had established his loyalty and affection with so much use of the word 'skipper' that finally Field could stand it no longer.

He had said forcefully, 'This is not a bloody square-rigged barquentine, Potterson my boy. This is a police force. For Christ's sake, come down out of the rigging, realize that the nearest point at which the Indian Ocean touches Africa is five hours' drive by car, and act like a down-to-earth copper. Off duty you can call me Bill, Mate, Cobber or whatever you like, but on duty I am Inspector or sir. Not—I repeat not—Skipper. Is that understood?'

'Yes, Skip—sir,' said Potterson humbly. But during the past few weeks the habit had crept back again.

'What have you been doing, Potterson?' he said, not because he wanted to know but because he thought he ought to say something.

'Duty roster, and station log completed, sir. Rainfall gauge checked, detained persons allocated work . . .'

'What does Strongbow want?' said Field. 'Not his bloody bicycle again?'

'Yes, sir, at least a constable's bike, sir.'

'If only Sergeant Strongbow would understand that the money he receives for his bicycle is for the purpose of maintaining it in good repair, not for spending on his girl friends and then complaining that he hasn't enough funds to repair it, we'd all be a lot happier,' said Field irritably.

'He's also got a man from the Mansuta Tribe,' said Potterson. 'He thought he might be useful to us.'

'How?'

'A bit of information, sir.'

Field raised his eyebrows. 'Are you suggesting we take over the job of Special Branch, Potterson?' he said dryly.

'Oh no, sir. But don't you think we should have our own sources of information without leaving it all to Headquarters?'

Field stared hard at him.

'Get Strongbow to bring him in,' he said.

Potterson opened the door and with a thunder of feet Strongbow approached the desk. The African slid in behind him almost without apparent movement.

'This is the man, sah,' he said, beckoning him to the desk.

Field looked at the African.

'Where did you find him?'

'He came to my house, sah, to ask for food.'

'So you ran him in?'

'No, sah. As he is a member of the Mansuta tribe, sah, near which district there have been many outbreaks of arson, I thought perhaps he might be able to spy for us, sah, and help us in our enquiries.'

'I congratulate you, Sergeant Strongbow, on your devotion to duty.'

Sergeant Strongbow's right foot crashed down to the floor in a thunder of delight. 'Thank you, sah!'

Field looked at the man. His hair was curled in a tight black fuzz against his skull; his forehead was high, his ears slightly pointed lay flat against his head; his nose was straight and flared at the nostrils. One dark eye swirling in the liquid white was bloodshot. He had a dark moustache which ran down beside his thick grape-purple lips to join a ragged fringe of whiskers around the point of his chin. He wore a ragged grey shirt and a ragged tweed coat, out at the elbows and torn at the collar, and his khaki shorts were stained and dirty. His legs were thin black sticks, his bare feet splayed and calloused, the pale khaki colour between his toes stretching under to the soles of his feet. He stood there, his face a mask, his eyes clouded. Whether it was apathy, resignation, despair or a pure withdrawn contemplation Field would never know.

Sergeant Strongbow repeated his story. The man had heard of the great wealth to be found in the new city of Salisbury. It had troubled him. Eventually he had abandoned his land where he had scratched a living all his life, left his wives and children, and set out for the great city.

It was a familiar story. But usually it was the younger ones who were attracted from the reserves and joined the hundreds of unemployed in the African townships of Highfield and Harare.

'Ask him,' said Field disapprovingly, 'why he, at his age, should do such a silly thing.'

The man replied slowly, hesitantly. Apparently Strongbow had some difficulty in understanding him.

'He says,' said Strongbow eventually, 'that a man must finally do what his heart tells him to.'

'What happened to him in Salisbury?'

Strongbow was confused over this also. Apparently he had found employment with a European household as a garden boy. He had not even reached the eminence of house boy or a cook boy, never been allowed in the house. After a year of this he had decided to go back to his village; he was now on his way.

'All right,' said Field. 'Take him off and find out more about him, and see if he is willing to co-operate.' As the door closed behind them he looked across at Potterson.

'Poor sod,' he said. 'He goes out to discover his pot of gold at the end of the rainbow called Salisbury, works for twelve months under the inspired tutelage of some disinterested emigrant from Tooting or Tottenham and goes back home as a police spy. A touch of Chekhovian tragedy about the whole thing, don't you think, Potterson?'

Potterson looked at him warily. 'Yes, sir,' he said dutifully.

There was a knock at the door. Sergeant Strongbow's dark face reappeared.

'I forgot it, sah,' he said. 'The bicycle, sah.'

'Come in, Sergeant,' said Field wearily. 'We have discussed your bicycle before, you know.'

'It is not my bicycle, sah, it is the bicycle of Constable Nimrod, sah. He complains that his bicycle allowance is not enough, sah.'

'What is his bicycle allowance, per month?' said Field heavily.

'Ten shillings per month, sah.'

'That is six pounds a year, Sergeant. How much did Constable Nimrod spend on his bicycle last year?'

'He tells me he wasted four pounds on it, sah.'

An African constable always 'wasted' money on his bicycle, he never regarded it as money expended upon necessary upkeep and servicing. It was a dichotomy of thought which Field found impossible to follow.

'That means he made a clear profit of two pounds, Sergeant.'

'But, sah, he wasted four pounds which he would like refunded, sah.'

Field was aware that this sort of dialogue could go on for hours.

'The allowances are laid down by police regulations, Sergeant Strongbow. I cannot alter them and I cannot raise the bicycle allowance without authorization from Headquarters.'

'But you could ask them to raise them, sah.'

'The next time I go to Umtali I will bring the matter to their attention, Sergeant,' said Field finally. 'But I warn you that I expect no results. Now go away and talk to the old man from the Mansuta tribe.'

Sergeant Strongbow marched out of the office and Field looked across at Potterson. He knew by the general air of depression that it was now his turn. 'Something troubling you also, Potterson?' he said.

'Mr. Michaelson's just been in, sir.'

'Yes?'

'He wants me to shoot his dog.'

'What's the matter with it?'

'It's got mange or something.'

'Why doesn't he shoot it himself?'

'He hasn't got a gun.'

'Well, lend him a gun.'

'I offered to, sir, but he said he couldn't do it. He likes the dog too much.'

Field was silent for a few seconds.

'You've shot a dog before?'

'Yes, sir, but I didn't like it.' He paused. 'I don't mind human bodies. I'm callous about bodies, but dogs . . .'

Field looked at him critically. He said, 'You can't come out here Empire building, my boy, without experiencing a bit of unpleasantness now and then. You're not a London bobby directing the traffic and rounding up long-haired teenagers. You're the father and mother of this country: the Law. And if nobody else will shoot the dog, you will. If the dog's sick you'll be putting it out of its misery anyway.'

Potterson looked at him with deeply depressed eyes. 'But the dog always seems to know, sir. They have that look. They get a sort of despair, an apathy; it makes me feel like a—a murderer.'

The telephone shrilled. Field reached for it, thought better and left it for Potterson to answer.

'Chapanda police post,' said Potterson mechanically. His voice brightened. 'Oh, hallo, sir. Yes, he's here. I'll put him on.' He looked across at Field. 'The D.C., sir.' Field picked up the phone and Potterson replaced his receiver.

Charlie Holland had been District Commissioner handling native affairs at Chapanda for two years now. Field liked him. They occasionally knocked a ball around the scarred and tussocky nine holes which served as a golf course behind the large, shed-like building which passed as a country club; they had shared a few late nights drinking Castle lager at the Chapanda Hotel bar.

'Hallo, Charlie?' he said.

Instinctively Field knew that here was trouble. The silence was so long that Field wondered if he was there at all.

'Charlie?' he said.

'Hallo, Bill,' said the well-educated, whisky-matured voice. Another long pause. 'For God's sake, what have you been up to?'

'I don't follow you,' said Field tonelessly.

'Listen, Bill. This is unofficial and absolutely off the record. I shouldn't be ringing you up, but you understand . . .'

'Yes, I understand,' said Field.

'I've just had your house girl, Lupin, in my office with

a native called Matshilobe, and, of all people, Ali Hassim Khan.'

'Yes?'

There was another long pause and then he said, 'She says you raped her in the storeroom at the police camp. She's made a full written statement to that effect.'

'I didn't know she could write,' said Field laconically.

'Good God, Bill,' said Holland, nettled, 'this is serious. I've got a Shangaan interpreter here.'

'I see.'

'Bill, don't you understand? I can't stop anything as serious as this.'

Field realized that Holland was waiting for him to deny, angrily, the accusation, waiting for him to shout, 'This is absolute nonsense' or 'I'll flay the hide off that girl' or 'Wait till I see that thug, Hassim Khan'. Instead he said, 'Of course not.'

'I've had to telephone the Provincial Commissioner at Umtali and tell him about it. God knows what will happen now.'

'I'll tell you,' said Field, his mind working out clearly the chain of future events. 'Your P.C. will get in touch with police headquarters in Umtali and the Provincial Criminal Investigation Officer will be informed. Let's give them three hours for the drive down from Umtali, shall we? That's say, three o'clock. At that time the P.C.I.O. will come bounding into my office looking like a tiger ready for a meal, together with someone like a Detective Inspector, a couple of Patrol Officers and a posse of African constables. Big stuff, boy, I can tell you. Rape is a very serious crime.'

The voice at the other end of the phone was mystified. It said, 'Bill, are you taking this seriously?'

'Very seriously,' said Field slowly.

'Bill, I couldn't do anything else, could I?'

'No, Charlie, you couldn't. Thanks for the tip-off. See you . . .' He was going to end 'at the club', but quick reflection told him this was unlikely. 'Soon,' he ended lamely. He replaced the receiver, and stared down at his blotting pad.

'Anything up, Skipper?' Potterson said.

Field looked across at him and grimaced. 'I suppose you could say so.'

'Can I help, sir?'

'I shouldn't think so. Though you will undoubtedly be called as a witness.'

'I don't follow you, sir.'

'You will. Would you mind telling me what I have done this morning, Potterson?'

'Sir?'

'A perfectly simple request, Potterson. Describe my movements from the time I arrived at the office this morning.'

'Well, you came in at eight o'clock and did the usual things. We made normal radio contact with H.Q. Umtali. You went to the Charge Officer, and came back here, and then you went to the storeroom . . .'

'At what time was that?'

'Oh, I suppose about 10.45, sir.'

'And I returned at?'

'About 11.25, sir.'

'Too many "abouts" in your testimony, Trooper. As the P.C.I.O. will arrive here from Umtali in about two and a half hours to place me under arrest, you'd better get your times exact.'

Potterson's eyebrows moved up. 'I don't understand, sir.'

'You will. Cultivate your powers of observation, Potterson my boy, if you want to rocket up the promotion ladder with the speed of light. Otherwise you'll probably end up like me as a run-down Inspector passed over for promotion and left to rot in the bush.'

'That's not true, sir,' said Potterson loyally but without conviction.

'Nevertheless, Potterson, if you're going to end up as an Assistant Commissioner with egg yolk all round your hat, you must be prepared to run around sucking up to superior officers . . .'

He stopped, hearing suddenly in his head, Milly's querulous voice. 'I know you only think you're being funny; you don't realize you have the ability to hurt people, and it's particularly objectionable when you do it to people who because of their lower rank can't answer back.'

He couldn't remember at which interminable quarrel she had accused him of this particular defect, but at the time he had thought she was probably right.

'Potterson,' he said, 'a distinguished posse of brass will arrive at the station in about three hours' time. By that time we'll have the place bright and shining—yes? Everything according to text book procedure. African constables sparkling like diamonds, prisoners working like white ants, you looking like something out of a recruiting poster—yes?'

'Yes, sir,' said Potterson doubtfully.

'They may be bringing a noose with them,' said Field. 'But I always believe in giving the hangmen a nice tidy place in which to work.'

'I don't under—'

'I know you don't,' said Field. 'Sometimes I don't either. But let's get started.'

'Yes, sir,' said Potterson, and got up from his seat.

Field waited until the door closed behind him, and then picked up the phone and gave Sarah's number. A few seconds later he heard the phone ringing and at once he formed a mental picture of that wide cool lounge, the french windows opening on to the flower-filled garden, the dark line of bush, beaten back, a hundred yards away; the house boy in his starched white coat would appear from the kitchen door, walk a dozen paces to the table. He would pick it up . . . now! 'Hello, hello,' said the voice on the phone and Field knew his timing was good.

'Go and tell Miss Sarah she is wanted on the phone,' said Field. 'You tell her it is important.'

'Okay,' said the houseboy. Field reflected he would now have to decide where she was: bedroom, lounge, garden, barn?

'Sarah, missus,' he would say, 'the telephone calls.'

Her voice, sexy, feminine, that peculiar mixture of inherited Afrikaans crossed with convent French, was suddenly against his ear. 'Hello. Who is it?' she said.

'It's me.'

'Oh!' There was a distinct hesitation. 'You!'

She had spoken but two short words, but in the box they would know at once that she was a hostile witness. This was how they had started, angry and antagonistic. And now they were back where they had started.

'My lord, I was about to offer in my defence that I became infatuated, indeed besotted by this white-skinned, black-haired girl. The contours of her body, the primitiveness of her passion induced in me such wild exhilaration, such a potent happiness . . .'

'I didn't expect you to ring,' she said.

'I know you didn't,' he said.

'There's nothing else to say, is there?' she said.

'Nothing else to say?' It sounded like the plug line of an absurd popular song, 'Nothing else to say, honey, except goodbye, nothing else to say until I die. No one else to hold me to keep me warm.'

'I thought you might like to know that I'm about to be arrested on a charge of raping an African girl . . .'

He heard her gasp. It was not, he supposed, the sort of conversational gambit she could be expected to appreciate.

'Who?' she said. 'Who?'

There was an urgency in her voice he did not expect. As if it mattered! 'Lupin,' he said. 'Lupin, you remember, one-time rain goddess high up in the Chimanimani mountains.'

He heard her pent-up expulsion of breath. 'Lupin, that nigger servant girl! You must be mad.'

'Nigger servant girl!' No, Sarah never would change. 'It is a point of view,' he said. He could have added, 'Your point of view.'

'Why?' she said vehemently. 'Why?'

'I suppose the news will get around pretty quickly and I thought I should tell you first. After all, it is a quick way of saying "Goodbye".'

He replaced the receiver closing out with a hollow final click the sentence forming at the other end of the line. Dramatic, juvenile, and silly. Yet strangely satisfying. Yes, the news would get around very quickly. Milly should be told. He picked up the receiver again and gave the number of the Downlands Welfare Centre in Salisbury. He added, 'Is there much of a delay?'

'Hardly any at all,' said the operator cheerfully. 'I'll ring you back.'

Three minutes later the phone rang and Field picked up the receiver. 'Your Salisbury call,' said the operator.

'Thank you,' said Field.

The line clicked, whined and crackled. After a few seconds a voice said, 'Downlands.'

'Can I speak to Mrs. Mildred Field?' he asked. 'This is her husband.'

'I think I can put you through to her,' the voice said. 'Hold on.'

There was another pause, a click and then surprisingly clear, Milly's voice. He could hear the sound of children shouting and talking in the distance.

'This is Bill,' he said.

'Oh Bill, how are you?' Oddly she sounded almost pleased to hear him. But then she always seemed to change her personality at the kindergarten. It was almost a physical change. He remembered the first time he had called to pick her up from work there. As he walked in through the front gates a small African girl about four years old with large, round, solemn eyes had skipped up to him and placed her hand trustingly in his. She was very black, woolly haired and wore a plain blue checked gingham dress. Quite at ease she walked by his side, her firm grip denoting absolute possession, perfectly content to be led or lead in any direction.

She had taken him to the playground at the back of the house. Twenty children, black and white, between the ages of about four and seven, raced and tumbled, squabbled and laughed there. Milly had been standing to one side arranging a queue into logical order to mount the steps of the slide.

He saw at once that there was something different about her. At first he couldn't understand what it was, and then with a small pang of guilt he realized he hadn't heard her laugh with such genuine pleasure for so long. The laughter seemed to have eased all the angular tension—sometimes an aggression—out of her body. She had seen them at last and moved across, laughing down at the little black girl and saying, 'So you've found yourself a new daddy, have you, Sheila?'

Driving home in the car, instead of being tired and peevish as he had expected, she had exuded a quiet happiness. 'They're all so beautiful, so innocent. And they all need love so badly.'

He understood then, for the first time, the desolation of a barren woman. Not a woman who didn't want children, or who didn't have children, but a barren woman. If that had been different, perhaps it would all have been different.

Remembering all this, with a quick flash of memory, he lost some of his confidence. Perhaps there was another way of telling her? 'I'm fine,' he said. 'How are you?'

'All right. What have you been doing?'

Should he really tell her? He said, 'Oh the usual. Nothing very interesting.'

The conversation was bogging down into the usual endless banality of most telephone conversations.

'I thought I might get next week-end off, and pop over to Chapanda. I need some more things.'

So she had to be told. 'I don't think I should,' he said, carefully trying to choose his words. 'I've just got myself into rather a mess.'

The voice at the other end suddenly became brittle, petulant, a voice he remembered. 'It's that girl again, I suppose?'

Her quick change of mood angered him. 'No, it's another girl,' he said brutally. 'A black girl. Lupin.'

'Lupin!' Her voice was incredulous. 'What do you mean? I don't understand.'

'I've been accused of raping her,' he said flatly. 'If they make the charge stick and I see no reason why they shouldn't, there'll be no point in coming back at all. I just thought you'd like to know. Within three hours I shall be under close arrest and it's unlikely I'll be talking on any telephone for some time after this.'

'Oh, Bill,' she said in despair, 'Oh, Bill!'

The sound of her voice made him ashamed of himself. He had to end it.

'Goodbye, Milly,' he said. 'I'll write to you.'

He put down the receiver and lit a cigarette. He knew he wouldn't write to her.

CHAPTER TWO

AT EXACTLY THREE O'CLOCK, as Field anticipated, two squad cars from Umtali roared up the steep hill from Chapanda, swerved in through the station gates, and with the typical melodrama of the C.I.D. braked to a skidding halt in the gravel outside the charge office. A touch of the Gestapo, thought Field, had brushed off on every police force in the world.

Potterson peered through the window and reported: 'Two section officers in the front seat, sir. The P.C.I.O. in the back with Superintendent Kingsley and, by golly sir, he's got an Assistant Commissioner with him. I think it's Mr. Dewley from Salisbury.'

'Big stuff, as I told you,' said Field grimly.

'In the second car two African constables in the front seat with another African civvy, Lupin, Ali Hassim Khan and that odd sod, Matshilobe, in the back.'

'Open the door, Trooper, and let light in,' said Field quietly. He sat squarely in his seat, arms on his blotting pad, hearing the car doors slam, the feet on the gravel.

Potterson opened the door and stood rigidly to attention. The huge bony nose of Assistant Commissioner Dewley surmounted by the gold braided peaked cap came in first. The face was stony, the tall, angular figure uncompromising. Following him was the shorter, stouter figure of Sam Kingsley, the super at Umtali, and Field felt a twinge of regret; he had never really thought of Sam as a policeman, more as an ageing avuncular friend. Sam wasn't going to like this.

Dewley at fifty-four years of age was six feet two inches tall, sunburned, muscular, athletic and quite immaculately uniformed. Field remembered his frosty dictum of some years ago. 'When an untidy policeman walks down the street, Trooper, the public don't think what a scruffy individual *he* is. They think what a scruffy police *force* it must be. Remember that, Trooper!'

Field had remembered. He remembered now as Dewley approached his desk in the short-sleeved, perfectly pressed khaki jacket with the silver insignia on the shoulders, that the man was utterly competent, absolutely ruthless, and if he had borne any resemblance to a human being would undoubtedly have risen to Commissioner. He carried a small rattan cane which he now cracked down sharply against the side of the khaki shorts and blue-topped stockings which were a model for every young policeman.

'Patrol officer,' he said viciously to Potterson, 'get out of here.'

'Power,' thought Field, 'plain, unbridled power to instil fear, to assert authority to quell mutineers, to cower subordinates.'

'Yes, sir,' said Potterson with plain relief. He slid out of the door and closed it behind him, and Field realized that he had left Ali Hassim Khan and Lupin out on the verandah.

'Well,' said Dewley harshly, 'isn't it usual for an inspector to stand up when a superior officer comes into the room?' He suddenly shouted, 'Stand up, man!'

'You repellent bastard,' thought Field and without moving stared up coldly into the other's face.

Thirteen years in the police force to reach the honourable rank of Inspector and this creature thought he could get away with Nazi sergeant-major tactics like this. He remained seated. At least they'd never get him hopping again.

'I was not expecting this visit—*sir*,' said Field. He emphasized the 'sir' with suitable irony. 'I understand that when senior officers visit a police post it is usual for the member in charge to be notified of that visit.'

Dewley put both hands on the desk and peered down into Field's face. At close quarters his long-shot veneer of good health and well-being deteriorated: there were baggy pouches under the predatory brown eyes, deep lines running from either nostril and ending in ridges of hard muscle at either side of the clamped, thin mouth. He said:

'The old barrack-room lawyer—eh? You haven't changed much have you, Field?'

Field had once served under Dewley. He disliked everything about him. His arrogance, superiority and intolerance had earned him the reputation of a piece of effluence, first class, a characterization they said, which often gave you some advantage in the slow climb up the promotion ladder. 'Any asset I may have learned in the police force can hardly be used as evidence against me—sir,' said Field slowly. He returned the unblinking stare. It was, after all, a technique open to anybody.

Dewley turned abruptly on his heel and crossed to Potterson's desk. He laid his cane down next to the blotter and placed his hat down beside it. He sat down, folded his hands and nodded to Superintendent Kingsley and the P.C.I.O. With an almost inaudible sigh Sam took a notebook out of his pocket and poised his Biro.

The P.C.I.O. was a tall spare man with a worried brown face and a thin black moustache. He was new in the province and Field knew little about him.

He said, 'You may or may not be surprised to see us, Inspector Field, but a most serious charge has been laid against you. An African girl named Lupin, whom I understand works for you, has been to the District Commissioner's office and made a statement that you raped her in the storeroom?' He peered up questioningly, and Field ignored the look.

Assistant Commissioner Dewley now intervened. Field knew he must be holding himself in with great difficulty.

'Perhaps we might examine the evidence, Inspector,' he said in even, almost kindly tones. 'We stopped at the District Commissioner's office on the way down to learn the nature of the complaint and we have Mr. Ali Hassim Khan and this girl outside whom we will bring in presently. No doubt you know him?'

'I know him,' said Field flatly.

'Apparently an African named Matshilobe was in the police compound when he met this woman who laid the complaint. He took her at once to Mr. Khan.'

'He would,' said Field.

'I understand she has been working in your house, Inspector?'

'Yes.'

'Your wife was there also?'

'My wife went to Salisbury a month ago to work in the welfare centre in Highfield.'

There was a short silence, filled with intangible but jagged question marks.

Dewley's voice was as cold and hard as a mortuary slab.

'Am I to understand, Inspector Field, that you have been *living* with this African woman?'

Field smiled mirthlessly. 'You are not to understand that. She was a servant, nothing more.'

Poor Lupin. What a way to describe the rain goddess! 'A servant, nothing more!'

'This man, Ali Hassim Khan—'

'You know as well as I do that he is the local boss of Z.I.P.P.'

'That is beside the point. He claims that this woman is his'—Dewley hesitated for a second over the word—'friend.'

'Friend!' Field gave a short, hard laugh. 'What does he mean by friend? That thug probably sleeps with a different woman every night.' He stopped, thinking Lupin might be one of them. He had not thought of it that way. But of course he had no idea what she did every night after she returned to her quarters in the police compound.

'He's been instrumental in seeing that the formal charge accusing you of raping this woman has been made,' said Dewley vindictively.

'What a God-sent opportunity for him,' retorted Field sarcastically.

'Have you anything else to say?'

'I reserve my defence.' Field looked across at Sam Kingsley to see his reactions.

'Very well,' said Dewley. He nodded at Sam who closed the notebook. The P.C.I.O.'s face was impassive. Dewley got up from behind the desk and paced up and down the office.

Off the record now, thought Field. What the Assistant Commissioner really thinks.

Dewley swung round and pointed his finger melodramatically at Field.

'That a man in this division, a police officer in a senior rank should have a charge of this nature levelled against him is the biggest disgrace this police force has ever suffered. You, Inspector, are a disgrace to that force. For seventy years men have come out here to Southern Rhodesia because they believed in the ideals, the integrity of this force . . .'

'Police Depot Lecture Number One,' thought Field. 'Ideals and Aims of Southern Rhodesia's B.S.A. Police.'

'. . . in its incorruptibility, its sense of fairness and justice. At this moment we are fighting for our lives in the face of world opinion which believes this is a police state where we exploit, brutalize and murder Africans. You are a symbol—'

'Go to hell,' said Field carefully, 'and take your bloody symbolism with you. You've been playing God so long, I'm surprised they haven't awarded you a "police issue-harp".'

He let out a long breath of relief. He did not know rudeness could bring such pleasure. Dewley paused in mid-stride. He was very angry and kept his voice under control with difficulty.

'Blasphemy won't help you, Field, and neither will bad language. We always knew there was something wrong with you, Field. Too much drink, too much womanizing, too much flippancy, too little respect for the force. As I'm sure you know, rape in this country, unlike Britain, is a capital offence. If you're found guilty, and it looks to me pretty obvious that you are, I hope to God they hang you.'

He strode to the door and pulled it open. 'Section Officer, will you bring Mr. Khan and the woman in, please. Yes, and the other African with the interpreter.'

Ali Hassim Khan came in through the door followed by Lupin, Matshilobe, and the police interpreter. Matshilobe wore a badly fitting sports jacket and creased grey flannels, an old pair of shoes without socks, a dirty red shirt and no tie.

He looked frightened.

Ali Hassim Khan wore a new pale grey suit, white shirt, dark blue tie, matching breast pocket handkerchief, and his expensive new brown brogues were highly polished. He was tall, powerfully built. The harsh contours of his bony face were pale chocolate shading to an even paler fawn. Heavy, black horn-rimmed spectacles jutted belligerently from the ridge of his triangular shaped nose and splayed nostrils. His thin mouth, constantly slightly open, revealed strong white teeth. He was, Field knew, a quarter white, a misfortune of ancestry to which he constantly referred in support of his misery and inequality when he addressed an audience: 'I hate the guts of the man who fathered me. I hate the whole white race who have inflicted this misery on us.'

As a Matabele boy he had been educated in an American mission school near Bulawayo and sent to the States as one of their most promising products. On his return to Southern Rhodesia he had found the Church too restricting for a man of his character and ambition, and to the distress of his church elders had changed his faith to that of Islam, a habit as fashionable among Negroes as the change to Catholic amongst English intellectuals. With a new name he had turned to the more opportunist field of politics. He had turned up in Chapanda two years ago, obviously appointed as strong-arm man for the district. Field knew him as a shrewd, clever and ruthless operator.

Dewley nodded to Sam Kingsley who reopened his notebook and again pointed at Field. 'Is this the man against whom you are making this charge?' he asked.

Ali Hassim Khan glanced briefly at the African by his side. The man nodded.

'Yes, that is the man he saw in the storeroom with this girl,' he said in a strong American accent.

For a second Field felt almost sorry for Dewley. God, this must be bitter for him. To enlist the aid of a well-known agitator to bear witness against one of his own officers, was galling indeed. And it was all so simple for Ali Hassim Khan, really. You learnt the law of the whites, the loose implicit freedoms of democracy, and then you gelded your opponent with them.

Dewley spoke to the police interpreter.

'Ask this woman if this is the man she alleges raped her in the storeroom?'

The interpreter put the question to Lupin who stood with her head averted. She mumbled indistinctly.

'I won't have this,' said Dewley sharply. 'Tell her to look at this man and identify him as the man who did or did not rape her in the storeroom.'

This time she lifted her head and stared at Field with those dark and now sullen eyes. She replied in Shangaan and Field knew enough of the language to know what she had said.

'Yes, that is the man.'

'Ask her,' said Dewley harshly, 'if she understands exactly what she is saying? She declares that this man took her by force? She did not surrender of her own free will? Make that quite clear to her.'

The question and answer between Lupin and the interpreter were conducted in undertones, then the interpreter said,

'She says this man take her against her will.'

'Right,' said Dewley. 'We'll now take her to the storeroom for further interrogation.' He turned to Sam Kingsley. 'Perhaps you'd care to have a word with this man, Superintendent. After all, he is under your direct jurisdiction.'

The door closed behind them and Sam Kingsley sighed heavily. He sat at Potterson's desk and with careful concentration extracted a plastic pouch of tobacco and a pipe. Field watched the therapeutic operation with interest; he had seen it many times before. Sam would now suck the pipe stem experimentally, light a match and hold it flaring above the bowl.

Sam Kingsley said, 'What's the matter with you, Bill?' He sucked at the pipe. 'Have you gone bloody well mad?'

'I think so,' said Field. 'At least I can't think of any other good reason.' Then he said, 'Change desks, will you, Sam? I'm not used to you over there.'

Field had known Kingsley for thirteen years. He had been member-in-charge at Chapanda station when raw recruit William Field had first arrived. The same relationship now existed between Potterson and himself.

Without protest Kingsley moved across and sat in Field's chair. He smoothed his hand across the top of the desk as he might smooth the flank of a horse.

'They were good days,' he said. 'The last of the good days.'

Field remembered him as a first-rate superior officer, logical, tactful and humane. In many ways he had tried to fashion his own conduct upon that of Sam Kingsley's. As an officer, Kingsley had moved up slowly through the ranks to the comparative eminence of Chief Superintendent. Now at fifty-four, a year away from retirement, he was greying at the temples, thinning at the crown, and specks of dandruff showed in the parting of his hair. The wrinkles around his jowl were like tiny folds of elephant skin, and two bags of the same material hung under each eye. But amidst the wrinkles and criss-cross of lines the eyes were as blue as thrush's eggs.

They narrowed as he looked at Field.

'Bill,' he said quietly, 'I know you were disappointed when the commission didn't go through.'

'I didn't give a damn,' lied Field. Kingsley ignored the interruption. 'I backed your application to the hilt,' he said slowly. 'I said "All right! So he's been a bit wild at times, inclined to have one too many on his night off, not overfond of discipline, but he's got that quality which makes a good copper: a fundamental belief in the rightness of law and order." '

'Thanks,' said Field ironically. Sam Kingsley was now at his most nauseating. God knows why, but as soon as most officers began to offer advice they made sound precepts seem like cant. Now the famous S. Kingsley philosophy was about to emerge.

'In this country,' added Field, 'law and order begins and ends with the colour of your skin. The African's idea and mine are usually as far apart as the anus and the adam's apple.'

'At a time like this,' said Sam severely, 'without a clear conception of law and order for all men, black or white, Rhodesia and the rest of Africa are going to disintegrate.'

'I can name you half a dozen black dictators who don't think so,' said Field cynically.

Sam did not argue. 'Why do you always seem to look for trouble, Bill? That girl, for example. I mean, Bill, if you want to take a bird away for a quiet week-end, why take her to a place where you bump into an Assistant Commissioner?'

'It was my own business,' said Field coldly. 'And I don't go out of my way to meet Assistant Commissioners.'

Kingsley nodded his head, 'Probably it was,' he said, 'but you know all that stuff about Caesar's wife.'

'I'm not Caesar's wife, I'm male. What do you expect coppers to be; computers? Or maybe you'd better grow a new crop without balls.'

'Now, listen,' said Kingsley, 'I believe that unless an officer is human, unless he understands a few human frailties a fat lot of good he'll be in the maintenance of law and order. . . .'

Field smiled faintly. 'This is your own philosophy I'm giving you back then, Sam Kingsley.'

Sam puffed at his pipe, peered critically at the bowl and carefully tamped back a bit of glowing ash with his matchbox. 'And in raping this girl you carried that argument to its logical conclusion?'

'Very funny,' said Field sourly.

'Sometimes, Bill,' said Sam Kingsley removing the pipe from his mouth to make room for his speech, 'I wonder what made us all become policemen. I know most of the force came out here like boy scouts to emulate Sanders of the River and play god to innocent, smiling Africans. For years that's just what we did. And we still do to a certain extent. But there's a great smoulder of anger in the air now.'

'The wind of change,' said Field flippantly.

'I sometimes wonder where we shall finish,' said Kingsley soberly. 'Shall we all end up like Auschwitz guards?'

He put back his pipe and sucked thoughtfully. 'Violence,' he said, 'is part of the air we breathe. The lion breaks the buffalo's back with one might swipe of his paw and tears out his guts. If violence isn't there we invent it. You should see my mother-in-law. If she hasn't got a problem a day she manufactures one. This case will be a godsend to her.' He paused and added, 'and she'll know it's really all my fault.'

'I'm sorry,' said Field shortly.

Sam Kingsley looked hard at him. 'You can't have been infatuated by this bint, can you? Why did you do it?'

'A dozen built-in reasons,' said Field ironically, 'a rape a day keeps the doctor away. You ought to start a new psychological warfare department, Sam.'

At that moment the door opened and Dewley and the P.C.I.O. came back. There was a new and threatening air about both of them. The P.C.I.O. took one pace forward in a stilted, military manner and said, 'William Henry Field, I am investigating a charge of rape which has been laid against you by an African girl, named Lupin. She alleges that this morning at this police camp of Chapanda you raped her in the storeroom. You are not obliged to say anything unless you wish to do so, but anything you do say will be taken down in writing and may be used in evidence against you.'

'I've nothing to say,' said Field.

The P.C.I.O. continued in the same official voice, 'William Henry Field, by order of O.C. Province you are under arrest. You are immediately suspended from duty and Section Officer Tarratt will be transferred from Umtali to take over your duties from tomorrow morning.'

Dewley now intervened. 'Field, you'd better go and stay in your quarters until we want you. You can pack a few things. We shall start back to Umtali later this evening.'

It was dark when Field heard footsteps on the back verandah and a voice saying, 'Bill, are you there?'

He went through into the kitchen and opened the door. It was Cohen looming against the stars, huge and hairy, dressed as usual in the grubby bush jacket, pockets packed with tobacco, matches, knives, papers, knees and thighs bulging out of abbreviated khaki shorts, thick woollen stockings rolled down over enormous deerskin boots. Cohen was Veterinary Officer of the Chapanda district and Field had known him a long time.

He followed Field back into the lounge, dropped into an armchair, fumbled in a crowded breast pocket for his cigarettes and said, 'I hear you've been cementing sexual relationships between the black and white races.'

'News travels fast.'

'You've heard of talking drums,' said Cohen equably. 'Let me tell you that throughout the settlement of Chapanda they're beating loud and clear. You are the best piece of talking drum that's hit the village since Doc Sinclair chased that bird through the streets omitting the functional necessity of wearing his trousers.' He held out a crumpled box of fifty Waverley to Field, and when he shook his head, struck a match to light his own. 'As a mate the D.C. rang me and explained the position,' he said. 'Are you really under arrest?' he asked curiously.

'Close arrest. You're breaking the law.'

'Going to arrest me, too?' Cohen's grin was crooked.

'In an hour or so I shall be escorted to Umtali and lodged in gaol to await trial,' said Field ignoring the flippancy.

'Just for knocking it off with a black Sheila.' Cohen was quite cordial. 'Times are hard. I'll have that cold beer now,' he added.

'I suspected a secondary reason for the visit,' said Field. He went back into the kitchen, collected two beer tankards from the dresser, swung open the fridge and extracted two bottles of cold Castle lager. He flipped off both caps and returned to the lounge placing a bottle and tankard on the small table beside Cohen.

Cohen held up the bottle to inspect the label. 'I don't understand you at all, Inspector,' he said seriously. 'I thought you were all boss-eyed over that other bit of frippet.'

'Just following your example. Never miss the golden opportunity. That's right isn't it?'

'Ha-ha,' Cohen was sarcastic. 'You convulse me. I've known you a long time, copper, don't forget that.' He filled his glass with reverent care and then, cocking an eye up at Field observed cautiously, 'You go mad or something?'

'Sam Kingsley asked me the same question,' said Field levelly. He didn't really want to discuss the matter with Cohen, but knew him well enough to understand that he hadn't driven up to the police post merely to ask curious questions. He wished he could get to the point. He said, 'I still don't know what you're doing here.'

Cohen swallowed almost half of his beer in one long draught and wiped his mouth with the back of his hand.

'When a mate's in trouble I like to see if I can help.' He lifted his tankard again.

'You mean you're going to confess?'

Cohen spluttered into his beer. 'Ah! Good! More like the copper I know. Confess? Christ, if I confessed to all my crimes they'd hang me.'

Field poured out his own beer. 'Not before time.'

'Listen,' said Cohen looking up out of the big, dark eyes, fashioned by some unlikely mid-European liaison a thousand years before, 'Why don't we beat it?' A gleam of big white teeth showed under the ragged fringe of whisker. 'I mean it.'

Field didn't understand. 'Beat it?'

'Scarper, disappear, vamoose, escape, eff-off, if you get my meaning.' He paused for a second. 'I've got the Land Rover at the bottom of the hill loaded with food, and guns, petrol and my V.D. kit. I've even packed my best suit,' he added defensively. 'We can walk out. You could even pack a bag and bring your guns.'

'And where would we go?'

'We'd be in Portuguese East in under three hours; down in the Union before dawn.'

'They could extradite from either of those places without much trouble at all.'

'All right then, mate, the Congo. That's the real place. I'm fed up to the teeth with this veterinary racket. We could take the back tracks up into Zambia and then across into the Congo. Some damned army or other is bound to need two nice well-fed recruits. Or we might even recruit our own army, occupy some nice little town and live on the fat of the land for the next few years.'

Field thought: How bloody, idiotically typical of Cohen, the man with a philosophy as uncomplicated as a punch on the nose.

'I've always known it,' said Field, 'you're just a villain at heart.'

'You mean no?'

'I mean, no.'

'Listen,' said Cohen, 'if you've raped that black girl they'll get you for it.'

'After the due process of law and order.'

'Law and order are words of pure expediency, my friend,' said Cohen softly. 'You're a copper, a calling undertaken by few and unappreciated by many. If you were born black in Georgia a hundred years ago, your "bloody nigger" life expectancy could be charted with a certain amount of logical and emotional certainty. You're in the same position: the difference being only that you're a white copper in a black country, which in the eyes of the outside world places you somewhere below the level of a Belsen oven-opener.'

'Rhetoric,' said Field.

'The fact that you might be a regular churchgoer, a paid-up member of the Save the Children Fund, a teetotaller and the devoted father of five doesn't mean a damn. Once upon a time it was just village gossip which condemned you. Now in our marvellous civilized society, communications have allowed the whole of world opinion to register their wolf howls of protest. Operate outside their established terrain and they'll destroy you.'

'A point of view,' said Field.

'This ethical malarky about being judged as an individual was scarcely viable when the lion bit the first Christian, and the second Christian burnt the third Christian. You're pre-judged, mate.'

'Who cares,' said Field flatly.

'Congo?'

'No.'

'I could do with a change. A vet's life in this part of the world is too humdrum. Let's start empire building again. With our experience a hundred a week wouldn't be too much for free-lance mercenaries. The whole of Africa to choose from: Egypt, Kenya, Tanzania, Ghana, but Congo best. Congo?'

'No,' said Field. The worst of it was he knew Cohen was dead serious and probably absolutely right. He had offended against the tribe's concept of ethics. His real crime was that he had been caught.

'I expect that bitch Lupin laid for you,' said Cohen casually. 'Knowing that bastard Ali Hassim Khan as I do it's just the sort of thing that would appeal to him. Shall we "do" him before we leave?'

'We're not leaving,' said Field.

Cohen leaned forward and stubbed out his cigarette.

'What still puzzles me, is why?' He paused and added, 'You know why?'

'No,' answered Field. He paused and reconsidered. He said nothing, but he knew he had one or two clues.

CHAPTER THREE

PULFORD STUBBED OUT HIS CIGARETTE in the dirty ashtray, lit another from the long flame of his butane gas lighter and blew a belligerent cloud of smoke in Field's direction. 'I don't think you're taking this seriously enough,' he said coldly.

Field stared with distaste around the long, bare room under Salisbury's High Court which served as Counsel's interrogation room. The walls were a nondescript fawn, the polished lino brown, the bare scrubbed table with a chair at either end gave it a barrack room air.

'Perhaps you're right,' he said without conviction.

'As an ex-policeman, you know as well as I do that under the Roman Dutch law of Rhodesia this charge carries the death penalty.'

It was strange, thought Field, that Pulford's emphasis upon the *ex*-policeman should carry such a sting. But no doubt at all about the truth of that remark; at the end of this little lot he would be *ex* all right. 'It was the first thing the Assistant Commissioner pointed out to me,' he said.

'And that doesn't worry you?' said Pulford.

'Should it?'

'They hanged Peter Poole in Kenya a few years ago.'

'He killed an African.'

'It was a case which could have been reduced to manslaughter. But he was convicted and hanged, many people thought, simply to prove the law is the same for both black and white.'

'But he killed an African. I didn't.'

'Oh, didn't you?' said Pulford hostilely. 'I was under the impression that somewhat earlier, you did.'

Field felt a flush of anger. 'You know damn well that has nothing to do with this case.'

'Oh, hasn't it? Well I assure you that given half a chance the prosecution will do their best to make it something to do with it. The newspapers are already coyly emphasizing the "coincidence" of the policeman who has not only killed a black man but also raped a black woman.'

'Who cares?' said Field dully.

'You should care,' said Pulford coldly. 'Whether you like it, or Rhodesia likes it, or Britain likes it, over the past decade a new concept of international morality has emerged and when it becomes more disciplined and less hysterical the Communist as well as the capitalist countries will have to take notice of it.'

'Look,' protested Field, 'I thought the idea was that you should defend me, not international morality.'

'The general idea, yes. What I'm saying to you is that with half a chance the prosecution will brand you as a black-hater, a bully, a killer and a rapist. If they get half a chance and the judge lets them get away with it they will turn this trial into a circus performance with you as the monster, a sort of junior Eichmann.'

'What about the judge and the twelve just men?' said Field tonelessly. 'They're all Rhodesians.'

Pulford laughed contemptuously. 'This isn't a jury from the deep south of the United States; these twelve men and women will be leaning over backwards to show that justice is twice as fair for the black man as for the white.'

He was echoing Cohen's words and Field stared curiously at this short, fat, balding man sitting across the table. Cigarette ash was scattered down his coat lapels, his eyes were creased, deep set, his trousers baggy, and a flake of yellow tobacco leaf stuck to his protruberant lower lip. He had known about Pulford's reputation as a barrister and especially as a defence counsel for the last ten years. Pulford was an acrimonious man, perpetually quick tempered, partly because of the diet inflicted upon him after his last coronary, partly because the legal antics of *homo sapiens* did not really amuse him. Half Jewish, half Lancashire, he had emigrated to Rhodesia at the end of the last war and built up a lucrative practice in Salisbury. He had a high, thin, unpleasant voice and an aggressive manner which terrified prosecution witnesses and juries alike and occasionally brought stern rebukes from the Bench. He was sardonic, contemptuous, malicious and, when he was interested in the case and felt like it, a very brilliant advocate. Field had accepted his services with alacrity and relief.

'Whom are we facing?' he said. Like practically every B.S.A. policeman of experienced rank he had done his stint as a police prosecutor on minor cases in the lower echelons of the magistrates' courts; he knew far more about many aspects of Rhodesian justice than most of its citizens.

'Mouncer Philips,' said Pulford. 'He's a bit of an old dodderer, but if he doesn't fall asleep too often we should get a fair trial.'

'Who,' said Field, 'is acting for the Crown?'

'Herbert Wallace. He's an uninspired "drip", but he's clever enough to lead in an "open and shut" case like this.'

'Nice to know I'm convicted already,' said Field sharply. 'You cheer me up no end.'

Pulford looked at him with a flash of bright, beady eyes. He was not amused and changed the subject. 'Now let's get a few of these things straight. You'd had this girl in your employment for how long?'

'Seven months.'

'Did she make advances to you? You know what I mean. Was she around at odd times wearing provocative clothes, standing there with a happy smile on her face waiting for action?'

'Look,' said Field in some exasperation, 'she'd only been out of the bush for nine months, she wasn't sophisticated . . .'

'Oh, for God's sake, man, all women are sophisticated in the sense that they know how to attract a man. It's born in their blood stream, they imbibe it with their mother's milk.'

'She was someone around the house that was all,' said Field, nettled.

'In fact you'd hardly thought of her as a woman, I suppose,' said Pulford sarcastically.

'Well . . .'

'I've seen her, remember,' said Pulford, 'and she's a bloody attractive piece of goods, and we've got to show that she's attractive and immoral, that she goes around jumping into bed with whoever is around as often as she can and that she came into that storeroom with the prime intention of making you . . .'

'Oh, for God's sake,' said Field. 'The police aren't such bloody fools as all that. You know as well as I do that her moral character has nothing to do with it. Even had she been a well-known prostitute she could still be raped. That is the charge and the police took bloody good care that she understood the charge.'

'Inspector Field,' said Pulford caustically, 'don't tell me my business. The forensic evidence is that you did poke the girl. We are not disputing that fact. What we are disputing is the fact that she was raped. If we can prove compliance—now there must have been occasions when you thought this girl was throwing herself at you.'

Field could think of at least three, but he said, 'You are suggesting I think that I should fabricate a story that this girl is no better than a common little whore, which in effect is perjury . . .'

'God damn it,' said Pulford, angrily stubbing out his cigarette, 'perhaps you'd like to conduct this case yourself. I don't know why I took it in the first place.'

'You needed the money,' said Field rudely and inaccurately but Pulford ignored the interruption.

'What is our case I'd like to know,' he said coldly, 'or are you admitting that you *did* rape her in the storeroom?'

'I don't know,' said Field, 'I was emotionally upset, angry, confused.'

'I don't give a damn if you felt like Elizabeth Taylor in her big love scene. Did you rape this girl?'

'I suppose so,' retorted Field angrily.

Pulford extracted a fresh cigarette from his box of fifty Waverley, which lay on the table. He lit it holding it between his lips with the thumb and forefinger of his right hand.

'I suppose so,' he repeated mockingly. 'At your age don't you know the difference between rape and consent? Is your knowledge of the sex act so abysmally small? To start again: do we have a case at all?'

Field kept his temper with an effort. 'I have heard it said by people who respect the law, that it is just as much an offence against justice and human dignity for a guilty man to escape punishment as it is for an innocent man to be found guilty.'

'My God,' said Pulford, 'an idealist! Self immolation!

Perhaps I'd better go into court and say we change our plea to "guilty"; we throw ourselves upon the mercy of the court.'

'Not if I know you,' said Field. 'You're a professional and you're going to defend me whether I like it or not.'

'Too damn right, I am,' said Pulford calmly. 'But I'd like a few things to go on.'

For once Field had said the right thing. Pulford was sixty-three years old, short of breath and running out of years. He observed his pudgy body in his morning bath, his lack of wind, the heart which had failed him once and would certainly fail him again, with utter contempt. He had no social graces, he could hardly bear fresh air, no one would ever suggest that he wrote his memoirs, and women moved away from him at cocktail parties. He thought all Rhodesian politicians were amateur lunatics and declared that if a whole boatload of them together with a similar number of their British equivalents were sunk without trace in the middle of the Atlantic no one would miss them. He believed that many of the old-fashioned decencies fashioned over the centuries disappeared at the end of the second world war, and he was not hopeful of their reappearance in the future. He was maintained as an upright human being by his professionalism, by his books, his case histories, by the fact that he had studied and polished his craft for more than forty years and that wherever jurisprudence was practised he would be respected. That Field should intuitively have been aware of this pleased Pulford; nevertheless he continued to stare at him suspiciously.

'All right, what do you expect to get?' he said.

'My sentence when found guilty you mean?' asked Field.

'That's right,' said Pulford.

'Three years if you're no bloody good,' said Field, 'two if you're very competent, eighteen months if you're a bloody marvel.'

For the first time Pulford smiled, a thin wry grimace which exposed his tobacco-stained teeth. 'That's better,' he said. 'Now we know where we stand. But satisfy my curiosity about one thing. You could have had this girl before if you really wanted her. Why bother with all this kinky business of maize sacks and storerooms? Surely you could have chosen a more leisurely and pleasurable occasion. I don't understand.'

'Neither do I,' said Field. 'I can only think that it was a protest. A silly, stupid, futile protest.'

'There are other ways of protesting,' said Pulford affably. 'I swear in my bath. I find it gets you into less trouble.'

Field had been over the events leading up to the scene with Lupin a hundred times in his mind.

'I don't know,' he said. 'I really don't know.'

'All right,' said Pulford. 'Let's go back and start at the beginning.'

PART II

CHAPTER FOUR

The beginning as far as Milly was concerned was that Saturday night of the dance and *braaivleis* at the Country Club with Field swinging the Vauxhall into the car park, tyres hissing on the gravel, headlights wheeling against the starry sky.

He braked next to the Johnson's station wagon and went round to help her out and as he opened the door she heard herself saying for the third time, 'Now remember, we mustn't stay too late and you mustn't get too drunk.'

His response was Pavlovian. 'No dear,' he said. God, how she hated these 'do's'. She knew exactly what was going to happen during the next few hours. It was the occasion for a binge, a sort of monthly springtime when under the influence of sufficient alcohol all the males over forty would suddenly feel seven feet tall and incandescently virile, a euphoria which would seep away as hangover Sunday arrived.

She knew exactly what Bill would do. He would glance regretfully at the bar as they went in, sizing up where that abominable man, Cohen, was standing so that he could make periodic forays in his direction. She simply could not understand their friendship. As she said to Angela, 'He's so rude. I don't think he ever washes and his conversation is just so much smut.' Then having parked her at some table with a few of their friends he would carefully dance two duty dances stepping on big heavy policeman's feet around the room. The strangest thing about this was that he always believed himself to be rather a 'dab hand' at dancing—perhaps all men who managed to slide around a dance floor with a woman in their arms deluded themselves with this peculiar piece of masculine egotism—and Milly had never bothered to shatter the illusion. He would make romantically coy remarks about the early days of their courtship because he could think of nothing else to say, and by the time he deserted her for the bar he would feel that conscientiously he had 'made an effort'. He would flirt openly with the women he didn't much care for, and more cautiously with the ones he fancied, especially that bitch Molly Crosby who really appealed to him, and who everyone knew would jump into bed with any man when her husband wasn't looking.

That Bill should be attracted to Molly Crosby was understandable. She was sexy all right. But Milly knew she had nothing to fear. An Inspector of Police in a place as gossip-ridden as Chapanda had no chance of extra-marital activities. What did perturb her was his disinterest. He took her for granted. She was just somebody around. Oh, he was kind and decent and a good husband, but she had known for some time that he regarded her as not much more important than a piece of household furniture.

This she knew was as much her fault as his. No, more her fault than his. Somehow she had failed him. Particularly in the deep urges of his sensuality. She had tried, oh God she had tried. But it had never really worked. At the climax of their physical collision they were two strangers seeking separate and different conclusions, and at the end of it all they were both alone, he to fall into a comatose sleep, she to lie awake staring at the dark ceiling, aware of their joint failure, aware of despair.

If only they had had children. Then it might have worked. But they hadn't had children and that was that. So now here she was at forty, with eleven years of childless marriage behind her, and Bill three years older and apparently quite able to find in his job and his pals and his pubs the answer to any frustration he might feel.

She swung her legs out of the car and stood up, patting her hair and adjusting her light blue stole, and they walked towards the low building surrounded by a wide verandah thirty yards away. From it came a steady background hum almost as if a giant machine were hidden within but which as they got closer could be separated into the sound of a radiogram, the buzz of conversation and the clinking of glasses. She knew exactly what she would find inside, for the Country Club despite its plushy title was only a large timber hut with a roof supported by a lattice-work of girders. Its functional interior was full of small tables covered with red and white check tablecloths arranged around a dance floor shiny with old French chalk. On the band rostrum stood a large, old-fashioned radiogram. The bar, focal point of life in Chapanda, was almost as long as the building itself, and drinks were served by African boys in white jackets and red fezzes.

As they got to the verandah steps Milly made her last appeal. 'Please don't spend *all* your time at the bar with that man Cohen,' she said.

'No dear,' he said automatically, and she doubted if he had even heard her.

But he had heard her, and he took refuge from hearing her by taking a deep breath, by drawing the night air deeply into his lungs. At this altitude the earth and grass blistered and bleached all day by the sun was now heavy with dew, cool and aromatic. Up on the mountain ledges he knew that a leopard or two would be staring down with curious yellow lambent eyes at the cluster of lights far below.

They climbed the three steps and in the lighted doorway met Molly Crosby. She was a blonde, masterful woman, wife of one of the wealthier farmers in the district, wearing a dark blue dress which revealed a splendid superstructure of sunbrowned bosom. She embraced Milly affectionately.

'Milly, darling, I haven't seen you for so long,' she said, and Milly, suddenly full of charm, answered, 'Oh Molly, I've been meaning to ring you for ages.'

Field sighed inwardly as she flashed her blue eyes provocatively in his direction saying warmly, 'Hello, Bill, healthy and handsome as usual,' before escorting Milly towards the ladies' cloakroom. Molly always took charge. Field had decided long ago that she came from a long line of lady prefects. One could be quite certain that long before the steaks, chops and sausages began to sizzle over the wood fires, Molly would have already dispensed order, tolerance and gay laughter. She was a 'cordon bleu' organizer.

Field stepped out towards the edge of the verandah and

looked up towards the peaks of Chimanimani. Beyond the mountains the moon was already starting up over the rim of the world, its silver pallor luminous in the sky. On the high plateau behind those peaks the elephants would be moving quite soundlessly, their immense sail ears swaying as if influenced by mysterious air currents. Far down below in the low veld, the wide black Sabi would be sweeping quietly through the night, the crocs making slow swirls near the sandbanks, the hippos, like small black islands against the lighter sky, occasionally erupting in frantic splashings and snortings. On the low banks between the long fleys of glistening water, the stunted ipane and ghostly fever trees with bark of a soft pellucid grey-green, would tremble in the faint breeze, and the giant beobabs, manufactured inevitably by some Walt Disney of early creation thrust their shrunken jagged arms from monstrously swollen trunks.

The contrast here between high, windswept plateau and mountains and the hot and humid low veld had always intrigued Field. In the villages on the low veld the huts would be quiet, the babies sleeping, a tiny light here and there; some of the women would still be awake awaiting the return of their beer-filled husbands from the village store. And all around, everywhere the wild creatures: deer and rabbit, impala and roebuck lifting timid heads and wet black noses sniffing the air, living through the night in a sort of nervous, trembling ecstasy.

Field drew in another deep breath. Africa never ceased to astound, mystify and enthrall him.

At the crowded bar Cohen caught him by the elbow. He was arguing as usual with Charlie Holland amongst others. It was typical of Cohen's social bravura that he would engage in a number of bar arguments simultaneously and like a skilled juggler keep all conversational balls bobbing in the air.

At that moment Charlie Holland was the target for his derision. 'D'you know what this silly roinek bastard thinks?' He did not continue his explanation because at that moment he caught the eye of the African barman and shouted, 'Hey, boy, two cold Castles.'

He turned back to Field whose eye had avoided the barman's but had been riveted by the soft, naked back of a girl farther along the bar.

'You're having a cold Castle, yes?'

'Thanks,' said Field. The back was bare. Two slender shoulder straps performed a miracle of suspension with a flowered silk dress cut down into a wide V. And powdering the marble skin down the line of her backbone was the faintest dusting of dark freckles.

Cohen threw down two half crowns and thrust a tall, cold glass filled to the brim with amber liquid in his hand.

'Oh, for Christ's sake, keep your feverish eyes off that bint and pay attention to us,' he grumbled. 'This Englishman here . . .'

'Rhodesians, please,' said Charlie, winking at Field.

'Rhodesians?' sneered Cohen. 'Well, is your passport Rhodesian or British—eh? That's really the test, ain't it?'

Cohen was thirty-four years old, a first generation South African Jew. Six feet two inches in height, fourteen stones, ten pounds in weight, he was fond of stating these facts aloud. His hair was dark and wild, his nose had been flattened in the boxing ring at Witwatersrand University, and for some inscrutable reason he affected a French student's skipping-rope beard which curved around the edge of his sunburned, pockmarked face. His eyes were black and restless, his entire attitude one of aggressive masculinity. His contempt for society in general and at that moment in particular, he expressed in his dress: old bush jacket, short khaki shorts and stockings rolled down over his huge boots.

'I see you're prepared to dance,' said Field ironically. 'I thought you might come in a tropical dinner jacket like Van Cleman.'

Cohen bridled, 'Some of us have got to do a bit of bloody work, haven't we? I've just driven up from the bloody Sabi, did you know that, and down there I was as hot as a hayseed in the belly of an angora sheep.'

'Apt,' said Charlie Holland, 'apt.'

Field liked Cohen. He was male and without artifice, the most uncomplicated, pugnacious, argumentative human-being Field had ever met.

Charlie Holland came from a different world. He had been

District Commissioner for five years now, Native Commissioner before they changed his title when 'native' became a dirty word. He was overweight, inevitably overdressed even in the hottest weather; at that moment he wore light grey flannels, white silk shirt, dark blue blazer with R.A.F. buttons and an R.A.F.V.R. striped silk scarf. He played the role of a bluff, sunburned, moustached R.A.F. prototype, *circa* 1940-45 because this pattern had been forced upon him during those dangerous yet carefree years when he had flown a Wellington Bomber with complete anonymity and malice towards none, and at the end of the war, having failed to discover a more satisfying emotional persona, he had become permanently attached to this protective camouflage. His marriage to a 'popsie' in 1943 had ended abruptly a year later when she ran off with an American lieutenant, although he still received friendly postcards from an address in Junction City. Now he lived alone in a large, rambling bungalow with three African servants, and played courtly and jovial attention to other men's wives without the slightest intention of romance or of ever again becoming involved with anything as dangerous as a female.

Not that he wasn't a good D.C., detached, clinical and conscientious, with a well-defined sense of justice and fair play, and a deep and compassionate understanding of the Africans whose interests he served. But in many ways he was an anachronism, still Empire building, still recalling the days of the British Raj with nostalgia. If Charlie Holland could have had his way, fast barquentines would still be tacking into Table Bay bearing the Queen's Mail, wagon trains rolling up from the Cape, and noble Zulus and their impis attending 'indabas' over which Charlie Holland presided. As these things were no longer possible Charlie accepted the *status quo*. Charlie was a conformist. Charlie kowtowed to authority, whereas Cohen with the rabbinical voice of an Old Testament prophet cried loudly and passionately in the African wilderness.

Cohen's parents had escaped from Nazi Germany in the thirties and his pregnant mother had arrived in South Africa just in time to produce her son.

'A refugee twice in my life,' moaned Cohen. 'Once in my

mother's belly and the second time because I couldn't stand the bloody Nats. Boy, that's tough!'

Cohen was imbued with a massive continuing ferocity against himself, against his neighbours, against mankind and all his works. In the great cask of his body raged a passionate anarchist anger which contradicted, confused and catapulted from one extreme to the other.

At the beginning of an evening he was likely to be defending apartheid with insults and epithets, to roar that black and white could never live together without abrasive injury to each other, and five hours later over his whisky chasers he would be lamenting the lot of the African under the white tyranny in the Cape, the feudalism in the north, the dictatorships in the west and the communist despots in the east.

Field knew that Cohen thrived on the emotional climate of Africa: there was room in this sun-filled continent for male expression. Here was fundamental reality. In a dozen hardly-discovered or openly-revealed places a man could own a harem, start a rebellion, kill animals or his own species without interference. This was probably the last continent where he could indulge in all the old-fashioned vices unrestrained by any law or appetite except his own. Here in all likelihood where the reign of *homo sapiens* first began, where the man-killing apes first picked up their weapons of stone and branch and established a continuous code of behaviour, he could carry on those traditions comforted by twentieth-century prophylactics, cold beer, air-conditioning and jet air travel.

As if by radar Field was suddenly conscious that the girl with the freckled back had turned on her stool and was now staring at him. He lifted his eyes. Her gaze was direct and uncompromising but there was no recognition, no glint of humour, no flirtation in her look. She was very pretty, with a high forehead, straight nose, softly rounded face and large blue eyes; her hair swept up high in front and then curved down into two soft wings on either cheek. She is, thought Field, more than pretty, she's beautiful.

Her eyes held his for perhaps two seconds, then she deliberately swivelled around on her bar stool, turning her creamy back to him, rejoining the conversation of the two men—one enormous—beside her. Field didn't know them.

Cohen had observed the by-play. 'You haven't got a bloody chance there, mate, so you needn't lick your lips,' he said sardonically. 'D'you think a fancy bird like that is left around in a dorp like this for more than thirty seconds?'

'She's married?' asked Field.

'No husband, mate, but she's got a bloody great South Springbok forward in tow. Christ, he's too big for anybody.'

'Who is she?'

Cohen leered. 'The question of course being asked as a good copper because you have to know everybody in the district?'

'Precisely,' said Field.

'She's old Van der Huizen's daughter . . .'

'You mean that kid—?'

'That you used to know when you were a trooper on patrol here ten years ago. Yes, that's her. She's been down in the Union getting educated for the past six or seven years.'

'I often used to stop in with the old man for a drink,' said Field thoughtfully. 'I hardly noticed her. Skinny kid with big eyes.'

'They grow up, mate. They grow up. Haven't you noticed?'

'I've noticed,' said Field.

Field glanced across again. All he could see was the perfect profile, the pretty curve of her neck. As he turned back he saw that Milly had emerged from the ladies' cloakroom escorted by Gwen Lloyd, the small, dumpy, excessively cheerful wife of a local tobacco farmer, and for a fleeting moment he compared the smooth, curved figure of the girl at the bar with Milly's angular frame. She stood there looking uneasy, clutching her bulky handbag in both hands, wearing a print dress which she seemed to have possessed all her life. Her hair was set in a strictly utilitarian bob and her skin was pale and unattractive.

At his side she said coldly, 'I see you've met your drinking partner already.'

'You must come and join us,' intervened Gwen Lloyd cheerfully before he could reply. 'Jack's got a table—look over there. Come on, Bill, you can give us all the inside dirt on the police force.'

She took Milly by the arm and, chattering, led them across to the table.

Lloyd was a small man with skin the colour of the African soil, reddish, dun-coloured, raddled. He had been working in the sun without his hat, and the sun had burned the white skin under the receding hair to an angry red. He smiled when he saw Field.

'Hello, Bill, how's tricks?'

'How's the crop?' countered Field.

'Great, absolutely great,' said Lloyd enthusiastically. 'That's why we're here. It's a sort of celebration.'

'Cured and ready for the sales?'

'Good Lord, you should see the colour of the leaf,' said Lloyd eagerly. 'We've never seen tobacco like it, have we, Gwen?'

'Nothing like it in the whole of Rhodesia,' she said proudly.

Lloyd had been born in Cardiff and brought to South Africa as a boy. He had married Gwen, also of Welsh parents, and they had come north after the war, primarily because of the political situation in South Africa, but also, Field suspected, because they couldn't make a go of it there. He had visited their farm a week ago and they had taken him through the curing sheds proudly exhibiting the huge bundles of golden leaf flecked with brown spots. As they left the shed a sack had fallen off one of the bales and Gwen had scampered back to replace it with the same care that she might replace the blanket over a well-loved child.

'God,' said Lloyd, as they walked back to the sparsely furnished farmhouse, 'you know we couldn't have gone on after this year. Four terrible years and I don't think more than ten cupfulls of rain fell on our property, at least not at the right time. The rain came up to our fence and you leant over and your hand got wet but nothing fell on my land. Nothing. Not a bloody drop. And the plants just wilted and died.'

'And suddenly it came right,' said Field. Lloyd's eyes narrowed in the hot sunshine. 'Absolutely right.' He paused. 'You know what this means, don't you, Bill?'

Field knew. Even with government controlled prices it

meant the difference between a reasonable standard of living and another year wondering if the bank would once more stand the cost of buying the seed and paying the boys. It meant new clothes for Gwen and a new suit for Lloyd, a bottle of whisky a week in the house instead of none at all, perhaps a bicycle for Priscilla, their eleven-year-old daughter. Two good crops and good prices at the sales and you began to think hopefully of a holiday at the Cape.

'Let's have a drink on it,' said Lloyd as the waiter came to their table. 'What's it to be? Two gin and tonics, and Bill—?'

'I'll stick to cold Castle.'

'Not a short, not a drop of Scotch?'

'Later perhaps,' said Field.

Someone turned up the radiogram and the sound of an old Glenn Miller record boomed around the room.

'Dance?' he said to Milly gallantly, and she rose rather unwillingly. 'Bill always likes to get his duty dances over quickly,' she said loudly. Gwen laughed a little warily. 'Oh yes, Jack's just the same. The trouble is, Milly, they're getting too old for it.'

They moved out on to the floor amongst the other couples. As they danced, beyond Milly's shoulder Field saw that the girl at the bar was still staring at him with the same bold look. What was her name? Sarah, that was it, Sarah Van der Huizen. Maybe he could introduce himself at an appropriate time later on. He could only just remember her as a child, thin and rather moody with little to say, hanging around the drawing-room at Van der Huizen's place. He had an idea he'd spoken to her a few times. He could hardly remember.

'Who is she?' asked Milly.

'Who?'

'The girl against the bar. I saw you staring at her.'

God, these women, they picked up the scent before you'd even spotted the quarry. 'Oh, come on, Milly, there's bound to be a bit of excitement with a new girl in the bar.'

'I'm sure there is.'

'She's old Van der Huizen's daughter.'

'A Boer! I thought she looked Jewish.'

Field prevented himself from saying, 'You would', and made a great effort to be charitable. The sweeping strings and brass of the old record aroused nostalgia. He tightened his grip on Milly, endeavoured to hold her more closely but she stiffened in his arms.

'Remember this tune?' he murmured, 'we must have danced to it a dozen times.'

'Did we?'

He persevered, 'You had it at your Aunt's house. I shall never forget it.'

His mind formed a quick mental image of the lounge in the small house in Cape Town. The blue wallpaper, the little silver clock on the mantelpiece which chimed so sweetly, her aunt peering in with a smile and saying, 'Oh, I see I'm interfering with the lovebirds.' Milly flushed, a little put out at her words. 'After all, we were only dancing.'

'I don't remember,' she said. 'It all seems so long ago. And I was younger and sillier.'

'Well, now you're old and wise, you can start enjoying yourself.'

She drew back a little. 'In this place?'

'I know this isn't Salisbury,' said Field doggedly, 'but other women find plenty to do.'

'I'm not *other* women.'

'I never said you were. I said other women find plenty to do.'

'I don't want to waste my life playing bridge and women's tea parties and talking about servant problems and the price of tobacco. That's all I'm going to hear at this place tonight.'

'Christ,' said Field, 'if you're not even going to try and enjoy yourself I don't know why you bothered to come here in the first place.'

Milly's face took on the closed, flat expression he knew so well. 'I could hardly let down the pillar of local society, could I? After all we do have our social obligations, don't we?'

Field blew out his breath in exasperation. 'For God's sake, Milly, if you don't like it here in Chapanda why don't you go back to your old job in Salisbury? You could get a room with the Edwards or even go back into our own house when the tenancy runs out.'

Her voice was very hard. 'That's what you really want me to do, isn't it? Get rid of me.'

'Milly,' said Field patiently, 'I'm stationed here. I shall be stationed here for another two years at least. I can't choose. I'm a policeman. But at the end of two years I can probably get transferred back to Salisbury. Now if you're not happy here you can go back and wait for me there. There's nothing unusual about it. Other wives in the police force have looked after homes and children in the city while their husbands have been out on a bush station.'

As he led her back to the table her silence was stony. The tension was relieved by the arrival of Molly Crosby. 'Come on, you two girls,' she said, 'I need your help.' To Field she added, 'It'll be ready in about fifteen minutes, then you can bring out the beer with you.'

Field watched them go. He raised his eyebrows to Lloyd. 'Women!'

Lloyd laughed and reached for his beer. 'Oh, come on, Bill, you know we couldn't do without them.' He took a long drink. 'I don't know what I'd have done without Gwen over the past few years. She's gone without—well everything. With bankruptcy hanging over our heads, trying just to stay afloat, it wasn't easy for her to keep smiling.'

Field finished his beer. 'Let's go and have a drink at the bar.'

'I'll sit here for a bit if you don't mind, Bill,' said Lloyd. 'You go. I'll come in a minute.'

Field got up and left him. He knew Lloyd didn't want to get involved in a heavy round with 'the boys'. He didn't blame him. He arrived at Cohen's elbow in time to hear old Bob Shields, who had retired after thirty years in a Salisbury bank to a bungalow at the edge of the village, saying, 'When I first came to Rhodesia fifty years ago it had the atmosphere of a rural English country village. No one hurried, there was a spaciousness about life. The sun shone every day, and the Africans, well, they were a pretty lazy lot. If you wanted a fence mended you stopped a couple of boys and offered them a couple of bob and they bought a tin of corned beef with the money and that's the way it went. You were free to go where you liked, black or white. If you went down into the Zambezi the mosquitoes ate you alive, and you were liable to catch blackwater and malaria wherever you went. But it was a country worth living in in those days.'

'I'm sure it was,' said Colonel Raderly. 'There was discipline among the Africans with their tribal standards and there was discipline amongst the settlers. . . .'

'Christ, man,' said Cohen, 'now the two old buzzards are going to give us a lecture. Remember this. Whatever trouble we have now, we brought with us.'

Colonel Raderly, a tall, thin man in a light black and white hound's tooth coat and immaculately creased trousers, said, 'Not at all. I believe the African has always needed discipline. I thrashed my horseboy the other day.' He caught Field's eye as he spoke and smiled thinly.

Field didn't like him. Raderly had moved down from Kenya when the troubles started and apparently failed to discover the same aristocratic milieu in Rhodesia. Field said coldly, 'If he'd punched you on the nose in return, Colonel Raderly, you'd have got no more than you deserved. And it would have been no use coming to us with a complaint.'

'You didn't let me finish, Inspector,' said Raderly, forcing a smile to his lips. 'I thrashed him because he was supposed to be looking after a very valuable horse of mine. The box was left open, the horse got out and it was the middle of the night before we found it in a very distressed condition. The boy deserved a thrashing. And, incidentally, and I think you might appreciate this, Inspector, the lad's father came around next day and presented me with a chicken.'

'Perhaps he'd have given you a side of bacon if you'd shot the boy dead,' said Field ironically.

Cohen guffawed. Raderly did not seem to think it funny.

It was Cohen, his voice full of honey, who went on, 'Colonel Raderly, I presume you are well acquainted with the African?'

Raderly, who didn't know Cohen very well, was cautious. 'I would say that people in Southern Rhodesia know more about the problems of the African than someone living say in Manchester or Birmingham.'

'I doubt it,' said Cohen.

'I'll buy a drink,' said Field leaving the familiar arguments behind and moving along the bar. There was an empty space behind the girl with the freckled back and he pushed in there. She did not appear to notice him. Her back was as smooth and beautiful close up as it was at a distance, and she was wearing a perfume which Field guessed was French and expensive. He ordered the drinks, collected the glass and elbowed back to his group. The imperious figure of Molly Crosby was now at the door calling loudly, 'The food's ready. Bring your beer out with you.'

Outside at the edge of the lawn under the trees, a fire had been lit in a long pit. The wood and charcoal had burned down to a thick bed of glowing embers, and laid above it upon a grill of chicken fencing wire, steaks and chops and sausages sizzled and spat. Already the children—about twenty of assorted ages—carrying huge rolls stuffed with pieces of steak or sausages, were racing about the grass. Field reflected that these days no matter how much they boasted about the love and loyalty of their African servants, very few people in Rhodesia left their younger children at home.

The adults, glasses in their hands, were clustered round spearing pieces of steak with long forks.

Molly Crosby came up to him with an enormous piece of steak sandwiched between a roll. 'Here, Bill,' she said, 'I've done this specially for you. I always believe in keeping on the right side of the police.'

'Thanks, Molly,' he said.

She looked straight up at him and said merrily, 'Did anyone ever tell you, that for a policeman you've got very attractive blue eyes, Inspector Field?'

'No,' said Field, his mouth full of steak. He had heard that Molly had been seen in Bretts in Salisbury with one or two escorts much younger than herself. She went into Salisbury about once a month, on shopping trips, and stayed at Meikles. Malicious gossip suggested that these were journeys in search of illicit bliss. Field looked at her rounded body and decided he would like some illicit bliss with her. Not that he had the slightest intention at all of making any approach. He had had no romantic affairs since he married Milly eleven years ago. What was the point of getting married and using it as a base for fooling around? Anyway, Rhodesia was far too small to conceal a policeman philanderer, or a philanderer of any sort for that matter. Recently, however, with Milly's increasing coldness and reluctance to share any sort of physical contact, he was less certain about this philosophy.

Molly Crosby seemed to divine his thoughts.

'You don't come and see us much these days, Inspector,' she said flippantly. 'I always thought it was part of your duty to visit the outlying farms.'

'It is,' said Field.

'Well, I suggest you come on Wednesday afternoons when Sam's in town,' she laughed.

Field grinned. 'You're going to show me the tobacco crop, I presume, Molly.'

Her voice was teasing. 'I'll think about it.'

Cohen appeared at their side, his mouth also full of steak, and Molly turned back towards the fire.

He watched her go. 'That woman,' he said. 'That woman! When I look at her I break into a cold sweat. D'you know what I'd like to . . . ?'

He broke off, lifting his head, staring up into the sky. They watched it together rising slowly up against the night, lifting high against the stars, leaving a long trail of sparks in its wake. Far away against the dark backdrop of mountains the rocket seemed to pause, and they heard the faint 'pop' as it shot five silver stars down towards the earth.

Field dropped most of his steak sandwich into a waste bin and said, 'Damn.'

'I would guess from the Tribal Trust lands, wouldn't you?' said Cohen affably. 'So, who's got rocket warning apparatus there?'

'Three of the chiefs and old Tzalo.'

'That old Zulu warrior?'

'He's no Zulu. He came up from the Cape with the pioneer trains. But I bet it's him.'

'Why?' said Cohen.

'Because he reported an attempt at intimidation a couple of weeks ago.'

He turned to go. 'Oh well, that's the end of my party.'

'There's plenty of time,' said Cohen, 'I'll keep the bar open and the women happy till you get back.'

Field walked back to the verandah steps. Several men were gathered there. They had all heard about or seen the rocket. Milestone who ran the garage came up saying, 'D'you think you'll need us, Inspector?'

How odd it was, Field thought, that at a time of crisis they should drop all familiarity and call him by his rank. Still they were, after all, members of the Police Reserve.

'Shouldn't think so,' he answered.

Field crossed the verandah to the phone. It had obviously just rung and Lloyd had answered it. He held out the receiver to Field. 'It's your Trooper, Bill.'

Field put the warm receiver to his ear and said, 'Hello?' Potterson's voice was worried. 'I've just had old Tzalo on the blower, sir. He says his farm's being attacked by a gang of men.'

'He probably heard someone walk past in the darkness,' said Field dryly.

'No, sir, his dogs started barking. He went out to investigate and someone fired a shot at him.'

'Fired a shot at him?' Field's voice was sharp. 'Was he hurt?'

'No, sir, but he scampered back and let off his alarm rocket, and now he's barricaded himself and his family in the farmhouse and he's sitting there with a shotgun across his knees.'

'I saw the rocket. What steps have you taken?'

'I've got a Land Rover, the Sergeant and four constables, sir. I've armed them with riot guns, sir. Shall I pick you up from the Club?'

'Right away,' said Field. 'I'll be waiting in the road outside.'

He went back to look for Milly. He found her sitting at one of the tables at the edge of the lawn still chatting to Gwen. She paused as he came up and Field guessed that the general subject had been the continuing deficiency of all husbands. 'I suppose you're off,' she said.

Field nodded. 'Probably won't be long. Almost certainly a minor accident. Possibly a false alarm.'

There seemed little point in saying more, but as he turned away the coolness of her attitude vaguely irritated him. At least she might have been a little more concerned. The group of men had left the verandah steps; practically everybody had drifted back to the food and the firelight, and in another thirty minutes they would all be inside, dancing and drinking. He strode along the verandah, swung around the corner and too late realized that a woman was coming quickly in the opposite direction. Instinctively his hands went out to catch her, but they banged together heavily. She twisted away from him as though he was contaminated, and stood back rubbing the place on her thigh where his knee had caught her.

Field's hands retained a memory of a soft, feminine figure, someone fresh and young. It was Sarah Van der Huizen.

'I'm sorry,' he began, but she took another step away from him angry and hostile.

'Bloody copper,' she said with venom.

Field blinked. 'Listen,' he began, 'I've said I'm sorry.'

She didn't seem to hear him. 'Like all policemen, big and clumsy,' she said angrily, 'crashing around the corner not caring who you knock down.'

He tried to mollify her. 'Like you, I can't see around corners.'

'I don't suppose you can see anything except your own self-importance,' she said trying to push past him.

This gratuitous rudeness astounded him. It was so unnecessary. And over such a small thing. He was so incensed he caught her wrist. 'Miss Van der Huizen,' he said coldly, 'you're not old enough to run in, and too old to spank, but your father should have performed the operation years ago.'

He could feel the hatred in her glare. 'You're hurting my arm,' she said furiously, trying to pull away. He was very close to her and he could smell the expensive perfume again. He released his grip and stood back to let her pass. She almost ran along the verandah away from him.

He watched her go, shocked by the encounter. What in the name of God had he done to deserve such a tirade? He walked on more slowly now, thinking of what she had said. When he reached the park he stood by his car with face set, trying to rationalize and reject the experience. Had some experience with the police down in the Union upset her? It was all very strange and unpleasant. He unlocked the door of the Vauxhall before he remembered that they were picking him up in the Land Rover. He put the keys back in his pocket and walked slowly through the darkness towards the road.

He stood there hearing the shrilling cicadas, hearing the muted sound of music, the shrill distant cries of children. Anger smouldered inside him, anger as much against himself as against this strange girl. He had allowed himself to be flattered by her glances; he had imagined that they had concerned him as a man. Well, now he knew they were merely an appraisal of a 'bloody copper'. The bitch! The bad-tempered Boer bitch!

He stood there watching the lights of the Land Rover threading down the hill which led around the village; the sound of its racing engine growing louder as the headlamps came thrusting towards him.

CHAPTER FIVE

WITH THE SPEEDOMETER steady at seventy miles an hour the Land Rover roared down the wide, perfectly cambered road completed when Timber Concessions moved into the Chapanda district. The wind buffeted in through the side windows warm and damp and smelling of the night. Occasionally with silver brilliance the headlights flicked against a soaring white moth, and twice a small 'duiker' deer, scarcely bigger than a hare, scampered across the road and dived into the feathery grasses at the roadside.

Potterson rubbed at the mist fogging the windscreen and lifted his voice above the noise of the engine.

'Which way, sir? Across country or round by the main road and then in through the back way?'

'Main road,' said Field. 'It's farther but much quicker. We'll bounce a bit when we hit the dirt road but keep your foot down.'

'How long d'you think, sir?'

'Fifteen minutes to the spur road into the Tribal Reserve and another twenty to reach old Tzalo. When we get closer we'll start the siren and fire a Very pistol just to cheer up the old buzzard. Not that he'll be downhearted. If he's still alive that is.'

Potterson changed down expertly into second, judging his engine revs perfectly to match the gear shift, and they bellowed exultantly up through the dark avenue of Timber Concession pines which crowned the hill. He put his foot down hard on the long straight descent and again lifted his voice above the engine.

'Why d'you think they're attacking Tzalo, Skipper? Usual political intimidation?'

'Of course.'

'Most of them pay up.'

'Not Tzalo,' said Field. 'He's a stubborn old black man, just like stubborn old Afrikaaners and stubborn old Englishmen. He's not going to be intimidated into the pretence of joining a political party, paying dues and all that crap unless he wants to. And he doesn't want to. He won't compromise. He won't be pushed around. The fact that he might get his head bashed in or his house burned down won't change him.'

'He's got guts.'

'He's an idiot,' said Field flatly. 'Logically, five bob a week isn't much to pay against having a petrol bomb thrown in through your front window.'

'But, Skipper—?' protested Potterson.

'He's about on the level of the "good" Germans in the early days of Hitler. The Nazis brushed them off the face of the earth with hardly a protest. To make good you've got to operate at either end of the pole—be an extremist. The "in-betweens", the "moderates", the "liberals" in this sort of situation never get to the starting gate. In the face of modern methods of intimidation, old-fashioned honesty has as much chance of survival as an ice cream in hell. You know that. Tzalo hasn't got a chance. Unless we protect him.'

'But we shall protect him,' said Potterson indignantly.

Field said flatly, 'Of course. That's our job.'

Fifteen minutes later they swung off the main road taking the dirt road into the Tribal Trust Lands, and within yards they were bouncing and swinging to miss the deep ruts and potholes. As they crested a low hill, they saw the glow lighting the darkness ahead.

'Fire,' said Potterson. 'Could it be his house?'

'Hope not. I'll fire a Very flare. If the thugs are still around —which I doubt—they might take fright.'

Field reached into the locker compartment for the squat-barrelled Very pistol, snapped open the breech, and forced in the heavy cartridge. He clicked the gun shut, pushed it through the open window and pulled the trigger. With a loud 'pouf' the single red star shot high into the night and hung there like a brilliant vermilion head.

'Okay! Siren!' he said.

Five minutes later, with the banshee wail rising and falling around them, they jolted in to the cleared space around Tzalo's homestead. The thatched roof of a pole and dagga hut was burning fiercely—two figures were running in and out trying to rescue its contents—but the house with its corrugated iron roof looked undamaged.

Potterson jammed on the brakes and Field swung open his door. He shouted to Ironside, 'Sergeant, take two men and scout around and see if you can find anybody. The rest help to get the stuff out of the barn.'

He ran over to the blaze and met old Tzalo dragging a sack of maize through the door helped by a young African boy.

The old man paused for a second to wipe the sweat from his face. His white teeth parted in a grin, 'Ah, Inspector, I'm very glad you have come.'

'They've gone?' asked Field.

'I think so. As soon as you fired your rocket and I heard your siren I knew we were safe to come outside.'

'Much more inside the hut?'

'A few sacks of maize and tools, that is all.'

'Right, let's get them out.'

Field followed Tzalo back into the burning building. The heat was intense. Sparks dropped on their heads from the blazing thatch. Field grabbed a sack of maize and towed it behind him out of danger. In five minutes, with everyone helping, they cleared the hut. There was no chance of saving it. All they could do was stand back and watch it burn.

Ten minutes later Sergeant Ironside stamped heavily towards them and reported that his patrol had found nothing.

'I didn't think you would,' commented Field.

Old Tzalo came back from his house walking slowly and wearily. 'I am a bit old for these adventures, Inspector,' he said. He added, 'You will come inside and take coffee? I am very grateful for your intervention.'

They followed the old man over a narrow verandah floored with rotten boards into the single-storey shack. The sash windows rattled in the wind. The large living-room was furnished with three rush mats, a wooden table and plain chairs. Against one wall stood a weatherbeaten dresser, holding cheap plates of willow pattern, three religious prints showing hazy angels revolving in cloud-filled skies hung on the bare wooden walls. It was the room of a poor man, yet Tzalo was far better off than most of his neighbours.

Two doors connecting with the bedrooms and kitchen led

off from the main room and through the doors emerged four African women and a solemn-faced collection of children.

'My sons' wives,' explained Tzalo. 'My sons are up in the Reserve, otherwise you can be certain this would never have happened.'

Field sat down at the table and looked at the old man. He was short, his face black, creased and weatherbeaten, his nose splayed, his lips thick. He wore an old blue shirt frayed and faded from constant washings, old grey flannels with a dark blue patch over one knee, no shoes. Yet he possessed a special sort of dignity, and his voice when he spoke in his formal, almost stilted English, was deep and musical. Field had known him on and off for ten years and always got on well with him.

'Any idea who did the damage?'

Tzalo pursed his lips thoughtfully, then smiled. 'Let us say, Inspector, that my intuition tells me very well who was behind it, but my intelligence also tells me very well that this would be difficult to prove.'

As usual, Tzalo was acting like Sherlock Holmes. Field knew that Conan Doyle was his favourite author.

'I would like to hear the source of your intuition,' said Field patiently.

Tzalo looked pleased. 'I had a visitor a week ago. In fact I reported his visit to your office, Inspector.'

Field nodded, and Tzalo went on, 'A very smart visitor, very well dressed, very polite. He informed me very politely that I had been elected to the Zambezi Independent People's party which of course was a great honour. He also added that the subscription was a pound a month, and that he was prepared to accept payment now.'

'Ali Hassim Khan,' said Field.

'Of course.' Tzalo paused, savouring his story. 'I pointed out that I was an old man. I told him I had come up from the Cape on an ox-wagon as a little servant boy before the turn of the century, and that I had had the privilege of seeing the great Mr. Rhodes himself.'

'I'm surprised they haven't been on to you before,' said Field.

'They have,' said the old man, 'but I am well respected in

the area, and I have five large sons in whose blood runs the blood of Zulu warriors.'

'Did he threaten you?'

'Of course not. He is much too clever. He simply said that he hoped I would reconsider his offer.'

'I bet he did,' said Field. 'And you can be certain he'll be at home playing cards with at least ten friends tonight. Did you recognize any of the others?'

'I think so,' said Tzalo. 'When the dogs started barking I went outside with my torch. It is a very powerful torch and when I shone it around I suddenly picked up the shape of a man wearing a yellow shirt. At that distance I could not recognize him of course, but I have seen an African hanging around here in the reserve several times lately wearing such a garment. One of my sons told me that he believes this man works at one of the farms in the district.'

'Which farm?' said Field.

'That of Mr. Van der Huizen.'

'Oh does he?' said Field with interest. 'We'll make enquiries.' It was, of course, typical that an African engaged on what should be a secret intimidation would wear a shirt that made him so conspicuous. A highly-prized shirt, no doubt. Possibly his only shirt. But he would have scarpered from the farm by now if he realized he'd been recognized.

'Someone fired a shot at you then?' said Field.

'Whether it was me, or over my head, whether to frighten me or merely to recall the gang and tell them to make off I do not know,' said Tzalo, 'but a shot certainly was fired, and it was then that I saw that they had set fire to the hut.'

One of the fattest African women wearing a faded print dress with a blue handkerchief around her head, brought in a large pot of coffee. The other women placed six chipped enamel mugs, a tin of Carnation milk punctured with two holes and a bowl of sugar on the table. The cups were filled, milk and sugar added and the first passed to Field, the second to Potterson and the third to Sergeant Ironside; the constables waited their turn.

Tzalo did not drink. 'It keeps me awake,' he explained. Then he added cheerfully, 'I am afraid we have big problems in Africa, Inspector.'

'I'll talk to Ali Hassim Khan on the way back,' said Field, 'though I don't suppose I'll get anywhere.'

'Do you know, Inspector,' Tzalo was off on his own track, 'when I was a boy in the Cape Province it was the best place in the world to live.'

'You did tell me,' said Field, uneasily aware from past experience that once Tzalo got started on a favourite theme it might be half an hour before he finished.

'Under the British flag there was freedom for all: the black man, the coloured, the European, the Afrikaaner. We lived together happily Mr. Field. Now what is Africa coming to when my own people attack me? Intimidate an old man like me, Inspector?' He shook his head and smiled happily. 'But they will not succeed.'

'Well, we must be going,' said Field. 'I'll leave a constable here just to make certain you're not disturbed again tonight, though I think it's unlikely.'

Tzalo stood up with him prepared to prolong the lecture until the very last minute. 'One thing is certain,' he said, looking at Field with wide, brooding eyes, 'the Europeans must remain. I do not say this to you because you are European, Inspector. I say it to you because it is necessary. The state of the world makes it inevitable that we must live like the Europeans merely to survive.'

As they bumped back towards the main road Potterson said, 'Does he really believe that stuff about the Europeans staying here?'

'Of course he does. He's old-fashioned. He doesn't understand that they buried what was left of the British Empire with Winston Churchill. Including Southern Rhodesia.' He paused and then went on, 'Let's call in at the Timber Concession compound, shall we? Ali Hassim Khan is bound to be there, and no doubt five hundred Africans have had their eyes on him all night long.'

Timber Concessions ran their own compound for African workers and their families. A beer hall sold thick mealie beer, and there was a dance hall attached. They were open every evening, but Saturday night was always a gala occasion and the place was packed.

A heavy gate barred the entrance. The uniformed guard

swung it open when they saw the police Land Rover, and saluted as they drove in. Potterson parked in the open space outside the barn-like wooden building. As they climbed the steps they could hear the loud syncopation of the band, the buzz of conversation, an occasional shriek, the shuffle of dancing feet. Randolph Brown, the company's welfare officer, was standing in the entrance. He was a tall, thin, long-haired young man with rather bulbous eyes, and his face sunburned a bright copper colour. He wore an open-necked white shirt, sleeves rolled up, and pale grey flannels. As soon as he saw them he looked worried. He hurried across.

'Good evening, Inspector. Not an official visit, I hope?'

'Sounds as though you're having a gay time here tonight,' Field said affably.

The young man brightened. 'About the usual amount of noise I would say. We get very little trouble here as you know, Inspector.'

'Yes,' said Field, 'but there's been a little trouble up in the Reserve. A barn has been burned down. Is Mr. Ali Hassim Khan here, by the way?'

The cheerful look on Mr. Brown's face faded. 'Yes, he's here. Been here all the evening in fact. I can vouch for that. I've been talking to him myself some of the time. You don't think—?'

'Just a routine enquiry,' said Field heavily, 'but I'd like to have a word with him. It would probably be better if he came out here.'

'I agree. I'll get someone to fetch him. It won't take a second.' Mr. Brown, now visibly worried again, disappeared through one of the doors which led into the dance hall.

Ali Hassim Khan watched Mr. Brown come down the hall towards him. He could see by the look on his face that he brought trouble and he knew exactly what the trouble was. He disliked Mr. Brown. He disliked all white liberals; they were neither one thing nor the other; they vacillated like emotional women and you could use them like women, playing on their black brother sympathies. Mr. Brown made him sick. With the police whom he knew would be waiting outside you knew where you were. They were enemies. They operated with the laws they had made against you, and they had power on their side and force on their side so you operated cautiously. History would end their rule, but he had no time to wait for history.

'Oh, Ali,' said Mr. Brown apologetically, 'I'm afraid there's some trouble. It's the police.'

'Yeah,' said Ali Hassim Khan, 'how many? A posse armed with riot guns?'

'Good heavens, no. Only the Inspector and a European constable.'

'Great,' said Ali Hassim Khan. 'Great.' Since his three years in Howard University, Washington, he had adopted an American accent and the American idiom. America had really made him. He had arrived there with no more than the usual chip on his shoulder, a nice anglicized African ready to learn all about democracy, God and the end of the colonial era. But in Washington he had learnt all about hate. The American Negro, more urbane, more intellectual, more dynamic with three hundred years of slavery, and white domination on his back, had kept up with the times. Oh yes, he had learnt a lot in those three years. They came in all sizes at Howard: the quiet ones who thought you could make it through compromise, the ones who said that economic equality was all that mattered, and the ones who hated, the ones who saw the future only in a blood clash between black and white. Ali Hassim Khan listened to all of them but believed the violent ones. Listened and learned.

'Let's go talk to the Inspector, shall we, boys,' he said.

Field paced half-way across the hall and back again. It would have been better if he had been in uniform. Uniform was a protective camouflage.

He said, 'Good band they've got by the sound of it. Damn sight better than the record player up at the club.'

'These boys have got real talent, sir,' said Potterson. 'And none of them reads a note of music, did you know that? Just born in them, I suppose.'

Field wondered how Milly was getting on. Of course the Jenkins would run her home if necessary. By now he would also expect Cohen to be leering avidly at Molly Crosby, or maybe he had transferred his attentions to Sarah Van der Huizen. He felt vaguely annoyed at the idea.

Ali Hassim Khan came through the door with Brown and two other Africans. By comparison with the other three men who wore pale fawn and light grey suits, white shirts and jazzy ties, Brown looked untidy. 'You wanted to see me, Inspector?' said Ali Hassim Khan.

'I wanted to see *you,* Mr. Khan,' said Field quietly, 'not your friends. Or you Mr. Brown.'

Mr. Brown looked disconcerted. 'Oh, of course, you want a private talk. Let's go back into the dance hall, shall we, fellows?'

The two Africans looked as if they didn't like the idea at all. However, Ali Hassim Khan spoke sharply in dialect and they followed Mr. Brown.

'I see you have your constable with you, Inspector,' said Ali Hassim Khan smoothly.

Like two boxers sparring, thought Field. Or rather, like two cautious diplomats making opening moves: you make a concession, I make a concession.

'Potterson,' said Field, 'go and wait in the Land Rover. I shan't be very long.'

For the first time Ali Hassim smiled, showing strong white teeth. He was as tall as Field, and equally heavily built. Field stared straight into his eyes: the policeman's look. More often than not it worked, but not this time. Ali Hassim Khan's eyes were cold and predatory, the planes of his pale brown face beneath them hard and muscular. No pushover, this one. No Bantu just in from the bush, wondering what it was all about. This was the new African, his blood laced with genes from Afrikaaner or European, and hating the alien infusion. A man demanding his inheritance, brooding over the old wrongs. There was going to be no compromise here. This was a violent man seeking violent solutions, well versed in the cult of the second half of the twentieth century, aware that blood, riot and trouble were the well-tried recipes which brought you to power. A man clever enough also to operate inside the law. He'd never capitulate like Nkomo and Sithole and go quietly into detention to appease his followers, and be ready for the premiership when the time came. This man operated on his own terrain like a jungle cat. What the hell he was doing out here in the bush at

Chapanda, Field couldn't understand. Just sharpening his claws, he supposed.

'So what can I do for you, Inspector?' Ali Hassim Khan demanded curtly.

'I understand,' said Field, 'that you visited old Tzalo's farm a week or so ago, and suggested that he became a due-paying member of your political party?'

'Perfectly true. And as a member of a law-abiding democracy, he refused,' said Ali Hassim Khan guardedly.

'And by the merest coincidence someone took a potshot at him tonight and burnt down his barn,' Field countered.

Ali Hassim Khan's voice was contemptuous, 'You are not suggesting that I had anything to do with such a squalid little affair, I hope.' His voice rose higher. 'You are not accusing me of that, Inspector?' He had to watch himself. The rage burnt deeply inside.

'If I had any proof I would charge you at once,' said Field levelly. 'But I will tell you as a favour that I suspect you. Your boys might get away with this sort of stuff in Highlands and Harare, but you'll have a little difficulty in getting away with it here. In the reserve they're not quite sophisticated enough for you. They're law-abiding, peaceful people, not unemployed layabouts like so many of your friends in Salisbury.'

Ali Hassim Khan was angry. 'Yes, as you say, Inspector, they are unemployed. And whose fault is that? The fault of the Europeans: the people who need a pool of slave labour from which they can choose a few hundred hungry workers and pay them slave wages.'

Field knew he was in too deep. But this was a private conversation and he might just as well go in over his head.

'Frankly, Mr. Khan,' he said civilly, 'I don't think you give a damn about the African unemployed or the reasons why they are unemployed. I think you are a cynical bastard who holds both your own people and the Mashonas in utter contempt. I think all you want is a quick ride to power on their backs, a quick ride to the expense account cars and hotels and airline tickets to romantic places. You may very well get there, for I'm pretty sure you don't give a damn for anybody except yourself.'

Ali Hassim Khan was cold and angry. 'Do you, policeman? Do you? I am sure that oppressing my people must give you a great deal of pleasure.'

'You started the speeches and I got carried away,' said Field a little wearily. 'I am not here to oppress your people, you know that. Only to keep the law. So I'm warning you, Ali Hassim Khan. I keep the law in this part of the country, and if I get any evidence that you're mixed up in any intimidation attempts, you'll be inside so fast you won't see your arse for dust. I hope I make myself clear.'

The two of them stood staring at each other in silence for at least three seconds, then Ali Hassim Khan said bitterly, 'You make yourself quite clear, Inspector. As you say, the law is on your side even though that law is a vicious and repressive law.'

'I am well aware of the provisions of the Emergency Powers Act.'

'So far,' said Hassim Khan, 'the repressive measures have been directed at the black Rhodesians, but in the fullness of time no doubt they will also be turned against the white Rhodesians.'

'Good night, Mr. Khan,' said Field, 'I hope you know what I've been talking about.' He turned on his heel and walking towards the door, aware that the other was standing still staring after him.

Outside in the darkness, driving more slowly now, Potterson said, 'Did it go all right, sir?'

'Everyone hates the police,' said Field, 'I should be a nice quiet bank clerk in Salisbury.'

Potterson laughed dutifully. 'But did it go all right, sir?'

'If the Commissioner heard a recording of our conversation I should now be applying for a job as office boy in the Zambian Sewage Company,' said Field. He paused. Then he said, 'It went all right. Ali Hassim Khan had a perfect alibi.' He added, 'May as well come back to the police post with you. The party at the club will be over by now.' He sat there in silence for a few seconds and then added, 'Got to admire his guts though.'

'Old Tzalo, sir?'

'No. Ali Hassim Khan.'

'I don't follow.'

'It's one thing to be an extremist agitator when the laws of the land offer minor penalties for transgression. It's quite another when the punishment is punitive. The death penalty could be the result of this little affair at Tzalo's.'

'Only theoretically, sir.'

'It's one thing to be a policeman in a force dedicated to keeping law and order,' said Field, 'it's quite another to be a policeman carrying out repressive measures for a government he didn't vote into power.'

'You don't really believe that, Skipper. No matter what you think about the lot in Salisbury, they're still democratic.'

'So far.'

Potterson sounded anxious. 'But you remember what it was like in sixty-two and three,' he said. 'The chaps told me in Salisbury. Riots every Saturday and Sunday. Duty every weekend to cope with them. Stand-by twenty-four hours a day.'

'I was there,' said Field heavily. 'The police force would have disintegrated eventually under the strain. But repressive laws are like income tax. They tend to stay. I like the old concept of law and order, Potterson, not the new. Sometimes I wish I was a London bobby with nothing to worry about but armed hold-ups, dope peddling, smash-and-grab raids, teenage hoodlums, rape, murder and train robberies. Not to mention those long lonely nights on the beat in the rain.'

'At least we've got the sun out here, sir,' said Potterson happily.

'Yes, Potterson. We've got the sun.'

CHAPTER SIX

AFTER LUNCH NEXT DAY he swung the Land Rover off the dirt road at the painted sign which said 'Van der Huizen', jerked into low gear and pointed the broad nose up the steep slope. The dirt track was well graded, dun-coloured in the sunshine, the bush on either side thick and verdant; between the trees the sky was a wedge of blue and the shadows across the road were purple and black.

As he climbed higher the vegetation thinned, and glancing sideways he could see the countryside stretching away into a haze of heat. Since his earliest days as a trooper in Chapanda, he had always envied the old Boer his long, low house sitting high on the hillside looking across the Sabi valley.

Field parked in a wide sandy area cut out in the hillside, alongside a dusty Land Rover and a pale blue Victor, got out and slammed the door. William, the African constable, slipped out the other side. 'Okay,' said Field, 'carry on.' It was William's duty to talk to the African farm workers and see if they knew anything about a man in a yellow shirt.

Field had not seen the Victor before and he spent a second examining it, before walking up the path through a terraced garden full of flowers and shrubs. When Van der Huizen had arrived here this country had been matted bush; it had cost him nothing to buy. He went round to the tobacco cutting sheds, windowless buildings of wood and corrugated iron with steeply pitched roofs at the back. Nearby a saddled horse held by an African attracted his attention—and he saw a yard or two away Sarah Van der Huizen on her knees working with great concentration.

Intrigued, Field walked closer. She held a small, fawn-coloured 'duiker' deer, not much bigger than a large hare, in her arms and was carefully bandaging a wound in its stomach. The small animal did not struggle. It lay inert, its eyes wide and dark, its tiny black nose moist. A little blood seeped through the bandage.

Sarah had found it an hour earlier as she rode quietly

along the track which ran along the edge of the escarpment. The mare had been quiet and tolerant beneath her, the steamy bowl of the Sabi Valley stretching far away into a misty immensity on her right.

Sarah Van der Huizen was twenty-three years old. She had been born on the farm at Chapanda and in her eyes it was the most beautiful place in the world. It had always meant freedom: in the early days freedom to explore the strange wild world of animals, spiders, scorpions and snakes that inhabited the bush around the farm; freedom to race down to the compound to hide and scream and play with the hordes of African children there; freedom from any authority except the gentle authority of her mother who up until she was nine years old had taught her to write and draw and paint.

When her mother died and she had been sent down to the Cape to stay with her maiden aunt and go to school there, it was almost the end of the world. She had hated the frowsty old nuns at the convent school who made her work at books and do sums and pray to a God who, she knew, if He existed at all, must exist out under the blue sky in the sunshine, and not here in these drab schoolrooms. School had meant discipline, authority, and the end of freedom, so she had learned to resent authority in any guise, schoolmistress, priest, nun or policeman.

She knew that she was pretty, that men desired her. In fact that great big oaf, Freddy, whom people spoke of in awe because he played rugby for some important team, had followed her all the way from South Africa and was now spending a week at the Chapanda Hotel in the vague hope that she would look upon him favourably.

At the Cape, David Mitchison had seriously and honourably proposed marriage and she had been tempted. He was good-looking and athletic and his family were wealthy. But when he kissed her nothing happened. She was young, romantic, and old-fashioned enough to think that an emotional flash of lightning and a roll of thunder should preface and climax this action. If you were in love anyway. And with David, nothing happened.

She had stayed at the Cape after she left school because

both her aunt and her father had thought she should have a chance to mix with people of her own age group. 'After all, Sarah,' said her aunt, 'you'll never find yourself a husband stuck away up there on Erasmus' farm.' She had mildly enjoyed the life of a pretty, unattached girl mixing in Cape Town society but she hadn't wanted any of the 'nice' boys who wanted her and she longed to be back at Chapanda. And now she was back. And she was happy. And she was never going to leave again.

She looked up at the policeman. She remembered him as a young man on a brown horse who used to ride up to the farm and drink a beer with her father. She had never thought of him as a policeman then and looked forward to his visits. He had patted her head and given her bars of chocolate and she had liked him, and they had been friends. But last night she had looked at him, remembering the serious young man of ten years ago and hardly recognizing the man she saw. Now he was older, tougher, more brutal, a symbol of the authority she resented, and when he had collided with her in the darkness all the resentment that he should have changed so much, flared out. She knew that she was volatile, quick-tempered, impatient, but the sudden physical contact had jolted words out of her mouth she did not know she could use. Now she looked up at him warily wondering if he was going to say nasty things about last night. But all he said was, 'What happened to it?' with a note of concern in his voice. She liked that. She bent again to the tiny animal and said, 'I don't know. I found it lying beside the track about a mile from here. I thought a leopard perhaps.'

Field bent down to examine the tiny deer. As he did so he noticed she was wearing pale fawn jodhpurs and that the front of the thin silk shirt, open at the throat, was stained with the 'duiker's' blood. Her hands were small and shapely, with oval, manicured fingernails, but they worked swiftly and competently.

'Definitely not a leopard,' said Field. 'Not at this time of day. And one little bite would dispose of a "duiker". More likely a wild dog got it and you disturbed him. Is it badly torn?'

'No, I don't think so.'

'It's probably suffering from shock more than anything else. Have you got a pad under that bandage?'

'No.'

'You really need one. And a shot of penicillin would help. I've got both in my medical kit. I'll fetch them.

'Thank you.'

Field smiled. 'It's a pleasure to know a bloody copper can help occasionally.'

Her eyes narrowed again and he stood up quickly. She obviously had not exhausted that subject. She looked very young and immature without any make-up, her dark hair held back behind her ears with a mother-of-pearl slide.

'Shan't be a minute,' he said.

When he came back Joshua, the old African servant, had taken the horse away and she had undone her bandage. Field examined the wound, dusted it with penicillin powder, applied the cotton wool pad and helped her bind it up again. He inserted the hypodermic needle into the phial of penicillin and wondered what Bill Marcus in charge of police medical stores would say if he saw his precious drugs being used on a small deer.

'Hold him tight,' he said. 'He might jump when the needle goes in.'

Her small white hands held the deer firmly against her body as Field injected the drug into the deer's hindquarter. It did not move.

Field stroked the velvety skin. 'I don't think we can do much more,' he said, 'and I don't think you should be too optimistic about its chances. These small animals die of shock very easily, you know. It's nature's way of letting them out without much pain. What will you do with it?'

She held it close to her like a baby as if her own warmth could somehow infuse strength into it. 'There's a small pen behind the barn where I used to keep my pet rabbits. I'll let it rest there and tell Joshua to look after it.'

'Good idea,' said Field. He stood up. 'I'm going in to talk to your father. Perhaps I'll see you later?'

'Perhaps,' she said. She didn't sound over-enthusiastic.

He found her father sprawled out in a chair in the lounge,

a glass of whisky by his side, half asleep. Erasmus Van der Huizen was a hulk of a man, his bald head bristling with a stubble of white hair, his thick neck creased with folds of fat. His huge, corpulent body was encased in a white shirt and baggy grey flannels, he wore carpet slippers on his feet and his face was as featureless as a lump of dough. Yet life still twinkled in the piggy blue eyes, boomed out in the heavy Afrikaans' accent. The years had made him fat and old, but he was still recognizably a male creature, arrogant, generous, tolerant, welcoming.

He sat up in his deep armchair, as Field came in.

'Hello, Inspector,' he said, extending his enormous hand. 'Haven't seen you around, man, for a long time. I suppose the news got out that I've got a pretty daughter home with me.' He trumpeted with laughter at his minor joke and Field smiled cautiously. He said, 'There was trouble in the Reserve last night. A gang attacked old Tzalo's farm.'

'Did they, now! A good nigger, that Tzalo. I like him.'

Field knew that to Erasmus 'nigger' was merely a name, like lion, tiger, Boer, Afrikaaner, Roinek, Eytie, Kraut. You recognized and discussed your fellow-men by these nouns.

'We think one of the gang might have come from your farm. A boy in a bright yellow shirt.'

Van der Huizen scratched his ear. 'I paid off about ten boys last week,' he said. 'Most of them were Nyasaland boys. He could have been one of them.'

'It's called Malawi these days,' said Field politely.

'What is?'

'Our neighbour to the north. The ex-British protectorate of Nyasaland.'

'Yah man. I forgot. Good job the bloody government's got our independence, eh man?'

'I suppose so,' said Field.

'But you're a bloody liberal man. I bet you didn't vote for it.'

'I didn't even have a party to vote for,' said Field. 'There was no opposition candidate in my constituency.' He paused, trying to get the conversation back to business. 'Do you mind if my constable has a look around, talks to your foreman and a few of the boys?'

The old man heaved himself up in his chair and subsided again with a grunt.

'Do what you like, man. But first you'll have a drink and meet my girl, Sarah.'

'Well—'

'Oh for Christ's sake man, of course you'll stay. The bloody police force can spare you for an hour or two. Besides it's a change to have someone to talk to.'

Van der Huizen liked the big policeman. He liked the big, dark-shaded chin, the level blue eyes, the air of seriousness, the masculinity. He remembered him coming to the district as a tall, gangling trooper in a brand new uniform which looked about three sizes too big for him, very self-conscious about both his appearance and his responsibilities: 'A beer? I don't think I'd better, Mr. Van der Huizen, I'm on duty you know.'

Well, times had changed. The African sun and food had filled him out, long weeks in the bush had given him confidence, years in contact with the frailties of bastard human beings had given him experience. Now he was big, the shyness had gone, he was no longer a bloody Englishman but a hybrid species, perhaps a little like that Yankee frontiersman who had rebelled against the German George. Some people never realized that people change as well as times.

'You'll have a cold beer, Bill?' said Van der Huizen, struggling out of his chair.

'Yes, I will, thanks.'

The old man went across to the enormous fridge which he kept in the living-room. Why shout for a boy when you can have a drink under your nose? He snapped open the polished door. 'Lion or Castle or I've got a Heinekens if you'd like that?'

'Castle,' said Field. Then after a pause, 'I was talking to your daughter outside, Mr. Van der Huizen. I don't think she likes policemen very much.'

Van der Huizen chuckled again. 'She's a fire-eater that girl. She likes fights. She picks fights. She's like her mother. Wild! You'd hardly remember her. Scotch, you know. A wild Celt. Came from some place up in the Highlands, Lochinver, I think. Had the same skin and those bright blue eyes. Her mother and father emigrated to South Africa, ran a little shop in Cape Town. Never made much of it. That's why Annie took me, I think, because she wanted security. I don't think she ever really loved me. Not the way I wanted her.'

Field had heard the old man's story many times. He'd arrived in Rhodesia when you could have bought most of the bloody country for a bob an acre. He'd been a plasterer back in Johannesburg, his father the youngest of a large farming family, so there'd been no money there. And what good, for Christ's sake, was daubing plaster on walls when to the north there were millions of miles of virgin land waiting for plough and seed? Oh yes, back in the '90's the Van der Huizens had had money but somehow, between the British, the gold rush, the diamonds, the Reformed Church and the booze, it had all slipped away. So he'd come north to Salisbury and worked there for as many hours as the daylight lasted at his trade, until he'd got himself a stake. Then he said to Joe, his boss boy on the building site, who came from Basutoland, what about heading out east and trying to farm a bit of land? Dirt cheap, they say, near Fort Vic. Joe said, 'Okay, boss.' So they'd bloody well walked all the way to Fort Vic, sleeping on the roadside or in African villages. And they'd put the money down for the land in Fort Vic and started walking again until they got there. They'd slept under that bloody tree, man, standing on the lawn over there; though it hadn't been a lawn then. He'd always had a soft spot for that tree; it had kept the rain off so often. A bag of seed, flour, and coffee, biltong, salt, and sugar, his rifle and ammunition and one bottle of whisky, for medical reasons you know man. Spades and hoes, and five thousand acres. He'd added to it since then; now he had sixty-five thousand acres which stretched from up here in the hills down to the banks of the Sabi.

They started to dig, they planted their maize, and that was the end of the stake. But it was a good crop and it sold well, and with the profit they bought a light plough, and he and Joe had taken in turn to pull the bloody thing. So that's how it began. Sleeping under a tree and pulling a plough by sweat and muscle because they hadn't got enough money to buy an ox. And all these stupid 'dumkopf' overseas bastards talking about 'settlers' as if you dropped like a swarm of locusts on the ground and it blossomed pound notes. Maize at first, and then a little tobacco, and Ferguson sixty miles away had lent them the use of his curing sheds and given them good advice. A bloody good chap, Ferguson. And after five seasons of just about making out he'd approached the bank manager in Fort Victoria and got a loan. They'd planted a thousand acres of tobacco that season and struck it rich. God had been good. Three good seasons in a row and they were on their feet. It was then that Joe bought himself a wife from the nearby Shangaan village, and told Erasmus that he should bloody well go down to the Cape or Salisbury and do the same. Stuck out here with nothing but mosquitoes and whisky was no good for anyone; a man had to keep some connection with life. A man should breed children from his own stock.

So he'd built himself a two-roomed house. From start to finish he built the whole bloody thing, then he'd ridden into Fort Vic and caught the train down to Johannesburg and on to the Cape. And met Annie.

His aunts had buzzed with annoyance. Surely, there were plenty of good Boer girls who'd make him better wives! Strong girls who could plant and hoe and run a farm. But Erasmus knew it had to be Annie. There was some magic about her; an incandescence about her body, her eyes, every movement she made. She inhabited his thoughts.

She had been serving behind the counter of the sweet and newspaper shop run by her parents just behind Adderley Street when he walked in casually for a packet of fags one day. He walked in not less than four times a day quite uncasually after that, and his smoking increased.

He'd courted her very respectfully, a visit to the bioscope first, then little walks up through the shady trees on the fringes of Table Mountain and on Sundays they'd climb the mountain by the easy route and sit on the top looking down at the great blue sweep of Table Bay and the little white houses far below. 'It's beautiful,' Annie said, in her soft clear Highland accent, 'so beautiful. And warm, too. That's what I like, warm!'

It was on the plateau top of Table Mountain, after he'd learnt to talk to her, that he approached the subject of marriage.

'Joe's my boss boy,' he said. 'We've built this farm together up in the Eastern Highlands. It's rough but it will get better and I'll make money and I'll be able to take holidays in the Cape and Mozambique. Last month Joe bought himself a wife.' He grinned, not at all sure of himself. 'I'd like to buy you and take you back with me.'

He looked at the wide, blue eyes which Sarah had inherited and was not quite sure if he'd said the right thing. But she smiled and then she laughed and she said, 'Well, good Scots girls aren't very expensive. You buy them with a pound of herrings where I come from.'

Annie had thought the 'buying' bit very original. She had prattled about it all the way down the mountainside, and for the first time she had taken him in to see her father and mother.

'Dad,' she said gaily, 'you'd better meet Erasmus. He wants to buy me and take me off to his farm in Rhodesia. How much d'you think I'm worth?'

The old Scot had looked at him thoughtfully over the top of his steel rimmed spectacles and said slowly, 'I suppose there are stranger ways of finding a wife?'

A month later they were married and travelling back north. They'd had their troubles but Annie was as hardy as any Boer woman and just as practical; she could bake and wash and run a house. And the magic he had found on their first meeting, her moments of tenderness, her passion, the quick furies which excited or exasperated him were always there. The fact that the good Lord had only seen fit to present them with a daughter was a disappointment, but Erasmus never regretted his marriage.

Erasmus paused in his story. 'You must excuse an old man, Bill. He tends to go on a bit long about his memories.'

Field took a long satisfying swill of his beer. 'Not at all,' he said.

He looked around the lounge. It was a beautiful room. Whether Annie or Erasmus or just good luck had designed it, didn't really matter; it existed. Heavy black beams supported the high ceiling, the immense stone fireplace was filled with a huge bowl of flowers, silver candlesticks and green candles stood on the mantelpiece, white walls, lime green curtains, dark green settees and armchairs made it comfortable. Rust and green rugs and carpets were scattered on the black polished floor, the sunlight poured in through the high french windows, and outside in the middle of the clipped green lawn stood a huge, shady flamboyant tree. All around the room were trophies, eyeless shells of white bone surmounted by horns of strange convoluted beauty. Field disliked them. He had never got any excitement out of killing animals although he'd tried hard enough; he'd seen all those bony relics as they once were, as wild beasts, in the evening light, in the dawn with the mist rising, camouflaged by nature against the pale greens and the soft golds, beautiful creatures with liquid eyes, velvety coats and quivering black nostrils poised and ready to spring away with quicksilver grace.

Erasmus caught his glance and looked up at the huge sable horns with pride.

'By gar, that fellow gave me a fight,' he said. 'Damn near killed me before I killed him.'

Field knew they were not trophies to Van der Huizen. They were trespassers; they had contended for his land; he had fought them over this terrain and won, and their heads were nailed against the wall to prove who was the victor. Sarah came into the room and Field saw that she had changed out of the jodhpurs and blood-stained shirt into a blue silk sleeveless dress with a low round neck. She had loosened her hair so that it fell back and soft around her face. She looked deliciously clean.

Van der Huizen introduced them. 'My girl, Sarah,' he said. 'You know each other?'

'Yes,' said Field.

Sarah simply looked. Then she said, 'You finished your beer, Inspector. You'd like another?'

'Thanks,' said Field, content to have this lovely, shapely girl waiting upon him.

She reached across for his glass, half bending to do so. The upper half of her white breasts flashed briefly beneath the blue silk dress, and as if she knew exactly what she had done she lifted her eyes quickly to catch his. It was a provocative female trait which Cohen would have applauded but which slightly confused Field.

He said, 'Did you settle the "duiker" all right?'

'Yes,' she said. 'I've put it on a bed of straw and told Joshua to keep an eye on him.'

She walked across to the fridge, opened the door and looked inside. 'We're a bit low on beer,' she said. 'I'll get some more.'

'She's a good girl,' said the old man when she had gone. 'But what she needs is a husband! Someone who could keep her in order. Like you.' He brightened at the thought. 'Like the job?'

'Very much,' said Field. 'Only one drawback. I'm married already.'

'By gar, you're right,' said Erasmus seriously. 'I hadn't thought of that.'

'Sarah's a bit young to settle down, isn't she?' added Field slowly.

'Too young? Man, in my day they were married with babies at their breast when they were sixteen years old. Mind you they couldn't read or write, but they could bake and sew and keep house, and I'll guarantee they were better in bed than most of these young hussies these days.'

Field grinned. 'I have a feeling some people might think you a shade old-fashioned, Mr. Van der Huizen.'

The old man stretched out his feet so that his carpet slippers lay in a pool of sunlight. He reached out for the whisky bottle, poured in two inches and added a minute drop of water. He held it up to the light. 'Whisky and women, man,' he said slowly. 'Two of the things that make life bearable. I've had plenty of whisky. Not enough women. No time for women. Too much work.'

Sarah came back with the beer and listened while they talked for an hour. When he finally got up to go, to his slight surprise she followed him out on to the verandah. She sensed his curiosity and said mockingly, 'Don't worry, Inspector. I'm only going to see how the "duiker" is getting on.'

They walked down the steps and along towards the tobacco sheds. It was now very hot; the bright splodges of colour made by the sky and bush, red earth and green grass were blurred by heat. She swayed along by his side just about reaching his shoulder and he was vividly conscious of her body. He smelt the perfume she had worn at the club the night before, and supposed it must be a fresh sprinkling. They walked slowly with Field keeping an eye open for William. He certainly did not anticipate her next move.

Suddenly with a little 'Oh!' of horror she darted away from him heading for the wire enclosure built against one side of a curing shed, and at once he saw the reason for her consternation.

Inside the enclosure stood old Joshua holding up the 'duiker' by its hind legs as he would hold a dead rabbit. And the 'duiker' was dead, the golden fawn body stiff, the now absurd bandage still twined around its middle. It was only when Field saw Sarah seize a heavy stick standing against the wire and push in through the gate that he realized her intention and started after her. Clearly she thought it was the old man's fault. She lifted the stick to hit him, shouting, 'Bloody stupid nigger. You old idiot, I told you to look after it, and you've killed it, you've deliberately killed it.'

Field, stepping quickly into the wire enclosure after her, caught the top end of the stick, holding it firmly. 'Miss Van der Huizen, you shouldn't do this,' he said reasonably. 'The "duiker" obviously died of shock; it was probably half dead when you picked it up.'

'Let go,' she said, tugging at the stick, but he still held on.

The scene was a bit farcical and Field said, 'Bloody niggers and bloody policemen. Miss Van der Huizen, your language is too violent. You must realize that other people have a right to live in this country besides you.'

His mockery was a fundamental error: she had been tugging at the stick with both hands, now she held on with one hand and swung the other up hitting him in the face. His head went back with the force of the blow. The smile was removed from his lips. He reacted instinctively, without pause for thought. He hit her back. A hard slap across her cheek. It sprawled her against the wire fence and she stood there, one hand held up to her face, her eyes so furious that he half expected her to leap at him like a cat.

The entire episode was suddenly so childish and absurd that Field wanted to laugh.

'I'm sorry,' he said lamely. 'I shouldn't have done that. It was instinctive retaliation. I was brought up not to hit ladies; I was not allowed to even punch my kid sister, and if ever a girl needed punching she did—'

He stopped and she backed away towards the wire gate, tears in her eyes and hatred on her face. She sniffed. To Field she looked distressed and beautiful. Near tears she said, 'I hate you. I hate you. You're like all policemen. A brute and a bully.'

She turned and half ran through the gate and turned up towards the house. Field knew she was weeping like a small girl, running a few steps and then walking. In the old days of course she would have flung herself on her father's chest and he would have comforted her; now Field guessed she would cry alone in her own room and he wished he could run after her and help her.

'Sarah,' he shouted after her, 'Sarah,' but she didn't stop.

Field heard old Joshua's voice quavering behind him.

'He was dead, boss, honest, boss. I come in to see if he was warm, and there he was dead.'

The old man's helplessness was humbling.

'It's all right,' said Field, 'it's all right. She was upset and didn't know what she was doing when she saw you holding the animal like that. Women are like that. She's got a soft heart for animals. Human beings are probably not her strong point.'

The old man looked at him with rheumy eyes, not understanding a word. Field patted him on the shoulder and threw down the stick. He found his constable in the curing sheds and together they walked back to the Land Rover. He wondered vaguely if he might find Sarah Van der Huizen aiming a shot gun at him from behind her blue Victor?

It was not a good afternoon. Charlie Holland rang him up and reported that Ali Hassim Khan had written protesting about Field's interrogation at the dance hall, and asking that his complaint should be forwarded to the Commissioner in Salisbury. There were other smaller irritations to do with police procedure, and when he got home at six that evening he needed a drink. Milly was, as usual, a little distant. He slumped into an armchair.

'Get us a cold beer, there's a good girl.'

She was doing the crossword puzzle in an old airmail edition of the *Daily Telegraph*. The flimsy paper crackled as she moved. 'Abdul,' she called, 'get the master a cold beer.' Field looked at her quizzically. She could argue lengthily on the rights of the Africans, but when it came to dealing with the servants in her own household she was as autocratic as any other Rhodesian housewife. It was a dichotomy of attitude he found hard to understand.

The old man brought in the beer on a tray and Field winked at him. 'Thanks, Boss,' he said.

Abdul gave a quick shriek of laughter and left the room.

'Very funny,' said Milly. 'What's upset you today?' Field thought of telling her about his brush with Sarah Van der Huizen and decided against it.

'I had Charlie Holland on the blower this afternoon. Mr. Ali Hassim Khan had been complaining about my interrogation last night. That bloody man. The trouble he can cause.'

'He has a right to his opinions,' said Molly pugnaciously.

Field sighed. 'In my own home,' he said gently, 'I have a right to mine. A man should be able to make loud, large generalizations proving exclusively that not only has he the finest brain in the world and by rights should be President of the United States, but also occasionally make a complete ass of himself without his wife picking him up.'

'You'd like that put in the marriage vows, I expect,' said Milly curtly.

'A joke,' said Field wearily. 'I was only being funny.'

'You are becoming more and more like the rest of them here. A colonist in mentality and outlook.'

'This was a colony,' said Field quietly, 'until we made ourselves independent. Now what's for supper?'

'Curry,' said Milly flatly. 'Abdul seems to think everyone likes it.'

'Well, he makes rather a good curry, I think.'

'The trouble with all you men out here is that you don't really need a wife at all. You've got cookboys who will cook for you, gardener boys who will garden, houseboys who wash up for you. I expect you've got girls too on the sly who will do all the other things.'

'Some hopes,' he said. His flippancy annoyed her. 'Well, it won't last much longer,' she said angrily.

'No, dear.'

'The African has culture and intelligence, and the right to rule himself.'

'Yes, dear.'

'And don't sit there with that superior smile on your face thinking you know all the answers.'

Field knew from long experience that you couldn't get away with this 'Yes dear, no dear' malarky for long. In this mood women had to have some sort of explosion, some sort of verbal bruising, and afterwards, after a period of icy silence or sulks or tears, they would be prepared to renew the relationship. On the tacit understanding that of course they were the aggrieved victim. The Arabs had worked it out long ago; the Africans also, to a certain extent. You put a woman out to work, and filled her belly with children, and kept her slaving from dawn until dusk and she was as healthy and happy as—as a female mule anyway. Those bloody suffragettes were the cause of all the trouble. For ten million years women had baked the bread and tidied the cave and produced the kids. And Mrs. damn Pankhurst and her followers had ruined it all.

'You're a bloody Fascist,' said Milly furiously. That startled him. Milly very rarely swore.

'More Roman than Fascist, I was thinking,' he said tolerantly.

'You care for no one except yourself. You have power and you abuse it.'

That nettled him slightly. 'That's not true.'

'It's obvious from your mental attitude.'

Field sighed heavily. Oh for a glass of beer, a loaf of bread and a little peace and quiet when a man got home from work. But Milly had to have an argument; it was becoming more and more like South Africa every day; argument, especially political argument, was an obsession, as if through its exhausting therapy some compromise could be reached.

'Law and order is the basic premise of any civilization,' he said. 'I'm a policeman, that's what being a policeman is all about—I'm just doing my job.'

'Just doing my job,' said Milly, mimicking him. 'When things reach this pitch you can't just do your job. You're *implicated* whether you like it or not. On one side or the other.'

Field considered the remark. 'Honest Bill Field, the hope of the fourth form, now turned black butcher,' he said.

Milly got up. She was angry. 'You won't take anything seriously, will you? You live in the middle of a tragedy and you won't take anything seriously. It's all flippancy and beer with the boys.'

The insinuation of beery blimpish conformism startled Field, probably because he realized that there was more than a grain of truth in it. He tried to change the subject to get back on to some sort of normal conversational terrain. 'Milly,' he said, 'I came home for a rest and a quiet beer, and here we are in the middle of some goddamn argument about nothing. I just wanted a quiet beer.' He was conscious that his voice had risen.

'You'll never have a quiet beer until you have fair shares in this country.'

Field stood up. 'All right,' he said angrily, 'let's have fair shares. And let's start right here in our own house. Let's share the house with Abdul. In fact, let's be generous, let's give him the house and we'll move into his little pigsty at the bottom of the garden. Let's tell him, shall we?' He shouted loudly, 'Abdul!'

'Don't be a fool,' said Milly coldly.

But Abdul was already at the door. 'Nkosi?'

'We have decided,' said Field grandiloquently, 'to make you an equal partner in the household. Madam and I will sleep in your housebox-de-lux. My wife will take over the cooking and cleaning. I shall get up every morning and polish the boots and make the tea. Is that understood?'

Abdul gave a long, hilarious cackle. He appreciated the boss in this mood. 'Yes, sah,' he said, 'very good, sah.'

Milly was poised and very icy. 'Get on with the dinner, Abdul,' she said. 'The master is joking.'

'Yes, Missus,' said Abdul doubtfully. He disappeared into the kitchen.

'Joking my backside,' said Field rudely. 'I am in complete earnest. It's the only logical answer to your stupidity.'

Milly's lips were tight. 'You're very good at laughing at other people,' she said. 'Especially Africans. In your terms there are only two sorts, servants or agitators.'

'Mr. bloody Ali Hassim Khan is an agitator all right,' said Field pugnaciously.

There was passion in Milly's voice. 'And why? Because you've never given him a chance to be anything else. Could he be a doctor or a lawyer or a professional man? No, if he's going to lift himself up from kraal level he's got to be an agitator. That's all you allow him to be.'

The ground was swept from under Field's feet. He had used the same argument himself. 'It'll happen in time,' he said weakly.

'And at least he's a man,' she continued angrily making Field pause before replying. He sensed trouble in this illogical statement.

'I don't follow you,' he said warily.

'Man enough to give a woman a baby even though he is black,' she said, hysterically.

So now it was out: the plain, brutal accusation, the enduring reason for man and wife; the failure now thrust upon his shoulders. Field could have hit her. 'I'm sure he'd oblige if you asked him,' he said contemptuously.

'You've never succeeded, have you. You can't.' Her voice was shrill.

'Milly,' said Field, trying to pacify her, trying to prevent the quarrel collapsing into abuse and hysteria. 'Stop it. We've been through all this before.'

'I want a baby,' she said. 'Oh God, I want a baby! And now it's too late.' She slumped back in her chair, her shoulders hunched and covering her face with her hands began to cry.

'Milly, listen . . .' said Field not knowing what he could say that she could listen to.

She made a wild gesture of dismissal. 'Oh, why don't you run off to the pub,' she cried. 'That's what you usually do, isn't it? That's where you find all your answers.'

He looked down at her, alone and abject in her misery. He wished to God he could find either words or reasons to comfort her. But he knew it was useless. He also knew that this abrasive conflict would drain away some of her despair and leave her, if not more reasonable, then more resigned.

'All right, if that's what you want,' he said. 'There's no sense in trying to talk to you in this mood.' He tried to feel a shred of righteous indignation, the wronged husband cheated of comfort and his evening meal, but he couldn't feel anything at all. Except sadness. 'I'll go and have a pint at the hotel and then I'll be back,' he added lamely.

He walked down the verandah steps, got into the Vauxhall and drove slowly down the drive. His headlamps picked out the huge boles of the trees at the side of the road. Overhead through the screen of leafy branches there were stars in the sky. Behind the mountains a faint smudge of crimson still glowed and below the lights of Chapanda were bright and inviting. But he was only vaguely aware of their existence. Damned impossible women: they probed for chinks in the armour and knew where to inflict maximum damage. He braked and swung the car around the hairpin bend. Of course on some counts she was probably right. A child, two children, a family and she would have been reasonably happy, her reason for existence at once self-evident. Perhaps it *was* his fault. But this was hindsight. How could he exhume and analyse the complex years of a marriage? On that first long leave in Cape Town he had met Milly out from Croydon, England, on a visit to her aunt. She had been pretty and gay with her English accent and he had been attracted by the London girl with her associations with the great town and its sophistications. He realized that she was not really enjoying her visit. Africa for Milly was too brilliant, too hot, too lurid, too flamboyant and too raw. Life at home was secure, it ran on rails; there was no District Six in Croydon where black humanity smouldered behind lace curtains. She was looking forward to the voyage home until Field began to lure her with his talk. Rhodesia was different, he told her. More like England. Easy going. Without the dramatic overtones of South Africa. She'd like it.

In those three months of his first leave they had decided to get married. After all, every young trooper had to have an eligible wife if he was ever going to become Commissioner.

He had thought at the time that his own love and hunger were duplicated by Milly; that his vigorous passion was shared and returned by her. But it had taken no more than a few weeks after the marriage to realize that this was an illusion. Oh, yes, she loved him in her way: the way of a woman still clinging to adolescent inhibitions, whose conception of the physical expression of love were based upon the women's magazines and influenced by those intimidating bits at the back in the 'Letters Answered Column' which said, 'Nothing really to worry about at all, my dear. Just have a little chat with your own doctor about it.' In physical love there was a measure of abandonment to which she could not commit herself, and did not want to commit herself. And their marriage foundered on this obstacle.

He coasted down to the bottom of the hill into the pallid glow of Chapanda's few street lamps and switched to sidelights. As Cohen put it crudely and succinctly, 'If you're both happy in bed, you can always get someone else to do the washing up.'

Oh well, he'd have one drink at the hotel bar and then go back and try and patch things up.

He knew at this time in the evening the Chapanda Hotel, which catered mainly for tourists, would have few people in the bar. He walked in through the wide glass doors, strode across the foyer past the settees, potted palms and armchairs, and pushed through the swing doors into the bar.

For some reason, known only to a long departed manager, the décor was South Sea Island. A thatched roof over the bar, a coloured picture of a South Sea lagoon behind the stacked bottles and glasses, cane chairs and tables, concealed lighting.

It was, as Field had surmised, almost empty. Empty

except for Cohen sitting at the bar on a stool, dressed in the inevitable bush shirt and shorts. He swung around as Field approached. 'Oh, the Inspector himself. Does foul play bring him to a bar so early in the evening?' Cohen was obviously a bit sloshed already.

Field took the next bar stool. 'You could call it that, I suppose,' he said. 'I'll have a large whisky, Sam,' he said to the barman. 'Water. No ice.'

Cohen's nose came slowly out of his beer. 'A large whisky, Inspector! At this time in the evening? It must have been a rough day.'

'It was,' said Field grimly. He added a lot of water to the whisky and drank. Then he turned back to Cohen. 'What's the matter with me? Do I look the sort of man that women love to hate?'

Cohen guffawed. 'You're probably using the wrong sort of toothpaste, old cock. In this world you've got to have your breath smelling of the wind on the heath, your eyes shining like neon lights, and your excrement dehydrated. You can't expect all the fresh young things to fall over backwards for hairy old sods like you. Smell like me and they'll all come flocking to your bedroom.'

He breathed heavily at Field, who recoiled from the blast. 'Christ,' he said, 'when did you start?'

'Lunch-time,' said Cohen. 'With a small pause for a nap. And back as soon as the bar opened. That's right, isn't it, Sam?'

'That would be quite right, Mr. Cohen,' said the tall, thin barman in a soft Scottish accent. Sam had been behind the bar at the Chapanda Hotel ever since the hotel opened fifteen years ago. He had a mysterious past somewhere back in South Africa, something to do with someone else's wife, Field had been led to understand. Now, thin as a hickory golf shaft and wrinkled as an old apple, he went about his business with dry, impersonal precision.

'You'd better tell Auntie Cohen all your troubles,' said Cohen with repulsive familiarity. 'Unburden yourself, Inspector. Let's have a good old heart to heart.'

'Get stuffed,' said Field vulgarly, draining the remainder of his whisky. But he was pleased to meet Cohen. He had something in common with him although not quite sure what. The whisky made him feel better.

Cohen was unperturbed. 'Now, now, temper.' He turned back to the bar. 'Sam, you'd better make that two more large whiskies. I can't leave my friend to drink alone.' He patted Field heavily and affectionately on the back. 'I'll tell you what us poor gelded males do. I said I'd meet that silly old bastard Holland at the club at nine. We'll go and fill ourselves up to the brim, and then go back to my place and engage some small black houris to wriggle in lascivious dance.'

Field thought of Milly's reference to girls.

'I'd sooner drink,' he said. 'Anyway, what are you supposed to be celebrating?'

'Celebrating,' echoed Cohen in mock horror. 'Man, I'm grieving. This is my last chance of civilized living. Tomorrow I go down to the Sabi Valley. A long, hot, sweaty, stinking week in the Sabi Valley.'

'Doing what?'

'Dogs. Bloody horrible underfed rib-caged Kaffir dogs. Vaccination or death for hundreds of bloody horrible dogs. Cohen, the killer, the stern arm of the Veterinary Department, the terror of the low veld approaches. Runners with forked sticks race through the villages crying, "Cohen cometh with syringe and hypodermic. Hide your dogs, take them to the hills, for Cohen cometh".'

Field felt the whisky warming his belly. He envied Cohen the trip. A week down there lost in hundreds of square miles of stunted bush under the impersonal blaze of the sun, away from all women and political argument. A great coolness and tranquillity as the orange balloon of the sun fell back over the horizon. Night with the stars and the cries of the animals and the dark peace. The dawn grey and shimmering with mist. . . .

Cohen read his thoughts. 'Why don't you come?' he said. 'Isn't it time you did a patrol in that direction?'

Field tapped his glass uncertainly on the bar. 'I suppose I might,' he said cautiously.

'We will pitch our tents together under God's great open sky,' said Cohen poetically. 'Brothers in God's fresh air and not a single woman to separate us. I will read you passages from that great work, *The Short and Happy Life of Sir Edgar Whitehead,* and you will recite "Is there a man with soul so dead who never to himself has said 'This is my own my United Nations Land' ".' He appealed to the barman, 'Who wrote that, Sam? Robert Louis Stevenson or Sir Roy Welensky?'

'I think it was Mister Shelley,' said Sam politely.

Cohen smacked the bar in applause, 'By God, you're a bloody genius, Sam. I'd never have known it was Shelley. Why don't you come down to the Sabi too? With a bit of luck we might even make up a four for bridge.' He tried out his pseudo-English accent on Field. 'What about that, my deah fellow—eh, old lad?'

Field said rudely, 'You have a nasal, flat, unpleasant Jewish-Afrikaans voice quite unlike that of any Englishman, reminiscent if anything of a domineering Nazi commandant. In fact you *are* a Fascist, and do you know that damn young bitch called me a "bloody copper".'

'Ah, now the truth is coming out,' said Cohen happily. 'He is spurned by the woman he lusts after.' He paused. 'I wonder if it would be better if I became a homosexual?'

Field grinned. 'I've never thought of you in that way.'

'I've never really thought about it either,' said Cohen, 'but just think how interesting it would be to be called a Jewish, Commie, bastard queer?' He considered the idea. 'No, I think not. I react like litmus paper to the soft rounded contours of sweet Mrs. Crosby. I shall say to her, "Come live with me and be my love, and we will all the pleasures of every gin palace in Salisbury prove!"

'You haven't got a hope.'

Cohen was disdainful. 'Stranger things have happened.'

'I've never heard of any,' said Field rudely. He turned to the barman. 'Same again, Sam.'

They swapped drinks and talk until eight o'clock by which time Field had decided to accompany Cohen down through the Sabi Valley. First thing in the morning he would send a signal to Umtali notifying H.Q. of his intention to go off on a week's patrol. His two bright patrol officers could look after the station while he was away.

By nine all idea of meeting Charlie Holland at the Club had disappeared and they left at closing time shouting noisy and affectionate goodbyes.

'See you tomorrow ready for the trip by nine-thirty,' said Field.

'If you manage to make it,' called Cohen fumbling unsteadily with the door of his Land Rover. 'You henpecked married men are all the same.'

'I'll make it all right. Just see you're ready by nine-thirty.'

To his relief the lights in the bungalow were out when he got back and he parked the car as quietly as he could. He decided against waking Milly by sleeping in the other single bed and crept into the spare room. He hardly remembered undressing and falling asleep.

CHAPTER SEVEN

AT NINE-THIRTY next morning Field pulled up behind Cohen's Land Rover outside the government offices. This old-fashioned double-storey wooden building of early colonial vintage, with wide, wire-screened verandahs and peeling paint represented the official heart of Chapanda. It housed the District Commissioner, the Magistrates' Court, the Veterinary Officer and other minor government departments.

Field had a hangover. He had been unable to face breakfast, jibbed at the thin green and golden slice of melon taken straight from the fridge. Milly had been unsympathetic, but to his surprise she made no strident objections to the Sabi patrol.

She said non-committally, 'Maybe it will do you good to get away for a few days.'

Field leaned forward and switched off the engine. It was very hot and humid. When the rains were delayed like this, late October and November were suicide months all right. Over the mountains the thunderheads came up every morning and hung there like black and purple bruises against the sky. Sometimes they were shot through with silver tongues of lightning and the thunder rolled down the gullies and canyons, but the rain did not come. Twigs snapped and broke with a dry crack underfoot, and out in the country the dust hung in the air never seeming to disperse. Chickens scratching round African huts surrounded themselves in small haloes of dust.

'Sergeant Ironside,' he said, 'go inside and tell Mr. Cohen that we are ready and waiting.'

Ironside got out swiftly and flung back the steel door against its frame with the force and precision of a discus thrower. Field flinched at the crash. He decided that a short walk might do him good. He got out and closed his door with a soft click. He walked through the warm air, across to the Voortrekker Memorial, observing that the square of grass, parched and brown from the long hot summer needed cutting; it was knee deep. The early Chapanda pioneers, stimulated by memories of English village greens, had planned the settlement around this central lawn. It was neatly flanked by the small stone church (Anglican) with a square tower, the government offices, the post office, the filling station, the general grocery store, the Standard Bank, the hardware shop and the draper's. There were several grass-grown building lots waiting for the coming of prosperity, but with the tall, graceful trees, the flower beds and red shingle roof of the Chapanda Hotel a short distance down the road, the scene was nostalgically reminiscent of England.

The memorial was of brown sandstone: a simple stone plinth surmounted by a small-scale replica of a covered wagon. Bronze plaques fastened against each side supplied details of the many treks which had first brought the white settlers to these empty highlands: the first Moodie Trek of 1892, the Martin Trek of 1904, and after them the Edenbergs, the Du Plessis Utrechts, the Woolmans and the Websters. And at the turn of the century by courtesy of the American Mission, one 'Miss H. J. Gilson, first teacher for Europeans'.

Miss Gilson had always intrigued Field. Had she been gay and pretty and crossed in love, coming out to the Dark Continent to heal her breaking heart? Or had she been matronly and grim, determined to convert the black-skinned heathen? No matter who she was and what she had done, her name was now fixed inexorably in the early history of Chapanda.

Field stood reflecting for a minute or two, then walked slowly back across the grass. As he reached the Land Rover Cohen was coming down the verandah steps. He looked at Field.

'Christ,' he said, 'You look as bad as I feel.'

'They tell me it's drinking on an empty stomach,' said Field, with an attempt at flippancy he did not feel.

'Christ, man, why didn't you make me stop?'

'If you'd had your way,' said Field, 'we'd still be knocking it back now. Are you driving with me?'

'I certainly am. You don't expect me to eat your dust all the way to Nikita do you?'

The interior of the cab was tropical.

'Only the bloody stupid white man would go working in this heat,' grumbled Cohen. 'In Arabia they'd lie in silken tents drinking sherbet served by luscious tarts in transparent trousers.'

'Fantasy world,' said Field, 'I like the sun. I like the way it burns and you drip sweat and you grow leaner and harder and your bones stick out. Besides the bloody sherbet would make you sick.'

'But the girls,' insisted Cohen with a moan of despair.

'Stick to dogs,' said Field. 'Cheaper.'

'Girls don't give you rabies,' said Cohen still licking his lips.

'Don't ask me to state the obvious.'

'All right, all right,' said Cohen irritably. 'What's keeping us?'

They started off: two Land Rovers with Field, Cohen, Sergeant Ironside and one African constable in the first, bicycles, tents and gear piled on top. In Cohen's Land Rover, his two African assistants.

Twenty minutes later, turning left on to the main road between Umtali and Fort Victoria, Field began to feel better. The road unrolled like a bizarre typewriter ribbon, an eight foot wide tarmac strip, the black central core edged on either side with red dust. The morning sunshine was golden, the dark green hills patched with darker shadows. They hooted past a herd of wide-horned native cattle driven by two small boys with khaki shorts, long sticks and toothpaste smiles and as soon as they were safely past, three skinny, hairless dogs sprang out from under the bellies of the cattle and raced after them barking shrilly.

'Horrible dogs,' said Cohen, 'tick-ridden, rabies carriers.' He lapsed back into silence.

They passed an African woman in a bright red dress who smiled and waved, and held up a small well-wrapped baby for their admiration.

The road curved up between two enormous kopjes of granite, vast round boulders of pebble smoothness, streaked with iridescent stains of green and dark brown, and pretty miniature Msasa trees splayed out gracefully from every crack where their roots could find purchase. At the top of a hill, surprisingly, they seemed poised like a trapeze artist at the highest point of a backswing, miles above a tremendous plain of mottled green, its edges smeared away in a distant haze of mist. Far away a blur of smoke indicated a forest fire. Below them the trees fell away, the road reappearing five miles farther on, a pale grey streak glistening in the sunshine. Above them, blue emptiness and long wisps of white cloud drifting across the horizon. The scene exhilarated Field. He was never bored, droning over these endless empty roads through hundreds of miles of isolation.

'Bloody dogs,' said Cohen morosely. 'All the medical profession to choose from and I had to decide to be a dog killer. To think I might have been some well dressed quack in Adderley Street placing my stethoscope with gentle precision on the left breast of some delicious female.' He brightened at the thought.

It was a long hot day. The sun was beginning to sink, flaring each telephone line with gold as eighty miles beyond Nikita they turned off on to a dirt road, and then there were no more telephone wires. Only the bumpy track which ran for two hundred miles southwards following the immense black configurations of the Sabi until it coiled away into Portuguese East Africa. On its lower reaches stone quays undated by history had been found and the people who built them were as big a mystery as the ruins at Zimbabwe. Africa was full of such enigmas.

The track was inches deep in dust and the second Land Rover fell far behind to escape the cloud they threw up. The grass and bushes edging the road were white with the floury stuff.

Beyond the grasses stretched the dark green stunted mpani trees and occasionally the elephantine trunk of a giant beobab; only the toughest vegetation could survive the droughts and white ants of the low veld.

This was all tribal trust land now, the perimeter of each village evident a mile or two before they arrived by the undergrowth eaten down almost to the grass roots by the goats.

'Bloody animals,' said Cohen. 'Almost as bad as dogs. Leave them alone and they eat Africa into desert like they did Babylon and the ancient lands of the Tigris and the Euphrates.'

'Now I know why you became a vet,' said Field. 'At heart you're an animal lover.'

Cohen made a rude noise. 'Keep your mind on the road, Inspector,' he said. 'The veterinary department can ill afford to lose its best man.'

They pitched camp just before sunset in a grassy clearing about two miles from a village, and Field sent Sergeant Ironside back to make a quick reconnaissance and inform the local Chief that the police were in the vicinity and prepared to listen to complaints.

'The British Empire showing the flag on arrival—eh?' said Cohen. The large tents, portable tables and canvas chairs were hauled down from the roof of the Land Rover, Abdul's cooking tent pitched, the primus lit, and half an hour later Cohen lounged comfortably in his chair while Field broke the seal on a new bottle of Teachers and poured a generous measure into two glasses.

Cohen added a little water, sipped leisurely, and observed in self-satisfied tones, 'One thing about being with the police, it really is camping de luxe.'

'The whisky is purchased privately,' said Field. He relaxed in the chair next to Cohen. 'Did I ever tell you about my second station? Lost in the Zambezi bush. We were inspected about once a year by a Superintendent we called Blue Neck. Bastard, he was. We had three bottles of brandy in the medical stores which occasionally we sipped on Saturday nights because there was nothing else to do, and topped them up with cold tea strained through a mosquito net. Trouble was it became a bit cloudy and we dreaded the next visit of old Blue Neck. Court martial offence you know. I'll never forget our terror as he went through the medical stores: "Ha-ha," he began, "medical comforts. Hum . . . Bovril, limejuice, brandy, three bottles . . . Ah, a little cloudy I see." He walked slowly to the door and I could feel my sergeant physically trembling in his boots. At the door he turned and said quite casually, "Sergeant, I've had a certain amount of experience in the B.S.A. Police. I found if you use distilled water and a little burnt sugar it doesn't go cloudy at all." '

'Decent feller,' said Cohen.

'Not really,' said Field. 'He just had a perverted sense of humour.'

The land sloped at a gentle angle towards the river a quarter of a mile away, and through the scanty growth of bush they could see the dying sun glittering on its surface. Across this landscape, a miniature black frieze against the light, a small herd of cattle passed lifting a faint golden haze of dust in the air around them. Above the low hills beyond the river the sky slowly became scarlet and a flight of river birds, tiny dots against the incandescence made shrill, sharp noises as they scurried southwards. From the direction of the village came the occasional muted yapping of a dog. It was all very peaceful and pastoral, and after the airless heat of the day and the long drive they enjoyed their whisky.

Behind them, the foothills of the mountains which separated Rhodesia from Portuguese East Africa rose steeply from the river plain, the highest peaks covered in swirling mist and cloud.

'I think,' said Field, 'we might get rain tonight.'

'About time too,' grumbled Cohen. 'I hate it when the rains are late like this. Man I'm tired of hearing every tobacco farmer in Africa moaning about the bloody weather. If the sun shines they want rain. If it rains they want the sun. God protect me from farmers.'

By the light of a pressure lamp hung on a tree which attracted myriad insects they ate a supper of fried potatoes and steak, followed by tinned fruit salad and sweet black coffee. Field called up the police office at Chapanda on the Land-Rover radio and talked to Potterson.

Potterson's voice crackled cheerfully behind the static. 'Nothing to report, Skipper. How are things going down there?'

'Fine. We've just pitched camp about sixty miles down the track leading to Crocodile Springs,' said Field. 'We shall stay here for a couple of days and patrol the villages. I'll make radio contact again at eight a.m. tomorrow. Right? Over and out.' He went back to Cohen who was listening thoughtfully to the distant sounds from the village.

'Daydreaming?' said Field.

'Nightdreaming,' said Cohen. 'When I think of all those munts lying on top of those soft muntesses my heart is wild with envy,' he said.

'Why don't you get married and stop drooling,' said Field.

'Do you find it such a success?' said Cohen politely.

'Just as much a success as you find bachelorhood.'

'You have the eyes of a married man,' said Cohen. 'I saw you looking lecherously at that new piece, Sarah Van der Huizen, the other night.'

'No point anyway,' said Field. 'She's a young, spoiled bitch.'

'But pretty rich,' said Cohen languidly. 'She will inherit old Papa Van der Huizen's farm. I'm getting tired of bloody dogs. I think I'll propose to her.'

'Do that,' said Field. He didn't really want to discuss Sarah Van der Huizen with Cohen.

At half past nine lightning flashed in the darkness, thunder rumbled and the first of the November rains exploded out of the sky. African rain falling in sheets and buckets with drumming fury. At half past ten with the rain pelting steadily on the canvas, Sergeant Ironside, back from his patrol, poked his head through the flaps to report.

'Ah, come in, Sergeant,' said Field. 'You've been gone longer than I expected. But Abdul's kept your supper hot for you.'

Sergeant Ironside wiped the rain from his spectacles and sat down. Cohen poured a large shot of whisky into a glass and shoved it across to him.

'You need something to keep out the mosquitoes on a wet night like this, Sergeant.'

Ironside's eyes gleamed behind his glasses. 'Thank you, sah,' he said. He drained the tot of neat whisky at one gulp. As far as Field knew alcohol had little effect upon him.

He began his report slowly, and Field knew that no power on earth would alter his slow mechanical delivery.

'As instructed, sah, I set out on my patrol at eighteen hundred hours from the camp to the local village where I first interviewed the chief Msitilonga. He reported to me that the villagers were very worried at the lateness of the rains; however they had managed a good maize crop and they had suffered no further outbreak of rinderpest since the small outbreak last year.'

'Very good,' said Field officially.

'All due to the effectiveness of the prophylactics supplied by the veterinary department,' intervened Cohen cheerfully, 'I hope you told him I was coming after his bloody dogs tomorrow.'

'Yes, sah, I said you would wish to inspect all dogs and licences tomorrow and that he would be responsible for all defaulters.'

'That'll send all the bastards to the hills,' said Cohen, his cheerfulness turning to gloom.

'Carry on with your report, Sergeant,' said Field.

'The chief also said he had been having trouble with one of his wives, sah. A young wife, sah. Aged sixteen.'

Field raised his eyebrows. 'How old is Chief Msitilonga, Sergeant?'

'I do not know, sah, but he is an old man. More than seventy years.'

'Having trouble in more ways than one, I should say,' said Cohen lasciviously.

'What was his complaint, Sergeant?'

'She has been throwing eyes at a young man in the village, sah. Msitilonga has beaten her, but he believes that the devil has not been driven out. Even the witch doctor has had little success.'

'Very serious matter,' said Cohen. 'Better raise a posse, Sheriff.'

'Shut up,' said Field. He turned back to Sergeant Ironside. 'A man as old as Msitilonga should be wise in the ways of young women by now, Sergeant. What does the old goat want with a young girl of sixteen, anyway?'

'He is a wealthy old man and inclined to indulge himself with frivolities, sah.'

'What did you do, Sergeant?'

'I interviewed the girl, sah, and pointed out that her father had received a very good "lobola" for her, sah. But I do not think I convinced her, sah. This man has been a houseboy in Salisbury, sah, and has been to evening classes. He seems to have intoxicated the girl with his ideas, sah.'

'Surprising what you can learn at evening classes,' said Cohen thoughtfully.

'I'll have a word with Msitilonga,' said Field, 'although the broken hearts department is really handled by the District Commissioner. What else, Sergeant?'

He knew from experience that Sergeant Ironside would be saving his titbit until last. It might be something quite inconsequential. On the other hand it might be important. You never knew with Sergeant Ironside.

'I established, sah, in conversation with Msitilonga that there has been no intimidation of his people by local terrorists, sah.'

'Yes, Sergeant.'

'And as I was about to leave a fisherman arrived at the village and requested permission to speak with me, sah,'

'Yes, Sergeant.'

'He had found a body, sah.'

As Field poured himself another whisky he caught the ironical gleam in Cohen's eye.

'Yes, Sergeant,' he said in quiet exasperation.

'The man lives four miles away on the banks of the Sabi, sah. A mile away from his kraal there is a dried up river which runs down from the mountains. In the hot season sah like now there is no water, but when the rains come it is very fierce with water, sah. I went with the man and he showed me the body, sah.'

'Go on, Sergeant,' urged Field, now considerably more interested.

'It was lying on a litter made of wood which was supported by a pile of stones at the point where the dried up creek joins the Sabi, sah.'

'More and more interesting,' commented Field.

'If I read your mind correctly, dear Sherlock,' said Cohen, 'you want to know why the body hadn't been thrown into the Sabi River itself and why it had been left for the rains to do the job?'

'Exactly, my dear Watson.'

'It was now getting dark, sah, but I examined the body and found the man dead. He had been killed with a thrust from an assegai, sah.'

'So what did you do?'

'As the rains were already falling and that I knew much water would soon come down the watercourse and wash the body into the Sabi I got the African man to help me move it to a hole under the bank. Then we piled up stones to protect the corpse from crocodiles or wild animals and I came back here to report, sah.'

'Very well done, Sergeant,' said Field. 'Give the man another whisky, Cohen.'

Cohen poured him out half a glass; and again Sergeant Ironside knocked it back in one swallow.

'Well, it's obviously too dark and wet to investigate until the morning,' said Field, 'and I must say you were damn lucky to get there just before the rain started. I've seen those dried-up gullies after the rains. Within an hour they're a raging torrent. We should certainly have lost the evidence. He paused, 'What about the fisherman?'

'I have brought him with me, sah. He is outside.'

'Oh God,' said Cohen with a guffaw, 'you haven't left him outside in the rain?'

'Yes, sah,' said Ironside with a disapproving blink at Cohen.

'It's not polite,' said Cohen mildly.

They called the man in. He was shining, middle-aged and scared. His ragged khaki shirt and torn faded denim trousers were plastered to his body. Field took a blanket from his bed, threw it across to him and said, 'Here, wrap yourself in this.' He turned to Ironside. 'Sergeant, after we've had a word with this man see that he gets a meal and then billet him in the Constable's tent.'

'Yes, sah.'

'Now, Sergeant, ask him when he first found the body.'

The Shangaan fisherman looked puzzled. Then he spoke haltingly and Ironside translated. 'He found it at the time the blue and white bird flew across the river.'

Cohen spluttered. Field who had conducted many such interviews motioned him to be quiet.

'Was it light when the bird flew across the river or was it dark?'

The fisherman considered. 'It was light.'

'Was it light by the sun or by the moon?'

'It was light by the sun.'

'Was the sun on this side of the sky or on that?'

The fisherman pointed to the east. 'It was on this side of the sky.'

Field suddenly began to feel tired. This sort of exploratory question and answer could go on for hours. It could all wait until the morning. A corpse was unlikely to walk away.

'All right, Sergeant,' he said, 'that's all for the time being. We'll set out at first light for the river. You've done very well, Sergeant.'

He saw Ironside's eye on the whisky bottle. 'All right, Sergeant, you deserve one.' He poured out two more generous tots and pushed them across to both Africans. The fisherman eyed his speculatively, and then copied Ironside's example. He was still spluttering when they left the tent.

'Regular Sherlock Holmes country, I must say,' said Cohen. 'I'm overcome with admiration. You have now established that the sun was shining and a blue and white bird flew across the river. What I want to know is whether it was a male or female bird.'

'Don't be daft,' said Field. 'He found the body this morning, lying on a litter waiting for the rains to carry it out into the Sabi. Obviously a ritual murder and probably to bring the rains. Very interesting indeed. Now turn in and get some sleep. You're going to get up early tomorrow. I shall need a medicine man to give evidence as to the cause of death.'

'Pneumonia,' said Cohen, 'as perfect a case of pneumonia as I've ever seen. Man, let's throw him in the river, forget the whole thing, and go back and get ourselves a good breakfast.'

The naked corpse of the young, well-built African lay composed and dignified on a rough wooden litter covered with green leaves, his hands folded on his breast.The gaping wound of a spear thrust showed under his left rib cage.

'Very funny,' said Field. 'Do you want to examine the body?'

'I have examined it,' said Cohen. 'From a distance I pronounce this man dead.'

The overnight rain had stopped. Overhead the rain clouds, huge bolsters of grey and white, sailed steadily across the sky. Between them through ragged corridors of blue, the sunshine spilled down. Yesterday it had burned down with a sullen corrosive heat; this sunshine was daffodil coloured, it sparkled; the rains had started and the world could breathe. The watercourse, dry for many months, was choked with rainwater now, a great torrent streaming down from the mountains to join the swollen Sabi.

At first light Field had made radio contact with Chapanda, leaving a message for Potterson to send down a second vehicle with a corpse box. Now he said, 'We may as well put the body back in its hole till the box comes. Sergeant Ironside, go back to camp, wait there and guide them here when they arrive. Then you can take the corpse back to Fort Vic and deliver it to the mortuary.'

'Yes, sah,' said Sergeant Ironside.

'I'll take Constable Brown with me to the head of this watercourse to have a look round.'

'For what?' asked Cohen interestedly.

'To find out who put the bloody body there. Any normal murderer would try and conceal his crime. As I said last night this is probably ritual murder probably to propitiate some rain god.'

Cohen looked sceptical. 'Oh very clever, Inspector. I must say it all worked out very well then with the rains coming so soon after the killing. Are you telling me that you believe in all this mumbo jumbo?'

'There are more things in heaven and earth, Horatio . . .' quoted Field flippantly.

'Listen,' said Cohen pugnaciously, 'I know the B.S.A. Police are a bunch of Victorian boy scouts at heart. But when the police start quoting Shakespeare into the bargain you can be dead sure they don't know what the hell they're talking about.'

Field turned to Ironside. 'Sergeant, ask the fisherman if he knows of any other people who live in the mountains above this watercourse.'

The Sergeant's conversation with the fisherman was long and complicated. Eventually he turned back. 'Sah, he says that men do live up there. They grow maize on the high land and hunt beyond the mountains. They do not come down to the river. He has never seen them. He has just heard about them.'

'Probably a branch of the Mansuta,' said Field. 'Shangaans at root. A nomadic people rather like the Masai. They drift backwards and forwards across the mountains between here and Portuguese East as the seasons and the mood take them. Shy birds. They don't like civilization.'

'Wise fellers,' said Cohen. 'So what now?'

'We go and look for them. Want to come?'

'I guess the Veterinary Department can spare me for a few hours to watch Rhodesia's answer to Sherlock Holmes at work. Which way?'

'We follow the stream as high as we can by Land Rover; then we walk.'

Field, Cohen, and Constable Brown, a tall angular young man, so thin that everything about him—sun helmet, khaki shorts and boots—looked a size too large, climbed into the vehicle. Field reversed and they bumped off, tracking the sandy, scrub covered bank of the watercourse. The rains had already started the miracles: the wet earth creaked, and ached with plant life which was a discernible physical force. Green shoots of grass forced through the sandy soil; mushroom fungi of incredible shape and variety thrust from the bole of every bush and tree; tiny blue and pink flowers interwoven with leaves made small green oases on the patches of dark soil. The air was cool and aromatic. The rains had come, the cycle of life could restart. The rains would continue intermittently for the next three or four months and Rhodesia would be green.

They drove upwards for two hours, covering perhaps ten miles of rough country, until the increasing steepness of the incline and the rocky outcrops brought them to a standstill.

'The climb starts here,' said Field.

They moved slowly, pausing frequently to look back and regard the view they opened up. It was not tough going; the stunted 'impane' trees gave occasional shade and the soil was dry and sandy and easy on the feet. It was tufted here and there with dry grass, and small lizards slid with a dry rustling sound across the outcrops of pitted silver-grey rock. They kept the stream on their right hand side; it fell in a series of abrupt waterfalls into narrow gorges, its low-pitched roar constant in their ears.

'The Gaboon viper inhabits these Eastern Highlands, so I believe,' said Field. 'The only one I've ever seen is in the museum in Salisbury. Stuffed! And I've never met anybody else who's ever seen one either.'

'Perhaps we'll be lucky,' said Cohen politely. 'I understand there's no known antidote to its bite; death's absolutely certain.'

'Correct.'

'Very interesting scraps of information you pick up, Inspector. I'll tell you if I tread on one.'

The first drop of rain splashed soft and warm on Field's pale fawn shirt, leaving a wet mark as big as a penny. A huge grey cloud was passing overhead.

'Only a shower,' said Field. A flock of tiny red and brown birds screeched past from a nearby clump of rushes as if the rain threatened them with immediate extinction, disappearing down the mountainside shrilling with wild excitement.

'We could shelter over there,' said Cohen indicating an overhang of rock. They stood there quite dry while the rain slanted down like a curtain of bright wires against the sunlight.

'I am afraid this is going to destroy all the spoor marks, Mr. Holmes,' said Cohen apologetically. 'There won't be a single clue left between here and the top of the mountain.'

'What's worrying me,' said Field, ignoring his flippancy, 'is the fact that the whole tribe may have scurried back into Portuguese East by now. Any villager with an eye in his head would have seen the Land Rover crawling across the flats and watched us climbing up towards them.'

'You still think it's a ritual killing?' said Cohen.

'I'll lay bets on it.'

'Oh come on, Sherlock, what makes you so certain?'

'I've told you. An ordinary murderer doesn't lay out his victim like a carcass of Canterbury lamb. There would be bruises and marks on the body, signs of a struggle. This man has been seized by one or two others and killed with a sharp spear thrust under the ribs into the heart. That's a Zulu method of execution, you know that, used by the warrior "impis" of Cetowayo, Dingaan and Lobengula. The Shangaans are Zulus; they came north at the same time as Mzilikali's "impis" and turned eastwards into this country when he decided to settle at Bulawayo.'

Cohen walked from under the shelter of the rock and held out his hand experimentally, 'It's stopped raining. Let's get moving. I can't wait to meet these old-fashioned executioners.'

An hour later the slope levelled out into a huge grassy plateau which led back into a deep cleft in the mountains. The stream, widening over a bed of white pebbles, ran through a series of shallow pools, and clumps of tall trees dotted this pastureland. Back in the cleft against the darkness of the mountainside they saw the thin, silver thread of a waterfall. The higher peaks were still concealed by thick mist. Now, also, there were signs that humans lived here: small fields of maize, their stalks withered and seared by the long hot summer, blackened circles where fires had been lit. They followed the stream until they saw ahead of them a dozen long-horned native cattle grazing at the edge of one of the pools. As they walked closer a small herdboy, quite naked, sprang back up the gorge at top speed.

'D'you think we'll be speared by a reception committee?' Cohen enquired with interest.

'I don't think so. We come unarmed and peaceful.'

The village was small. Two dozen thatched houses lay within the natural protection of the gorge, and Field guessed it housed sixty or seventy people. Men and women crowded around inquisitively. They showed no sign at all of unfriendliness or apprehension.

'Constable Brown,' said Field, 'ask them if we can see the Chief.'

A fat woman in a faded flowered dress, brightly coloured Shangaan beads in a band around her head and on her forearms, chattered loudly in reply to Brown's question and pointed farther up the gorge. Constable Brown looked puzzled. He was a handsome young man in spite of this thinness; his pale brown skin and black eyes went well with his khaki sun helmet and uniform. 'She say that the Chief and the witch doctor and the elders are farther up the gorge with the—?' He paused and turned back to the fat woman, confirming his information, 'with the rainmaker.'

'Let's get a move on,' said Cohen. 'First time I've had a chance of seeing one of these geezers at work.'

The fat woman yelled into her hut, and a small naked boy popped out. His eyes were round and frightened.

'He will guide us,' said Constable Brown. 'It is not far.'

They clambered for three hundred yards up the gorge, following the small naked figure bobbing along in front of them. The rocky walls were choked with vegetation; the atmosphere wet and humid. They crossed and recrossed the stream, jumping from rock to rock and hearing, quite close now, the sound of falling water. It was a gloomy place. At last the small boy stopped and pointed ahead. Obviously he believed his errand over for before they could question him he had darted off back the way they had come.

They went forward. Field was conscious of a peculiar sense of anticipation, an awareness that something strange might be about to happen. They panted up a short steep incline and came out in a clearing below the waterfall. They stopped.

The thin waterfall, thirty feet in height, leapt out from a black ledge cascading down into the shallow pool below. To one side of the pool stood a small group of natives: Field knew at once they were the elders. Capering around the edge of the pool waving a horsehair flywhisk and shouting unintelligibly was the witch doctor.

In the Zambezi and Northern Rhodesia Field had seen African ceremonies far more colourful and bizarre than this: occasions of a vast tumult of drums and costume, chanting and whirling naked bodies glistening with sweat. This was decorous by comparison. But what was strange about this scene was the girl. She stood on a rock in the middle of the pool. She was naked. She stood with her back to them, her arms raised as if in supplication as the spray streamed down over her glistening skin and long matted black hair.

'By God, man, it's a white girl,' said Cohen in amazement.

For a second Field thought he must be right. The girl's skin was so pale that she looked European. Then he realized that it was a trick of the water and sunlight; the girl's skin was *café au lait*, paler than that of most Africans, but her features although not conspicuously negroid were African; her long dark hair looked more Indian than anything else. She must have been seventeen or eighteen years old. Quite oblivious of their arrival, lost in some trance of either her own imagination or that of the ridiculous witch doctor still prancing around the pool, she stood motionless.

The witch doctor was absurd. He wore patched denim trousers, soggy from the knees downwards, and a belt of green reeds; his chest and face were daubed with white ashes and a conical hat of python skin was perched on his head.

The seven elders were also dressed in this unlikely mixture of European and African dress. Ordinary trousers or shirt with a few bits of greenery, a feather or two and a daub of ashes. Field always wondered why they never found such things incongruous. Only one man stood out amongst them with dignity. He was the tallest. Grey-headed, dressed in the ancient Zulu ceremonial costume of monkey tail, kilt and leopard skins, his headdress was plumed with waving black ostrich feathers.

A little to one side stood two middle-aged women in long Mother Hubbard style dresses. Their only concession to the powers of magic seemed to be the few leaves stuck in their hair.

The tall grey-haired man saw them almost at once and shouted angrily to the witch doctor. His reaction was comical. He spun round in alarm and stood staring in consternation as they approached. The girl, sensing the disturbance, also turned in alarm almost slipping from her rock. Then seeing the three strangers she scampered in a scurry of fear through the shallow water towards the two women. One held out a large piece of scarlet cloth and wrapped it around her.

Field held up his right hand as a salute and walked forward. He knew that Africans hated Peeping Toms at their sessions of magic or ritual. Although no one in the group appeared to be armed, the man found at the end of the watercourse was very dead, and there was no point in taking chances. He found Constable Brown by his side.

The dignified grey-haired African stepped forward and returned the salute.

'Ask this man if he is the Chief,' said Field. Constable Brown interpreted and then nodded affirmatively. 'This is the Chief.' He added, 'The Chief says that it is forbidden for strangers to witness the ceremony of the rainmaking. We have offended him.'

Field always preferred Constable Brown's literal and more romantic translations to the factual dullness of Sergeant Ironside. Particularly at this moment.

'Tell him that I apologize for our interference,' said Field. 'We were unaware that they were conducting this ceremony. However, will you also point out that we are the police, and keepers of law and order in this territory. Will you say that the dead body of a man has been found at the end of a water-course leading directly from this village. It is my duty to investigate this crime and I would like to ask him some questions about it.'

Constable Brown turned back to the Chief. His conversation appeared long and involved.

'Well?' said Field a little impatient at the length of the dialogue.

Constable Brown's face was slightly surprised. 'He says that it is Tuitsala, the body of one of his young men, sah. He asks whether we removed the body, and I said we have done so. He replied that this is not good because the body should have been washed into the great river to propitiate the rain gods.'

Field decided to avoid controversy.

'Does the Chief admit that he killed Tuitsala?'

Constable Brown turned back to the Chief and conferred. 'No, sah, he did not kill him. This was carried out by two of his young men.'

'Where are these young men now?'

In answer the Chief waved contemptuously to the mountains. Constable Brown's interpretations were now swift and certain.

'They have gone back into the mountains.'

'Why did they kill Tuitsala?'

'Because he violated the rain goddess.'

'Is this the rain goddess?'

'Yes, this is the rain goddess.'

'Did the Chief give the order to kill Tuitsala after this violation?'

Constable Brown hesitated. He took longer over this bit. Then he said slowly, 'The Chief says it is the custom of these people. The Chief says that this girl was bought from a people who live far away across the mountains. She cost many cattle, and her powers are great. But if her violation had not been avenged the rains would not have come.'

Field decided to leave the forensic evidence regarding the nature of the violation until later. Now he said, 'Constable Brown, you will tell the Chief that he and his witch doctor and those of his elders who are implicated must come with us to Umtali to answer questions about the cause of the death of Tuitsala.'

Cohen had listened with interest to these exchanges. Now he said quickly, 'I am prepared to sign a death certificate to the effect that the death of this man Tuitsala was due to pneumonia.'

Field looked at him in surprise. He didn't know what Cohen was up to. 'Don't be an idiot,' he said.

The Chief spoke again and the constable translated, 'He says that now the rain goddess has been cleansed of her violation by blood, the rains have come. This water flowing from the mountain is proof. All men black and white will now benefit.'

'Go on, Sanders of the Sabi River,' said Cohen coldly. 'Big white master now utter words of wisdom about inches of rainfall.'

The trouble was Cohen meant what he said. Field could tell that from his voice; he didn't know what was the matter with him but he wasn't making things any easier by his attitude. 'Oh, for Christ's sake shut up,' said Field. To Constable Brown he said, 'Tell the chief it is not necessary to kill a man to bring the rains. The rains fall every year. The fact that they were later this year was an incident of meteorology, nothing more.'

The Chief answered slowly, and Brown said, 'The Chief remembers many years in his lifetime when the rains did not come and many men and women, children and cattle died. He says that blood is sometimes necessary to bring the rain or to bring freedom from oppression.'

'Well, give us another quick answer from the *Handbook of What Every Young Policeman Should Know,*' said Cohen.

Field turned on him angrily. 'Look. You forget there's a corpse with a stab wound on its way back to the mortuary at Fort Victoria. You forget that I've been in contact with H.Q. by radio and informed them of the murder. I'm a policeman obeying orders.'

'That's what they all said at Auschwitz,' said Cohen bitterly. 'I am not responsible for my own actions. I'm just obeying orders. I am just a nice married man with three kids and a blonde wife and I'm just dropping these cyanide pellets down amongst these Jews in the gas chamber because I am ordered to do it. Absolve me from all guilt, please.'

Field could have punched him on the nose. 'You're damn mad if you can't distinguish between a normal policeman who serves society and a Nazi criminal who destroys it. This is a murder I'm investigating.'

'You were calling it a ritual killing earlier on.'

'Whatever I was calling it, a man has been murdered. Whether or not he deserved death I don't know. I'm not a judge. Simply a police officer.'

Constable Brown said, 'The Chief does not understand why you wish to arrest him, sah. The rains had not come. Without the rains the rivers will dry up and there will be only a land of dust and rock. The cattle will die and the maize will wither. The sun will rise every day into a burning sky and the bellies of men and beasts will swell with agony and there will be no life left on the earth.'

Field looked at the Chief. The old man must have been seventy or more. . . . He may have served with Lobengula's 'impis' as a boy; certainly the history and ceremonies of Dingaan, Cetowayo and Mzilikali, would be known to him and lie deep in his bloodstream. Now, one of the last of the noble savages who had lived far from the corruption of the white man's civilization, he had been caught by the power he sought to avoid. Proud, almost naked in his dress of monkey tails and leopard skins he stood there resigned, awaiting Field's decision and Field would have given much to have been able to avoid it.

Cohen's face was angry. 'Let this man take his cattle and women and his rain goddess and go back over the mountains. He's got a concept of law and order that's different from yours and mine. He's no murderer and you know it. This is his law not yours and you should respect it.'

'There's a body on its way back to Fort Vic—'

'You've said that before, so what? You climbed these mountains to investigate and whoever might have been responsible has disappeared back into Portuguese East.'

'Now listen . . .' began Field.

'You're going to condemn this man to a living death in one of your stinking gaols.'

'They're not my stinking gaols,' said Field angrily. 'You own them as well. And I'm not condemning him. I'm simply doing my job.'

Cohen was almost inarticulate with rage. Field had never seen him so angry. 'Then you can bloody well do it without me. I thought mine was bad enough when I have to shoot these rabies-ridden starving dogs, but I can see it's clean healthy fun compared with yours. And I'd sooner be bloody well shooting dogs than mixed up in this business.'

Field watched him stalk off down the gorge. Damn the man! He knew that this romantic Cohen standing up for the rights of the minority was in character, but he had never known him take such a quick and angry decision before. Usually he stayed to argue; usually his moral position was open to a dozen permutations. For the first time Field realized he had never subjected their friendship to a rational scrutiny. He knew he liked the man. They shared a male understanding. Perhaps in Africa these things cut deeper. Back in England this sort of association depended upon a casual drink in the local, the Saturday football match, a trip with a couple of girls. This was wilder terrain. And if, at intervals, a jet might loll across the sky, a tiny metal capsule high against the sun, drawing a thin vapour trail between each centre of so-called civilization, outside this web of airlines, telephone lines, and radio communications there was an immensity of distance, a remoteness, a strangeness, a danger. Things were slightly larger than civilized life. Friendships were of the same dimensions. Damn the man!

He turned back to Brown. 'Constable, it's going to take quite a time to get depositions made by all the people connected with this episode. However, we'd better get started. Ask this—this rain goddess to come over here.'

Constable Brown went across and brought the girl to him. Wrapped in her thin red sheet she was now quite calm. Her dark brown eyes regarded him without fear. She is enjoying it, thought Field, she has been savouring every minute of this experience. And why not? Here was an ancient purpose of womanhood: the vestal virgin, the instrument of magic, the one who gave birth, the mother, with a power of fulfilment beyond the imagination of man.

Her dark hair, still soaking wet, was matted down her back. Her hands he could see were pale brown and shapely; she had been cared for as befitted a goddess who brought the rains. And who could disprove her power? See, her body was wet with the water she had brought from the sky. The waterfall arched out from the mountainside, a great stream of silver falling downwards and then erupting upwards into a pale cloud of mist as proof of her divinity.

'Tell her,' said Field, 'that she must also come with us to the city to answer questions.' He added, 'We shall need her as a material witness.'

They got back to camp with their four witnesses late in the afternoon. Field was tired and hungry and in no mood for any of Cohen's histrionics. But Cohen's mood had changed completely. He was subdued and depressed with his own problems.

'Bloody Africans,' he said. 'Bloody dogs. I shot ten today to put them out of their misery. They were starving, nothing but skin and bone, and I fined each of the natives who owned them two quid each on the spot; I told them they were damn lucky I didn't put a bullet into them instead.'

'You mean your conception of the noble savage has suffered a setback,' said Field ironically.

'No,' said Cohen, 'the other lot were different. Who've you brought down with you?'

'The chief, with witch doctor, one of the elders and the girl.'

'She's not guilty, surely?'

'Nobody's guilty,' said Field in exasperation. 'You've been watching too much television. She's a witness, that's all. I'm taking them back in the Land Rover with me right away.'

'Look, Inspector Field,' said Cohen flatly, 'don't try and bullshit me. The Chief's admitted he at least acquiesced in a crime of murder. What'll he get?'

'God knows. With a good lawyer who makes a strong emotional plea as you did this morning, plus the fact that they didn't actually commit the crime, two—three years—six months—acquittal—I don't know.'

'The Chief will never live that long.'

'They're not convicted yet.'

Field went back to the radio transmitter and gave Potterson a breakdown of what he intended to do, and twenty minutes later they were driving down the long trail towards the main road. It was soft and muddy, shining with pools of water. The trees dripped water and the sunset was sullen and waterlogged.

CHAPTER EIGHT

FIELD STOOD AT THE CORNER of Stanley and Second Avenue and decided he needed a beer. Not a beer in a sleazy bar full of gravel-voiced characters in sweaty shirts and dirty shorts talking of the tobacco crop, the bloody British, and who was going to win the two-thirty at Borrowdale. A beer in a glossy bar full of city girls with silken legs and cascading silver voices.

He had just left the selection board of senior officers who would decide upon his suitability for a commission. This was the reason he needed a drink.

They had cross questioned him at length about the 'rain-goddess case' as it was now known. The fact that it was more than five months since that journey to the Sabi; the fact that the story had received little attention in the press—stories of witchcraft, African ceremonies and crimes were commonplace and anyway it had clashed with an American moon probe and an Afro-Asian declaration in the United Nations that something terrible must be done about Southern Africa as a whole—did not seem to diminish the board's interest. Field sensed their mood of disapproval about his handling of the case.

They knew as well as he did that the two young men who were alleged to have committed the murder had disappeared for good into Portuguese East, that the Chief had received two years as an accessory, but on they went, chipping away at him with lightly barbed questions as if he had made a dozen obvious mistakes. Did he think there was any way in which he could *possibly* have apprehended the murderers? Perhaps if he had signalled Fort Vic and asked for C.I.D. help? Perhaps if Special Branch plain clothes Africans had infiltrated into the area?

Field had been keeping his temper with difficulty. Now he abandoned discretion. 'You mean,' he said tartly, after a few minutes of this sort of oblique suggestion, 'that barging straight up there in a police Land Rover blew the gaff and ruined the case for the C.I.D.'

There were a few seconds of anguished silence. Then the Senior Officer tapped the table delicately with the end of his pencil and said coldly, 'There is no need to take that attitude Inspector Field. This is not a Court of Inquiry. But you must understand that in the selection of officer material we must consider the candidate's past record, and an analysis of any case in which he has been concerned is most helpful.'

'And balls to you too!' said Field to himself in angry retrospection as he crossed the road skirting the green oasis of Cecil Square heading for Meikles and the Causerie. Since his earliest days as a trooper he had always enjoyed a visit to the big city. Six months in Chapanda with only the village store to stare at, and Salisbury's shining glass windows looked like Aladdin's Cave.

The shop windows dazzled in the morning sunshine, full of gorgeous, red-lipped, slender-breasted, life-size plastic girls exhibiting bras and belts, fur coats and silken gowns. Shoppers both black and white hurried purposefully or dawdled as if hypnotized by the continuous show. Even in Field's time Salisbury had changed from a sleepy town of twin-storey buildings with a country atmosphere, into a modern city of singular beauty and elegance. In this climate an architect could conspire with nature, raising his pastel-coloured wedges of pre-stressed concrete, certain that the coalescence of sunshine, light and sky would enhance his ambition.

He looked up at the skyscrapers. Not skyscrapers by New York measurements perhaps but thirty storeys by Central African standards was high enough. Towers of imperial symmetry; blue and ivory, soft red brick edged with white; the Pearl Insurance building like a colossal and almost edible fawn coloured biscuit perched on one end; the Ambassador Hotel a pale blue and white column soaring into the sunshine, and down here at eye-level, above the shrubs the jacarandas and scarlet-plumed flame lily trees of of Cecil Square, the bronze memorial flagstaff, and the memorial tablet proclaiming that a few yards from this place upon the 13th of September 1890 the Pioneer Column had first raised the Union Jack to mark the occupation of Mashonaland. His mind could hardly accept the reality that out of the virgin bush within the span of one man's lifetime this great city had grown.

As usual at Saturday lunchtimes the Causerie was filled with the 'dry martini, gin and tonic, scotch and soda' crowd. Ladies, mainly young and pretty were dressed fashionably; gentlemen wore casual clothes, blazers, light tweeds, silk scarves in regimental colours, old school ties. Rhodesia had inherited the full weight of the Edwardian empire. Field in his new, dark grey, lightweight worsted suit, 'two vents in the jacket, really most fashionable, sir', white shirt and dark blue tie felt perfectly at ease. He had just drawn twenty-five new pound notes from his Standard Bank at the corner of Cecil Square. He was equipped to deal with life.

There was a crowd against the bar. He side-stepped a young man emerging with three full glasses, turned sideways to edge past another and arrived at the bar. A voice on his right side said, 'Well, goodness gracious me, the man from Scotland Yard.'

It was Sarah Van der Huizen. She had just removed a glass containing a gin and tonic from her coral pink lips and her eyes were intensely blue. It seemed a long time since their first militant meetings. Christmas had come and gone, the rainy season had petered to its close and the cool green days of Spring had arrived and he had passed the time of day with her on half a dozen occasions in Chapanda but their encounters had been guarded. To his surprise she smiled at him. She looked very pretty.

'Hello,' he said.

'Why, Inspector Field,' she said, 'aren't you a little off your beat?'

'Well, aren't you?' retorted Field.

'I'm staying for a week with friends here.'

Field said, 'I came down here for a board. And Milly's having a short holiday. She drove me to Salisbury in her car.'

'What's the board for?' she demanded curiously.

Field hesitated. 'A commission.'

'Will you get it?'

'Shouldn't think so. The board didn't like me. It's my second attempt anyway. If you're officer material they snap you up first go. My second application was just to show I'm an ambitious policeman. Anyway they didn't approve of my handling of the rain goddess case.' He was surprised he was telling her so much. Perhaps he was trying to impress her? Or maybe he just wanted to talk to someone.

She giggled and Field wondered if she was a bit tiddly. Perhaps that was why she was friendly?

'What happened to the rain goddess?' she asked.

'Lupin?'

'Is that her name?'

'Nearest we could get to it with all the Zulu clicks and clocks in between.'

'But what happened to her?'

'She works in our house in Chapanda.'

Her eyebrows signalled surprise. Field explained, 'There are no special hotels for female witnesses. She stayed in our police compound with one of the African sergeant's wives while she was waiting for the preliminary hearing, and then she came to work for Milly. She's been working for us and living in the police compound ever since. She can't go back to her own people—they weren't her people anyway—they bought her in exchange for a few cattle from another tribe over in Portuguese East. And there's really no great demand for violated rain goddesses.'

'So what will happen to her?'

'She'll marry someone quite soon, I expect. Might even become a policeman's wife.'

Sarah smiled again. 'You lead a very interesting life, Inspector. When are you going back to Chapanda?'

'Monday.'

'Oh, I'm going back on Monday too. Isn't that a coincidence?'

'I'm looking for a lift,' said Field boldly. 'My own car's still in Chapanda.'

She looked at him without speaking for a second then she said, 'All right.' She added, 'I'd better give you my phone number here in Salisbury so we can arrange how I pick you up. Have you got a bit of paper?'

Field produced a small notebook and pencil. 'Police equipment,' he explained. As she scribbled down the number he said, 'Perhaps we can continue the fight?'

Her eyes caught his again but she didn't laugh, and he thought so the lady is still of uncertain temper! She wore a lemon silk dress patterned with white flowers, white gloves and white shoes; her dark hair was shining and sculptured; small blue earrings set closely against her delicate ears matched her eyes. He became aware then for the first time that she had a man with her, a tall, thin, well-dressed young man in a dark tropical suit who had been chatting to someone else. Sarah Van der Huizen introduced them. 'Oh you haven't met David Mitchison. He's from South Africa.'

The young man did not offer to shake hands. 'Hello,' he said with disinterest. Field nodded with equal hostility.

'And this,' said Sarah Van der Huizen, 'is Inspector Field of Scotland Yard.'

David Mitchison's eyes opened in disbelief. 'Really?'

'No, not really,' said Field firmly. 'Of the Rhodesian B.S.A. Police.'

Mitchison's mouth turned down at the edges. 'Oh,' he said, 'one of those.'

Sarah seemed to be enjoying the friction but to Field it seemed that she came down on his side. 'Well David doesn't do anything at all,' she said, 'you see he has money and he goes all over the place thinking of great things he might do. That's when I first met him, thinking of what he might do.'

'First meetings are often dramatic,' said Field sarcastically. She is a little drunk he thought. He caught the barman's eye and said 'A gin and tonic.' He usually drank beer at lunch-time but the absence of pint glasses on the tables made him wonder if it was spirits only. He added, 'Would you like a drink?'

'No, thanks, we must go,' said Mitchison firmly.

'Thank you, a gin and tonic,' said Sarah, ignoring his statement. She drained her glass and set it down on the bar.

Field gave the order. He didn't press Mitchison. If he didn't want a drink that was his lookout. He turned back from the bar to hear Sarah saying, 'D'you know, the second time I met this man he hit me, he slapped my face.'

'Brave feller,' said Mitchison ironically. 'It's the courage one gets from living in a police state.'

Field let it pass. He was, in any case, much more interested in this new, vivacious, slightly drunk and infinitely friendlier Sarah than any supercilious young man.

He said, 'Joshua could have laid a complaint against you for assault.' He saw her eyebrows rise in disbelief and he added, 'and you could have laid the same charge against me.'

She smiled again. 'Oh, Inspector. Can I blackmail you?'

'I expect so,' said Field. 'The Commissioner takes a very dim view of policemen who go around slapping the faces of pretty girls.' Her eyes were still fastened on his and he felt vaguely disconcerted.

Mitchison was impatient. 'I hate to break up this mutual admiration society,' he said, 'but Sarah we did say we'd meet Pat and Arthur at the Colony at one and it's now twenty past.'

'All right,' said Sarah, 'I'm coming.' She finished her drink, placed the glass on the counter and picked up her handbag. 'Nice to have met you, Inspector. We're dancing at Brett's tonight. Why don't you drop in and I'll buy you the other half.'

'Maybe the Inspector's wife doesn't like him staying out late,' said David Mitchison coldly. He took Sarah's arm possessively.

'Thank you,' said Field ignoring him. 'I'll see what goes. I might take you up on it. In any case I'll ring you about the lift.'

He watched Mitchison lead Sarah Van der Huizen away, finished his drink slowly and then left the bar. He wondered if she had really meant what she said or was it just a social remark signifying nothing? Perhaps she liked a flotilla of men around her, new recruits arriving at regular intervals to keep her other escorts alert? An older man amongst her admirers would flatter her? In any case she was slightly high so she'd probably forget the entire thing. In their first two meetings she had shown plainly what she thought of him; she was probably discussing him at this very minute as she swung along on David Mitchison's arm. 'But, darling, it's just as well to have the local constabulary on your side.' Oh well, to hell with her; she meant nothing to him.

Outside, he blinked in the bright sunshine. He walked across to a taxi on the rank, swung open the door and said,

'Police Depot.' The African taximan tipped down the meter flag, said, 'Yes, sah,' and shot off into the traffic.

Field sat back and supposed he should contact Milly. She was staying with her girl friend Angela who lived in a modern block of flats in Highfields. The flat was small and orderly with only one guest room so fortunately there was no room for Field. He stayed in the Mess at the Police Depot.

Field disliked both Angela and her flat. She had some high-powered job with an insurance firm; she was about seven feet tall, a culture-vulture, elegant and blasé. In the flat, discs of Bach preludes were prominently displayed in their coloured sleeves, reproductions of Modigliani nudes decorated the walls, and a copy of a Benin bronze she had picked up in the British Museum on her last visit to London stood on the sideboard. She was a rampant femininist and Field said, 'If the Suffragettes were still operating she would be permanently chained to the Houses of Parliament.' He also added rudely, 'bloody old Les.'

That night in the N.C.O.s bar at the police depot he ran into an old friend, Bob Mellons. He had met Bob on the boat coming out from England as recruits, and they had served together through their six months police depot training, enduring peppery drill sergeants, endless lectures and making their first exploratory trips into Salisbury.

Mellons' smile was slow, his laughter a sort of gentle internal exploding. He bore malice towards none, he was reliable, even-tempered, stubborn, and romantic to a point of imbecility.

To a certain extent his romanticism was practical. 'Three years in the Rhodesian Police,' he said, 'your fare paid out, and a nice little gratuity at the end of it. See the world at their expense. What could be better? Three years and then off to the South Sea Islands.'

The fact that he'd stayed nearly fourteen years in a perpetual euphoria about animal life, sunsets, the Queen of Sheba's mines, the power of witchcraft, the Zimbabwe ruins and other bits of romantic trivia had escaped his notice.

Sex drove no demonic impulses through his loins; he was a man's man, legends of knights in shining armour, pale Genevieves sorrowing by shadowy lakes sublimated or anaesthetized his passion. Until he met Mrs. Annie Summers. Without Annie, a pretty widow of thirty-four with two young sons, who made it her business to help at police fêtes and jumble sales, he would have remained quite content with the knowledge that babies were found under gooseberry bushes and man's best friend was his mother. Annie altered all that; she spread her silken nets and brought him to her bed with ease and serenity. Field had been best man at their wedding, quite certain then, as now, the Bob Mellons would live happily ever after.

'Dice to see who pays for the first drink,' said Mellons. 'Best of three, and as you're the guest you get first throw.'

Field picked up the leather cup, shook the dice and upended it on the bar.

'Four aces,' he said. 'Four in one. I'll stick.'

Mellons gathered up the dice thoughtfully and slid them back into the cup. 'Four in one and you decide to stick. I can see you're a wild gambling man.'

'A simple policeman like you can afford to buy the beer,' said Field. 'What else have you got to do with your money?'

Mellons rattled the cup gently against his ear as if the quiet chatter of the dice might whisper some aural magic. 'Met any pretty girls lately?' he said.

Field who had been thinking vaguely of Sarah Van der Huizen raised his eyebrows; Mellons rarely made such intuitive remarks.

'What brings this up?' he asked guardedly.

Mellons smiled, and went on shaking the dice. 'I knew you were in town. Tubby Lloyd spotted you in the Causerie Bar this lunch-time talking to a smashing piece of stuff.'

Field ignored the implied question. 'You'll wear the spots off those damn dice unless you throw them. Shoot, or let me buy the beer.'

Mellons flicked the cup over on to the bar and shielded the dice with his hand. 'What's the betting I've got five queens,' he demanded solemnly.

'Twenty to one,' Field offered.

Mellons looked up with innocent eyes, 'Salisbury girl?'

'No.'

'Keeping her to yourself?'

Field smiled. 'What a hope. You are breeding scandal where no scandal exists, Bob Mellons. Her father's an Afrikaaner farmer up in my district I've known for years. He has sixty-five thousand acres, and I imagine a tidy bit of money. The chap who's after her obviously has more loot than he knows what to do with.'

'Which lets us poor old policemen out.'

'Right out.'

'You disappointed?'

'No.'

'But you do think she's smashing?'

Field pursed his lips thoughtfully. 'Yes,' he said simply. Then he added, 'We were supposed to be playing for the first beer.'

Mellons slowly removed his hand from the dice revealing two threes, an eight, jack and queen. He looked hurt. 'Obviously the dice are loaded in this joint,' he said.

'I'll have a cold Castle,' said Field.

Mellons called the barman and ordered. Then he said, 'Too bad you're an old married man with only your pension to look forward to. It's a rough life.'

Field stared at him in surprise. 'I miss your point?'

Mellons looked innocent. 'Isn't there something in the good book about lusting after virgins?' he said. 'Especially when you're above that dangerous age of forty.'

'You're putting two and two together and making two hundred,' said Field unperturbed.

'Probably that's why they never made me an officer.'

Field said, 'They never made you an officer, my boy, because you've never wanted to be captain of the first fifteen; you don't possess those qualities of leadership upon which the British Empire was built.'

'Amen,' said Mellons, 'but let me draw your attention to Conditions of Service, point nine. I quote from memory, "Promotion is open to all. Up to the rank of Inspector it is by competitive examination; to the higher rank of Chief Inspector it is by selection. Appointment to commissioned rank is by selection from warrant officers with not less than ten years' service".' He paused. 'They must have forgotten we have both served nearly fourteen long and sober years.'

'They haven't forgotten,' said Field grimly, 'they have ignored the fact. You and me, mate, are two forgotten legionnaires.'

At that moment they were interrupted at the bar by the noisy arrival of sergeants Petrie and Diggan. Field didn't like either of them very much, but then you couldn't be expected to like every man in a large police force. Petrie was a tall, thin, Glaswegian with a bony protuberant nose and jaw, large hands and bony wrists, with the reputation of being a great jester. Diggan was a South African, tall, sunburned, muscular, with a long vacuous face, kept perpetually amused by Petrie's sallies of wit which Field usually found both derisive and unkind. Petrie had a story to tell them. 'A "shabeen" raid last week,' explained Diggan.

Mellons said, 'I never did quite understand why we have to raid "shabeen" parties.'

Petrie was amazed. 'Blimey, give over. Supposing you were in England or in South Africa and you bought half a dozen bottles of gin and whisky, provided a room and a record player and then invited all your friends, but charged them ten bob entrance fee?'

'Why should it be against the law?' insisted Mellons.

'Against the law! Blimey, you're contravening the liquor laws, the licensing laws, the registered premises act, fire regulations and a dozen other things. Didn't you know we had all these laws for the express purpose of stopping people enjoying themselves?'

Diggan laughed at the joke. 'Go on, Pet, let's hear the story,' he said impatiently.

Petrie put his beer on the bar conscious that he had now alerted his audience. 'All right then. You see, we got a tip-off about this "shabeen", so I was told to take a van and a police patrol down and break it up. I parked the wagon in a side street; it was pretty late.' He paused and winked. 'I thought we'd give them plenty of time to warm up—get it? The sergeant and I went in round to the back garden while the others waited for our signal. The blinds were drawn but there was a little crack in one of them and I looked through. Got a great view. . . .' He whistled appreciatively, and reached for his beer to maintain the suspense.

'Oh, go on,' said Diggan impatiently. 'Go on.'

'Well, there was this munt dancing with this girl and she hadn't got a stitch on, and he was taking his clothes off as they went around dancing. All the others were standing around cheering, all shagged up to the eyebrows with liquor. The African sergeant kept nudging me and saying, "Shall we go in now, sah?" And I kept saying, "No, wait a minute, Sergeant, wait a minute" with me eyeballs almost popping out of my head. And then at last I couldn't stand it any longer and we busted in through the front door, and there they were performing away in the middle of the room with everybody clapping and screaming.'

'Any trouble?' said Mellons.

'Trouble!' Petrie did an open-mouthed, goggle-eyed, funny face look which had Diggan rocking. 'Everyone was having a marvellous time. That the police should bust in when he was right on the job was the funniest thing that had happened for years. They were so creased with laughing we had to carry half of them out to the wagon with laughing exhaustion.'

At that moment the telephone on the bar a yard away from Field's elbow shrilled and the African barman picked it up. He listened, said, 'Yes, sah,' and looked helplessly at Field.

'Okay,' said Field, 'I'll take it.' He took the instrument and said, 'Inspector Field, Sergeants' Mess.'

'Oh good,' said the voice at the other end. 'Duty Officer here. Emergency down in Harare. Would you pass the word around that everyone, repeat everyone, is to report as per emergency drill at once.'

'Yes, sir,' said Field. He paused. 'Does this include personnel on leave, sir?'

The voice on the other end chuckled. 'Well, I certainly think we can find something for you to do, Inspector Field. The rendezvous is Salisbury Town Station. We're sending people out to Harare as they arrive. There seems to be about half a dozen outbreaks of violence down there. Planned too, by the look of things. Fires, rioting, the usual stuff. We can use all hands.'

'Very good, sir.' Field replaced the phone and turned to the others.

'Don't tell me,' groaned Petrie. 'Emergency?'

'Right first time. All personnel to report at Salisbury Town Station as per instructions laid down.'

'Damn,' said Petrie, 'and I'd got a lovely bit of crumpet arranged for nine o'clock. Oh well, come on, Dig.'

Field turned to Mellons, 'What about you, Bob?'

Mellons finished his beer. 'I've got a Land Rover, one sergeant and four constables laid on as my part of the act. Why don't you join us? It'll be someone to talk to if the patrol gets long and boring.'

'Doesn't look like being very boring. Rioting and fires down in Harare.'

Mellons placed his empty glass on the bar. 'You know it's often only a false alarm. As soon as they glimpse a police vehicle you won't see their arses for dust.' He paused. 'Tell you what we do, Bill. We'll wear our riot overalls and steel helmets over our civvies. Then after we've shown the flag for a couple of hours we can stow our kit and have a few beers together on the town. How's that?'

'Right,' said Field. 'Where do we pick up your vehicle?'

'Back of the armoury.'

It took them five minutes to dress in riot kit, another five to walk to their assembly point. Mellons' posse of African constables under an African sergeant were lined up beside the Land Rover, its windows and windscreen protected by heavy wire grills. They drove round to the issuing depot and Mellons signed for riot guns and ammunition. Field signed for his own Smith and Wesson revolver and ammunition. It felt heavy and absurd in the holster at his side.

As Mellons drove out through the Police Depot entrance he turned to Field, obviously sharing the same feelings. 'You know, wearing this thing always makes me feel like someone in a television serial. I've never fired a single shot in anger in my life.'

'Lucky you,' said Field. 'And when you think that the entire bloody force is absolutely unarmed practically all the time, it's probably a miracle that no one's ever been seriously hurt.'

'Careful,' said Mellons, 'cross your fingers when you say that my boy. There's always a first time.'

CHAPTER NINE

THEY DROVE through the centre of Salisbury. The shops were shut but the windows were still brightly lit and there were plenty of people around, both black and white. It was warm, pleasant and peaceful.

Mellons halted at the red at the first Stanley Street intersection and said sourly, 'Five miles away Harare is burning to the ground and around here nobody gives a damn!'

'Oh, come off it,' said Field reprovingly. 'If they *did* know, what could they do about it? Walk around with a worried look on their faces? Feel sick?'

The red changed to green and Mellons selected his gear and let in the clutch. As they moved forward he said, 'All right. We won't have a fight about it.'

He tooted his horn warningly as two Negroes, the man immaculate in a pale grey suit and black and white shoes, the girl encased in a dress of shining red silk, paused at the edge of the pavement, and added, 'I was just feeling sorry for Harare.'

Field grunted. 'You can be sure of one thing tonight. Zipp will be trying to burn down Zapu's headquarters and Zapu will be trying to return the compliment to Zipp.'

'And the best of British luck to both of them,' said Mellons enthusiastically.

They drove in silence for a few seconds and then Mellons asked, 'Were you in Salisbury in '61 when we had our first famous riots, Bill?'

'No.'

'I was stationed in Harare. A politician who is now regarded as one of the leading supporters of the African lobby came down next morning to inspect the damage. I drove him and my senior officer around and at the end of it he said very seriously, "If this happens again tonight, Superintendent, you will open fire. We can't allow a breakdown of law and order like this." '

'And it didn't happen the next night?'

'No, the African had had his fun. The famous politician

missed the chance of ordering his own personal Sharpeville and is now ready to take his place in the United Nations without a stain on his character.'

'Olé,' said Field. 'We all need a bit of luck.'

'I've thought about resigning,' said Mellons.

'Me too,' said Field sarcastically. 'I can see the advert. Two ex-coppers nearing forty-five on small pensions need rewarding open air work.'

'What really disturbs me,' said Mellons thoughtfully, 'is that sometimes I feel that some people would be really happy if the streets of Salisbury were empty and bloodstained, if armed men were crouching behind overturned cars, if dead bodies littered every doorway, and the cameramen could take those touching pictures of kids wandering about the ruins wounded or frightened or howling.'

He drove the car into the compound next to Salisbury Town Station. 'All out! We're here.'

They crossed the yard, walked up the stairs and into the Ops room where every telephone and radio microphone was manned, the room buzzing with incoming and outgoing messages. The Assistant Commissioner stood by the huge map of Harare talking to the Duty Superintendent. He looked up as they came in and said, 'Good. More reinforcements. They can do the rescue job.'

He walked across. He knew them both. 'Mellons, Field, good evening,' he said pleasantly. 'We've got a special job for you. It looks as if something very clever is going on in Harare tonight. Seven outbreaks of arson and violence in different parts of the township. Obviously planned to make as much trouble as possible. They've cut a lot of telephone wires and wrecked a sub-station. There's no electric light. Come over here, will you.' He led them over to the huge map. 'Now we've just had a report that they're attacking the Church of Christian Spirit at the corner of Drysdale and Fifth. Apparently even the servants of God are not as sacrosanct as they might be. Your orders are to take your vehicle in and get the Minister out. If he's got a wife or family get them out too. If you want any reinforcements get on the "blower" and let us know. You are to avoid any unnecessary violence. Play it by ear and as softly as possible. Get going.'

'Yes, sir,' said Mellons. They went outside. The Land Rover was ticking over and Mellons' African sergeant was now at the wheel. The four constables, riot rifles between their knees, sat immobile in the back.

'Okay, Sergeant,' said Mellons swinging open the side door, 'I'll drive. Inspector Field will sit with me. You get in the back with the constables. I expect we shall meet a bit of trouble, bound to be stoned on the way through Harare. Our orders are to rescue a Minister from the Church of Christian Spirit, and remember this, no one is to open fire without a direct order from me. Understood?'

'Yes, sah.'

The sergeant scampered round to the rear door and was in the back before Field had climbed in beside Mellons.

The partition between the front cab and the rear was closed. 'What's your African sergeant like?' asked Field. 'Seems pretty keen.'

Mellons revved the engine and eased the nose of the Land Rover out through the police station gates. 'Sergeant Mushiwara? Fine chap. Very solid.'

Field noticed that a shade of excitement revealed by stronger cadences of Somerset had crept into Mellons' voice.

They turned into the Manica Road and Field reached forward to unhook the microphone from its place on the radio set.

'I'll give them an identification call,' he said, pressing down the speaker button, 'This is Inspector Field and Inspector Mellons reporting in for radio check. Inspectors Field and Mellons reporting in for radio check. Over.'

The operator's voice crackled through the loudspeaker. 'I read you Inspector Field, loud and clear, loud and clear. Over.'

Field had the mike an inch from his mouth. 'We are proceeding to Harare and will contact you again from the township. Over and out.'

'Message received and understood. Good luck. Over and out.'

'Nice to be in touch with the outside world,' said Mellons softly as clear of the main traffic now he drove swiftly through the dark streets, and turned down Pioneer Street.

Seventy years ago it had been the single main street of civilization in a wilderness of veld and mountain: the place where the wagon trains unloaded their supplies from the south and bearded settlers congregated to drink and pick up mail before travelling out to their lonely farms. Their headlamps picked out the low, single-storey, graceful Dutch colonial façades of the old stores and shops. Pioneer Street was now decrepit and Field always thought it should be preserved. After all it was rare in a country's history that the trunk and branches of its growth could be seen and protected. At the entrance to Harare township they were flagged down by a police patrol with a red lamp. The sergeant in charge was talkative, obviously informed about their mission by radio.

'Not a damn light in the whole of Harare except the fires,' he said, indicating the red glare in the sky. 'About a quarter of a mile down the road you'll find a gang of thugs skulking in the bushes and front gardens of the houses so I should pick up speed at that point as you're bound to be stoned. Good luck!'

As Mellons accelerated away Field unhooked the mike and contacted H.Q. 'We are now entering Harare,' he said. 'So far our progress unimpeded.'

H.Q. acknowledged the report and they drove on, their headlights cutting a wide white track through the darkness ahead until Mellons said, 'Hello, here they are.'

Vague figures in white singlets or shirts loomed in the darkness on either side and they heard shouts and whistles. Stones and milk bottles banged against the coachwork. Mellons flicked his headlights up and down, pressed the horn in a sustained bray of warning and shot past. The road was quickly quiet and deserted again.

On the next corner a small shop—a general store by the look of the blackening advertisements outside—was burning, the flames bursting through the two small windows of the concrete, box-like structure, the sparks swirling up against the night sky. No one watched or tried to put out the fire; it could have been burning in the middle of a desert for all the attention it attracted.

Mellons blew a long blast on the horn in a fury of

exasperation, 'Where the hell's the fire brigade? Why doesn't someone do something?'

'Look at the sky,' said Field, indicating the red glare covering the sky overhead. 'There are probably twenty fires twice as big as this in Harare tonight. Anyone with his head screwed on locks his front door, hides under the bed and keeps out of trouble.'

'Bloody disgraceful,' said Mellons.

Field turned his head to watch the small store disintegrating as they drove past, seeing the faces of the four constables suddenly flushed with red as their skins reflected the blaze. He said, 'That probably belongs to some poor little sod of an African shopkeeper who's refused credit to one of the "boys", or who's refused to pay his political dues in the mistaken belief that law and order can be maintained.'

'And so it can,' said Mellons shortly.

Suddenly ahead they saw the waving white mushrooms of many torches, and in the long glare of the headlights glimpsed perhaps twenty Africans armed with sticks and waving them to stop.

'Straight through,' said Field impatiently.

Once again Mellons pressed the horn in a long screech of warning, and jamming the accelerator down to the floorboards hurtled the machine towards them. They had scattered to the side of the road before they got within twenty yards. 'You call that maintaining law and order,' said Field sarcastically.

'At this minute I am the law,' said Mellons coldly. Field made a rude noise.

'Don't kid yourself. You're just the overpaid instrument of the law, that's all.'

'Now listen to me,' began Mellons, belligerently, then glanced sideways to see Field laughing. He shook his head. 'Bastard!' he said quietly.

'I think it's the next on the left,' said Field.

Mellons took the Land Rover around in a tight turn and accelerated down the dark empty street. The red glow filled the sky between the black buildings and each little block of a concrete house was shuttered and quiet.

'Like a graveyard,' observed Mellons.

'Dead right,' said Field, 'ninety per cent of Harare's citizens are hiding away, wondering who wants to pay off old scores, and wishing to God daylight would come.'

They roared past another group of youths who brandished sticks, yelled threats and threw stones.

'A few of the citizens still up,' said Mellons cheerfully.

'Turn right at the end here,' directed Field, 'and it should be at the bottom on the left-hand side. According to my local knowledge it's got a big white cross painted on one side which we can't miss.'

Mellons turned right and started to slow down.

'Better give H.Q. a buzz on the blower,' he said, 'I'd hate to disappear without trace.'

'Okay,' said Field and picked up the microphone. 'This is Inspector Field calling H.Q. Field calling H.Q. Over.'

Immediately the operator's voice broke in. Plainly he had been told to stand by on their frequency. 'H.Q. getting you loud and clear, loud and clear. Over.'

'We are now within three hundred yards of our target,' said Field, 'approaching the Church of the Christian Spirit. Yes, I can see the white cross painted on its side. The street itself seems quiet but we are approaching cautiously. . . .'

Mellons let the engine idle. He peered intently through the windscreen.

Field said urgently into the mike, 'Hang on, there's a group of Africans around the Church. God knows what they're doing. I'm signing off now, but will report back. Over and out.' He replaced the mike. 'What d'you think, Bob?'

'Better be prepared for trouble,' said Mellons quietly.

'They don't seem to be belligerent. Strange?'

'I don't like it much.' Mellons was uneasy.

Field said, 'Let's run up to the front door and pile out together. A couple of warning shots will probably scare them off if necessary.'

'I hope so,' said Mellons, 'I'll pull up hard against the church to keep that flank covered and come out through your door. Warn Sergeant Mushiwara.'

Field slid back the glass panel, 'Sergeant, we're almost there. Once we stop, jump out at once. No firing unless you get a direct order from me or Inspector Mellons, but be prepared to put a couple of shots into the air to frighten them. Is that understood?'

Yes, sah,' said Sergeant Mushiwara. His teeth glinted as he smiled and Field thought, 'My God, he's enjoying himself.'

He extricated his revolver from its holster and thumbed off the safety catch. As they drove in towards the church the party of Africans converged upon their vehicle. To Field s relief he saw they were grinning.

'I believe they're on our side,' he announced.

Field swung open his door before the Land Rover stopped. He heard a voice shout, 'It's the police, the police!' And another closer to him, 'Don't shoot, don't shoot. Friends, sah, friends!'

Field sat poised above the semi-circle of Africans dressed in the usual singlets and shorts, white shirts and denims. They were laughing at him, quite happy, non-belligerent, anxious to be friendly.

'What's going on?' he asked.

A huge African pushed forward to act as spokesman. He wore a stained white vest which revealed enormous biceps, his face was flat and ugly, his white smile childlike and happy. 'We are very pleased you have come, sah,' he said.

'Glad to hear it,' said Field, stepping down amongst them. 'We understood this church was in danger?'

He felt at once that the revolver was overdramatic, and shoved it back into his holster and repeated, 'We thought this church was being attacked?'

The big Negro answered, 'Yes sah, it was, sah. But we are the parishioners here, sah. I am a church warden. When these fellers started this trouble we banded together to protect our property. We chased those fellows off, sah. They are no-good idlers, sah.'

'Good God,' said Field surprised, and then hastily, 'Well done.' He turned to Mellons still poised in the car door behind him. 'Better give H.Q. the happy news, mate,' he said. He turned back to the Africans. 'You chased the attackers away?'

'Yes, sah,' said the huge African benignly, 'we took twenty prisoners, sah.'

'Twenty prisoners. For God's sake!' said Field. 'Where are they?'

'We have locked them in the shed at the back of the Church.'

Field lifted his voice as everyone began talking at once. 'Better report that too,' he called to Mellons, who was now busy with the mike. 'Ask them if they want us to ferry back twenty prisoners?'

'Some bloody hopes,' said Mellons caustically, and then hastily into the mike, 'No, sir. I wasn't referring to you, sir.'

Sergeant Mushiwara and his four constables, rifles at 'port' position, were now lined up a few yards away from the side of the Land Rover. Field said, 'Where's the Minister?'

'The Minister's name is Father Brown, mine is Mr. Williams,' said the large African politely. 'He is in this house next to the church. You can go in, sir. The door is unlocked.'

'Fine,' said Field. He turned to Sergeant Mushiwara. 'Post your men out around the church, Sergeant, and tell them to keep their eyes open.' He lifted his voice again so that Mellons could hear. 'I'll go in and get the vicar, Bob.'

'Okay,' said Mellons.

He followed the Mr. Williams up the short path which led to the vicarage. It was an unpainted shack leaning against the side of the church. The Negro opened the door and called into a thin black corridor. 'Father? Father Brown? I have a visitor for you.' It was then that Field realized for such an enormous man he had an astonishingly mild voice and manner.

He said, 'I should go through, sir. I think he knows you are coming.'

A crack of light appeared at the end of the corridor and Field, edging past, felt his way towards it. He opened a door. Father Brown was a plump, jolly-looking African dressed in clerical black, his dog collar disconcertingly white against this sober background, a man in his early fifties, Field guessed. He wore heavy horn-rimmed spectacles and he sat at a small, plain wooden table reading his Bible by the light of the smoky oil lamp. There was a faint film of perspiration on his chin. He lifted the horn rims from his pudgy nose and stared up as Field came in. 'Ah, good evening, Officer,' he said cheerfully, 'we were expecting you.'

Field went closer.

'I see, sir,' he said politely, 'that you're getting instruction from the good book. How would Jesus Christ have dealt with this little lot?'

He realized as soon as he had spoken that it was what Milly would have called one of his unfortunate remarks. However, the Minister seemed to think it apt. He beamed. 'He would have scourged them, Officer,' he said cheerfully, 'he would have scourged them. Do sit down, Officer.'

Field sat down on a chair opposite him. He liked the man's unhurried composure. 'You must be a Matebele, sir?'

'Yes, Officer, I am a Matebele.'

Field decided he must disillusion him immediately about his rank. 'I am afraid, Father,' he said, 'I'm not an officer. Merely an inspector.'

The Minister disregarded the reply with a cheerful wave of his hand. 'We are all officers under God,' he smiled. His broad white teeth flashed in the lamplight.

'I'll pass your message on to the Commissioner,' said Field patiently. 'Now, sir, if you'll get yourself, and those of your flock you wish to move, into the Land Rover, we'll get moving.'

The large dark eyes behind the glasses opened.

'But I do not wish to leave. This is my church. My parishioners and I are perfectly capable of looking after ourselves.'

'Sir,' said Field with an infinitesimal increase of authoritative patience, 'may I remind you that several thousand young hooligans are on the rampage tonight, and outside you have twenty or thirty devoted parishioners. In an hour or two every liquor store in Harare will be broken wide open and the contents guzzled. You know as well as I do what a Matebele or a Mashona with a mixture of brandy, whisky, gin, crème de menthe, not to mention South African sherry, inside him is likely to do . . .'

Father Brown grinned. 'It would be an interesting cocktail, I must admit,' he said. Field warmed to him. 'No doubt, sir, it will prove effective,' he said, 'and we know from experience that before the night is out there will be looting, burning, rape and possibly murder here in Harare. They will turn their attention first to the easiest places to loot and burn: the churches, cinemas, dance halls, rape at the girls' hostel will come later.'

Father Brown looked uneasy. 'I hope you have taken care of that problem,' he said.

'Since the events of July, 1960, yes,' said Field, 'although I see it was advanced in a recent book by an African nationalist that the girls were only raped because they refused to boycott the buses in a local strike.' He added, 'Quite interesting sociological reasoning, I suppose?'

Father Brown closed his Bible firmly. He wasn't letting Field get away with that one. 'There are many faults on both sides,' he said severely.

'Nevertheless, sir,' said Field. 'I still think you should leave. Your parishioners may be able to save the church, but if a bigger mob returns, your life and their lives might be in danger, and without you to defend they could slide away into the darkness. Tomorrow when the grog's worn off and the looters are suffering from hangovers you'll be able to return.'

The Minister considered this logic for a few seconds and then relented. He got up from the table, a small fat black man with a cherubic black face, possessed of an air of dignity and decisiveness.

'I think you are right,' he said. 'I will accompany you.'

Outside Mellons was surrounded by a semi-circle of cheerful Africans. He saw Field and Father Brown and said, 'Ah, good. H.Q. says things are hotting up and we're to bring the Minister straight out. No larking about. They were rather rude about the prisoners but eventually suggested that if the parishioners could hold them until daylight tomorrow a waggon could probably pick them up.'

Mr. Williams said mildly, 'We will hold them until tomorrow, never fear.'

'If you'll sit between us in the front seat, Father Brown,' said Field, 'we'll get started.' He stood back to allow the priest to clamber up and then turned to Mr. Williams. 'You may be attacked by a bigger mob,' he said warningly. 'The fact that the church burns down isn't the end of the world. You can always rebuild it. But it's difficult to get a new head, Mr. Williams, remember that.'

Mr. Williams laughed appreciatively. 'God is on the side of the righteous,' he said stoutly. 'We shall defend our church against any attackers, and we shall keep those we have apprehended until we hand them over to the forces of the law.'

'All right,' said Field. He swung up beside Father Brown and rolled down the window so that he could say, 'Good luck.' As they moved away he said, 'Cromwell would have approved of Mr. Williams.'

'There are many Africans who wish to solve our difficulties through peace and goodwill,' said Father Brown quickly. 'But it is very hard for the voices of the moderates to be heard. Education and tolerance at all levels between both races is what is needed.'

'Hear, hear,' Mellons butted cheerfully into the conversation as he got into top gear. 'As Livingstone once observed, 'Commerce and Christianity must go hand in hand.'

'Dr. Livingstone was a great man,' Father Brown said, 'but these days I feel that we have had enough of commerce and a larger quota of commonsense would be much more useful.'

'Hear, hear,' said Mellons again politely.

He picked up speed going up the slight hill and swung the Land Rover round the right-hand turn. The road stretched ahead, dark and straight in the headlights, and after two minutes' driving Field, peering through the windscreen, said, 'Take it easy. Something in the road up ahead.'

The 'something' vaguely black and menacing stretched completely across the road. 'Looks like a barricade,' said Field, and Mellons eased his foot off the accelerator and idled towards it.

It was a barricade, a home-made affair, a jumble of dustbins, boxes, tree trunks, branches, one upturned cart. Mellons took his foot off the brake and coasted. 'Reckon we could bash through that little lot without much trouble,' he said, eyeing the pile speculatively and he revved the engine again, taking the Land Rover to within a few yards of the obstacle. 'Shall I give it a go?'

'Yes . . .' began Field, then glimpsed in the shadows on either side of the barricade the flash of white singlets, the quick glitter as a match was struck. 'No, no! Back Reverse!' he shouted intuitively guessing what was about to happen. 'Quick! Petrol bomb!'

Mellons slammed on the brakes, swung sideways and crashed the gears into reverse. As they spun back in a half circle, debris from the barricade crackling under their wheels, Field saw the flaming wick of rag stuffed into the bottle full of petrol flying through the air. It struck the pile with a great roaring 'whoof' and the whole world disintegrated into flame. The interior of the Land Rover was suddenly filled with its glare.

'Oh, my God!' cried Father Brown, crouching back. They were still five yards away but the heat was intense, the flames unbearable. All around the figures of Africans leapt and howled with hate. Bottles, stones and sticks rattled, banged and broke against their bodywork. Finishing his reverse lock Mellons bashed into first gear and they swung forwards in a jolting semi-circle bouncing up the pavement and removing the neat, white painted fence of a small house on their way, and then straightening up he roared back the way they had come.

Field released his breath. 'Very subtle,' he said. 'They'd soaked that barricade in petrol. We'd have been in quite a mess if we'd gone through that little lot.'

'Where do they learn these things?' Mellons demanded sarcastically. 'D'you think they see it on television?'

'Probably,' said Field. 'Have you any idea where we're going now?'

Father Brown, now recovered from his fright, spoke up. His eyes were shining. 'This is a great adventure, isn't it?' he said. 'Do you often experience such excitement?'

'We really prefer a quieter life,' said Field civilly, 'but it is often denied us. And the point now is how do we circle round to miss them?'

'I know a way back which will extricate us,' said Father Brown quickly. 'It will bring us out near the sub-post office on the Melling Road. And then we join the main road which will lead us straight out of Harare.'

'Lead on, Father Brown,' said Mellons, and to Field he added, 'I think we'd better warn H.Q. about that roadblock.'

'Will do,' said Field and picked up the mike. 'Inspector Field to H.Q. Field to H.Q. Come in, please. Over.'

'H.Q. reading you loud and clear. H.Q. answering. Over,' came the immediate reply.

'We have picked up Father Brown and he is with us in the Land Rover,' said Field. 'We have just dodged a roadblock in Circus Road, a pile of wood soaked in petrol which is now blazing merrily. There are a few gangs of youths skulking about and we have been stoned intermittently but no serious damage has been caused. Over.'

The loudspeaker crackled and Field heard someone clearing his throat authoritatively. He recognized the Super's voice on the line. 'Superintendent Harrow here, Inspector Field. Now listen to me. You are to leave the township at once and return to H.Q. I will repeat that. You are to leave the township at once and return to H.Q. Confirm message received. Over.'

Field pressed down the mike button. 'Message that we are to leave Harare at once and return, received and understood. Over.'

Harrow's voice crackled on the air once more. 'Get the hell out of there as fast as you can. Things are hotting up and we are considering pulling all police units out of the township until daylight when, if necessary, troops will be used to restore order. Over.'

Field said, 'Wilco. Over and out.' He replaced the mike and said bitterly, 'Troops. Why in the name of God do they have to consider troops. The police can restore law and order. What do the bloody troops know about it?'

'You will turn left here,' said Father Brown, 'and at the T-junction at the bottom we shall turn right which will bring us to the Melling Road Post Office.'

They roared down a narrow gut of a road, the sound of their engine reverberating from the banks and walls on either side. Mellons hurtled round the corner in a noisy sliding skid, banged up into second gear and tore up the side road towards a great blaze of light ahead.

'You training for Le Mans?' said Field ironically.

'By the look of those flames ahead we should be training for the fire brigade,' said Mellons seriously.

They came out of the side road at a slight elevation above a small triangular shopping area intersected by the main road. All the shops were burning brightly and all were in the process of being looted. The light of the soaring flames revealed figures scurrying out of the liquor store, the supermarket and a shoe shop. Every window was smashed; the area was wrecked. There were close to a hundred rioters in the small square all urgently intent upon running into the burning buildings and reappearing with arms loaded with loot. This they deposited in small piles guarded by their friends while they dashed back for more. To the left stood the post office, its doors smashed open. Against its walls a group of men were struggling, sticks and arms rising and falling, and Field's head jerked towards them. 'Good God,' he said, 'they've trapped two African police reservists. We've got to give them a hand. Swing her across towards them, Bob. Put the headlights on them. Hurry!'

He turned round to shout into the back, 'Sergeant Mushiwara, we're going to quell this riot. When we stop, pile out and fire two warning shots into the air. Reload and stand by. Understood?'

'Yes, sah,' said Sergeant Mushiwara, and again came the quick flash of the white teeth.

'The Super said, "Get out at once",' grumbled Mellons, flicking up his headlights to impale the struggling figures against the post office wall.

'Bugger the Superintendent,' said Field rudely. 'We'll clean up this little lot. We can't leave those African reservists. They'll kill them.'

'I know that,' said Mellons as they jumped and bounced across the rough earth between them and the post office, 'I'll take the two constables and scare them out of the shops. You take Sergeant Mushiwara and the others and rescue the reservists.'

'What about me?' asked Father Brown eagerly. 'I could help.'

'You stay here, Father,' said Field grimly. 'A little prayer may help. We may need assistance from upstairs.'

Horn blasting, headlights isolating the struggling figures against the post office wall, Mellons bounced the Land Rover in towards the fight. He jammed on the brakes, and only then did the rioters appear to hear them. One shouted a warning and the others turned, freezing into momentary immobility, a frieze of thin figures and angular shadows like a Congolese primitive painting, against the burnt ochre background. Then abruptly the scene disintegrated and the rioters scurried away into the darkness like beetles caught under a strong light.

Field, revolver in hand, leapt out of the Land Rover and sprinted towards them. Behind him he heard the rear door crash open, Sergeant Mushiwara's sharp command, the 'bang-bang' as the two riot guns fired their charges into the air, the blast punching him twice in the back. He slid to a halt beside the two police reservists. They were dazed and shaken. They leant back against the wooden wall of the post office in an abandonment of exhaustion.

'You all right?' said Field, breathing heavily. In the light from the flames their eyes rolled. One nodded dumbly, the other, blood streaming down his face, was just about able to speak. 'Yes, sah. We glad you came, sah.'

'Go and get in the police van,' said Field. 'We'll take you out of here.'

'They're robbing the post office, sah,' whispered the reservist weakly. He was a tall, bony young man. He touched the side of his face where the blood had matted. 'We tried to stop them, sah, and then this gang came along, sah.'

'You've done very well,' said Field reassuringly. 'Now go to the van and take a breather.'

He glanced around. The violence of the guns had cleared the square completely of rioters. Mellons and his constables had seen the looters race away from the blazing shops and supermarket, and were now returning, jog-trotting back up the slight slope towards them. Sergeant Mushiwara arrived at his elbow; the other two constables had disappeared chasing the rioters who had been attacking the reservists.

'Right, Sergeant,' snapped Field. 'Into the post office to see if anybody's left.'

He ran past the barred window set in the post office wall

and followed by Sergeant Mushiwara charged in through the wrecked front door. In the red light he saw an African who looked as if he might be the postmaster stretched out on the floor, his head battered, blood on the floor about it; he was unconscious or dead. At the far end of the room behind the wire grille and wooden counter over which stamps, postal orders and pensions were issued, a tall Negro in a dirty singlet and faded denims was hacking at a locked drawer with a large, shining axe.

Field sprang forward, opening his mouth to yell at him. Then to his utter surprise he heard a loud bang somewhere inside his head and a bright yellow light suddenly flashed across his eyes. He was vaguely conscious of trying to ward off an unknown danger with his left hand. Then there was another bang, another burst of yellow flame. His hands scrabbled across coarse hard material. There was a great leaping pain in his head. A round white object rolled near his face. Bewildered, he realized it was his helmet. He was stretched on the floor. What was he doing on the floor? Someone must have knocked him down. The simplicity of this deduction astonished him. That was it. Someone must have been waiting behind the door to hit him. Bloody nerve! He rolled over and tried to push himself up, tried to shout in his loud policeman's voice. A noise, half croak, half groan emerged. The room was blurred, full of shadowy figures. There was noise, struggle, hate, violence. Then the blur cleared and objects came into focus. Sergeant Mushiwara was wrestling with an African. That must be the one who had hit him and knocked off his helmet?

Suddenly his eyes focused on the other Negro, the one behind the counter at the other end of the room. Even at five yards' distance the malevolence of the man's hatred penetrated through into his muzzy brain. The bastard was after him! The bastard was going to try to kill him! The man was scrambling over the counter, his face red in the blotchy light, his lips tight back over his big white teeth. Field had seen the same intense hatred in the face of a trapped animal. And this man with the swiftness of an animal charged at Field, axe lifted high to cleave downwards. He was above him, enormous, malignant, destructive.

Somewhere, a thousand miles away he heard a voice screaming, 'Shoot, Bill, shoot, shoot!'

An instinct fashioned by ten million years of self-preservation forced him to roll desperately to one side. His right hand, still holding his revolver, pushed up towards the man's chest. His index finger snatched at the trigger and with a mild malicious life of its own the gun roared and jerked. The African made a noise which was half cough, half choke, and axe and man crashed down on Field. Spurred at once by a terrible fear, Field tried to struggle away, to push him off, then he realized that the other body was slack and inert. He sat up and the man rolled away, sprawled flat on his back. There was blood on Field's overalls. He felt sick.

Mellons knelt beside him. He was panting as if he'd run a hundred yards at top speed. He put his arms around Field's shoulders and Field leaned back against them as if he could take some strength from their solidarity. He just wanted to sit there and be sick.

'God, Bill!' said Mellons, 'I looked in through the window. I thought he'd got you. I thought you'd had it. I screamed at you. Did you hear?'

'I heard,' said Field. 'I think I've killed him.'

'God, you nearly had it. It was self-defence. You had to shoot.'

'Did I?' said Field. He felt numb, cold, drained of energy.

'Murderous bastards. I think they've killed the postmaster. Can you walk, Bill? We've got to get out of here. They won't leave us alone for long.'

'Yes, I can walk,' said Field. He didn't want to walk. He just wanted to sit there, leaning against Mellons, and feel sick. Then he said, 'We must get him to hospital.'

Mellons eased him away and stood up. Now he looked down in surprise. 'Who? You mean this one you've shot?'

'Yes,' said Field angrily, 'I mean him.'

Mellons's voice was mild, "All right. We've got to get all of them—the postmaster and the two reservists—as well as this chap to hospital.'

He turned to Sergeant Mushiwara who now held the rioter who had hit Field. He had handcuffed him. 'Get that man into the vehicle, Sergeant.' As he spoke the four African constables came crowding through the door. One spoke quickly to Mushiwara who said, 'They say the rioters are forming up again across the main road, sah. They will try to stop us, sah.'

'Oh, will they?' said Mellons grimly. 'We'll see about that.' He turned to help Field off the floor. 'Sergeant, place your constables around the Land Rover and fire over their heads if necessary. No, wait. Two constables help to get these wounded men into the truck. Put blankets on the floor for them to lie on. Then we'd better clean out any valuables left in this post office. Better force open that drawer or someone else will do it for us after we've gone. Then we'll get out of here.'

He put his arm round Field's shoulders again. 'Come on, Bill, let's get started.'

Field wobbled a couple of steps. 'Christ,' he said, 'what did they hit me with?'

'An iron bar. The first blow must have knocked your helmet off and dazed you. Then he hit you a second time and knocked you cold. By the grace of God you put up your left hand and warded off some of the force of the blow. Look at the back of your left hand.'

Field stared down at the broken skin and blackening flesh. 'I don't remember,' he said, 'I just don't remember.'

'Sergeant Mushiwara got to him just before he could hit you again. I came up to the window just in time to see that one go for you with the axe. Thank God you were still functioning. Now come on, let's walk. The fresh air will do you good.'

Outside at the edge of the circle of light spread by the fires they could see the crowd of rioters reforming. Father Brown was still seated patiently in the cab. 'This machine,' he said, indicating the radio, 'has been talking. It has said constantly, "Inspector Field or Mellons, will you come in please. Will you report please."' He added cautiously, 'It sounded very annoyed.'

'Must think we're bloody disc jockeys,' said Mellons sourly.

'I heard a shot?' said Father Brown simply.

'It was me,' said Field. 'I think I killed a man.' Mellons who had gone round to the back to supervise the closure of the steel doors came back to the driving seat. He overheard the remark. 'We don't know yet,' he said, 'wait till we get him to the hospital. Anyway you had no choice.'

Father Brown was silent for a second. Then he said, 'These are terrible times. Terrible times.'

Mellons started the engine and in bottom gear they crawled slowly down the slope towards the shining tarmac of the main road. He eased the front wheels carefully down the kerb, allowed the rear wheels to do the same thing, straightened up, and came back into neutral as he saw what lay ahead. He said, 'Our friends don't seem to want to part with us.'

Fifty yards in front the rioters were seeping back across the roadway like a slow stream of black water. They edged through between the burning buildings; they came out from behind the post office and moved slowly down the hill. Now there must have been nearly two hundred of them: youths, half naked or in singlets and khaki shorts, in dirty overalls, in denims. They approached menacingly, sticks, bicycle chains, half bricks in their hands, ominously quiet yet moving with a deliberation of purpose which was frightening to watch.

'Straight through, I think,' said Mellons bluntly, 'and no arguments.'

Field considered. 'A slight show of force might not be a bad idea.'

'Meaning what?' said Mellons.

'Four shots over their heads would tell them that we mean business and could clear a quick path for us,' said Field, 'then bang through as hard as we can go.' Surprisingly he felt better at the thought of action.

'Good idea,' said Mellons, 'blow me a hole down the main road, and I'll be up it like the proverbial salmon.' But his voice was tight and hard; he did not sound like the slow, cheerful, Somerset man that Field knew.

Field turned to speak through the partition. 'Sergeant Mushiwara,' he said quietly, 'take out your constables and line them up in front of the vehicle. I shall join you. I shall give the order to fire. The constables are to shoot over their heads. Make that quite clear. We shall give the rioters three seconds to disperse then we shall jump into the back and go through them like a dose of salts. Make sure everyone understands what is going to happen.'

'Yes, sah,' said Mushiwara, and Field saw the round-eyed constables turn their heads towards him as he broke into Shona.

Field opened his door and Mellons said protestingly, 'You're not fit enough to do it.'

'Don't be so bloody silly,' said Field. 'Or would you prefer to slip away and fetch a magistrate to read the Riot Act?' He left his door open, 'Stay in gear and be ready to bash on. And for Christ's sake don't run out of petrol for the next five minutes.'

'Ha-ha,' said Mellons mirthlessly.

Field walked slowly around to the front of the truck. As soon as the rioters saw him they stopped their slow advance. They stood poised, perhaps forty yards away, sticks raised but now uncertain. There was silence. Only the constables' boots made a noise as they marched officiously around to form up in front of the truck.

'Right,' said Field. 'Load.'

A vague quiver of uneasiness stirred the rioters as the breech blocks snapped shut. They swayed slightly like grass in the wind.

'You two,' said Field indicating individual constables, 'will fire over their heads directly in front. You to the right, you to the left. Now keep your aim high. Get that quite clear. Well into the air over their heads. Right! Firing positions!' There was a swelling murmur from the crowd as they saw the guns raised, a movement away, the beginnings of consternation which presaged panic.

'Aim!' Field yelled the word loudly. Then 'Fire!' The riot guns hurled flame and noise and a flailing hail of lead pellets high into the air. With a great yell of fear the rioters ran away, falling over each other, pushing, scrambling to safety.

Field counted slowly to three. 'Now,' he snapped, 'back in the truck. At the double. Quick!'

The Land Rover was moving before Field scrambled back into his seat. He peered through the partition to see the last of the constables being yanked in unceremoniously. The door slammed; he saw the bolts go home.

'All aboard,' he yelled to Mellons. 'Put your foot down.' The great burst of power as Mellons accelerated threw him hard back against his seat. He saw the rioters hesitate in their mad charge for safety, sensed their frustration and hate as they understood that they had been outwitted and they turned to charge back into the path of the moving vehicle. Stones banged in a typewriter tattoo against the sides. A thin screen of rioters raced across the road in front, and Mellons roared towards them like an express train. The rioters thickened around their flanks and they seemed literally to burst through a white surf of shirts and vests throwing them back like a bow wave. They screamed threats, banged on the sides with their sticks and fists. But suddenly the screen of bodies in front had gone—none of them wishing martyrdom under the hissing two-ton wheels—blown away as if by a strong wind.

They were clear. The howls of derision faded in the night behind them. Their headlamps threw twin beams down a black deserted road. Mellons blew a triumphant 'toot-dida-toot-toot' on the horn and said, 'I don't think we'll stop for tea on the way back.'

Father Brown said in a puzzled voice, 'I do not understand?'

'It is a little joke,' said Field. 'My friend is full of little jokes.'

Father Brown chuckled. 'Oh, yes, I understand,' he said. 'A little joke. I see. We will not stop for tea. I understand.' He gurgled with laughter.

'I'm glad you came along,' said Mellons. 'Rarely am I so appreciated.'

The radio loudspeaker crackled. They recognized the Super's voice again. He was angry. It said, 'Inspectors Field and Mellons. Do you read me? Come in, please. Over.'

'Gawd!' said Mellons. We forgot our masters. Answer it, Bill. Say you're suffering from a sick headache and we stopped at a chemist to get some aspirin.'

'I am,' said Field. He picked up the microphone. 'Inspector Field answering H.Q. I read you H.Q. We have encountered some trouble and were temporarily out of touch. A crowd of several hundred rioters are burning and looting in the square near the Melling Road Post Office. We stopped to rescue two African reserve policemen. We have four casualties. Two are very badly injured. I would suggest a doctor and ambulance standing by at Town Station. Over.'

The Super's voice did not seem any less angry, 'I don't care where the hell you've been, or what you've encountered. Your orders were to come straight back. Over.'

'The two police reservists might have been killed,' said Field, 'we had no alternative but to stop. Over.'

The Super's voice was bleak. 'Don't argue with me, Inspector. You had clear orders. We have already pulled all units out of Harare. The situation is quite out of control. Now get the hell back here as soon as you can. We will have a doctor and ambulance standing by. Over.'

'Message received and understood,' said Field. 'We are on our way. Over and out.'

He replaced the mike. There was no sound in the cab except the steady hum of the engine for at least five seconds, then Father Brown said, 'It was Nelson I think who put his spy-glass to his blind eye.'

'And a fat lot of good that did him,' said Mellons disgruntedly. 'One of the earliest maxims implanted in me by my drill sergeant was, "Never volunteer for anything, and never try and be a hero." We should have known better.'

'We had no alternative,' said Field, 'none at all.'

In the back yard of Salisbury Town Station a fat, square ambulance stood waiting, headlights dimmed, engine running quivering like some species of strange white cow.

Field went around to watch as the medical orderlies brought along their stretchers and prepared to lift out the two injured men. One of them said, 'Not much point in bringing these two back was there? They're both dead.'

CHAPTER TEN

FIELD PICKED UP HIS DRINK and held it up to the light, squinting owlishly through the clear amber liquid as if he'd never seen a glass of whisky before. 'Some are darker than others,' he said. 'I don't suppose it means anything.'

Constantine behind the bar, grave and reserved in his Savile Row dark suit and owlish horn-rimmed spectacles, went on polishing a glass. He owned the bar and restaurant, presiding over it with the elegance and firmness of a dowager duchess caring for a crowd of debutantes.

'Look,' said Mellons quietly, 'there is no use brooding about it. It's done. It's happened . . .'

'And the man's dead.'

'It was him or you. He was probably responsible for the postmaster's death anyway.'

'That could have been the other chap.'

'The lightest coloured Scotch we have is J and B,' said Constantine taking a bottle down from the shelf. He poured an inch and a half into two glasses, and pushed it towards them. 'Here, try it.'

'It's my turn,' said Mellons.

'On the house,' said Constantine, pouring himself a measure. Constantine was Greek, thirty-two years old, tall, lean, handsome, enigmatic.

The small bar behind the long thin restaurant was empty. From the loud-speaker above the rows of glittering bottles and polished glasses issued the soft, reassuring background of somebody's latest long play. All was peaceful and comfortable except the conscience of Inspector Field which tried to find rescue and reason in whisky.

'I could have shot him in the shoulder,' said Field.

'Don't be a bloody fool,' said Mellons irritably. 'You had no time to decide how or where you were going to shoot him. You just shot in self-defence. Bloody miracle you didn't miss him.'

Field drained his whisky and poured an inch of water into the J and B. His head felt a little fuzzy. He had been drinking now pretty steadily for an hour. The doctor had said he could have a drink, and he had taken him at his word.

'It was him or me,' he said, seeking reassurance again.

'That's right. That's what the old man said, isn't it?'

Field nodded. 'He was curt but understanding. In the circumstances there was nothing else I could have done, he said. The publicity would do the force no good, but that was unavoidable. He understood that it was self-defence. He didn't say I was a bloody hero or a bloody murderer. Merely that it was self-defence.'

'There you are,' said Mellons.

'What sort of a job is it?' Field said bitterly, 'Where you have to go around killing men to make a living?'

Mellons did not answer and Field picked up his whisky and drained it. He patted the bandage covering his left hand which still felt sore. He shook his head slightly to try and clear the muzziness. How absurd it all was. An hour and a half ago he had been storming into a wrecked post office, an hour and a half ago he had shot a man dead; and now he was sitting in this posh bar in the centre of Salisbury slowly getting drunk while that black body of the man he had killed lay stretched out on a slab in the mortuary like a starfish. His eyes had been open when they carried him across to the ambulance; cold, dead eyes like empty glass reflecting torchlight. He pushed a pound note across the counter. 'Two more of the same,' he said, 'and do join us.'

Constantine smiled vaguely, inclined his distinguished head slightly and said, 'Delighted.' Mellons said, 'No more for me, thanks. Besides, I'm driving.'

'I need bottles,' said Field bluntly.

'Bill,' said Mellons emphatically, 'stop being so bloody dramatic.'

'Dramatic,' said Field, picking him up angrily. 'What the bloody hell is it but dramatic? If a man's death isn't dramatic, what is? He was a bus driver. He earned twenty pounds a month. He had a wife and three children. He was not a known agitator. He was probably drunk like I am now.'

'He killed the postmaster.'

'The other chap could have done that.'

'He was smashing open the till.'

'You don't kill people for smashing open tills.'
'He would have killed you.'
'Yes,' Field admitted, defeated. 'He would have killed me.'
'And he would bloody well have enjoyed doing it,' Mellons said quietly. 'Listen, Bill, drink that whisky and I'll take you back to the Depot. Now come on, there's a good chap. You've had a nasty crack on the head, you should be in bed. What did the doctor say?'
Field poured a drop of water into his scotch. 'The doctor said, 'Have a drink''. He also said that without the helmet my brains would now be decorating the post office floor.'
'There you are then.' Mellons got off his high stool. 'Come on, Bill. Constantine is waiting to close anyway, aren't you?' He appealed to the tall young Greek.
'It is quite all right,' said Constantine politely. 'If Mr. Field wishes to stay on he can do so.' He came closer to the bar and regarded Mellons curiously as if he was seeing him for the first time. 'Sometimes it is necessary to behave without logic,' he said gently. 'I will keep Mr. Field company if you wish to go.'
'Well,' said Mellons doubtfully.
'Oh, go on home,' said Field irritably. 'For Christ's sake, Bob, go on home. I know I'm acting like a bloody fool, getting drunk like one of those unshaven Hollywood actors in a bad film. It's terrible when you can't do anything nice and normal without feeling that you're copying something out of crappy television or a movie. I'm getting drunk. It's as simple as that. I shan't get into bad company, or pick a fight or roll in the gutter. I shall just have a nice long maudlin session with Constantine here, pop into a cab, be sick behind a hedge, and end up at the Police Depot quiet and orderly, and feeling like death. I won't disgrace my uniform or the flag under which we serve. Now for Christ's sake just go home. Drive carefully and I'll see you tomorrow. Right?'
'I was only trying to help,' said Mellons, affronted. 'But if that's the way you feel, okay.'
Field caught him by the shoulder pulling him back. 'I've insulted you,' he said. 'You won't ever speak to me again. When you see me coming in the mess you'll hide behind a cocoa cup and look the other way.'

Mellons grinned. 'You're a bloody big clown,' he said. 'I hope you get so drunk some young copper runs you in. That would just serve you bloody well right.' He turned to the bar, 'Good night, Constantine. If he does do any damage you can always appeal to the police comfort fund for redress.'

'Good night,' said Constantine politely but without warmth.

There was a long silence after he had gone. Field liked Constantine without really understanding why. He had frequented this bar in the old days when he had been stationed in Salisbury. Now Constantine continued to polish glasses and occasionally hummed a few bars in unison with the background music.

'You know what it's all about?' said Field. 'I mean you couldn't help but hear what we were talking about?'

Constantine carefully placed the glass he had just polished in a rack behind the bar and pulled up a stool against his side of the bar. He sat down carefully, placed his perfectly manicured white hands palms downwards on the counter.

'I knew half an hour before you came in. They said there had been trouble down in Harare and that an African had been killed by the police.'

'You see in front of you, the killer,' said Field loudly.

Constantine turned over one hand and examined his palm. 'You British do not like killing very much,' he said, conversationally. 'To be ruthless and implacable the British need a big reason and with a big reason they kill without conscience or remorse. We Greeks are different.' He lifted the hand under scrutiny and carefully examined a finger-nail. 'We quite enjoy killing on a reasonable, personal scale.'

'Killing in a war is one thing,' said Field, 'killing privately—'

'I was not talking about war,' said Constantine, 'only about killing. In Africa it is a constantly recurring factor like drought and famine, the sale of women, and the death of animals.' He turned back, reached for a bottle of whisky from the shelf, and placed it on the counter between them. 'As we are interested in ceremonial drinking,' he said, 'we may as well drink the best. This is a single malt. You like a single malt?'

'I have no great experience of the stuff,' said Field, 'but I am willing to try anything more than once if I like it.'

'There is Glen Grant, and Glen Livet, Glen Fiddich, Laphroaig, and several others. This is Glenmorangie, which comes from the Scottish town of Tain just below the Dornock Firth. It is very much to my palate.'

'I thought the Greeks were only interested in shipping, oil and women,' said Field.

'It is possible you have that list in the wrong order,' said Constantine. He produced clean glasses from under the counter and poured out two drinks. 'Add only very little water,' he said.

Field picked it up and sniffed. 'It smells like whisky.'

Constantine nodded approvingly and sipped his drink, rolling the liquor round his mouth with his tongue.

Field drank a little from his glass. 'It tastes like whisky.'

'You like it?'

'Yes,' said Field. 'But this is your bar. And my round?'

Constantine's eyebrows rose slightly above the rim of the glass. 'You are my guest,' he said disapprovingly. 'We are drinking to the dead.'

Field looked at him suspiciously. He appeared to be quite serious. 'So be it,' he answered gravely. He was silent for a second. Then he said, 'I was thinking of going to Bretts tonight to see a girl. D'you think that's madness? I mean in my condition? Half drunk? And I'm pretty certain she only asked me so as to make the fellow she was with jealous.'

Constantine asked, 'Is it the girl you were drinking with in Meikles this morning?'

'Yes.'

'Then it is not madness. She is very beautiful,' said Constantine thoughtfully.

Field knew there was something odd about this statement. 'How do you know about me drinking in Meikles Bar this morning?' he said.

Constantine looked at him quizzically, 'I was there,' he answered. 'I saw you. I like drinking in other people's bars. I find it entertaining.'

'How long have you been in this country,' said Field, 'if that's not a rude question?'

'It is a rude question,' said Constantine solemnly. 'It is rather like asking a guest when he is thinking of leaving. But as I know you I will accept it. My father brought the family over from Athens after the war. How long have you been here?'

'You've been here longer than me.'

'And the girl?'

Field did not see the relevance of the question but he answered, 'She was born here.' He had another thought. 'Why don't you come to Bretts too? Then I can buy you a drink.'

The Greek did not answer at once. He considered the suggestion. 'All right. It is quiet here. I'll get Joseph to close up.' He got off the stool and passed through a door at the back. Field slowly finished his whisky. He felt light-headed, the fumes of the whisky anaesthetizing his vision into something smaller, more confined than usual. He knew he was pretty drunk but the knowledge did not worry him. It seemed appropriate to be drunk.

Outside Constantine said, 'We will take my car.'

'It's not far,' said Field, 'we can walk. Do us good. Do me good anyway.'

'We will take my car,' said Constantine firmly, taking him by the arm. 'It is here.' He led him towards a brand new, white Ford Zodiac standing by the kerb.

'I know,' said Field. 'Ashamed to be seen walking through the streets with a bloody copper. Specially a drunk copper.'

Constantine unlocked the door. He did not answer. As Field lurched in the other side he said, 'After Bretts I shall go home. There is no point in walking back here to pick up my car.'

They found a parking space almost opposite the night club and walked across to the neon sign. The doorman swung open the plate glass door and almost touched his forehead to the ground when he saw Constantine. As they walked across the soft carpet of the foyer Constantine said, 'He comes from the same suburb of Athens. We Greeks are a close-knit community.' Four steps later he added, 'Like the Jews.'

At the entrance to the restaurant and dance hall stood a burly dark man in a dinner jacket. He smiled when he saw

Constantine and shook him warmly by the hand. Constantine said over his shoulder to Field, 'A table? Or do you want a drink at the bar?'

'A table?' said Field, impressed. 'You mean we can get a table? On Saturday night? No, let's have a drink at the bar.'

He felt strangely unreal as he followed the tall handsome Greek through the door towards the inner bar which was crowded with small tables and people. Through the archway which led to the dance floor he could see couples amorously packed together. An Italian beat group filled the place with electronically boosted instruments and voices at an ear-deafening level. He could not see Sarah Van der Huizen anywhere.

Sarah watched them come into the restaurant, the tall elegant Greek and the more heavily-built police inspector, with a rising surge of excitement. What attracted her to this man twenty years her senior she did not know; she did not understand it and she did not try to analyse her feelings. Her convent education, her upbringing, the influence of the Dutch Reform Church throughout her childhood which equated sex with sin, and breathed fire and brimstone over most carnal relationships intimidated her. Yet she could not help herself and she did not care. In Chapanda since their fight she had avoided him because she was frightened of her feelings. Bumping into him that morning at Meikles had revived the old excitement. She suspected that Englishmen were cleverer than South Africans therefore she distrusted him, but this man was strong, powerful, arrogant and male and he made her shiver.

She turned to David Mitchison. 'I've just seen two old friends,' she said quickly. 'I'm going to talk to them for a minute.'

There were six of them at the table, all having a good time, all gay and a little drunk. Sarah had drunk far more than she did usually and she knew this accounted for some of the excitement. But not all of it. 'Don't be long,' said Mitchison, 'else I'll come and fetch you.'

At the bar Field and Constantine found two empty stools.

'Why do you wear those glasses?' said Field. 'The sun's not shining.'

'They are real spectacles tinted to look like sunglasses,' said Constantine coldly. 'All modern African dictators affect them.'

'Two whiskies,' said Field.

'She is here,' said Constantine calmly, 'she has found you.'

Field looked over his shoulder and saw Sarah pushing through the crowd towards them. She had her hair done up in some modern fashion which he liked, leaving two wings curving round her cheeks; she wore a black low-cut dress. Her skin was dazzling white, her eyes wide and excited.

'Oh God,' thought Field, 'it shouldn't be allowed. Such beauty. Such skin.' He said ineffectively, 'Hallo.'

She stood beside him smiling. Then as she saw his hand and the look on his face, the smile faded. She reached out and took his bandaged hand in both of hers.

'What's the matter? What's happened? Are you hurt?' she said. It was such a spontaneous gesture of warmth that for a moment Field could not reply. She held his hand gently like she had held the small 'duiker' deer that morning at the farm. She was really concerned about his small injury. He could not believe it.

As soon as Sarah saw his face she knew something was wrong. He was pale, his mouth had a set rigid look, his eyes were strained. He had lost all his arrogance and bravado and he was sick with despair. All this she knew without knowing how she knew it and she wished she could comfort him. 'I heard there was trouble in Harare,' she said quietly.

'Old wives' tales. Let me introduce you to my old friend Constantine.'

'I know Constantine,' she said.

'How do you know Constantine?'

'Everybody knows Constantine,' she said.

The young Greek lifted his shoulders in wry resignation. 'It is the penalty for keeping a bar,' he murmured. 'Everybody knows Constantine. Even the police.'

'Have a drink,' invited Field.

'I'm drinking brandy,' she said, 'expensive French brandy. I had three martinis before dinner and then we had wine and now I'm drinking brandy and I'm getting drunk and it's lovely.'

'Everybody who's anybody is drinking tonight,' said Field solemnly. 'Do join me as we sink to the floor in a drunken stupor.'

'I'd sooner dance,' she said.

The brandy arrived and Field fished for his money.

'It is not necessary,' said Constantine calmly, 'these people are friends of mine.' He nodded to the barman who smiled and went away.

'From the district of Piraeus,' he said. 'A second cousin.'

'Very useful indeed,' said Field. 'You don't have any cousins in the police force I suppose?'

'Not yet,' said Constantine, 'but my older cousin is in the army.'

'Would you like to join our table?' said Sarah.

Field peered at her seriously. 'Is that fellow Mitchison with you?'

'Yes, and two of his friends and two other girls.'

'We mustn't keep you then,' said Field.

'You don't want to come?'

'No.'

She was immediately hostile. 'All right then, I'll go back and—'

He took her arm. 'You said you'd rather dance,' he said placatingly, putting his other arm around her waist and holding her tightly. She did not move away. She did not want to move away.

'All right,' she said.

On the dance floor she clung to him. 'Oh God,' he said, 'I think you're marvellous.'

She tilted back her head to look at him. 'Inspector Field,' she said, 'you're drunk in charge of a woman.'

He laughed. 'Why do we always have rows?' he said.

'I don't know.'

'Why did you call me a bloody copper?'

'I don't know. I just felt like it.'

'I suppose that's a reasonable female answer.'

They danced in silence for a little while. Then she said, 'Something's happened tonight. What is it?'

'How do you know?'

'I can feel it through your skin and your hands and your

body. My mother was a Celt from a far off misty isle, half a witch and half a saint so my father says, and she knew about everything.'

He looked down at her. 'You're dark and passionate and primitive.'

'I don't know what I am,' she said taking his remark quite seriously, 'only what I feel.' Anxiously she said, 'Tell me what happened.'

'I killed a man tonight,' he said slowly.

Her head went back again and her eyes were clouded. 'You mean you had a car accident and someone was killed?'

'No, I shot a man.'

'An African?'

'Yes.'

'In Harare? In the riot?'

'Yes.'

'An African?'

'Oh, yes, only an African. Not really a human being. He was quite black.'

He felt her stiffen in his arms. 'You don't have to mock me.'

'But that's what you meant, wasn't it?'

He felt her begin to break away from him and he knew that it had all gone wrong again. But suddenly she stopped and said, 'Inspector Field, *you're* picking the fight tonight.'

His face felt stiff. Perhaps he was drunk. Perhaps he didn't know what he was saying. 'I'm sorry,' he said. 'And you're right. I am tired. I think I'd better go home.'

'I'll come with you,' she said. 'I shouldn't have had that last brandy. It's made me feel giddy.'

'But what about your party?'

'What about them? They don't own me.'

'All right,' said Field, 'we'll go and say goodnight to Constantine and we'll get a taxi.'

'I've got a car,' she said. 'One of us can drive. I'll get my coat and see you in the foyer in five minutes.'

At the bar David Mitchison stood talking to Constantine. 'You've been long enough,' he said rather rudely to Sarah, and Field thought hazily, 'Trouble, trouble, here comes trouble.'

Sarah was frigid. 'I've been dancing,' she said defiantly.

'Good evening,' said Field with an attempt at mild diplomacy and he saw Constantine smile.

'Hallo,' said David Mitchison shortly, and then to Sarah, 'come on, let's go back now.'

'I don't want to go back,' she said.

'Well, where are you going?'

She said coldly, 'I'm going home.'

'Then I'll take you,' said Mitchison.

'No, thank you. I can take myself. Good night, Constantine.' Without any other explanation she left them.

Mitchison glared menacingly at Field. 'She's going home with you!'

'That's right,' said Field apologetically, 'I said I was tired and she offered to give me a lift and I accepted it.'

'Now see here,' began Mitchison pugnaciously.

'Gentlemen,' said Constantine consolingly. 'David! When a lady decides to do something by herself there's nothing you can do about it.'

'If this chap thinks he can walk off with my girl . . .'

'He's not walking off with your girl. He's had a hard day and he's going home. Miss Van der Huizen has had an enchanted day and she's going home. That's all there is to it.'

'*I* could take her home.'

'She doesn't want you to take her home. Just relax and let me buy you a drink and tell you some delightful stories of ancient Greece.' He took him by the arm turning him towards the bar. With the other hand he raised his dark glasses, swivelling his head towards Field, and the eye farthest away from Mitchison produced an enormous conspiratorial wink. 'Good night, Inspector,' he said. 'Sleep well.'

Field paused. 'I don't understand how you lost to the Romans,' he said slowly.

In the foyer there was no sign of Sarah but the doorman indicated the exit. 'She is waiting outside.'

Ten yards away beside the kerb stood the pale blue Victor which Field had first seen at the Van der Huizen farm. Sarah was sitting in the passenger seat wearing a light pale blue coat buttoned up to the neck which he knew must match the colour of the car. He slipped into the driver's seat.

'Smooth,' he said, 'very smooth. Do you always treat your boy friends like that?'

'He's not my boy friend,' she said irritably. 'He's just someone I know.'

'Someone who wants to marry you?'

'Yes.'

'But you don't want to marry him?'

'No.'

'I've no objection,' said Field. 'I approve of one of us taking the other home.'

His head felt a little woolly but he knew he was perfectly fit to drive. He held out his hand, 'Keys.' She fished in her bag and produced one small chromium key.

'You want me to drive?'

'I feel a bit funny,' she said. 'Are you all right?'

'Yes, I'm all right.'

He inserted the key in the ignition and turned it. The engine caught at once and Field revved it up. He examined the gears experimentally, pulled the lever down into first and they moved away from the kerb.

'That's the light switch,' she said pointing at a knob. He switched on the side lights.

'Nice chap that Constantine,' he said conversationally.

'Yes.'

'How long have you known him?'

'I don't know. On and off for quite a while.'

'Good looking?'

'Quite good looking.' Her eyes flashed across at him. 'They tell me Greeks have a drama about them which appeals to a woman.'

After a few seconds' pause Field said coldly, 'You find Constantine attractive?'

She laughed without amusement. 'If you mean by that, is he, or has he been my lover, the answer is no.'

Field considered again then he said sadly, 'Yes, I suppose I did mean that. Who is your lover, anyway?'

'I have no lover,' she said. 'And I have no lovers in my past. Does that answer your question?'

'I wasn't asking one,' said Field. 'Who's picking the fight now?'

She laughed, warmly this time.

'A truce,' she said, 'let's have a truce.'

'If I drive me to the Police Depot do you think you can find your own way back?'

'Yes.'

'All right then, that's what we'll do.'

The centre of the town was quiet now, the shop lights out, the people gone. One policeman patrolled the darkened streets with an Alsatian on a lead. Driving up the broad leafy avenue leading to the police depot they could see the bright stars, the white glimmer of a moon somewhere behind the trees. Field drove in through the main entrance past the shrubs and hedges and lawns.

'I've never been here before,' she said. 'It's quite pretty. And no armed guards or barrier at the gate?'

'All in bed,' said Field. 'It's a peaceful country.'

'Yes,' she said.

'On your left behind that high hedge is the officers' mess,' said Field. 'Here is the flagstaff where the Union Jack is raised and lowered to trumpet ceremony at dawn and sunset.' He indicated the wide stretch of lawn behind it. 'That's where you do the equestrian drill for your passing out parade. A company of mounted men. Very colourful in best uniforms, white topees and carrying lances. Sometimes the white ants eat holes under the turf leaving a thin crust overhead, and many a young recruit trotting along like the Charge of the Light Brigade suddenly feels a proper Charlie as his horse puts its foot in a hole and pitches him straight over its head. Most bruising to the pride.'

'Did it happen to you?'

Field grinned at the memory. 'Of course. And my horse knocked over the one next to him and he brought down three more riders behind us. The Commissioner almost died of apoplexy. If he'd had a Bren gun we'd all be dead now.'

He pulled up under the trees a hundred yards farther down.

'I can walk from here,' said Field. 'It's just across the lawn.'

He turned towards her sliding his arm along the back of the seat. 'Thanks for everything,' he said like a small boy being polite to his hostess at the end of a party. Her head leaned towards his and he kissed her, a light stranger's kiss, feeling her lips cool and soft like doeskin.

He looked across at her, 'I suppose if David Mitchison had brought you home you'd have kissed him.'

'I expect so.'

Field decided not to ask any more questions. It surprised him such imaginings could be painful. He was not prepared for her next reaction. Suddenly she moved very close to him lifting her mouth and this time she kissed with such passion and urgency that he could hardly believe it. But he too was swept up by this surge of passion. He felt a wetness on her cheeks. He stopped kissing her. 'Tears?' he said gently. 'Why?'

She put her face against his shoulder. 'Why do I have to go and fall in love with a rotten old married man like you?' she sobbed. 'Why can't I fall in love with David Mitchison and live happily ever after?'

'Just a second,' he said blinking, trying to clear a path of understanding through the confusion this remark engendered. 'In the first place you're not in love with me. You're just confused by a mixture of brandy and animal magnetism.'

'I am in love. I am!' she said, and wept again.

'In the second place,' said Field realizing that the fumes of alcohol in his own head were slightly interfering with his dignity, 'I'm only forty-three and that's not so damned old. It is true that I am married and for that I apologize. But I was young at the time.'

She did not seem to be listening to him. She kissed him with such passion and ferocity and whispered. 'I love you, I love you,' that Field began to believe her.

She drew away, 'I do feel sick.'

'God!' said Field, 'Is that the effect I have?'

'Oh dear,' she said, 'I feel so sick.'

'Hold on,' said Field, 'there's a bush over there. Hold on.' He slipped out of the driving seat and hurried round to let her out. With one hand around her waist he helped her across the grass and in the dark shadow of the bush stood behind her, two hands clasped around her waist while she bent over.

Now at last he was aware of the African silence, the ragged shadow of the trees on the silvered lawn, the huge bolsters of trade clouds edged with phosphorescence sailing slowly across the wide clean sky. And Sarah retching.

She straightened up, leaning back against him heavily, and he gave her his clean breast-pocket handkerchief.

'Oh, dear,' she said. 'What a fool! What a fool! I feel so ashamed.'

'Sarah,' he said, 'don't worry. I'll drive you home and you can jump straight into bed.'

'Please,' she said. 'Please.'

Back in the car he left her side window open and drove swiftly. She lay back with her head on the window ledge, her hair blowing in the wind. She said, 'I feel awful.'

'Hold on,' he said, 'you'll soon be home. 'What number Highland Woods was it? Twenty-nine?'

'Yes,' she said, 'you turn right at the bottom and it's the big house on the right-hand side. Take the car and drive back to the Police Depot in it. You can bring it back to me at Meikles tomorrow. One o'clock at the Causerie.'

'Thanks,' he said. 'I don't think I'd get a taxi at this hour.'

'This is the drive,' she said.

The house was large and in darkness and Field parked in the wide area near the double garage.

'I'll be all right,' she said starting to get out. 'Just leave me. No, don't kiss me. I taste awful.'

She stood outside the car looking in through the window, the moonlight on her face, her dark hair blown awry by the wind.

'Oh dear,' she said. 'I feel so awful.'

He leaned across and placed his hand across hers. 'Sarah Van der Huizen,' he said, 'I love you, too.'

'Do you?' she said softly. 'I'm glad.'

Then she was gone, leaving him only half aware that they were no longer strangers but victims, doomed and blessed to be at the beginning of that long journey through the sensory delights and senseless despairs of the condition loosely defined as love.

CHAPTER ELEVEN

IN MELLONS' CAR next morning, neat, shaved and showered, Field felt like hell. He had woken early and slowly gone over the events of last night in his mind. The feeling of exaltation over what had happened between him and Sarah Van der Huizen had gone, replaced by a feeling of nausea. He didn't feel like talking, but made an effort. 'I suppose you missed breakfast, too?'

'Not on your life,' said Mellons cheerfully. 'I had grapefruit, bacon and eggs, coffee, toast and marmalade. How do you feel?'

'Grim.'

'You really *want* to call on Milly before we go to Town Station?'

'I ought to.'

'You could wait until this afternoon.'

'No, I'll get it over with. Milly might be worried. Anyway it'll get me in the right sort of mood for the questions they're going to ask at the enquiry. I expect all the top brass will be there.'

'Dead right they will. Every one of them, plus coroners, undertakers and civic dignitaries.'

Field was bitter, 'I can imagine what they'll say. "We deeply regret this occurrence Inspector Field. Now are you quite certain that this action of yours was absolutely necessary?" '

Mellons laughed cynically. 'Tell them that next time you'll let him bury the axe in the top of your skull. That might satisfy them.' He changed gear expertly as they swept around a corner. 'Don't worry, mate, you've got me as a witness as well as Sergeant Mushiwara. You're in the clear. Relax.'

The morning was fine and sunny, the suburbs through which they drove neat and green, the hedges clipped, the flower beds brilliant areas of colour, the water sprinklers erupting showers of water over shaven lawns. Mellons came to a stop outside the modern block of flats where Milly was staying with Angela. It was a tall building of red brick with corner stones and facings of white. Its entrance hall was tricked out with wide glass doors, an Italian mosaic floor and a small ornamental fountain. Lifts rose smoothly to each of its eight floors and every flat boasted an exterior sun balcony.

'Aren't you coming in?' asked Field as he realized that Mellons was making no attempt to leave the wheel.

Mellons grinned and shook his head, 'I'll wait here if you don't mind. It's too damned early to be polite and social.'

Milly and Angela had finished breakfast and were sitting out on the sun balcony, the Sunday papers strewn around them. Last night's rioting was headlined in all of them so Field had no doubt that they knew all about it. Both were flippant and slightly distant as if they had formed some secret feminine pact against him; he was shut out, an intruder into this inner sanctum of women. He recollected that he often felt like this when Angela was around. In this situation in some subtle way Milly always managed to reverse her loyalties.

No, she did not want to discuss 'last night'. While Angela was tactfully out in the kitchen reheating the breakfast coffee she made that quite clear. 'It's your business not mine,' she said coolly. 'Besides it will only upset me. Save all the gory details for that dear friend of yours, Cohen, when you get back to Chapanda tonight.'

Generally she was bleak and unfriendly and Field was irritated by her attitude. If she'd known that he'd been kissing Sarah Van der Huizen last night she would have every reason for coldness, but dammit she didn't know. As far as she knew he'd been risking life and limb to protect her from the rampaging blacks. 'I wasn't going back to Chapanda tonight,' he said bluntly.

'Oh, weren't you?' said Milly airily. 'I thought perhaps that after all this fuss they might send you back to Chapanda at once.'

Field didn't understand what she was getting at. It could of course be her inimitable way of saying that she was on holiday and didn't want to see him again for a couple of weeks. In any case the conversation seemed quite purposeless. He drank the thick strong black coffee with two spoonfuls of sugar which Angela set before him, said goodbye and took the lift back to the ground floor.

'Okay?' said Mellons with a quizzical look in his eye as Field climbed back into the front seat.

'As "okay" as it will ever be, I suppose,' said Field morosely. 'I'll never understand women as long as I live.'

'Better men than you have said that,' said Mellons complacently. 'That flat must cost at least fifteen quid a week?' he added enviously.

Field was a bit vague. His mind was upon other problems. 'Not so much as that. I'd say about four fifty a year excluding rates.'

His mind was turning over a small, nagging idea which had woken with him and had now grown into almost a conviction. Shouldn't he do something about the widow of the man he had killed? Reflecting upon it he knew the idea was absurd, and might even be dangerous. But the thought kept obtruding. He considered how he might do it as Mellons pressed the starter and accelerated away.

'Has she got any money?' said Mellons.

'Who?' said Field and tried to bring his mind back to the present. 'Oh, Angela? I shouldn't think so. I think her father left her some sort of small private income. Can't imagine the insurance company she works for paying her much.'

Mellons said, 'I suppose this enquiry business will last until lunchtime. You coming back to the mess for a drink afterwards?'

'No,' said Field and wondered if it was a good idea to confide in him. 'No, I've got a date at the Causerie to deliver a car.'

Mellons took his eyes off the road for a second to glance at him. 'Same girl?'

'Same girl.'

'None of my business?'

'No.'

'Nevertheless be careful, Bill.'

'Be careful?' Field opened his eyes in mock astonishment. 'What have I got to be careful about?'

'She's a pretty girl, isn't she?'

'Yes, she's a pretty girl of twenty-three and I'm an old man of forty-three. You told me so yesterday.'

'Rubbish,' said Mellons emphatically. 'You were a gay roistering blade before you got married.'

'That's a nice Somerset way of putting it, I must say. Just because I went to a few dances and kissed a few girls on their front doorsteps? A gay roistering blade! Christ! Give up this Three Musketeers' dialogue and get back into the twentieth century.'

'Balls,' said Mellons forcefully.

Field glared at him. 'And what's that supposed to mean?'

'It's your business, not mine,' said Mellons with studied disinterest, 'but I do know that if I brought *my* wife into town for a week-end there would be none of this "I'm staying with my girl friend and you stay at the Mess" sort of thing.'

'I'm not a sex maniac like you.'

'It's nothing to do with that,' said Mellons primly. 'It's not what Annie would call "right".'

'Listen,' said Field in exasperation, 'I've said I've got a date at the Causerie. I'm going to have a lunchtime drink. That's all there is to it.'

Mellons was silent for a few seconds, then he said guardedly, 'She obviously likes you.'

Field laughed aloud. 'Oh, come off it, Bob!'

Mellons was insistent and rather self-righteous. 'I may be an old frump but I can tell you that if she's half your age, and knows you're married, and also knows you're a bloody horrible policeman, and still wants to meet you, then she must like you. Even Perry Mason could work that one out.'

Field squared his shoulders against the back of the seat and said loudly, 'You're mad.' He hadn't expected to be facing this situation so soon.

They did not speak again until they arrived at Town Station. The enquiry was not quite the ordeal he had expected. The questions were short and to the point. No one seemed to think it was his fault. In fact, to his immense surprise they seemed to think he had done pretty well. When it was over Roy Henderly called him into his office.

Roy Henderly was one of the most popular officers in the force, tipped as a future Commissioner. He had risen from the ranks through the force of his personality and the reliability of his judgement. He was a big man—from Suffolk farming stock in the first place—well over six feet tall, greying at the sides with a hammered, impassive face and a taciturn manner. He had large, well manicured hands which he now clasped on the desk top in front of him.

'I suppose you didn't sleep too well last night, Bill?' he said.

'No, sir,' said Field cautiously, not knowing what this was all about. The use of his Christian name was an indication that the meeting was probably going to be friendly, but he was taking no chances.

'You've been having rather a heavy time lately, haven't you? The rain goddess thing and now this.'

Field played it off the cuff, the modest British public school reply. 'Luck of the draw, I suppose, sir.'

'Brought your wife up to Salisbury with you?'

Field paused, a fleeting moment of panic passing through his mind. Christ, what was he getting at? Surely he hadn't seen him dead drunk with Sarah Van der Huizen, or maybe somebody else had and had passed the word back? Was this going to be one of those cosy 'Now we're all old enough to know what we're doing, *but*—' chats? 'Yes, sir,' he said.

'I would suggest a little leave.'

Mentally Field expelled a great breath of relief. He said quickly, 'I'm really not due, sir. . . .'

Henderly raised his eyebrows. 'No, I expect not, but as these are special circumstances I think I might arrange it.' He picked up the phone and said, 'Hallo. Get me a line to the Assistant Commissioner at Umtali, will you, please?' He listened briefly and seniority emerged. 'Yes, I know it's Sunday. I expect he'll be at home. Try that number. Good.' He replaced the receiver and looked back at Field. 'Get away somewhere. Go hunting or fishing. Play golf. Go to Beira. Costa Brava Holiday Camp. I was there only two weeks ago. Run by a chap called Sequiros. Damn nice fellow. Tell him I sent you. Chalet all to yourself. Buy your own food. Cheap. Something about sea breezes which lifts you out of yourself. Only thing we haven't got in Rhodesia, sea breezes. Take my advice—go to Beira. The Portuguese couldn't be more pleasant. Tell Sequiros I sent you. Friend of mine. He'll make you welcome.'

'Yes, sir,' said Field.

The phone rang and Henderly picked it up. He smiled. 'Hallo, George,' he said. 'Just caught you, did I? Sorry to interfere with your Sunday morning. Trouble? Yes, it was a bit hectic last night. Yes, one of your chaps was mixed up in it. You've heard, of course? Yes, Field. I've got him in the office with me now. I thought it might be a good idea to let him have a few days off. Say a week? You think so, too. Good. What about coping down at Chapanda? His two erks can cope, can they? Good. Right, I'll relieve him of all duties as of now until Monday week.' He changed the subject, 'How are things in Eastern Province? You seem to be having it pretty easy these days. You're coming down for the "Dining In Night" at the mess next week? Good. I'll see you then. Might even buy you a drink. Cheers, George.'

He put down the receiver and grinned delightedly at Field as if they were two schoolboys who had just pulled off a coup. 'It worked,' he said. 'Nothing simpler. Now you get off as soon as you can. There will be a few more details to do with this business to be cleared up, I expect, but they can wait until later. Have a good time.'

Field took a taxi out to the Police Depot and picked up the blue Victor. Driving back to keep his appointment with Sarah, Field felt a great sense of elation. He was a free agent for a whole week. And, of course, one important point arose at once. Should he tell Milly? Should he reappear on that sun balcony of Angela's and interfere with the private and happy lives of the two women once more or should he be tactful and leave them alone? He thought he would leave them alone.

The Causerie Bar as usual during a Sunday lunchtime session was full, but the first semi-circular velvet seat was occupied only by one whispering young couple sitting close together and taking up little space so that there was room for Field. The waiter came up and he ordered a gin and tonic, ice and lemon. At five past one Sarah Van der Huizen walked in. She was wearing a pale pink dress and pink earrings. Her hair was no longer swept upwards and coiffeured but combed out, loose and glossy.

As soon as she sat down Field realized with a slight chill of disappointment that her euphoria of the previous evening had disappeared. Last night they had been lovers, this morning they were merely acquaintances.

Within seconds this suspicion became a certainty. He said, 'How do you feel?' and her eyes turned to regard him as if he were a stranger asking a personal question.

'Terrible. I've got a terrible hangover.'

'That makes two of us. Try a gin and tonic.'

'It'll make me sick.'

'No, it won't.' He signalled the boy and added, 'Anyway, it was worth it.'

'Do you think so?' she said, and confirmed that their relationship was back where it had started.

He swallowed his own drink and ordered two more. Perhaps he should have expected it? Last night she had been celebrating; this morning she was cold stone sober. Last night it had been dramatic and romantic. Now both a hangover and a conscience were bothering her.

He gently swivelled the ice left in the bottom of his glass and said very carefully, 'You mean everything last night was the result of music, moonlight and too much brandy?'

'I suppose so,' she said, and then added defensively, 'anyway you needed . . .' she didn't complete the sentence.

'God damn it, woman,' he said, unable to control his vehemence, 'just because I'm boozed up and mentally beaten up you don't have to say you're in love with me!'

'I'm sorry,' she said miserably.

'So am I.'

She was sitting rather stiffly on the seat, now she turned as if to move. 'Perhaps I'd better go,' she said.

The waiter arrived with the gin and tonics and Field said, 'No, have your drink first. It'll make you feel better.'

Desperately he tried to think of some way to salvage just a fragment of what had existed between them. 'It doesn't matter,' he said. Then, 'I must give you your key.' He fished in his pocket.

He laid it on the table and she picked it up. 'Thank you,' she said, and then quickly and unhappily as if it would explain her entire situation, 'You're married.'

'I was married last night,' said Field sourly.

'I must have been drunk.'

'You were.'

'I'm sorry. I behaved terribly. I'm ashamed of myself.'

He took a deep breath. 'You didn't behave badly. You were wonderful. I shall never forget last night as long as I live. You were the most marvellous girl in the whole of Africa.'

Her eyes to his surprise were full of tears. 'Oh, Bill,' she said, 'don't say that. We shouldn't. I mean . . .'

He touched her hand. 'Don't talk. I understand. Just drink your drink. We'll call it summer madness and stay friends.'

She sipped the gin. 'I'm sometimes like this,' she confessed. 'I change my mind. I get frightened. And it's just that—'

'Yes?'

'We hardly know each other.'

'That's true.'

They were silent for a few seconds. She said, 'How did you get on this morning? At the enquiry or whatever it was?'

'Not bad. They asked me a lot of questions. They didn't seem to blame me. At the end of it all Roy Henderly called me into his office and gave me a week's leave. He said, "Go to Beira, have a holiday." So I think I'm going. Like to come?'

She smiled for the first time that morning but didn't answer. Then she said, 'I've never been to Beira.'

'Neither have I.'

She finished her drink. 'Does it really do you good?' she said.

'The gin? Oh certainly. You feel better already, don't you? Have the other half and you'll feel like last night.'

'No, I'd better not.' Her eyes glinted as she looked at him. 'I'm in enough trouble as it is!'

'You mean with your boy friend?'

'He's not my boy friend.'

'He wants to marry you, doesn't he?'
'That doesn't make him my boy friend.'
'I see.'
'He rang me this morning and tried to be all stiff and condescending.'
'And what did you say?'
'I said I couldn't be bothered to talk.'
'I felt the same way,' said Field, remembering Milly.
She said, 'What are you going to do now?'
'I'm going to Harare.'
Her eyes widened. 'After all the trouble last night?'
'Oh, that's all over. The tearaways have had all their fun. If I'm any judge they'll all be sleeping off their hangovers.'
'As we should be doing.'
He smiled. 'I suppose so.'
'What are you going to do in Harare?'
Field hesitated. He didn't really want to tell anybody. He said, 'Oh, just making a call.'
She paused. 'Maybe I will have that second drink. Let me buy it.'
Field signalled the waiter. 'No, you won't. Ladies are not allowed to keep gentlemen. Even elderly policemen.'
Her eyes turned directly to his. 'I don't think you're old,' she said. And then, 'Please let me buy it.'
'All right.'
The drinks came in tall frosted glasses, the pale lemon rind lying on the opaque surface, the ice cubes rattling gently in the liquid. 'Have you got a car to go to Harare?' she said.
'No.'
'Do you want me to give you a lift?'
Field considered the offer. It would mean he would have to explain his journey. 'All right,' he said, 'thank you. Shall I tell you what I want to do?'
'If you want to.'
'It's probably stupid.' He hesitated for a second. 'I want to go back to Harare to find the widow of—' he was going to say, 'the man I killed last night'; but this sounded so absurdly melodramatic that he couldn't get it out, so he went on, 'The widow of the rioter. I want to say I'm sorry

but I couldn't help it, that it was either him or me, and—I won. Do you understand?'

'Yes,' she said quietly, 'I understand.'

'I'd like to give her some money, say I'll try and do my best for her kids if they need help.' He paused and finished lamely. 'Sentimental nonsense, isn't it? They'd probably kick me out of the police force if they heard about it.'

'I don't think it's so odd.'

They finished their drinks and went out into the sunshine. Around the square the polished shells of the parked cars tethered to their meters were burnished by its rays. Beyond them buried deep in the green shade of the park the fountain shot feathery plumes of water high in the air. The atmosphere was somnolent and half a dozen African youths sprawled and yawned on the wooden benches. Another group, more lively, chattered and laughed near the flower stalls which were kaleidoscopic with massed colours so intense that they looked unreal: scarlets, pinks, mauves, yellows and blues. As they walked to the car, one of the youths, skinny, gangling and graceful in his tight, faded jeans, white singlet and floppy pink-soled feet, grabbed the hose used for watering the blossoms, and squealing with delight turned it on his friends. The effect was pandemonium. They ran away, fell over, doubled up, sprawled into the hedge, dissolved into helpless ecstasies of laughter. Field grinned at their antics. Yet these same youths could have been advancing menacingly on his Land Rover last night!

In the car she said, 'How will you find her?'

'I'll ask at the church where we rescued Father Brown. He or one of his parishioners are bound to know.'

As they pulled up at the police post at the entrance to Harare the young policeman on duty came across. He recognized Field. 'Afternoon, sir, going inside?'

'A private visit,' said Field. 'Everything quiet?'

'Quiet as any other Sunday afternoon, sir.'

'Good,' said Field, 'we can't be long.'

As he accelerated away Sarah said sadly, 'It's a bit like going into a game park, isn't it? A place set aside for wild animals and wired off.'

Field had never thought of it like that before. 'I suppose you're right,' he said.

After a few more seconds she added, 'I expected to see the whole place in ruins, but there's very little damage.'

'Darkness and flames in the sky make it look much worse than it really is,' said Field. He indicated the shop they had seen burning the night before. 'There's one bit of damage for you.'

The township was peaceful: Africans in their Sunday best strolled casually about the streets. At the spot where the blazing barricade had barred their way there was little evidence of last night's drama: someone had swept up the bits into a neat pile and mended the flimsy white fence which they had knocked down.

They parked outside the church and Sarah followed Field up the path to the house. He knocked on the door. After a short interval it was opened by a European priest wearing a white dog collar and a black cassock.

The surprise in Field's face must have shown because the young priest smiled and said, 'Can I help you?'

'I was looking for Father Brown, I'd like to have a word with him. He was here last night.'

The priest nodded. 'Yes, of course. He's not here at present and it's unlikely that he'll be back today. My name is Wilkinson and we share this church. Is there anything I can do for you?' He was a young man with a long oval face, thinning light brown hair, no eyebrows and a thin mouth overcrowded with large white teeth. He displayed them in a professional smile as his eyes went past Field to Sarah.

'Perhaps you would like to come in and talk?' he said. 'Yes, please do come in.' He did not take his eyes off Sarah.

He led the way along the narrow hall to the room Field remembered from the previous night. 'I'm afraid I didn't get your names?' he said apologetically, pushing forward a chair for Sarah.

'This is Miss Sarah Van der Huizen and my name is Field, Inspector Field of the B.S.A. police.'

A look of anxiety flitted across Mr. Wilkinson's face. 'Oh, my goodness, not an official visit, I hope, Inspector?'

Field relieved his anxieties at once. 'No, not an official

visit. In that capacity I was here last night.' He added, 'I had hoped to talk to Father Brown.'

The priest was relieved. 'Oh, quite so. Father Brown. A very fine African minister. With some African ministers, of course, it is very difficult to judge the true depth—er—the true depth of their spiritual feeling. But not Father Brown. Oh, indeed not Father Brown. Not, of course, that I will have a word spoken against any of them, but the depth of faith, that is the true test.'

'Quite,' said Field and added, 'You're from England?'

'Oh yes, from Nottingham actually. I've been here four years. Of course, I'm primarily concerned with administration, the financing of our church schools, that sort of thing. . . .' With difficulty he took his eyes away from Sarah's legs and went on: 'In many ways I feel the Catholic priests out here—although celibate, yes indeed, although celibate—are more fortunate. Yes, more fortunate. If they are teachers with degrees they get allowances up to fifteen hundred a year, and of course you can, if you're careful, keep yourself on two hundred a year. . . .'

Field was not even slightly interested in the good fortune of the Catholic priests. He said rather brusquely, 'We came to see if we could find the widow of the man who was killed in the post office riot last night.'

Father Wilkinson paused, his mouth slightly open. 'Oh, did you? Yes, dreadful, dreadful, but of course in many ways an act of God. Oh, certainly an act of God.'

'I don't follow you?' said Field politely.

Father Wilkinson passed a limp hand over his high bald brow, 'This man Nyandazi who was shot. He was in many ways an uncouth fellow. Oh, indeed a very hard man to deal with. A drunkard. Treated his wife very badly. I don't think she'll grieve very much.'

'You mean I've done her a service?' said Field brutally.

The priest was startled. 'I beg your pardon?'

Field put it bluntly. 'I'm the policeman who shot her husband.'

The priest's mouth stayed wide open; he looked more like an egg than ever. 'How very unfortunate. Yes, how unfortunate. But of course you couldn't help it. No, of course not.'

Field said slowly, 'I understood he was a respectable bus driver?'

'Oh, he was, he was. But you know he spent far too much of his time in the beer hall drinking and causing trouble. That was his curse, you know, drinking, drinking.'

'Perhaps that's why he broke into the post office,' said Sarah. 'He needed money to buy drink?'

Her intervention gave Mr. Wilkinson time to recover his composure. He beamed at her gratefully. 'Indeed, indeed. You may very well be right.'

'I wanted to see his widow,' said Field, 'to give her a little money, to see that she is being looked after.'

Father Wilkinson looked surprised again. 'Oh, you need not worry. The "Helping Hand Club" will see to that. It is an organization of European and African women who attend to the less fortunate . . .'

'I've heard of them,' said Field shortly, 'but I still want to meet Mrs. Nyandazi.'

'Oh yes,' said Father Wilkinson, 'yes, of course. I quite understand.' He pondered for a few seconds. 'She lives just around the corner. I could take you to her now if you like.'

'Thank you,' said Field, standing up. 'I would be grateful.'

Mrs. Nyandazi's house was a small concrete house surrounded by a tiny unkempt plot of ground. The woman who answered the door was young, thin, flat-chested and confused to find them on her doorstep. She smiled in deep embarrassment keeping one hand over her mouth to hide her bad teeth. She wore a blue and white handkerchief over her woolly hair, and a long, patched and faded Mother Hubbard dress. She had a baby in her arms and another toddler clinging to her skirt. Both howled with anguish as they saw the deputation. She hushed them into silence and opened the door wide so that they could come in.

'Hah, Mrs. Nyandazi,' said Wilkinson adopting a loud scoutmaster's voice as if the girl was stone deaf, 'this—ah—gentleman has something to say to you.' Over his shoulder as he passed through the door he said to Field, 'I'm afraid she doesn't speak very good English—in fact, I'm not quite sure what language she does speak.'

The house was poorly furnished, a rush mat on the floor,

a table covered with threadbare blue and white check oil-cloth, three rickety chairs. A small wide-eyed girl stood in one corner, a finger in her mouth.

Once inside Field felt the expectant eyes of everyone upon him, all waiting for his speech. He could sense that even Sarah expected something of him. Immediately he felt a complete fool. He did not know how to begin and his opening was inauspicious. 'Do you understand me?' he said to Mrs. Nyandazi, and she giggled and hid her mouth behind her hand once more. She wouldn't look at him as he tried again in Sindabele and Chishona, and still she only giggled and averted her head. Sarah said gently, 'Let me try. I have an idea she might come from the Chierandi district near us. I know a bit of the language.'

When Sarah talked, her voice was warm and sympathetic and Mrs. Nyandazi immediately stopped giggling and looked at her with big round eyes of recognition. Then she answered in a soft voice, turning to stare at Field with mute, melancholy eyes. She nodded as if in agreement. They talked together for perhaps five minutes before Sarah said, 'I told her that you were in the post office last night, that you went to rescue two African policemen who were being attacked, and that you fired the shot which killed her husband. I told her that you were sorry about this but that you yourself would have been killed if you had not acted in self-defence.'

Field was grateful. 'What did she say?' he asked anxiously.

'She said she understood,' answered Sarah. 'She replied that her husband should not have been stealing in the post office. He was a good man except when he was in drink and then he did not know what he was doing.'

'Thank you,' said Field. 'Would you tell her once more that I'm sorry and that if ever she needs any help in the future for herself or her children I'll do my best.'

'Yes,' said Sarah simply, I'll tell her that.'

As she turned back to Mrs. Nyandazi, Field fumbled in his pocket and produced the ten pounds he had folded into a small wad. He held it in his hand not wanting to hold it out to the woman and all manner of ready-made headlines passed in quick succession through his mind: 'B.S.A. policeman offers widow ten pounds for murdering husband. . . .' 'B.S.A. policeman bribes widow after killing husband.' Oh, well, to hell with them. He knew his action would leave him open to all sorts of misinterpretations; he knew he was sticking his neck out. He didn't care.

Sarah understood his embarrassment. She quickly took the money from him, opened Mrs. Nyandazi's hand and closed the slim brown fingers around the small wad of money. 'For the children,' she said to her in English and Mrs. Nyandazi hung her head.

In the car going back to Salisbury, Field was overwhelmed with the feeling that he had made a fool of himself. Anyway, there was nothing he could do about it. A man made a fool of himself and that was that. Sarah sat staring through the window.

Then she said suddenly, 'If we left by three o'clock we could be in Beira by late this evening, couldn't we?'

Field drew in his breath sharply. The implications behind her words were unbelievable. 'You mean . . .?'

'I'll come to Beira with you if you'd like me to,' she said simply.

Field kept both hands on the steering wheel and drove very carefully at a measured distance from the kerb. His throat suddenly felt dry. 'If you want me to,' she said urgently 'If you weren't joking.'

'Oh no,' said Field quickly, 'I wasn't joking.' The road was fairly empty. He leaned forward, switched off the ignition key, and as they coasted he braked into the side of the road and stopped. He put his left arm along the back of the seat and as her mouth turned upwards towards him, his right hand caught the curve of her breast. Her lips were cool and soft as Field remembered them.

'Oh God,' she said, 'I meant it last night. D'you hear me! I meant last night. I'm mad but I meant it. D'you hear me?'

'Yes, I hear you,' he said quietly. 'We can talk about it on the road to Umtali.'

They arrived at Umtali at four-thirty, and Field parked the car near the Cecil Hotel. He locked his door and went round to help Sarah.

'Tea at the Cecil?' he suggested.

She looked at him with amusement. 'You wouldn't dare,' she said mockingly.

'So far,' said Field reprovingly, 'there has been nothing between us but a couple of kisses. Long, passionate kisses I admit, but nothing more. Why should I worry about the gossiping harpies who inhabit the verandah of the Cecil Hotel?'

She lowered her eyes. 'So far,' she said, swinging two slender, nylon-stockinged legs out through the door.

Field always thought of Umtali as one of the prettiest towns in Rhodesia, with its shaded suburbs buried beneath pale blue jacarandas, flaming poinsettias and cascading bougainvillea. He liked the long, wide, straight-ruled main street which stretched away tilting up slowly against the sky until it lost itself in the haze, the pastel-coloured single- or double-storey shops on either side, the air of indolence and peace, and, despite the new office blocks and the rows of parked cars, the visible evidence of pioneering days. Of Umtali they said, 'It's humid,' but that was about the only criticism you ever heard.

The Cecil Hotel had emerged like a carotid artery from the heart of the British Empire; any white face became the tacit inheritor of 'sahib' or 'memsahib' immediately it climbed the steps to the verandah or entered the main door.

Field and Sarah sat in wickerwork chairs at a small round cane table next to a potted palm and an empty elephant's foot, while a tall, black waiter dignified in starched white uniform, green epaulettes and white gloves served them with tea in a silver pot, moist, thinly cut cucumber sandwiches, scones with delicately browned tops, thin brown bread and butter, strawberry jam and fruit cake.

'Marvellous,' said Field, seizing a scone. 'When I'm in heaven I shall have tea every day at the Cecil.'

'Is that what you think of heaven?' she said curiously. 'All the best things?'

'Of course. You come back here invisible and do exactly what you like.'

Her eyes were innocent. 'What about making love?' she said. 'You can't be invisible for that.'

Field, slightly disconcerted, spread jam on his fingers as well as the scone. 'That might need a little more arrangement,' he said carefully. 'Now be a good girl and eat your bread and butter first.'

'But you're eating all the scones,' she protested.

'I've only eaten two.'

'You're giving the others a very funny look!'

He laughed and passed her the plate.

'Why do you like the Cecil?' she said.

'Because I always expect to run into Rudyard Kipling, Rider Haggard or Somerset Maugham,' he said. He looked round at the ladies in flowered chiffon dresses with picture hats, the small boys with cropped hair in white shirts, grey flannel shorts and red and yellow cricket ties, the old gentlemen in faded alpaca coats and yellowing panamas. This was tea on Sunday in the Empire on which the sun had set but the inhabitants hadn't even noticed. Across the road through the trees he could see the pale fawn plaster of the police station tower, the red tiled roof, and even as he looked he saw Sandy Belmont come out of the side door, jump into a police Land Rover and drive off.

She caught his glance. 'Anyone you know?' she asked.

He took a cucumber sandwich. 'Someone I know about ten times better than you,' he answered.

'Are you scared?'

'Never so scared in all my life,' he said calmly. It was strange how quickly he'd settled into a behaviour pattern of running off to Beira with a girl; he felt light headed and euphoric about the whole thing. He added paternally, 'You can have a bit of fruit cake now.' He offered her the plate.

'I don't like fruit cake.'

'Then you can pour me another cup of tea.'

She took his cup and smiled secretly. 'You're a bullying brute,' she said. 'Do you treat all your women badly?'

'I've got a dozen chained to the wall back home.'

She poured the clear amber tea into the china cup, added milk and sugar. 'It's lovely,' she said. 'I love being with you.'

He covered her hand with his for a second. 'My fingers are jammy,' he said, 'but they're full of love.'

After tea, Field paid the bill and they went back to the

car. They turned right at the traffic lights and drove quietly through the curving green foothills which separate Southern Rhodesia from Mozambique. At the Rhodesian customs post a young clerk in a white shirt and grey flannels glanced perfunctorily at their passports, and with more interest at Sarah. There was even less formality on the Portuguese side. The small Portuguese officer in a smart uniform saluted and waved them on.

Field accelerated and they buzzed away. 'A sort of freedom descends, don't you think?' he said, 'as if "they" can no longer catch up with you.'

'It's like eloping,' she said quietly.

They hummed down the fine, wide empty road for the first fifty miles at sixty in a sort of golden haze, hardly speaking yet each acutely conscious of the proximity of the other. The sun went down directly behind them so that the small fat shadow of the car running before their bonnet gradually grew into a monstrous elongation. The tall plumed feathery grasses along the verges shone with a pink radiance, there were low hills in the distance, and then suddenly there were stars overhead. Field switched on the headlights. The wind was warm and a thin new moon, bone coloured and horned, rode along in the sky with them.

Eventually the good road ended, and they reached a nine foot tarmac, badly potholed in places, running like a black cheesewire through tall bamboo and thick bush. Occasionally the lights of another car blazed towards them and at the last moment each driver had to swing his nearside wheels off the tarmac strip and into the rutted dust. The road seemed to stretch on endlessly, but at last the country opened out again and there were huts at the roadside with dim oil lights inside, and eventually they halted at the red lamps of a closed railway crossing gate.

Field got out of the car and stretched his arms above his head. He peered back in through the window at Sarah. 'Tired?'

'No, I'm enjoying every minute,' she said. 'We can't be far from Beira now?'

'On the outskirts, I think.'

The air was very warm. It smelt musky: of blossoms,

tropical vegetation and damp. Two Africans leant indolently on bicycles waiting for the train to arrive, and quite abruptly it came out of the darkness, one great golden eye cutting a flarepath along the bright steel rails, and then with pistons plunging in and out like the arms of a runner, a hiss of steam, quick, flaring orange silhouettes of driver and fireman it thundered away into the night. The long line of goods trucks clanked along monotonously behind.

The gates swung open and they moved forward. Ten minutes later their headlights picked up a notice which said, 'First left for Costa Brava Holiday Resort'. They drove for two miles along a wide, well graded dirt road until they saw lights ahead and realized by the sudden freshening of the air that they were near the sea.

They came out by an enormous sprawling concrete structure with a jazzy modern façade six storeys high, with shops, a coffee bar, a café with outside tables, and at pavement level a wide, well lit entrance. Groups of holiday-makers in shorts, summer dresses, swimsuits, sat at the small tables sipping drinks, strolled by the shop windows, or re-crossed the road to an entrance which led to the holiday camp.

'My God,' said Field in amazement. 'One minute you're in the jungle and now this! Who would have believed it?'

They made enquiries at the reception desk, and the small dark clerk led them out to Señor Sequiros, the manager and owner. He sat at a small table entertaining a middle-aged couple from Bulawayo. The middle-aged man was florid, sunburned and happy. 'Great place,' he said to Field, 'lovely sands, marvellous bathing, you and your wife will enjoy it here.'

Señor Sequiros pulled up chairs for them. He was tall and lean with a dark moustache and elegantly greying hair, cut into a very smooth hairstyle indeed. He was impeccably dressed in Latin colonial style: white silk shirt, pale grey scarf, pale grey linen jacket, pale fawn whipcord shorts and pale grey stockings. He looked at Sarah with hot Latin eyes and murmured, 'So my old friend Roy Henderly recommended us, did he? In that case we must certainly look after you. Let us go into the office and arrange some comfortable accommodation.'

He excused himself to the couple from Bulawayo and led the way back through the front entrance. Behind the desk a huge chart on the wall showed the extent of his empire. He was childishly proud of his enterprise.

'It was seven years ago that I started this resort,' he said. 'Rhodesians need a holiday by the sea, I said to myself. And they do not wish to pay for expensive hotels. They are open air people who need a degree of comfort and privacy, so I thought of this chalet idea.' He tapped the map. 'Here, as you can see, is the hotel which is full of ordinary apartments which we let to people who like that sort of thing, but the cabins,' he indicated the little coloured squares running out along a wide tongue of land which stretched into the sea, 'go right out to here. It is five miles to the end of the peninsula, and one day perhaps we shall have cabins right out to the very end. Before I laid on water and electricity it was purely a sandy wasteland. Now we end here.' He placed a long, graceful forefinger upon a distant red square, and looked at them gravely. 'You could have this one if you like, Mr.—er—'

'Field, William Field.'

'Mr. Field. Your wife would perhaps enjoy it.' He smiled enigmatically. 'It is very quiet—for how do you say it—honeymoon couples.'

'Yes, we'd like that,' said Sarah suddenly.

Señor Sequiros turned towards her. 'It is new and quite well-furnished, frugal but quite comfortable. There is a cooking stove and all the pans. You can buy food at our stores or eat at our restaurants. Would you like to drive out there behind me and I will show it to you.' He glanced at his watch. 'After all, it is nearly eleven o'clock and you must be tired.'

'Yes, we are tired,' said Sarah.

'All that stuff about honeymoon couples,' she went on, as they climbed into the Victor to follow Señor Sequiros' scarlet Mini Minor into the camp. 'Do you think he suspects?'

'My dear girl, we look like a very old married couple,' said Field severely.

Sarah giggled. 'I don't feel like one,' she said happily.

They followed the red Mini across the road and into the maze of chalets. Naked electric light bulbs strung between telegraph poles lit the sandy stretches between the cabins. Near the dunes the camp opened out into a wide square. From a dance hall open on all sides to the sea winds hot pop boomed from a juke box, and they could see a jostling crowd of youngsters dancing; there was a large supermarket, and a restaurant on stilts.

'Enterprising chap our Señor Sequiros,' observed Field.

The road of hard sand now ran along the edge of the sea through the dunes themselves. The lights grew fewer in number and then ended and blindly they followed the rear lights of the Mini. On the seaward side the dunes were immense, fringed with spiky grass. They drove for a mile before Señor Sequiros stopped outside an isolated cabin. They watched him leave his car and walk across to a wooden post set amongst the dunes. He opened a switch box and pressed down a lever. A single naked bulb strung above the roof of the cabin flashed on.

'Our little cabin by the sea,' said Field. 'Let's take a look.'

With the engine quiet the sea boomed in their ears, and they could hear the wind scything through the coarse grass. Inside the chalet Sequiros switched on the lights to reveal a neat, tidy interior: two single beds on either side of the hut with blue check coverlets. He lifted one to reveal new blue and white striped mattresses and said, 'The sheets, blankets and pillows you will find in that cupboard.' He added, 'It is never damp at this season.'

There was a small sink with running water, a stove with three gas rings, a round table covered with a blue and white checked tablecloth, blue check curtains, a large rush mat on the concrete floor.

'Water and gas cylinders are brought in whenever necessary,' he said gravely. 'I think you will be comfortable here.'

'I'm sure we shall,' said Field.

'How long do you intend to stay?' said Señor Sequiros politely.

'About a week.'

'Good, then perhaps as friends of my friend Mr. Henderly, I shall be able to show you around?'

'We shall be delighted,' said Field.

At the doorway Señor Sequiros paused. 'You wish to eat at the restaurant tonight?'

Field glanced at Sarah, taking his cue from her; she shook her head.

'No,' he said. 'We're rather tired after the journey. We shall probably turn in early.'

Mr. Sequiros nodded gravely almost sadly. He stood in the doorway for another second before he left. 'There are,' he observed, 'sharks in the Indian Ocean. So far, no one in living memory has ever been taken at Beira, but personally, for myself, I do not advise you to swim out too far. Good night.'

The door closed behind him and they looked at each other without speaking. They heard his car start, heard him drive away, then she came towards him and he kissed her gently.

'You want to go and eat?' he said.

She stood close to him, her arms linked around his waist as if reluctant to let him go.

'Oh no, I'm far too excited, let's do all that tomorrow. We must still be miles away from Beira. It must be farther along the coast somewhere. Let's walk on the sands and look at the sea.'

On the top of the dunes in the darkness, the gigantic curve of the beach stretched away from them, the lights of the chalets marking its wide semicircle. The breeze blew in strongly from the Indian Ocean and they could see the flurry of phosphorescence as the breakers rolled in to crash on the sand.

She stood very close to him and he put his hand around her waist. It felt very slender and he could trace the curve of her hip. He kissed her again, and this time his kiss was not gentle and their bodies clung together.

'We'd better walk,' he said hoarsely.

'No, let's go inside,' she whispered.

His mind was confused and excited by her nearness and her voice; he said, 'Damn those single beds!'

'Never mind. We can push them together.' She tugged his hand. 'Come on, let's go back.'

They ran, ploughing down the steep side of the sand dune, staggering and almost falling until the impetus of the downward slope brought them up against the door of the chalet. They went inside.

Outside the night and the wind shivered against their windows and away in the bush little animals ran on terrified feet to familiar holes they had dug for themselves, and owls sat in the high trees and looked at the high white moon with round and condescending eyes. In India, small brown men came out of their houses feeling the coolness, watching the smudge of crimson dawn on the horizon, and in Sydney the cars piled up in a jam across Sydney Bridge, and long-limbed girls with Amazon breasts strode purposefully towards their typewriters. In the South Seas, in Suva, Arpia and Papeete, they dreamt somnolently under their coconut trees through the long hot day, and the Pacific Ocean clear and blue rolled casually up to a thousand coral beaches. In San Francisco farther to the north, they huddled in overcoats against the keen winds and the sea fret, and in New York the lights in the immense phallic columns set up in worship of commerce were already bright and a million inhabitants thought lovingly of the six o'clock martini. In England, with the children already in bed, they stared fascinated at the television screen and waited for the weather charts to tell them it would be wet tomorrow. Babies fell from the womb and men made love, and aircraft soared endlessly through the sky, murders were committed and people died, business men worried over income tax and teenagers worried over love affairs and statesmen worried over their immortality, and here in this tiny cabin, stuck like a pimple on the finger of sand stretching out into the turbulence of the Indian Ocean, they did not worry about anything. For one fraction of time in a time which passed uneasily or too quickly, time had no meaning and was expendable.

'Darling,' she said, 'I love you, I love you, I love you.'

He woke later some time in the middle of the night wondering where he was, then realized that Sarah was soft and warm and breathing quietly in the narrow bed beside him, and that they hadn't bothered to push the beds together.

He also realized that Señor Sequiros had mentioned nothing about a lavatory and indeed perhaps they did not possess one at all, but in any case he had to go.

He slid out of bed and did not seem to have wakened Sarah, and went outside closing the door softly behind him. He stood there looking at the stars filled with a great sense of exaltation, and then acting on impulse he climbed to the ridge of the dunes.

The lights in the camp were all out now, and he could see nothing of the circle of the bay. The wind moved steadily against his face and he could hear the constant roar of the sea. The stars were incredible, the milky way luminous over his head, the whole sky down to the horizon alight with stars.

He crouched there, a small naked human being on top of a sand dune beneath the enormous starlit bowl of the universe, a speck of human flesh in the middle of eternity, not knowing where he had come from or where he was going or what it was all about.

And he was exultant; he could have sung and shouted against the wind. He was male and human and alive. His hands could still feel the soft skin of Sarah, his mind was drenched with the enormous ecstasy and peace she had brought him.

He stood up stretching his arms towards the sky, aware of his nakedness and the wind on his body, and then he turned and raced back towards the hut. It was dark inside, much darker than the night, and he fumbled his way across to the bed.

She woke as he slid under the single sheet beside her, and said sleepily, 'Where've you been? Oh, you're cold, come closer.'

She was warm and soft. Outside the night and the wind and the stars set him problems he could not answer, stirred his mind with a yearning he did not understand. Here, lying close to Sarah, there was security.

CHAPTER TWELVE

NEXT MORNING at ten o'clock Field took the car and drove the mile along the sand dunes to the supermarket. He bought coffee, a carton of milk, sugar, a loaf of brown bread, butter and eggs.

'Just the essentials,' he said coming back into the cabin, and then stopping to look at her. 'We can get all the luxuries later.'

She was wearing a minute green bikini; her hair was done up in a knot at the nape of her neck. Her skin was very white and she looked very young and lovely.

'God,' he said, 'I don't think I want any breakfast.'

'We are going for a swim before breakfast,' she said firmly, 'so you can take that look off your face. Get into your costume at once.'

Hand in hand almost blinded by the glare of the sun on the dry golden slopes of tussocky sand and grass they struggled to the top.

Field collapsed, feigning exhaustion.

'Hell,' he said, 'that's it for the day!'

She prodded him experimentally with her toe then dropped on her knees beside him. 'You should have gone to bed early,' she said.

'I did, that's mainly the trouble,' he said.

'Then you should have stopped in your own bed,' she said, reprovingly.

'You're wicked,' he said. 'You're a lovely wicked girl. And I love you.'

She slipped down next to him, warm and heavy against his shoulder, and touched his lips with her forefinger.

'A week,' she whispered happily. 'That's almost as long as till the end of the world.'

The beach, wide and golden, sloped at a gentle angle from the dunes towards the sea. Two hundred yards from the shore it was stained brown from the slow and spreading emergence of the Pungwe River, but the breakers were sparkling white and, whipped up by the strong breeze, ran landwards to explode on the sand in a continuing barrage. Seething up the beach and then retreating, the foam left fat glistening mushrooms of spume behind, and within seconds the wind had blown them to shreds.

'Come on,' said Field, struggling over on to his side, 'race you down to the sea.

She was faster than he thought. Streaking away with an early lead, choking with laughter she almost beat him in that first exhilarating plunge into the breakers.

The waves were enormously powerful. They knocked them over, washed them under, hurled them back towards the shore. They struggled up and flung themselves back into the surging ocean, only to be rolled over again, submerged and washed ignominiously ashore.

In the shallows Field rolled over on to his back, gasping air into his lungs, panting 'Talk about a morning shower, more like a morning tidal wave!'

On her stomach, her wet black hair matted about her head, stuck in wet strands across her face, she dug her feet and hands into the wet and yielding sand.

'Oh, it's wonderful,' she sighed. 'I'd forgotten how wonderful it was to feel the sun and the sea.'

'The waves must run straight across from India,' said Field, 'that's why they're so powerful. Come on, let's walk a bit. If we go far enough we can have breakfast in Suez.'

'D'you think the beach really stretches that far?' she said, wonderingly.

'Our beaches go as far as our imagination reaches,' said Field. 'Come on.'

They walked along the beach away from the direction of the camp towards the farthermost spit of sand. The world became empty and endless, the sun reflecting on the bright sea and sand and the glare so filling their eyes that it was like walking in an immense and burnished bowl of light; their ears were filled with the roar of the sea, and only the occasional shell or black pebble and the twin trail of footsteps dragging behind them, showing that indeed they were walking. Eventually they turned away up towards the dunes again, and here the wind was at full strength plucking at the muscles of their legs and bodies and moulding them into unfamiliar shapes. They crouched in a deep hollow sheltered by the soft slopes and the fringes of spiky grass, and suddenly it was possible to talk and see and breathe again.

'Lord,' said Field, 'suddenly I'm so hungry I could eat you . . .' He took one soft arm and buried his teeth gently in her flesh.

'Ouch!' she said. 'You brute.'

'Don't you ever sunburn? All this lovely white skin, and this black black hair.'

She smiled up at him, and put one small finger on the end of his nose. 'I casserole to a nice medium brown.'

He said, 'I think I like you white best. Though I'm sure I haven't got a personal colour bar.'

'I hate you,' she said.

'Not about you anyway,' he said.

Laughing they struggled back to the cabin. Sarah fried eggs while Field made the coffee. Then she dressed in a pale blue, low-necked dress and white sandals, and he put on his thin dark blue trousers, and a dark blue short-sleeved sports shirt.

'You look dishy,' she said. 'Do we have to go into Beira?'

'Yes,' he said, 'we have to go into Beira. And we need a shopping basket.'

Beira was about twenty minutes drive away along a sea front road of holiday homes. It was a sprawling town of upended concrete boxes tilting pastel rectangles up towards the hot sun: soft blues, prawn reds, pale chocolates, delicate eau de nils, primrose yellows, and in the constant ciné glare of the sun which provided light, shadow and beauty where little really existed, the boxes with windows added an inconsequential, flippant dimension to the holiday and port.

They parked the car in the shade of a block of flats and walked around the streets.

They passed the end of the Paiva de Andrada, where 'Caldas Xavier, 1853-1896, Heroi da Integridade de Mocambique' stood on his pedestal, legs astride, hat in one hand, the other resting on his sword. The breeze blew softly through the casuarina trees, and with Sarah walking quietly at his side his happiness was total. The ships—their funnels and derricks sticking up above the warehouses at the end of the town—added to the seafaring atmosphere, and occasionally they heard the muted thunder of a siren, as a tramp steamer breasted out through the muddy estuary.

Almost nothing was left of the old, red-painted, corrugated iron town, which had seen so many pioneers at the turn of the century, and resisted and survived the yellow fevers and malaria, except a few decrepit old bungalows, their verandahs fenced in with mosquito netting, and the Standard Bank, red-bricked, double-storeyed, Roman Dutch in style, thrusting two empty flagpoles from its balcony as if uncertain what flag to fly. In the modern bars and cafés chromium Italian espresso machines hissed melodramatically, and the citizens and holiday-makers sat somnolently under coloured umbrellas at little plastic-covered tables.

'Let's have a beer,' said Field. 'I feel like a beer.'

They sat down at a small table. He hardly noticed the couple who came to sit a yard away to his right. Fortunately he was just paying the bill when a voice said, 'Good morning, Inspector Field?'

Surprised he turned to look and hoped his face didn't reflect his instant horror. It was Assistant Commissioner Dewley from Salisbury. Field knew him well enough; he had been the big frog in the small pool of Field's early years as a trooper and there was an official arrogance about him which Field found intolerable. Most of the senior officers managed to be both your superior and some sort of father figure; after all they'd come up through the ranks like everybody else. And of course Dewley invariably did the right thing. Dewley married the right girl: the wealthy daughter of a South African merchant who sat with him now, plain, angular and forbidding, a diamond pendant hanging against her leathery chest and a cluster of diamond rings on her fingers. When Dewley retired having just missed the crowning accolade of being Commissioner, he would undoubtedly live unhappily ever after in South Africa on his wife's money with no one to boss about except the poor black bastards who worked for him.

'Good morning, sir,' he said politely.

'You know my wife don't you, Field?' said Dewley affably, and Field noted the speed at which he had dropped the

Inspector and returned him socially to the non-commissioned ranks.

In that case he would play it on that level and escape as soon as possible.

'Good morning, Mrs. Dewley,' he said in his lower ranks addressing superior officers' wives voice.

'Good morning, Inspector Field,' she said in her slightly guttural South African accent. 'Such a surprise to find you here.' Field sensed that she could scarcely prevent herself saying, 'catch you here'.

He said, 'I would like to introduce Miss Van der Huizen. Assistant Commissioner Dewley and Mrs. Dewley.'

Everyone nodded politely and said 'Good morning', and Field left a tip for the waiter and began to move. Dewley anticipated the tactics.

'Are you from this part of the world, Miss Van der Huizen?' he asked loudly.

'I'm from the Union,' conceded Sarah, revealing nothing and finishing her drink.

Mrs. Dewley seized her opportunity.

'From Johannesberg—eh? I'm from Johannesberg.'

'No,' said Sarah politely, 'my relatives are in the Cape.'

'Where are you staying?' demanded Assistant Commissioner Dewley addressing himself to Field, but actually including Sarah in the question.

'I'm staying out at the holiday camp,' said Field pointedly and then quickly reversing the subject back to Dewley. 'Where are you staying, sir?'

'At a hotel on the front.'

'Pretty good place, I imagine?' said Field beginning to stand up.

'Not bad,' said Dewley, and then realizing that his subordinate was escaping, 'How is the wife?'

'Oh, very well,' said Field coolly. 'Very well indeed.'

He knew that the next question undoubtedly would be 'I suppose she's here?' but forestalled it. He had had enough of this cross-examination. After all he was on holiday, this was a foreign country and Dewley could go jump off the harbour wall for all he cared. 'Well, sir,' he said, 'we must be off. I hope you have a good holiday, sir.'

Sarah had already taken her cue from him, slipped from the chair and was now two yards away. She smiled her good-byes. Twenty yards distant, she said, 'Who was he? I didn't like him.'

'One of the most important men in the police force,' said Field.

'It's worried you?' she said perceptively.

Field took her arm. He couldn't care less if Dewley saw them. 'No—not worried. Irritated is the better word. I don't like him either.'

'He'll tell people back in Salisbury he saw you with me?'

'I expect so.'

'Oh, Bill,' she said, 'does it matter?'

'No.'

'But it will do you no good?'

'I've never worried very much about what did me good.'

'But this man's important?'

'Yes.'

'And the fact that he's seen me with you and that your wife isn't here will start the gossips talking?'

'I expect so.'

'Damn him,' she said, 'why did we have to bump into him?'

'It doesn't matter,' he said sharply. But he knew it did matter. He knew that meeting Dewley had somehow cracked the crystal bubble. Dewley was reality, Dewley was police procedure and promotion and annual reports and quiet conversations at the bar of the Officers' Mess. 'Yes, good chap Field, many good qualities. You know the Assistant Commissioner bumped into him in Beira camping out with a smashing bit of stuff? Yes, ditched his wife and gone away for a crafty week-end. Oh, dead cunning! Can't blame him I suppose. All like to do it if we had the chance, but of course not the sort of thing a policeman really should get up to!'

'Let's find a quiet place and have lunch,' he said.

They found a small restaurant facing the harbour. A woman two tables away sucking voraciously at a plate of fish soup looked familiar.

'Who are you staring at?' said Sarah. 'Not somebody else you know?'

'That woman. She reminds me of someone.'

Sarah said, 'Some old flame, I expect.'

'No, nothing like that.' Then he remembered. The woman's white dress with the filmy white edging rather like a nightgown, brought it back to his mind. 'Oh yes,' he said.

'Well, tell me.'

'It's not very pleasant.'

She frowned at him. 'Oh, go on. I'm old enough.'

Field smiled. 'It's a long time ago. I was a young trooper at a police station in a suburb in Salisbury. Very quiet. Very peaceful. Until one of the local housewives started being naughty. We knew all about it because one of her neighbours rang up practically every night to lay a complaint. Apparently as soon as the husband went off on night duty, she slipped off down the garden path into her gardener boy's hut. And she didn't emerge until very much later.'

Sarah said perceptively, 'They must have been watching very carefully from their back windows?'

'Undoubtedly they were.'

'Maybe she was a welfare worker taking him a bowl of soup.'

'She always wore her nightgown. Usually soup is not served in a nightgown.'

'But what does it matter? Supposing she did make love to him.'

'It was against the law.'

'I can't believe it. This is not South Africa.'

'In those days—about twelve years ago it was very much against the law. A white man could cohabit with a black woman, and everyone wished him luck. No penalty. But a white woman was allowed no sexual frivolity with a black man. Not on your life.'

'How unfair.'

'The law has now been repealed, and everyone can sleep with whom they please.'

'Lucky for us,' said Sarah, 'so what happened?'

'The police don't like to take action in these cases. This is supposed to be something between a husband and wife. The station sergeant—he was quite a decent chap—went to all sorts of trouble to duck the issue. He even tried to get one of the husband's pals to tip him off, to get him to change to a day shift, but of course it didn't work. And eventually the charming neighbours, having had a perfectly lovely time peering from behind their lace curtains and imagining the goings-on, threatened to report the matter to headquarters unless the Sergeant took action. He couldn't avoid it. He rang up H.Q. and asked for a ruling, and some snotty nosed superintendent tore him off a strip and told him he was there to carry out the law not evade it.'

'But it didn't affect you, did it?' said Sarah seriously.

'Oh yes, it did. One dark night the Sergeant told me he had a little job lined up for us, and off we went to wait behind a hedge in the lady's garden. And as they'd said, as soon as the old man had gone off on night shift down the path she came tripping in her nightgown and slippers, and into the gardener boy's hut she popped. You know, "hut" is a nice word for it; it was purely a small concrete box with a door and window. The light went out and I said, "Oh come on, Sarj, let's get it over with!" But the Sergeant said, "Not on your life. If they want me to do the bloody job, I'll do it properly. So keep your bloody mouth shut and obey orders."

'So we waited ten minutes and then we wriggled through the hedge and the Sergeant banged open the door which hadn't got a lock anyway, and switched on the light. The entire thing was so—' Field searched for a word and couldn't find it—'It was their business, not ours. The Negro was a nice sleepy young man who thought the whole thing was quite normal and wasn't this the way that God had arranged it, and into the bargain wasn't he lucky? We took the woman back to the house and I'll never forget the way she sobbed all the way up the path, and she was still crying when the Sergeant made the formal charge and I rang up the husband to tell him to come home from work because there was something he had to know about. So when the poor little blighter got home he began to cry too, and I felt slightly lower than the skin on a snake's belly. And somehow dirty.'

'What did you do?'

'Later that night I said in a burst of confidence to the Sergeant precisely that. I also said that if he expected me to take part in any more such capers he'd better have another think coming. I also said that if my three probationary years were up I'd quit the bloody spying, prying police force anyway!'

Sarah smiled, leant across the table and held his hand. 'And what did he say?'

'He said, "Field, you're a bloody young idiot, and don't talk to your Sergeant like that else I'll punch you on the bloody nose."'

'Was he a big man?'

'No, he was only a little chap. He couldn't have reached my nose standing on a step ladder let alone punched it. Still, I understood his sentiments. He said, "You'll find a lot of nasty things about this life and this job which you won't like at all, but you're just administering the law not making it, and if you're not man enough and big enough to take it on you'd better quit and get a job as a shop assistant in Salisbury."'

'But you didn't?'

'No.'

'Why not?' She still held his hand.

Field hesitated. 'Because I hadn't completed the three probationary years you have to sign on for, and because I was hooked.'

'I don't understand.'

'I liked the life, I liked the force, I liked the people. Very few are like Dewley. This is the greatest police force in the world, uncorrupt and honest. I liked that sergeant who gave me hell. And besides, I was posted away from Salisbury shortly after that to a country district. In those days we even had a horse patrol. I'd set out on my old nag with two African constables and their bicycles, and we'd be away for a month, deep in the bush. Pitch our tent, visit the isolated villages, talk to the chiefs about crops and unruly wives, witch doctors and rainfall. There was no hate or bitterness. Just loneliness and peace, and me Big White Chief administering justice. In those days I don't think the United Nations had ever heard of us.'

She smiled slowly, 'It couldn't last.'

'No, it couldn't last.'

'What happened to the housewife?'

'She got off with a fine. And of course the law's been repealed long ago.'

'This new lot might bring it back?'

'I doubt it.'

'How do you feel about mixed marriage?'

'Are you asking me how I'd feel if my daughter married a black man?'

'Yes.'

'Well in the first place I haven't a daughter, and if I had I'm sure anything I said to her wouldn't make any difference at all.'

'But how do you feel?'

'I don't feel anything. It's been going on since the world began. Like the sun rising and setting.' He put his other hand on top of hers. 'Sometimes it's right, sometimes it's wrong. I mean, as if I can talk about happy marr—'

He stopped, lifted his eyes to hers and found she was looking at him with unblinking, sympathetic. eyes.

'You stopped because you didn't want to be disloyal,' she said quietly.

'Disloyal as well as unfaithful,' he said. He held her hand tightly. 'Listen, I'll tell you this without the benefit of background music and with no more than a drop of white wine in my veins, here over the debris of our cold lobster in this unromantic restaurant. I've never met a girl like you before. I've never met anyone as beautiful as you before. I've never made love to anybody like I've made love to you, before, I've never felt like this before. I suppose it means that for the first time in my life I'm in love and I'm beginning to get a terrible presentiment that it's going to turn out absolute hell.'

'Don't say that,' she said.

'I'm forty-three and married, and you're twenty-three and your life in front of you. We came away on impulse, we ran away if you like—'

'Stop,' she said, 'please stop.' She paused and added softly, 'D'you want me to go away now?'

'Oh God, no,' he said in despair.

'We have a whole week. That's more than some people get ever.' She was silent for a little while and then she said, 'Sometimes you don't like being a policeman.'

'I didn't like having to kill a man as part of my job. I didn't become a copper for that sort of thing.'

'Do you take some sort of oath?'

Field looked at her seriously. 'I learnt the whole thing by heart,' he said. 'I William Henry Field . . .'

'I didn't know your second name was Henry,' she said. 'Isn't that sweet.'

'I, William Henry Field, on appointment as a police constable, do solemnly and sincerely declare and affirm that I will well and truly serve our Sovereign Lady Queen Elizabeth the Second, her heirs and successors, that I will act as a constable for preserving the peace and for preventing offences against the same and I will to the best of my skill and knowledge discharge all Police and Military duties faithfully according to Law, and that during my service in the Force I will obey all such lawful orders as may be given to me and will observe all Laws, Orders, Regulations pertaining to the Force, which may from time to time be in force.'

'How lovely. It sounds just like the Boy Scout's Code.'

'A lack of punch in the ending, I always thought,' he said gloomily. 'Those two "forces" coming so close together,'

'I was always rather scared of policemen until I met you,' she said.

'The law and its penalties is for villains, for rogues, not for decent citizens who make a slip, or ladies frustrated by their husbands.'

'Oh, Inspector Field of Scotland Yard, I do love you,' she said. 'Will you have some more white wine? And then will you take me back to our home and make love to me on a sand dune?'

'Nothing would give me greater pleasure,' said Field politely. 'Would you like some fruit salad first?'

CHAPTER THIRTEEN

THEY ARRANGED IT before they got back to Chapanda.

'After all,' said Field, 'you might easily have met me in Umtali and given me a lift. Just drive straight up to the police post and look as if you hardly know me.'

'It's gone so fast. The first two days stretched on for ever and then suddenly it flew. Oh, Bill, what are we going to do?'

'I don't know,' said Field.

It was three-thirty in the afternoon when she drove past the Chimanimani Hotel and up the hill swinging in through the gates of the compound to pull up outside the charge office. As he opened the door Field could see Potterson peeping through the window.

'Better not kiss you,' he said. 'Might have a bad effect on the morale of the other ranks.'

Sarah smiled. 'I'll see you tonight, we'll be more private.'

They'd arranged dinner on the way back. Milly was away for another week. After all what was wrong with such innocent social meetings?

In a louder voice which he thought might penetrate through to Potterson, Field said casually, 'Well, thanks for the lift,' and stood back watching her reverse and drive away.

He dropped his bag on the verandah and went into the office. Potterson stood up smartly.

'Welcome home, Skipper,' he said enthusiastically.

'All right, relax,' said Field. 'I haven't just come back from my honeymoon.' He realized immediately that he'd said the wrong thing. To cover up he added, 'Anything happened while I was away?'

'Only the usual routine, Skipper,' said Potterson.

'Any mail?' said Field.

'In the tray on your desk, Skipper,' said Potterson.

Field went across and thumbed through the envelopes. 'Official bumph,' he said. He noticed that Milly didn't seem to have written to him; maybe that was just as well.

Potterson hesitated. 'Your wife rang up yesterday, sir.'

'Oh?' said Field carelessly. 'Is she having a good time in Salisbury?'

'I think so, sir.'

Potterson had relapsed defensively into the official 'sir'.

'What did she want?'

Potterson looked nervous. 'She wanted to speak to you, sir.'

'So what did you say?'

Potterson swallowed his adam's apple. 'I said you weren't on the station, sir, and I didn't quite know when you would be back.'

'You were informed by Umtali that I was on a week's leave?'

'Yes, sir.'

'You could have passed on that information.'

'Yes, sir, but I thought she would know, I mean, sir . . .' Potterson trailed into confused silence.

Field thought, so everyone in Chapanda will know eventually that Inspector Field disappeared mysteriously for one whole week and his wife didn't know where he was. Everyone in Chapanda would make inspired guesses and sooner or later the news would get around that a gay week in Beira had been passed by their respected Inspector of Police. Oh well, it would give them something to gossip about.

'It is always safe to hazard a guess that your superior officer is away on a fishing trip,' said Field, and decided it was time to let Potterson off the hook. 'Even wives understand fishing trips,' he said kindly.

'Yes, sir,' said Potterson, relieved. 'Is Mrs. Field coming back soon, sir?'

Field extracted an envelope which had O.H.M.S. stamped on the front and tore it open with a sense of gloom. 'I don't know,' he said. 'Who knows about women?'

The envelope contained an official circular concerning outbreaks of rinderpest. He dropped it into the waste paper basket and the phone rang. He picked it up and said, 'Inspector Field.'

'Had a good time?' said a guttural voice which he recognized immediately as Cohen's.

'Christ,' said Field, 'news travels fast. I've been back just five minutes.'

'I know,' said Cohen and Field could almost see his leer. 'You drove back with a bird in a blue car. I've got my spies on every tree.'

'I'll tell you about it sometime,' said Field. 'Sometime in about fifteen years.'

'Listen,' said Cohen, 'I'm not interested in the sordid love life of the police force. But I thought we might have a quiet one this evening? I know you don't have a wife to henpeck you. What about six o'clock?'

Field didn't feel like conversation with Cohen at that moment. Later perhaps he would feel differently. 'All right,' he said, 'six in the club.'

'No, not in the club,' said Cohen. 'Raderly inhabits the club these days and I can't stand the man.'

'All right the hotel bar,' said Field, thinking that Cohen must have altered if he was ducking a chance of a verbal punch-up with Raderly. 'The bar at six.' He replaced the phone and looked across at Potterson. 'I suppose I'd better go and change into uniform. Can't sit around here looking like an idle member of the C.I.D.'

'I'll get a constable to carry your bag, Skipper,' said Potterson promptly.

'Don't bother,' said Field, 'they're not hotel porters. I can manage.'

He left the charge office and walked along the path to his bungalow; he climbed the verandah steps and found Lupin in the lounge arranged graciously in an armchair flicking through an old copy of *Vogue*. She leapt to her feet, her face contorted like a small child caught with a guilty secret. She flew across to the duster lying on the sideboard and began to work industriously.

'Oh relax,' said Field knowing she didn't understand a word he was saying, but hoping she would get the meaning from the tone of his voice. She did. She smiled bewitchingly at him and stroked the polished sideboard with a long caressing glide. For the first time Field thought maybe she was being coquettish? Those dark eyes of hers held a very strange look. Perhaps after his week in Beira she sensed some change in him? Women were supposed to have that intuitive ability. Anyway she was no more than a child; a child growing up pretty fast though, that was very plain. He went through to the kitchen to tell Abdul that he wouldn't be home for dinner and then went into the bedroom to change. He could hear Lupin singing quietly outside in the lounge as she continued her dusting and a few seconds later there was a knock on his door. Field, wearing only shorts, opened it.

She stood there waving her duster and making motions that she wanted to come into the bedroom to work.

'Not now,' he said, 'later. Buzz off.' He saw her eyes appraise him and felt slightly embarrassed. He shooed her away, 'Go on,' he said, 'scarper!' She thought it was very funny and went back to the lounge giggling.

Back in the office he caught up with various chores.

'No more trouble with Ali Hassim Khan?' he asked Potterson.

'No. sir. I thought perhaps he might have gone in to Salisbury to get mixed up with the trouble you ran into, Skipper? There was a questioning note in his voice and Field said, 'All right I know you want all the details, but not today. I'm too tired. Later.'

'Okay, Skipper,' said Potterson understandingly.

He was glad when six o'clock came and he could change out of uniform back into civvies. Somehow that made him seem closer to Sarah.

Cohen was sitting at the bar with a schooner of beer when he arrived. 'Why, the wandering policeman himself,' he said welcomingly. 'I hear you made a great hero of yourself in the rioting down in Harare.'

'It comes naturally to me,' said Field.

'Go on,' said Cohen, 'tell me about it. Tell me how you saved the entire white race from massacre.'

'Some other time,' said Field. 'Has Ali Hassim Khan been causing any more trouble lately?'

'Not according to the way he sees it,' said Cohen draining his beer and ordering two more. 'He's got a power complex like every other politician, black or white.'

'And a hate complex?'

'He has every reason to have a hate complex,' said Cohen,

'and where do you think the hate comes from? It comes from the blood in his veins, mate—white blood, the blood the white man put in the negress, the trigger for his own destruction. D'you think the average "munt" in the bush cares about "freedom"? Like hell. He cares about his belly and his bints. A bit of hunting, a lot of shagging, a bellyful of beer and a long sleep in the shade. Wise man. But of course neither Ali Hassim Khan nor ourselves are going to let him get away with this. He's got to learn that the world is full of shiny cars and consumer goods and that you've got to slave for eight hours a day to keep up with your neighbours. Don't you want your children to be a success like President Kennedy and get assassinated and have an airport named after you? It's taken one man's lifetime to bring him out of the bush and to the attention of all those educated chaps at the United Nations. It'll take another lifetime to make the world one long High Street full of Woolworth's and Marks and Spencer's stretching from Peking to Poplar and with a bit of luck everyone will be literate enough to read comics on their week-end trips to the moon.'

'I thought you were the great believer in freedom for the human soul?'

'Freedom is for a few mad dogs and a handful of eighteenth-century Englishmen,' said Cohen, 'most of us are only in love with the idea, we'd be terrified at the reality. Serfdom is our natural state. From dawn to dusk and from birth to death we are chained and encompassed by circumstance, situation and environment.'

'I must put that in my next annual report,' said Field sarcastically.

'Do that,' Cohen agreed graciously. 'And I think it's about time I turned to that noble drug whisky. Are you getting drunk with me tonight?'

'No, I've got a date for dinner.'

'Anyone I know?' Cohen asked casually.

'You know damn well,' said Field. 'Just leave me alone will you?'

'Have I said a word?' said Cohen innocently.

'I can hear the noise your mind is making a mile away,' said Field.

'I hope you have a pleasant evening,' said Cohen cordially.

Sarah met him at the door and lifted her lips to be kissed. Her eyes were bright. When he said, 'Where's your father?' she replied, 'Darling, he's in the lounge, but stop looking so worried, he's too old to care now, and I'm old enough to know what I'm doing.'

Field followed her down the wide hall walking carefully to avoid slipping on the rugs which covered the polished floor. 'Do I look worried?' he said. 'I didn't realize it.'

In the lounge the old man waved a hand from his usual armchair. 'Hallo, Bill. How are things?'

'Pretty fair. How are you getting on?'

'Not bad. I don't expect to feel great at my age. As long as you're alive that's all that matters.'

Dinner was fairly quiet, Sarah, looking relaxed and happy, but the old man seemed thoughtful.

At the end of the meal Sarah went out to make the coffee herself, and Erasmus produced a new bottle of Johnny Walker from his drink cabinet. He poured two inches of whisky into two heavy crystal glasses and handing one to Field sat down in his armchair again.

'Skol,' he said.

'Cheers,' said Field.

The old man said slowly, 'I hear you've been away with my girl?'

There was no accusation in his voice, no suggestion of a threat, merely a calm statement of fact, but Field was so astounded he almost choked on his whisky. The old man's blue eyes were staring directly at him and Field stared back.

'Yes,' he said simply. Then more to fill in the silence than anything else he added, 'how did you know?'

'Sarah told me,' said Erasmus. He added, 'She's very fond of you.'

'The same goes for me,' said Field lamely.

He could sense that Erasmus was regarding him with the same hard, critical gaze with which he regarded animals, crops, human beings, the vagaries of wind and weather, tobacco blight and rinderpest. Erasmus knew that you had to observe realistically if you were a farmer; emotion or self-deception ruined the harvest and piled up the creditors.

Erasmus liked Field because he sensed in him a realism which was not harsh, a humanism which understood frailty. He knew Field was right for his girl Sarah who in spite of her swift rages had so many of the gentle, hidden shynesses that Annie had, therefore he was pleased at this turn of affairs.

He knew that his years were diminishing. Anyway he was old now, it was time he had a rest. He would like to spend a few months down in the Cape, visit his relatives. The farm for better or worse would go to Sarah. He had tried to find a man for her. He had three managers, three young agricultural college idiots who didn't know a cabbage from a cow's arse and they'd all had their eyes on Sarah from the very first day. He hadn't objected to that; after all that was the purpose of the employment, but Sarah had turned her nose up at the lot of them. And now she had picked this one for herself and as her father he would do what he could to help her.

He said to Field, 'You're married?'

Field didn't know what was coming next. He said simply, 'Yes.'

'You've got a barren woman,' Erasmus said curtly.

Field felt angry at the old man's contempt. It was no bloody business of his anyway. A real piece of Afrikaans thinking, this.

'She's my wife,' he said coldly.

'Yes, but she's given you no little children.' His guttural pronunciation of 'little children' made Field wince. 'Sarah's a fine girl. She's full of babies. She's the woman for you.'

'I'm married,' repeated Field emphatically. 'I'm married in the eyes of God and the church and all that sort of thing.'

Erasmus grunted. 'That's only a matter for the law anyway,' he said. 'You've been sleeping with my girl, haven't you?'

Christ, thought Field, what was this going to be, a shotgun divorce? At any time this logical farmyard appraisal of Sarah and himself would not have amused him; now it chilled him with apprehension.

'Look, this is something between Sarah and me,' he said bleakly. 'We've got to work it out.'

The old man drained his whisky.

'I didn't say it wasn't,' he said, 'I'm just telling you that Sarah will take over this land after me and there's sixty-five thousand acres of it and it's good land and you could do a lot with it. I don't cultivate a tenth of it. You could pump water up from the Sabi, make it fertile. They've done it over at the sugar estate at Triangle and elsewhere.'

'I'm not a farmer, I'm a policeman.'

'Every man's a farmer at heart. You'd learn. Besides, she needs a man like you.' He added slowly, 'I'm just giving you my feelings—straight. It's up to you to make up your own mind.'

'Yes,' said Field. 'Thanks.'

He drained his whisky too and put it back into the outstretched hand. 'I will have another—yes.' He tried to smile and found it impossible. Sarah came back into the room with the coffee and the old man changed the subject.

'We seem to be getting on all right as a free country don't we?' he said. 'After that first fuss about the petrol things are just the same as before aren't they?'

'Yes,' said Field.

'It'll all settle down in the end,' said the old man. 'It has to. Someone has to till the land and grow the crops so it has to settle down. Bloody politicians think they run things. All they do is gas.'

'Yes,' said Field, not listening to him.

It was, he supposed, the way the aristocrats and the big landowners had always disposed of their property. You saw your daughter made a suitable match and left your property to your grandchildren. It was fundamental, deep in the bloodstream, but somehow the old man's realistic understanding of these facts was a shock to Field. He had gone away to Beira in a mood of romantic enchantment; he returned to find himself under consideration as a stud bull!

'Black or white?' said Sarah looking at him over her father's head with innocent eyes.

'Black,' said Field carefully and wondered whether she had put her father up to this.

They chatted inconsequentially for another half hour before Erasmus eased himself out of his chair and announced he was off to bed.

'No hurry, Bill,' he said, 'take your time. You're both young. You don't need the sleep I do. Good night.'

When he had gone Field said guardedly, 'Why did you tell him about us?'

Her eyes were clear. 'You're not angry?'

Field considered, 'No,' he said, 'just mentally winded. But why did you tell him?'

'He asked me,' she said simply. She came closer and sat on the arm of his chair and put her arm around his neck. 'You *are* angry?'

'No, I'm not,' he said, 'but you must admit it does come as a bit of a shock when a father accuses you of seducing his daughter.'

She laughed delightedly. 'Oh, he never said that. He wouldn't say that. He doesn't know what the word means. He just asked me where I'd been so I told him. After all I'm old enough to know what I'm doing aren't I?' She bent down and kissed the top of his head. 'You haven't objected before.' She slid off the arm on to his lap.

'This is pure seduction,' said Field. 'You're after me.'

'I know,' she said happily. 'Isn't it wonderful?'

The moon was high and hard in the sky when Field left the farm and walked quietly down to pick up his car. It was facing downhill so he released the handbrake and coasted the first two hundred yards listening to the tyres crunching quietly on the gravel before starting the engine. Chapanda was dark and deserted and his wristwatch told him it was a quarter to two as he climbed the steps to the bungalow. He sat in a deckchair there for a while to consider the events of the evening and wonder what he should do. She had told him again as she had told him on every one of those long nights in Beira that she was in love with him. Was there any doubt in his mind that he loved her? He knew he was possessed by a deep, primitive obsession. But the obstacles, the thistles, the impossibilities reared up in his mind like a succession of steeplechase jumps. He just couldn't ring up Milly and say, 'Sorry old girl, it's been nice knowing you. We've had eleven reasonably happy years together but now a change will be good for both of us.' He could hardly ring up Sam Kingsley in Umtali and say, 'Oh, just one other small thing Sam, I'm getting a new-model wife.'

He slept badly that night and the next morning there was a letter from Milly in the post. She wrote, 'Dear Bill, during these last few days I've been mixing with some of my old cronies from Downlands and to cut a long story short, Beryl Penbourne is going off for a three month trip to the Cape and they want someone to stand in for her. I've said I would. If you remember you said some months ago that if I felt like working in Salisbury for a bit you'd understand so I hope you do. Angela's been very understanding and she says I can dig with her as long as I like so you know I'm in good hands. I'm starting on Monday and I don't need to tell you how much I'm looking forward to working with children again. I shall have to come back to Chapanda either next week-end or the one after to collect a few more clothes but I'll give you a ring to tell you when I'm arriving. I'm sure Lupin and Abdul will look after you all right and you'll be just as well off without me for three months. Love Milly.'

She added a postscript of Borgian subtlety, 'I hope you enjoyed your leave in Beira.'

Field showed the letter to Sarah. 'What do you think she means by that last sentence?'

'It means she knows,' said Sarah with deep satisfaction.

Milly, as she had promised, rang up to say she was coming back to Chapanda the week-end after next. As if in retaliation Sarah, whom he saw practically every night at the farm—they kept away from places where people would recognize them and gossip—announced that David Mitchison was arriving from Salisbury to spend a week-end at the farm.

'I thought that was all over between you,' said Field suspiciously.

Sarah looked at him with curious hostility. 'There was nothing ever *on* between us,' she said. 'But after all, if you're having your wife down for the week-end you can't blame me for having a friend down for the week-end also.'

'Some friend!' announced Field. Sarah said with prim coldness. 'Well, I shan't be sleeping with him anyway.'

'How shall I know?' said Field belligerently.

'Yes, how will you know? After all, you won't be there to find out, will you? You'll be in bed with your own wife.'

It was the first childishly stupid quarrel they had ever had and it left Field feeling depressed and irritated.

Milly arrived on Saturday afternoon, and to Field's annoyance brought Angela with her. Angela's implied criticism of the police force as a career, Chapanda as a whole and mankind in general, never failed to goad and anger him. To avoid prolonging the confrontation, he decided to take them both to the Saturday night dance at the Country Club.

Angela surveyed the barn-like building, the screechy radiogram and the enthusiastic drinkers with distaste. Tall and elegant, dark and sophisticated, she made Charlie Holland whom Field had rallied to his side, and who was generally recognized as the only eligible 'man about town' for miles around look almost provincial. Charlie did not help matters either, with a succession of fatuously gallant remarks to Angela whom he addressed as 'old gel'. While he was away at the bar she said to Milly, knowing that Field could overhear, 'What a silly old man. I really fail to understand why men of his age behave in this way.'

Feeling that her arrows were also falling on his territory Field protested mildly, 'He's only doing his best. Back in 1942 he was probably the wit of some R.A.F. mess.'

'It is no longer 1942,' retorted Angela coldly, 'and it's about time he realized he is twenty-five years older.'

'Everyone gets older,' said Field defensively. 'It happens to the female sex as well, you know.' He stood up. 'If you'll excuse me I'll go and help him with the drinks.'

At the bar Cohen was delaying Charlie Holland's return to the table. Cohen always reiterated his hatred of these functions and always turned up to express his hatred in loud and resonant tones to anyone he could find to listen to him.

'Like me to join you and make up a five?' he leered as Field approached the bar. 'Maybe I could do the tall dark one a bit of good.'

'Why don't you try?' agreed Field flippantly. 'A little light conversation about rinderpest and swine fever should go down very well.'

'Great, man, great,' said Cohen, grinning. 'I can see that wit and gay repartee are abroad tonight. Gee, the lady's got real class. She must come from the big city. Lead me across.'

'Thanks, but I'm having enough trouble with Charlie,' said Field, as Holland left them to carry the tray back.

Cohen's eyes were fixed beyond Field's shoulder. 'I see your other lady friend has arrived,' he said maliciously. Field glanced round just in time to see Sarah dancing past in the arms of David Mitchison. She was wearing a pale green dress which exposed her lovely shoulders. Field had never seen it before. To Field she looked the most beautiful girl in the room, and he looked at her with such hunger and pain that as if the physical wavelength of his longing had reached out and touched her, she glanced up to catch his eye. She smiled, distantly: she smiled superficially, the fixed smile of the Lady Mayoress opening the fête, she smiled over the top of his head, away from him, against him, this girl whose lips he had kissed, whose body he knew, whom he loved so deeply that it had become an inner conflict now poised half way towards despair. She looked up and smiled at him as if he was the milkman, or the man behind the bar or some elderly friend of her father's and then she turned her head back to say something with a gay radiance to her partner as he whispered into her ear and they were gone amongst the swirl of dancers. Field was left stunned and silent.

His face showed his feelings. He turned back to the bar where the barman looked at him expectantly.

'I'll have a large—' he began, but Cohen had seen his face, and as if he understood the enormity of his hurt, laid a restraining and somehow kindly hand on his arm. 'No, he won't,' he said to the barman. 'We'll have two beers, two nice cold beers for a start.'

'Now wait a minute,' said Field angrily, but Cohen's voice, gentle for once and without a trace of its usual sarcasm, was compelling.

'Take it easy, man, take it easy. There's plenty of time. The booze will still be here. There's no conclusive place where a mate can prove his manhood and that includes both the bed and the bottle. We've got all evening before us, all evening before I have to carry you home to bed. Relax.'

His sympathy seeped through to Field's brain. All right, he knew he was being absurd. A girl gives you a tiny frigid smile instead of the warm conspiratorial look you were expecting and the world falls down on your head. He drew in a deep breath and expelled it slowly. Cohen took his hand away from his arm and spoke very quietly so that no one could overhear, which was strange because usually Cohen intended everyone in the African continent to benefit from his intellect.

'Women,' he said, 'are hell. They can't help it. Perhaps it's what we do to them. Haven't I ever told you of the wise words of Sekeloto, Great Chief of the Makololo, when Livingstone first arrived at his kraal covered in sweat, presbyterian zeal and carrying a bloody great black bible?'

'As good as your one about the young lady of Gloucester?' said Field disinterestedly.

'Listen,' said Cohen, 'this is a *true* story. There was Livingstone armed with bible and feverish intent to convert the black heathen, and Sekeloto, Great Chief of the Makololo, took one look at the bible and said mildly that he did not want to learn from "the book" because it might change his heart and make him satisfied with *one* wife. He, Sekeloto, Great Chief of the Makololo, wanted at least *five* wives.'

'Madman,' said Field, aware that Cohen's conversation was meant to be helpful.

'*One* is trouble,' said Cohen. 'Be like Sekeloto, Great Chief of the Makololo, and have more than a poker hand. Back to the harem, I say, back to the good old days of chastity belts and ducking stools.' He added, 'Now you drink up that nice cold beer and go back to your guests. Your two nice ladies are transmitting very funny looks in my direction.'

When he rejoined the table Milly said acidly, 'I see your lady friend has another string to her bow.'

This first revelation by Milly that she knew anything about Sarah Van der Huizen was a slight shock to Field. He decided to ignore it. 'Oh, come on,' he said, 'who's going to dance?'

But nobody was going to dance. Charlie Holland was sipping his scotch and staring contemplatively at the ceiling as if awaiting the arrival of the Graf Zeppelin so Field guessed that he and Angela had severed diplomatic relations. The only thing left was counter attack. He said to Angela, 'Cohen over there thinks you're the sexiest woman in the room. I've said I was sure you'd like to meet him.'

'No thank you,' said Angela coldly. A few moments later she stared round the room as if she was trying to place the location of a bad smell. She said, 'I can understand what Milly means when she says there's no one to talk to. I mean, don't you feel *cut off*?' This was addressed to Field.

'Not in the slightest,' he said mildly. 'What dynamic experiences of life or lust—spiritual, emotional or intellectual—could you be having in Salisbury that you can't have here?'

Angela was patronizing. 'If you don't understand that, you really don't understand anything,' she said.

They left before the end with Field bearing away with him the gnawing memory of Sarah sitting cosily at a corner table chatting animatedly to David Mitchison. He knew by this time that Milly knew something about his relationship with Sarah and was incubating the right moment for confrontation. When the two women had arrived early in the afternoon she had confirmed with a quick look that Field was sleeping in the spare room, and then ostentatiously ordered Abdul to take both her own and Angela's bags into the main bedroom.

'Coffee or a drink?' he said with an attempt at cheerfulness as he switched on the lights in the lounge.

'Neither, thank you,' said Angela coolly. 'I think I shall go to bed very shortly.'

'Me too,' said Milly. 'Really, these exciting evenings at the country club do wear one out, don't they?'

'It's the scintillating conversation that makes time pass so quickly,' said Angela. 'All that gay banter about tobacco virus and the uselessness of the African.'

Field began to smoulder; he hadn't really had much to drink, but enough.

'It is possible they might be able to get along without you,' he said shortly.

'I hope so,' said Angela. 'I shall miss these gay week-ends at Chapanda.'

'So shall I!' chimed in Milly.

'Well, it'll be the last you'll have for some considerable time,' said Field, annoyed.

'But not the last one *you* expect to have, I'm sure,' said Milly with a rush of anger.

Field did not answer. There was a spot of colour in Milly's cheeks. She had probably had one gin too many.

'Of course she was with her other boy friend tonight I notice,' she said contemptuously, 'I suppose you have to take it in turns.'

'There's always Lupin if the supply runs out,' added Angela with a light flippancy.

'I don't know what you're talking about,' said Field, angry himself now.

'Don't you? Don't you really?'

'News leaks out,' said Angela sweetly. 'You'll be surprised how many "friends" are so willing to reveal your secrets.'

'I can include you amongst that number, I suppose?' grunted Field wishing he could get out of this.

'Don't talk to Angela like that,' snapped Milly. 'What do you expect when you're seen all over Beira quite openly with that Van der Huizen girl. What d'you expect me to think? What sort of a position d'you think it puts me in?' Her face was set, her voice high. Field didn't try to deny the accusation. 'I thought you made it quite plain that you couldn't care less what I did,' he said, his anger evaporating at the sight of Milly keyed up and near hysterics. He hated these scenes; this screaming break-up of any sort of civilized sanity, this verbal bitterness which left mental bruises so hard to heal, and above all he hated the look of triumph on Angela's face that she should be sitting so securely in the middle of this marital row.

'Well, don't think you can get away with it,' shouted Milly. 'If you make me, I'll sue for a separation, but don't think you'll get a divorce; don't think you can use me as a convenience for all these years and then toss me aside for some little Afrikaans whore. . . .'

Field felt sick and ashamed that his actions should have provoked this torrent of self pity, this trite yet tragic female cry for justice. He wished there was some way he could explain and say, 'I didn't meant it to happen like this.' But he knew she would not understand or want to understand and only sneer at his sincerity.

'I'm sorry,' he said. And then, 'I think I'll go for a walk.'

'That's right,' said Milly victoriously, 'you go for a walk! Is that all you can do? You go for a walk? You're just running away as you always run away.'

Field stepped out on the verandah. He walked down the steps and behind him he heard Angela's voice saying, 'They're all the same Milly, all the same; I've told you often enough.'

Outside the night was cool and the stars were bright in the sky. He walked slowly down the hill away from the police post and then down to the green and the Voortrekker Memorial. He sat on the seat behind it. Christ, what a mess he'd got himself into.

He sat there for perhaps half an hour and then walked back up the hill to the bungalow. The lights were still burning in the lounge but the door of the main bedroom was shut. He went into the kitchen for a glass of water and heard a slight movement in the scullery. He went over to turn on the kitchen lights, thought better of it and said sharply, 'Who's there?'

A head came slowly round the corner. It was Lupin. She held a packet of sugar against her chest cuddling it almost as if it was a child. She indicated it with her eyes.

'I forget,' she said.

Whether she had crept back to pinch the sugar while Abdul was sleeping or whether it was really her own Field didn't know, and didn't care.

'You shouldn't be here,' he said.

She came out from the scullery and in the half light from the lounge, he saw the dusky skin, the glimmer of her eyes turned towards him, half afraid. Then she whispered.

'Missus, she come back?'

She must have been away in the compound when Milly and Angela had arrived that afternoon. 'Yes,' said Field, 'she come back.'

Lupin had learnt a little English in her few months in the household. 'She go away?' she said encouragingly.

Yes,' said Field, 'she go away tomorrow.'

He was unprepared for the beatific smile Lupin awarded him as if some secret and precious dream had come true. She took a step towards him, sensuously, her figure supple, inviting. Looking at her he could understand why Sekeloto, Great Chief of the Makololo, had preferred the continuance and abundance of his provoking yet complaisant young women to the secrets of the intimidating 'black book'. What could an alien religion upon which was grafted all manner of strict and demanding Victorian philosophies offer compared with this warm and immediate flesh?

Field opened the kitchen door and stood back to let her pass. 'Now you go home like a good girl, Lupin,' he said severely. 'It's past midnight. Mrs. Strongbow shouldn't let you out at this time of night.'

She smiled at him again, secretively, intimately, not understanding a word. This man was a chief amongst his people. All the African policemen in the compound as well as the great dolt Strongbow jumped at his command. Even the two younger white ones were subservient to him. He was strong and male and his wife was a whinnying ninny who did not understand her good fortune. As she went through the door quite deliberately she brushed against him with her body.

He heard their car drive off when he was only half awake and as he padded into the lounge across the bright yellow bars the sun thrust through the Venetian blinds, he saw propped up against a flower vase on the low table a letter addressed to him. He opened it and read: 'Dear Bill, I'm sorry I lost my temper and about the quarrel but I do think I have good reason. The sooner you get over your silly infatuation for this girl the better, after all she's only half your age and if you're not careful you'll ruin her life too. Angela tells me that men in their forties often have these silly infatuations so perhaps it's just as well I shall be away for a bit.

'I didn't have time to tell you about my work with the children because you were so preoccupied and I don't suppose you care anyway. But I have joined Angela's dramatic society and she thinks there's a good chance of me getting a part in the next production. Take care of yourself and write to me. Love Milly.'

'Listen, Sarah,' said David Mitchison persuasively, 'I know you've got a thing about this damn policeman, but where's it going to get you? He's twenty years older than you. He's solidly married and I know these middle-aged types. Their wives never let go, ever! And in their hearts they never want to go anyway. Good God, when you're forty he'll be sixty. D'you realize that? You can't imagine that, can you?'

'No.'

'We could get married in Johannesburg in a few weeks' time. Society wedding, really big, reporters and everything, pictures in the *Argus*—it would be great. Then we could go wherever we wanted for our honeymoon. Europe, England, America, anywhere. You'd like that, wouldn't you?'

'I suppose so.'

'I'll be taking over the family business in a couple of years, and there's a lot of money in it, but we could really enjoy ourselves until then and still have a good time afterwards. I mean, you don't want to be stuck away here in the middle of Africa with a flatfoot copper, do you? You'll never get a better offer, darling.'

'No, I don't suppose I will,' said Sarah quietly.

Field rang her at eleven o'clock and said, 'Has he gone?'

'No,' she said, 'he's driving back at six o'clock.'

'I'll see you at seven then. . . .'

He heard the long pause. Then she said, 'D'you think we—'

'Oh, God, yes!' he said urgently. 'I've got to see you. Please! I'll call for you at seven and we'll drive somewhere.'

'All right.' She replaced the receiver slowly.

For Field the rest of the afternoon was endless. It was his day off and he didn't know what to do with it. He thought of going to the club but the chances were he would meet someone he knew and start drinking and he didn't want such anaesthesia. He knew that this was the moment of crisis. If he did not resolve the situation by saying, 'I love you, I'll leave Milly,' he would lose Sarah. And that thought was intolerable.

She was waiting for him on the verandah when he arrived and she sat defensively so far across on the front seat of the car that after a few seconds Field said, 'I don't really have a contagious disease you know.'

It was almost dark and Field switched on the headlights. She still hadn't spoken when he said, 'Has your . . .' he was about to say 'boy friend', but he knew he would only sound antagonistic and malicious, so he changed it to: 'Has Mitchison gone?'

She said in a small voice, 'Yes, he's gone.'

'What did he really come for?'

'He told me he was in love with me. He asked me to go back to South Africa and marry him. He even asked my father's permission.'

'Did you tell him about us?'

'No.'

'Why not?'

'He knew I had a thing about you, but didn't want to know about it. He said you were far too old for me and it would never work out.'

'What did your father say?' Field did not care if his voice revealed his private agony.

'He thought it was entirely up to me.'

Field realized that he had been gripping the steering wheel so hard that his fingers hurt. Slowly he released his hold and said very carefully, 'Yes, I suppose it might be the best thing.'

He saw her turn her head to look at him. Then he added, 'Milly's gone back to Salisbury. She left me a letter saying I should be careful not to ruin your life as well as my own. So you getting married would be a way out I suppose.'

'Yes,' she said, with quiet despair, 'I suppose it would be.'

In the headlights he saw an opening in the hillside, a small, now overgrown, quarry which had once provided stone to make the road. He braked, swung in off the tarmac and switched off the engine. It was suddenly very quiet. He paused wondering how he dared ask the question which he wanted to ask: the absurd emotional question which had weighed him down with its intolerable consequence for the past few hours; the question that had woken him that morning with a sickness in his stomach.

'Did you,' he said, and he tried hard to keep any shade of emotion out of his voice, 'did you make love to him?'

The pause she gave seemed to last for an age; actually it could not have been longer than two seconds, then she said in a rush of words, 'Oh no, how could I? Of course not! Oh Bill, you didn't think . . .'

She slid, she almost leapt across the seat towards him. Their lips met and clung as if their warmth and touch could assuage their private desolation and give some rational perspective to their grief. He felt her tears wet against his cheek.

'Oh, what can we do, Bill,' she sobbed. 'Those women at the dance last week were beastly, they said awful things so that I could overhear. I felt—I felt like . . .'

Field remembered her in the corner talking vivaciously to Mitchison. 'I thought you were enjoying yourself,' he said.

'Jealousy is something you can't comprehend. Until it happens to you.'

'Enjoying myself! It was horrible! And not being able to talk to you. Or look at you. Oh, I couldn't stand it!'

'I couldn't either,' said Field.

'If it was Salisbury or London we might manage, but here it's too small, everybody knows everybody.' She wept again on his shoulder.

Field said hoarsely over the top of her bowed head, 'Maybe if we hadn't fallen in love it would have been all right.' He paused for a second then continued, 'I should have known better.'

She sniffed and raised her head and tried to smile. 'We should both have known better, but you don't know it's gunpowder until you light the match.'

He said, 'We can't stay here. Let's go to the hotel and have a drink.' Now he needed a drink.

'But we can't, people will see us.'

'Who cares?' said Field. 'I don't care if every bloody inhabitant of Chapanda is there.'

'And my face will look terrible. All this crying.'

'It's beautiful.' Field leaned down to kiss her. 'It will always be beautiful.'

It was past midnight when he took her back to the farm and nothing had been settled. They had been bold and courageous and discussed every aspect of their relationship. They had said it would be better if they could part, or if they could forget each other, better if they could treat this as a private and wonderful interval in their lives and go their separate ways. Better, but not possible.

'No, it's not possible,' said Field firmly, but somehow he felt she was not convinced. She sat there in the car with him, unwilling to get out, unwilling to leave him and walk up the path to the house. He added, 'When does Mitchison want you to go away with him?'

'Now, at once. He wants me to drive to Salisbury tomorrow or the next day and go to Johannesburg at the end of the week.'

'Oh no,' said Field, shocked. 'So soon?'

'Yes,' she said, 'so soon.' She added intensely, 'Maybe it is the answer to break off cleanly and quickly, for me to go away so that you can forget all about me.'

There was a note almost of relief in her voice as if she had finally worked out the best solution.

'No,' he said sharply. 'No!'

'I'd better go now,' she said, 'it's late.'

'But you won't go tomorrow or the day after? You can't.'

'I don't know Bill. I don't know what is best.'

'You can't,' he said urgently. 'You mustn't. I'll ring you tomorrow morning and we'll meet again tomorrow night.'

'What's the use?' she said. 'We shall only talk and talk and get nowhere.' She added sadly, 'And that does neither of us any good.'

She opened the door and got out.

'Good night Inspector Field,' she said softly, 'good night.' She went away into the darkness.

Field slept badly again that night and when he got down to the charge office at eight o'clock next morning Potterson looked at him very oddly.

'Night on the tiles Skipper?' he said cheerfully.

'No,' said Field shortly. 'Where's Patrol Officer Longman?'

Potterson looked surprised. 'You told him to go into Umtali for the Jenkins case,' he said.

'Oh yes,' said Field wearily. 'Of course. I forgot.'

He sat down at his desk and saw at once the official looking envelope marked 'Personal' sitting on the blotting pad in front of him. He had seen a similar one once before. He tore it open knowing that it was from the Selection Board, and knowing even before he read it that they had turned him down. In curt 'officialese' it pointed out that his application to be considered for a commission had not been successful; this was not to say that future applications would not receive the fullest consideration, etc., etc. He folded the letter back into its original creases and eased it back into its envelope, then slipped it into his breast pocket. He had now got to face the fact that he would probably keep the rank of Inspector for the rest of his service career, that the rank of Superintendent and above were forever beyond his reach. He said nothing to Potterson. His mind was on Sarah not upon his failure to obtain a commission. When he thought he could safely call her he said to Potterson, 'I'm just slipping back to the house for five minutes. If anybody wants me you can ring me there. Okay?'

'Yes, sir,' said Potterson.

Field walked slowly back to the bungalow. He could hardly say this rejection came as a bitter disappointment; he had barely given it a thought during the past two weeks. Sarah had occupied his mind to the exclusion of anything else. He wondered if the meeting with Dewley in Beira had had anything to do with this? Probably it had. Overall the police were a puritanical lot of bastards. But of course they had to be. It would be ironical, however, if Sarah, having cost him his commission and his marriage, was now to walk out on him. And that seemed highly likely.

He went into the lounge and on impulse took the letter out of his pocket and read it again. There was nothing he could do about it. He laid it on the table, picked up the phone and asked the operator for Sarah's number. The houseboy answered the phone and after a pause he heard Sarah's voice.

'Hallo,' she said, 'hallo, Bill.'

By the very sound of her voice, from the very first 'Hallo' he knew he had lost her; he knew that she had made up her mind to go away and marry Mitchison.

'It's the best thing,' she said tearfully, 'it's the only way, Bill. I've been awake all night thinking about it. We'll drive ourselves crazy trying to work it out. The best thing is for me to go away, at once. Yes, this afternoon.' She was crying now. 'No, not to see you again tonight. I couldn't bear it. Goodbye, Bill. Goodbye.'

The receiver clicked emptily in his ear. He sat there looking at the receiver as if it personally were responsible for this catastrophe. His brain as he walked back to the charge office simply said over and over again, 'She's gone! She's gone!' He opened the door and walked across to his desk. Potterson was busy writing. He looked at the blotting pad and the in-tray and the out-tray and didn't know what to do. He simply could not imagine how he was going to spend the next ten seconds, the next minute, the next hour, the next ten years. He couldn't sit at his desk any longer. He had to walk out in the sunshine, he had to breathe, he had to convince himself that he was still alive, he had to swim up to the surface through this great swamp of despair that engulfed him. He looked across at the keys hanging in their glass-fronted cabinet on the wall, keys to the safe, the armoury, the storeroom. The storeroom, yes, that would do; that was a hundred yards away across the compound. He could sit there in the darkness and think, or cry, or beat his head against the wall.

He stood up, walked across to the cabinet, flipped open the glass door and took out the storeroom key. 'I'm just going to check the storeroom entry book,' he said, 'I shan't be very long.'

'Yes, sir,' said Potterson in a mystified voice.

Outside in the bright sunshine Field saw the prisoners on their work rota, the guards with slung rifles, but the retina of his eyes did not register or pass on the information to his brain.

He unlocked the storehouse and went inside. It was small and dark and cool. The sunlight came in through the dirty window panes and lay in small squares on the floor. The piles of mealie sacks were stacked neatly in a double tier. He sat down on them his head in his hands. Then he heard someone at the door and he stood up quickly turning to see who it was. It was Lupin. She came in and closed the door with a firm click behind her. She held a letter in her hand and Field realized that it was the commission rejection and a small wave of anger against officialdom of all sorts began to rise inside him. Why the hell should his life be controlled by them? Why the hell should he be judged by senior officers, administrators, parsons, by the small-minded, the mealy-mouthed, the impotent! There was really no need for Lupin to have come all this way to give it to him. She came closer, her skin dusky in the gloom of the hut, her teeth glimmering as she smiled.

'Nkosi,' she whispered, 'you forget.'

She stood very close, her eyes and mouth turning up to him and he realized she had dabbed herself with Milly's perfume. Milly could spurn him, Sarah would leave him, but this girl was available, welcoming, wanting. . . .

'Girl, you are a fool,' he said angrily, 'why don't you leave me alone! Why don't you learn. It will do you no good! Love is madness. Utter destructive madness!'

She didn't understand what he said but he saw the sudden apprehension in her eyes, her mouth opening to protest if not to scream . . . He put his hand over her mouth and caught her soft body in his arms, forcing her down on to the maize sacks.

PART III

CHAPTER FOURTEEN

COHEN BRAKED the Land Rover to stop outside the company welfare centre. 'You think I'm mad, don't you?' said Sarah.

'Yes,' said Cohen, 'bloody mad!'

'You think I'm putting myself into an indefensible position.'

'I know what position I think you're putting yourself into,' said Cohen crudely, 'but I'm too delicate to mention the matter. You want me to come in with you?'

'No, you'd ruin everything.' His words had upset her.

'Thanks,' said Cohen tartly.

'I'm sorry, but you know what I mean.'

'Yes, I know what you mean. . . . Are you certain he's going to be here?'

'Yes, I rang up and made an appointment.'

'What did he say?'

'He was cautious. He wanted to know why I wanted to see him.'

'I bet he did,' said Cohen. 'I'd like to shoot Mister bloody Ali Hassim Khan.'

'He probably feels the same way about you,' she said, putting her hand on the door handle. 'I shan't be long.'

Cohen said, 'Scream if you need any help, and I'll send up a rocket for the B.S.A. police.'

She swung the door open and got out. 'I don't suppose Mr. Ali Hassim Khan rapes white women.'

'No, he leaves that sort of thing to our splendid white policemen,' said Cohen sarcastically.

She lifted her head angrily and Cohen raised his hands in mock defence. 'I take it back! I take it back!'

'So you should.'

'I thought sex might be your last line of appeal if all else fails,' he said bluntly.

She turned away from him and said, 'Oh, you're a beast! You really are impossible!'

Cohen didn't intend to spare her feelings. 'I'll be surprised if money's enough for Ali Hassim Khan,' he said darkly. 'Remember he's also read all that malarky about the greatest sacrifice woman can make.'

She walked towards the building and he called after her. 'Be intelligent! Woman's greatest gift isn't where she thinks it is. It's in the top of her head!'

Sarah climbed the steps to the club premises angrily reflecting that Cohen had placed his finger with diabolical accuracy upon the thought which had pushed into her mind and which she had resolutely rejected as too melodramatic to even warrant consideration. Melodramatic and absurd. If money didn't work, nothing would.

The doorway opened on to a long corridor with empty offices on either side. A young well-dressed Negro was obviously waiting for her. 'You come this way, please.'

As she followed him she could understand why Cohen thought her action illogical. He admitted that her idea might work but thought that Ali Hassim Khan would suspect a trap. But how else could she try and help the man she loved and could not have. She believed she was behaving realistically in leaving Field and marrying Mitchison. She knew she was partly if not wholly to blame for the crime he had committed. The least she could do therefore was to try to help him. He might never know about it, but she could go away comforted by the thought that she had tried.

Ali Hassim Khan's office was bare and uncomfortable. A wooden table with a chair either side, a steel filing cabinet in one corner. He saw her eyes examining the room. He did not get up but motioned her to sit. He said with his peculiar American accent, 'Sorry about the lack of luxury, Miss Van der Huizen, but we're always expecting a raid from the police and they're not particular about the mess they leave.' He lolled back in his chair, looking at her with uncomprising eyes. He pushed a packet of Lucky Strike across the table towards her. 'Smoke?'

She shook her head and he nodded at the young man who still stood in the doorway. 'Okay,' he said shortly.

There was a long silence as she met his bold, almost contemptuous scrutiny. His face was arrogant and hard. Behind the large, black-rimmed spectacles his eyes were dark and hostile. He wore a light-weight, dark blue, worsted suit of American cut, a white shirt and navy blue knitted tie.

He looked at her coldly. He saw a very pretty girl in a suit of heavy turquoise silk; an expensive suit from Italy or some other part of Europe, he knew that; the sort of suit that only white women with money could buy; she had never bought her clothes as yards of coloured cloth from the local Indian trader. Her body would be clean and perfumed. He had known several of her sort in the States, some eager to prove their inexhaustible racial tolerance by jumping into bed with a succession of poor down-trodden Negroes. This one was not like that. She had been raised knowing that the Negro was an inferior being. The suggestion of any physical contact would be repellent. This was the policeman's girl friend; she would be prepared to use her femininity to get what she wanted but sex would not be amongst her bargaining counters. He snapped his Ronson lighter and touched the end of his cigarette with the butane flame, 'What do you want?' he demanded curtly.

She fiddled nervously with her handbag and then, conscious of her action, tightened her fingers around it.

'You brought this case against Inspector Field?' she asked.

He was annoyed that this girl could come to his office and face him as an equal; no African woman within five hundred miles would have the effrontery, the education or the opportunity of such a privilege. 'So that's it.' His voice was cold.

Sarah sat stiffly in her chair. She had known Africans all her life, but had no experience of this sort of man. Intuitively she knew he disliked her. She found this confusing. As a pretty young woman she was treated with absurd deference by older men and as legitimate prey by younger. She understood and appreciated both points of view. But this man was withdrawn, predatory and without warmth. She knew it was going to be difficult.

'You brought the case. You can drop it,' she said.

'The Crown are prosecuting. The African girl provided the evidence. There's nothing I can do.'

'You are one of the chief prosecution witnesses. If you and the other African witness didn't testify there would be no case. You could probably make the girl change her story.'

Ali Hassim Khan tapped cigarette ash gently on to the floor. 'You are trying to pervert the course of justice, Miss Van der Huizen. I'm sure this is a criminal offence.'

The mocking tone of his voice encouraged her. 'I'm sure it is, too. But I thought a subscription to your personal party funds might help you to change your mind.'

The dark eyes narrowed. 'You're cool,' he said. 'Very cool.' Then he added, 'Why the deep interest in Inspector Field?' He knew the answer, but wanted to see her reaction. She had humiliated him by the calculated effrontery of her bribe; he would make it his business to humiliate her in return.

'He's a friend.'

'A *friend*?' The sarcasm was pointed.

She reacted angrily. 'It's none of your damn business anyway.' The words jumped out; she couldn't help herself.

His eyes never left her face. 'Now, now, Miss Van der Huizen,' he said calmly, 'if you want my help you'd better be civil to a poor coloured man.'

Once again his tone mollified her. She said quickly, 'You mean, you *are* interested in this—this proposition.'

'This proposition . . . ?' He regarded her carefully, his eyes deliberately wandering over her body. He knew the fact that he was deliberately misconstruing her meaning was in itself an insult.

She flushed. 'I am willing to pay a thousand pounds into your party funds or your personal bank account.'

'Is that all?' he murmured.

Her voice rose higher. 'I don't know what you mean.'

'Your father is one of the wealthier farmers of the district.'

'Oh, I see.' She tried to cover her confusion, and he added to it by saying, 'What else could I have meant, Miss Van der Huizen?'

She avoided that question. 'It's nothing to do with my father. He wouldn't get mixed up with—' She stopped.

'With dirty niggers,' said Ali Hassim Khan sardonically.

'I wasn't going to say that,' she said, angry again. 'You're putting words into my mouth. Are you interested or not?'

'A thousand pounds,' said Ali Hassim Khan, 'is not enough.'

'It's all the money I've got in my bank account.'

'Ten thousand pounds is not enough, Miss Van der Huizen. A hundred thousand pounds is not enough. You come here with this childish scheme believing that because you are a woman with what they refer to in the West as sex appeal you can bribe me. In Africa women are a cheap commodity, Miss Van der Huizen, to be bought and sold, and we do not set a high price on copulation or the production of children. You and your money and anything else you might think of offering are also cheap commodities. But we do put a high price upon justice. Justice for my people which you are now trying to pervert to save your lover.'

Sarah stood up. 'I'm sorry I came.'

He grinned at her scornfully. 'Oh, don't be sorry, Miss Van der Huizen. We all have to crawl sometimes. You have had little experience. I have had much. You will get better at it as time goes on.'

Cohen saw her come down the steps with a white set face and swung open the door of the Land Rover. She got in and sat there saying nothing. Cohen started the engine.

He drove for five minutes before he said, 'No luck?'

She shook her head. 'He made a fool of me.'

Cohen nodded. 'You gave him the opportunity.' Then he added, 'Don't you want to burst into tears or do something female?'

'Oh, shut up,' she said flatly and Cohen laughed. 'That's better. And at least you tried.'

'I was a fool, an absolute fool. If I'd offered him twenty thousand pounds he'd still have turned me down.'

'Of course he would. What's money compared with victory. And anyway you'll never beat him. Or them. If we have a war and murder each other we've still got to live with the corpses and the survivors. You've got to come to terms.' He paused. 'History will beat us anyway.' He grinned. 'I like making speeches.'

'I know,' she said.

'What are you going to do now? You still going to Johannesburg?'

'Yes.'

'When are you leaving?'

'Friday.'

'Catching a plane Saturday?'

'Yes.'

Cohen paused. 'I shall take a couple of weeks off when the trial comes up. I think he deserves one friendly face amongst all the enemies.'

She hesitated, 'You're real friends, aren't you?'

'Yes.' He paused. 'I don't know why. Never cared much for bloody Englishmen really. Men and women are one thing. With men it's different.' He added hastily in uneasy explanation, 'I don't mean to say we're a couple of old queers. . . .'

'No, I never thought you were.' She added quietly, 'I think you're lucky.'

'So do I,' said Cohen cheerfully. 'I'm surprised women don't make friends more easily. Friendships are often completely illogical, and women qualify on that ticket. Strange. Perhaps they're frightened to make friends?' He thought about it for a second. 'Maybe they haven't got enough time. Maybe it gives away too much of themselves. . . .'

'I don't think you know what you're talking about!' said Sarah.

Milly saw that he'd lost a little of his tan, but he still looked hard and fit. He cocked an eye at her without turning his head, a habit she knew so well and said, 'Didn't think we'd ever meet in a police cell, did we, Milly?'

'This isn't a cell, Bill.'

'Well, I wouldn't exactly call it a drawing room.'

The conversation faltered for a moment. 'You read the letter I sent—about going back to England and getting a divorce?'

He nodded his head. 'Yes, I read it.'

'I just couldn't write a letter and go away, could I? I mean I had to come and see you.'

'I suppose so.' He was not helping very much.

It seemed so strange to her that she could be sitting here talking to the man she'd been married to for more than ten years, arranging the break up of her life, and really not feeling very disturbed about it. It didn't seem real. But then a lot of her life in Africa hadn't seemed real.

'It is the best thing, isn't it?' she insisted.

'I suppose so,' he said dully.

'I expect I should be stronger. I suppose I should be able to put up with gossip. But I can't, Bill, I can't. I've tried and I'm sorry.'

'No need for you to be sorry. You haven't done anything.'

They sat in silence again and she reflected sadly that he was right: she hadn't done anything. Perhaps that was part of the trouble? She'd always been slightly disapproving, slightly against him. In all his enthusiasms, she'd been lukewarm. That he was sitting here waiting to be tried for this dreadful crime must be partly her fault. And she had to get away. She couldn't face up to the women surreptitiously nudging each other in shops and whispering, 'That's her . . . the wife of the one . . . you know . . . with the black girl . . . on the maize sacks.'

'What will you do in England?' he asked.

'Angela's coming with me. We shall live with my folks at first and then we shall get a flat together. I can brush up my shorthand and typing, there's plenty of jobs.'

'I see.' Then, 'I'll get some money from the police and I'll send you some. You can arrange the alimony at the divorce. I'll do my best to keep you going.'

'Money from the police?' She didn't understand.

'The money I've been paying into my pension scheme. They owe me that. I've resigned anyway to save them the trouble of kicking me out.'

'But what will you do, after—after—'

'After I've served my sentence? I don't know. Get a job. Might go to New Zealand or Australia.'

She nodded and continued hesitantly, not knowing quite how to put it, 'That girl. What about that girl?' She tried to keep the bitterness out of her voice.

His voice was flat, non-committal. 'She's gone off to Cape Town to marry someone else.'

'Trust her,' said Milly angrily. 'Cause all the trouble and then go off. . . .'

'She didn't start the trouble between us,' said Field quietly. 'It was there before she arrived.'

'But she's run off now?'

'She knew there was no future with a married man.'

'And now?' Milly's voice was cold.

'Like you, she knows there's no future with a convicted rapist,' he said flatly.

She softened. 'Oh Bill—' she began. Then a memory of Angela's voice echoed in her head. 'You've got to be hard, Milly. He'll be low and you'll feel sorry for him. Cut your losses. He'll never be any good to you. He'll never make you happy.'

Of course, Angela was right as usual. And into the bargain what Bill had said about the other girl's position made sense. Who did want to be married to a convicted rapist?

'So you see, it lets everybody out, doesn't it?' said Field as if reading her thoughts.

There was nothing else to say. She stood up and paused uncertainly. 'Goodbye, Bill. I'm catching the plane next week. The solicitor says that with the evidence he's got . . .' She stopped, not quite certain how to continue, and Field, with a sudden return of his old flippancy, said, 'Oh, there'll be no trouble about the decree. You can call the newspaper headlines as your main witnesses. Adultery on the maize sacks.'

'I didn't mean it that way,' she said, stiffening. 'It's just that . . .'

'Have a good time in England.' He stood up but making no move towards her. 'Goodbye, Milly.'

He watched her leave: awkward and angular, and felt a twinge of regret at seeing her go. But he knew that she would be happier without him. She would settle down with Angela in some flat off the Bayswater Road or in South Ken, go to all the plays, read the right Sunday newspapers, watch television on BBC2; they would fill their minds with enough social and political trivia to give themselves the necessary degree of commitment and an adequate reason for living. She was a nice girl and they had been totally unsuited to each other from the day they first met.

CHAPTER FIFTEEN

The Crown Prosecutor stood up, and cleared his throat. 'The charge is that you, the said William Henry Field, did on the 9th day of July in the storeroom at Chapanda Police Camp unlawfully ravish and carnally know Edze Lupiniyari, an African girl, without her consent and against her will. Do you plead guilty or not guilty to the charge?'

'Not guilty,' said Field. He sat down and caught Pulford's approving nod.

The sunshine streamed through the windows of Salisbury's large, old-fashioned high court room, roofed with black beams, colonial in character. Up on his dais, the scales of justice behind his head, splendid in his wig and robe, Chief Justice Mouncer-Philips peered through his spectacles as Counsel for the Prosecution prepared to outline the case for the Crown.

It was, thought Field, the law in all its majesty, as full of ritual as a witch doctor's ceremony, histrionically satisfying, constitutional, reassuring, predictable.

Herbert Wallace, tall, lean and scholarly, placed one hand on his lapel, 'My Lord, the Crown Case is that the accused who is an Inspector in the B.S.A. Police was the member-in-charge at the police station at Chapanda, when upon the morning of the 9th July the complainant Edze Lupiniyari, who is employed in the accused's household, went to the police camp to deliver a letter to him. He was not in the charge office and she looked around the camp and found him in the small storehouse where the prisoner, it will be found, had gone to check the inventory. She will say that when she entered this man forcibly and against her will raped her and I will bring medical evidence to show that this woman has been assaulted. Other expert forensic evidence will be called to show that semen was found on a maize sack in this store and I will introduce other evidence and exhibits as the case proceeds. My Lord, I would like to bring in my first witness, the Provincial Criminal Investigation Officer. . . .'

He knew his job pretty well. Outline the main facts.

Don't lead with too much technical evidence. Don't bewilder the jury so that they were not sure which was Exhibit 'A' or Exhibit 'F'. Keep the procedure simple and orderly.

Pulford hardly glanced at most of the prosecution witnesses. Dewley gave evidence, breathing official thunder and lightning and the horror of the police department and, to his bitter disappointment, Pulford did not even bother to ask him a single question. Field, knowing that Pulford would recall any prosecution witness he liked, was not perplexed by his tactics. He knew it was very unlikely he would want to recall Assistant Commissioner Dewley. When Sam Kingsley took the stand, however, and corroborated the police evidence, Pulford showed more interest. When the prosecution had finished he approached him. 'Chief Superintendent Kingsley. You have known the defendant for how long?'

Sam Kingsley sucked in his cheeks thoughtfully. 'I should say on and off for nearly fourteen years.'

Field felt a twinge of relief when he heard that homely voice. Here at least was a prosecution witness who would testify on his behalf. He had told Pulford as much.

'That is practically as long as the accused has served in the police force,' said Pulford.

'Yes, sir.'

'Could you elaborate on this a little, Superintendent? How long did the defendant actually serve under you?'

'On numerous occasions,' continued Sam. 'I was the member-in-charge at Chapanda when he arrived straight from police depot recruit training. He served with me for three years. Later he served under me at Banket and Bulawayo and even more recently I was his immediate superior at Umtali.'

'In other words, you probably know as much as or more about the character of the defendant than any officer in the police force?'

Sam did not hesitate. 'Yes, sir.'

Pulford changed his tactics. 'Would you say that the B.S.A. Police Force has great traditions of integrity, justice and fair play behind it?'

'Most certainly.'

'Has this man, in your opinion, been a credit to the Force?'

Again Sam did not hesitate. 'Yes, sir.'

Chief Justice Mouncer-Philips stirred slightly on his bench and adjusted his spectacles. He hadn't intervened for some time; obviously he felt he should remind the jury that he was still alive.

'I would hardly like to suggest to a Defence Counsel of such experience that he is leading the witness and extracting opinion rather than facts, Mr. Pulford,' he said, 'but is this all really relevant?'

Pulford turned towards him, his face innocent of all guile. 'You are quite correct, Your Honour. However, I do feel that this "opinion" of character is of considerable relevance to the defence of my client. In fact, I would like to crave Your Honour's indulgence for a few moments to explain that I am recalling the great traditions of honour surrounding Rhodesia's B.S.A. Police Force for a special reason. One might even say, your honour, that without this police force there would have been no Rhodesia as we know it today. The defendant, for example, is responsible for an area larger than the whole of Wales. This he polices with two European deputies and twelve African constables. . . .'

'Quite so, quite so . . .' murmured Mouncer-Philips, a little impatiently, but Pulford, making his first point to the jury whether the judge liked it or not, went on.

'This police officer has served in the Force with distinction for nearly fourteen years, m'lud. He is a happily married man with a pleasant home. Is it likely that a man of such integrity should lightly toss this away for a few moments of passion . . . ?'

'Mr. Pulford,' interrupted Mouncer-Philips severely, 'you know as well as I do that this rhetoric should be reserved for the time when you address the jury. I see no reason at all for this outburst at this moment. Please continue with your cross-examination and I should be obliged if there are no more digressions of this nature.'

'I have finished my cross-examination of this witness, thank you, m'lud,' said Pulford cheerfully, well satisfied with what he had achieved.

Field saw through his tactics as plainly as Mouncer-Philips and the Prosecuting Counsel. It was always a good idea to get the jury thinking along the lines you wanted them to think as early as possible. How, indeed, they would now ask themselves, could a respectable police officer with such a fine record rape a girl, and a black girl at that? Something very funny must have been going on. Possibly it was all a hideous mistake?

With the police evidence completed, the prosecution counsel took the medical witnesses slowly through their evidence. Whenever it was necessary he went over it twice and, as Pulford said afterwards, he was surprised he did not draw them diagrams. Pulford did not contest either the forensic or the medical evidence; he asked no questions, but when Matshilobe, the first African witness, took the stand he immediately became much more interested. Matshilobe gave his evidence through the Court Interpreter, Mr. Medzedzi, well-known and respected servant in Salisbury's courts, who spoke half a dozen African languages fluently. He was tall, silver-haired and seemed to carry as much authority as the judge.

Again the counsel for the prosecution cross-examined the witness with skill and care. Matshilobe stated that he had been passing through the compound to call on one of his friends when he had heard a noise in the storeroom. Purely by chance he had glanced inside and seen the accused lying on the maize sacks with the woman Lupiniyari. A few seconds later he had seen her run from the storeroom in a distressed condition and, thinking she needed help, he had caught up with her in the house where she worked for the accused. She had then told him that she had been raped by the accused so he at once had her taken to see Mr. Ali Hassim Khan. The cross-examination was exhaustive and lengthy. Herbert Wallace sat down, well satisfied, and Pulford got up.

'You say you "took" this girl to see Ali Hassim Khan?'

'Yes.'

'You took her of her own free will, you did not threaten her?'

'No.'

'Why did you take her to see Ali Hassim Khan? You were

on police property; why did you not go to the charge office and make a complaint there?'

Matshilobe hesitated but Pulford's attitude seemed harmless enough; he did not appear to be threatening.

'As a policeman was committing the offence it did not seem to be of any use to complain at the police station.'

'But why go to Ali Hassim Khan? Why not the District Commissioner or even your own chief?'

'Ali Hassim Khan is a good man who protects the interests of the Africans.'

'I see,' said Pulford a shade more belligerently. 'He is the leader of a political party in this area, I understand?'

'Yes.'

'Are you a member of this same political group, Mr. Matshilobe?'

'Yes.'

'And you work for Mr. Ali Hassim Khan?'

'Yes.'

Pulford did not press the point. 'One last question,' he said cordially. 'You are a Mashona?'

'Yes.'

'Thank you, that is all.'

Ali Hassim Khan was the next witness for the prosecution. As usual he was immaculately dressed in a pale fawn suit, a white silk shirt and a tan tie; Field had to admire his taste in clothes. He corroborated Matshilobe's evidence down to the last detail. And again Pulford rose to cross-examine.

'Mr. Ali Hassim Khan. When this woman Lupiniyari was brought to you by your employee, Mr. Matshilobe, what condition was she in?'

'She was weeping and distressed.'

'And what did she say?'

'She said she had been raped against her will by Inspector Field.'

'You talked to her and established this fact?'

'Yes.'

'Might I ask you what you do for a living?'

Ali Hassim Khan hesitated and looked at the judge, and Mouncer-Philips, leaning over, said reprovingly, 'Is this really relevant, Mr. Pulford?'

'Quite relevant, your honour,' said Pulford coolly.

'Well, if the Prosecution has no objection, you may proceed.' The Prosecution had no objection and Pulford repeated his question.

'I represent the Zambezi Independent People's Party in this part of Rhodesia,' said Ali Hassim Khan warily.

Pulford was as mild as the spring sunshine. 'Which means you collect party subscriptions and send them to your headquarters in Salisbury?'

'Amongst other duties, yes,' said Ali Hassim Khan. He added pugnaciously, 'Is that against the law?'

Pulford sighed as if his feelings had been bitterly hurt. 'Mr. Ali Hassim Khan, I am not suggesting that it is against the law. But I *am* suggesting that you are here to *answer* my questions, not ask them . . . Now your name, Ali Hassim Khan, was not the name which was first entered on your birth certificate?'

'No.'

'What was your name before you changed it?'

'Tutani Nyanadali.'

'Are you a Mashona?'

'I am an African,' said Ali Hassim Khan with hostility.

'Mr. Ali Hassim Khan,' said Pulford wearily, 'we are all Africans, but for the purpose of identification we separate ourselves into various tribal structures, Hausa, Fulani, Ibo, Kikuyu, Masai, English, Irish, Welsh, Scots. I will accept you as a citizen of the world if you will accept the fact that you were born Mashona.'

'Yes.'

'Thank you,' said Pulford. 'That is all.'

It was a long hot day and Field was glad when it was over. In one of the interview rooms beneath the High Court where Pulford and he usually talked together the barrister said, 'Well, how d'you think it went?'

'They wiped the floor with us. I expect the jury thought you'd had a mental block.'

Pulford waved his cigarette airily in the air, scattering ash over the wide square wooden table which occupied most of the room. 'Perhaps,' he said, 'perhaps.' He darted a quick glance at Field. 'But you weren't particularly worried?'

'Not particularly.'

'Why not?'

Field was blunt and matter of fact. 'Because I think you're an old fox and you've got something up your sleeve.'

Pulford showed his discoloured teeth in a slight grin.

'That is no way to talk to the Honourable Counsel for the Defence,' he said. He paused. 'Tell me, Inspector Field, do you know how many languages exist in Africa?'

'A hell of a lot.'

'Correct,' said Pulford affably. 'Seven hundred, to be fairly precise, of which more than three hundred have never been transcribed or recorded.'

'Fascinating,' said Field.

'I think so,' said Pulford, obviously well pleased with himself. 'I'm not sure that old poop Wallace will think so tomorrow when we have little Lupin in the box.'

'You're not going to try any rough stuff, I hope,' warned Field.

'Rough stuff? Why, Inspector Field . . .'

'I am not an Inspector any longer. I am a plain civilian. Remember that.'

'All right then, Mr. Field, as you have seen I am the very personification of patience and tolerance with the witnesses, especially with those two wide boys, Mr. Ali Hassim Khan and his friend, Mr. Matshilobe.'

'You won't shake *their* evidence.'

'I don't want to.' He paused and glanced at his watch. 'By the way, after you've served your time what do you intend to do?'

Field smiled cynically. 'Know any good jobs for ex-policeman rapists? I'm sure you could give me a reference.'

'I'm being serious.'

'So am I. I think I probably will leave Rhodesia. New Zealand, I thought, or Australia—a nice open-air life for a healthy man.'

Pulford went across to the door. He opened it and spoke to the warder standing just outside the door. Then he turned back to Field.

'I forgot to tell you,' he said. 'A friend of yours called on me and wanted to see you. We'll meet in court tomorrow.'

For a fraction of time a wild hope rose in Field's heart. But of course it was impossible—impossible!

It was. Cohen's ugly face with its familiar grin appeared around the doorway. 'Hi, man,' he said. 'Any of these prison warders been torturing you lately?'

Field sighed heavily. 'God,' he said, 'doesn't your sense of humour ever alter?'

'Someone's got to be the life and soul of the party,' said Cohen, at once belligerent.

'Sit down,' said Field indicating the second chair at the far end of the table, 'make yourself at home.'

'Quite palatial, isn't it,' commented Cohen looking at the plain wooden chair with distaste. 'Don't they even provide cushions?'

'No particular reason you came, I suppose?' asked Field warily. 'You haven't got an armed gang outside waiting to storm the court?'

Cohen's eyes opened innocently. 'Me?' he said in an injured voice.

'You're not going to slip me a stick of dynamite or a capsule of hydrocyanic acid?'

'Listen,' said Cohen, hurt, 'just because I suggested we did a bunk into the Congo or some civilized state farther north instead of you rotting for ten years in gaol . . .'

Field winced. 'Ten years! Leave that to Mouncer-Philips, please.'

'. . . For an offence which is purely an athletic exercise . . .'

'I must ask Pulford to try that line on the judge . . .'

'I once met a small black Negress in the back streets of Duala,' said Cohen dreamily. ' "Not many gentlemen find their way into the dark corners of this town," she said. "I would be grateful therefore if you will take this opportunity of possessing me. See, here you have the apparatus for the act and the price is low. Four hundred Cameroon francs for an interval of pleasure the memory of which you will carry to your grave . . . " ' Cohen paused. 'She was a very polite girl,' he said, 'missionary educated. I am sure Mr. Livingstone would have been pleased. Such politeness. Such a picturesque turn of phrase.'

'How are things out in the backwoods?' asked Field.

'Chapanda?'

'Yes.'

'No different. I'm still after Mrs. Crosby but she seems disinterested.'

'You surprise me,' grinned Field. He paused, wondering if he dare bring up the subject of Sarah. Plainly Cohen knew a lot about their affair. He decided to risk it; he wanted to know very badly.

'Any news of Sarah Van der Huizen?' he asked quietly.

'Oh, her,' said Cohen. 'I wondered if you'd ask that.' He grinned and Field was piqued. 'What's so funny?'

'Well, actually she's waiting outside. That's the real reason I came. She approached me in Chapanda and I said the best thing we could do was to go and see your lawyer and see if he could wangle us in.'

Field sat bolt upright. 'She's here in Salisbury?'

'She's just the other side of that door waiting to know if you want to see her.'

'Oh, God,' said Field, 'do I want to see her?'

'I take it that means you do. All right, hang on for a second.'

Disbelievingly Field watched him walk across to the door, open it and walk through. Five seconds later Sarah, in a white sleeveless dress, without a hat, came in. She walked across to the table and sat in the chair vacated by Cohen. She put her white handbag on the table in front of her. She looked small and forlorn, a little frightened.

'Hello, Bill,' she whispered. 'Is this what I'm supposed to do?'

'I don't know,' said Field hoarsely, 'I've never done it before.' The table now seemed enormous, stretching between them, a great plain of scrubbed wood.

He stammered, 'I thought—I thought you were in South Africa—married?' A terrible thought ran into his mind. Perhaps she was married, just back from the Cape on a visit?

'Are you married?' he demanded desperately.

'No,' she said, 'I couldn't.'

'Why not? Why couldn't you?'

'Because I love you,' she said quietly. The silence was long and complete.

She went on in a rush, 'Bill, I tried. I tried! I thought it was best that we should forget each other, and when you told me about Lupin I thought, "It's come true, we'll ruin each other." So I raced in a sort of terror to Salisbury and went to see David. And he kissed me, Bill, and I couldn't stand it. And at the airport he put his arm around my waist and I remembered you putting your arm around my waist at Beira that night; and in the plane he put his hand on my arm as if he owned me and possessed me and I thought, "What's he doing? He doesn't own me and possess me. I belong to Inspector Field of Scotland Yard," and by the time we landed at Cape Town I knew it was no good. I knew that if I went through with it I'd bring terrible unhappiness to him as I'd brought terrible unhappiness to you, and he's really a very nice young man, Bill. I tried to tell him all this, but I don't think he understood and he got angry and said it was just because I was infatuated by that "bloody copper" . . .'

She smiled across at Field and he could see that her eyes were full of tears. '. . . So you see, Bill, I got my own words thrown back at me.'

Field was finding it hard to say anything.

'I couldn't stand him touching me, and I couldn't stand him kissing me. I'd given myself to you and I couldn't give myself to anyone else. It's silly and old-fashioned, isn't it?'

'No,' said Field. 'No, it isn't.'

'I knew it was no use. But I didn't know what to do. So I stayed in Cape Town with my aunt. And then I found I couldn't live there either. I kept thinking of that week we had in Beira.' She paused and said slowly, 'I remember every second of it.'

Field found himself smiling. 'So do I,' he said, 'and I've had a long time to think about it.'

She smiled, too. 'What do you remember?' she whispered.

'That first time. When we'd just arrived. I woke in the middle of the night and you were sleeping quietly so I tiptoed out to the top of a sand dune and looked at the stars and the sea and thought of you warm and soft and only a few yards away . . . I understood then why man had danced fertility dances and burnt bonfires to the seasons and raised great stone images in his own little likeness. I didn't know life could be lived at such a level until I made love to you. I didn't know such emotional territories even existed to be explored . . .'

'Oh, Bill,' she said quietly. She lowered her head and stared at the table.

'I love you, Sarah. Everything I've done, and I've probably done some terrible things, were all because I loved you . . .'

'You haven't done any terrible things,' she said protestingly. 'You're a man.'

Field smiled again. 'That doesn't really excuse much, Sarah.' He added after a pause, 'What did your father say?'

'He told me to go and see you. He insisted you were a good man, and if a woman finds a good man, she should stick to him.'

'Your father's straight out of the Old Testament,' said Field affectionately.

'What will they—I mean—how long will you—'

She was confused and Field helped her out. 'The sentence one can expect for a crime of this sort is three years. There was one other case about thirty years ago and he got three years. The best one could expect is two, with remission about nineteen—twenty months.'

She looked down at the table and said in a low voice, 'I suppose—afterwards—you'll want to go back to your wife.'

'No,' said Field. 'No, she's going back to England. She said she couldn't stand life out here and what I'd done made it even more impossible. She said she would divorce me; it would be better for both of us.'

There was a long, long pause this time. So long that Field wondered if she'd heard his words. Then she said in a very quiet voice, 'If I wanted—if I wanted, would you come—do you think that we—I mean—' She stopped.

It was Field's turn to be silent. 'Sarah,' he said gently, 'is it fair on you? I'm twice as old as you are. I'd be three years older when I came out. And I'd be a convicted criminal. It wouldn't be very nice. And you're young . . .'

'I'd be three years older myself,' she said passionately.

'But it's such a long time.'

'Tell me,' she pleaded, 'just answer my question. Say "yes" or "no". Please!'

'Yes,' he said, 'yes. It's madness and unfair to you and you'll have time to change your mind. But yes—yes.'

'Oh, Bill!' she said, 'Oh, Bill!' And she left her seat to rush around the table. He stood up and caught her in his arms. Her body was soft and warm. She clung to him as if it was the last time they would ever meet.

The door had opened and the young warder, coughing politely, was at the door.

'All right, Officer,' said Field. 'She's going now.'

She lifted her mouth to be kissed and, as she drew away, she said in tears, 'I'll pray for you. Oh, Bill, I'll pray for you.'

Field looked at Lupin as she took the witness stand, a pretty, milk-chocolate skinned girl in a new print dress, a gold bangle on her arm, silver earrings dangling against her cheeks, and thought how strange it was—how odd that a chance meeting should end in such a conclusion. You met someone at a dance or an office, in a bus queue and they haunted or plagued, depressed or delighted you for the rest of your life. If he hadn't walked up the mountains to find the rain goddess, he would not be standing in this dock.

'You are,' said the Counsel for the Prosecution, 'Edze Lupiniyari?' Mr. Medzedzi offered the question to Lupin and she smiled happily. She liked nice simple questions.

'Yes,' she answered.

'Medical evidence has established your age at about eighteen years old. You would agree that you are eighteen years old?'

'Yes.'

'I believe that from November last year until quite recently you have been a housemaid in the home of the accused at Chapanda?'

'Yes.'

'What sort of work did you do?'

'I dusted and I washed the floors and I made the beds and I cleaned the house.'

'Now will you please tell the court what happened on the morning in question.'

'I was working in the house of Inspector Field and he came in. He was reading a letter which he put on the table.

Then he went out again, and I saw that he had left the letter on the table. I thought that he might need it so I decided to take it to him. He was not in his office and I saw him walking across the compound. I followed him and I saw him go into the storeroom. I followed him into the storeroom and it was there that it happened.'

'What happened? Please tell the court what happened.'

'This man took hold of me and threw me down and tore my blouse and took me.'

'He seized you forcibly?'

'Yes.'

'Did you resist him?'

'Yes.'

'Did you scream?'

'Yes.'

'Why was it you were not heard?'

'He covered my mouth with his hand.'

'And he had intercourse with you?'

'Yes.'

'And this was against your will?'

'Yes.'

'You did not accept this man?'

'No.'

The Prosecution Counsel took her through her evidence very slowly and very thoroughly and, after a rather hesitant start, as her confidence grew, Lupin began to enjoy herself.

When Herbert Wallace sat down and Pulford approached her, however, Field could sense her nervousness. No doubt she had been warned that he would be rude and rough. Instead he smiled at her with great friendliness and Lupin, sweet innocent creature that she was, smiled back.

'You,' he said, 'are Edze Lupiniyari?'

'Yes.'

'Now, I am going to ask you a few questions, Miss Lupiniyari, and I do not wish you to be frightened or worried. If you do not understand the question, I will repeat it for you. Do you understand me?'

'Yes.'

'I do not wish to frighten you or worry you. All I wish is to hear your story. Do you understand?'

'Yes.'

'Now, when you first met Inspector Field you were the rain goddess of a tribe of nomadic people called the Mansuta who lived in the mountains?'

The Interpreter seemed to have a little trouble getting that across to Lupin, but eventually she said, 'Yes.'

At this point the Prosecuting Counsel, who obviously did not trust this pacific charming Pulford, got up to object. 'My Lord, surely all this has been established earlier and is purely irrelevant to the case?'

Mouncer-Philips leaned forward. 'I must say, Mr. Pulford, there seems to be some substance in the objection of the prosecution. What is your line of reasoning?'

Pulford was equally patient. 'My Lord, I feel that it is essential that the relationship between the accused and this woman should be clearly delineated. If I seem to be spreading myself unduly, then I beg the court to bear with me as the purpose of this cross-examination will quickly become apparent.'

'Very well,' said Mouncer-Philips, 'you may proceed.'

Pulford turned back to Lupin. 'Did you enjoy your life as a rain goddess? Were you happy with those people?'

This question again confused her. Sometimes she was happy. At others, she was not.

'Now, Inspector Field took you down from the mountains and you appeared as a witness in another court case some time ago?'

'Yes.'

'Were you well treated during this period?'

'Yes.'

'But when the trial was over and you were free to go back to the Mansuta tribe, you did not do this?'

'No.'

'Why?'

'I was afraid. And besides I did not know where they were.'

'In other words you preferred to stay in Chapanda, in the police compound where you had been living before that first trial took place?'

'Yes.'

'You lived quite happily in the police compound with Mrs. Strongbow, the wife of an African police sergeant, and during the day you worked in the household of the accused?'

'Yes.'

'Now, after the alleged rape in the storeroom you rushed out and you met Mr. Matshilobe?'

'Yes.'

'Where did you meet him?'

'He came to the house.'

'And he took you to see Ali Hassim Khan?'

'Yes.'

'But he does not speak any of your language. He only speaks Chishona and probably a little English. What did he say to you?'

'He said, "Come".'

'You understood that in Chishona?'

'Yes.'

'Where did you meet Ali Hassim Khan?'

'At the Timber Company in an office at the back.'

'I see. And how did you get there?'

'I went on Matshilobe's bicycle.'

'You mean you sat on the crossbar while he pedalled?'

'Yes.'

'I see,' said Pulford. 'A most edifying spectacle, I am sure.'

A rustle of laughter ran around the courtroom. Mouncer-Philips looked displeased and the Prosecution Counsel got to his feet to protest. 'My Lord, it seems to me that the Defence Counsel is raising matters which are quite irrelevant to the case. I feel . . .'

Mouncer-Philips stared at him coldly. 'It seems to me that the Defence Counsel is raising perfectly legitimate issues, Mr. Wallace. Pray continue, Mr. Pulford.'

'Thank you, m'lud,' said Pulford politely. He turned back to Lupin. 'And when you got to see Mr. Ali Hassim Khan you could not speak to him in your language?'

'No.'

'Why not?'

'He does not speak Shangaan.'

'So what did you do?'

'They got an interpreter.'

'Did he speak your language?'

'Not very well.'

'But sufficiently for you to understand?'

'Yes.'

The Prosecution Counsel was again on his feet. 'My Lord, I really must protest at this line of questioning. The girl was examined by a police interpreter at the scene of the alleged offence; he spoke her language perfectly. Whether or not my clients speak perfect Shangaan seems to be of little consequence at this time.'

Mouncer-Philips looked over his spectacles at Pulford. 'Perhaps you would care to comment on this point, Mr. Pulford.'

'My line of reasoning is this, my lord. Neither Matshilobe nor Ali Hassim Khan speak one word of the intricate Shangaan dialect which is the mother tongue of this girl. Matshilobe claims he saw this alleged rape committed and took this witness to Ali Hassim Khan, but he also speaks no word of this language. I am sure the Prosecution will not wish to argue my contention. If they do, we have with us, acting as Court Interpreter, Mr. Medzedzi, who as you know has been a faithful servant here for many years and speaks very many African languages and dialects fluently. He will within a few seconds be able to corroborate that indeed neither Mr. Matshilobe nor Mr. Ali Hassim Khan speaks this Shangaan dialect.'

The eyes of the court turned towards the Prosecuting Counsel. He made no move to intervene; he knew Pulford too well for that. However, Mouncer-Philips was not letting Defence Counsel have it all his own way. 'The line of your reasoning still seems a little unclear to me, Mr. Pulford,' he said.

'I am suggesting, your lordship, that the very idea of rape was put into this girl's mouth by the two witnesses for the prosecution—not maliciously, perhaps, but by virtue of the fact that they did not understand what she was trying to say. This girl, remember, has been the willing tool of men from her very earliest days; as a child she was beaten and ill-treated by men; as a young girl she was sold as a rain-maker to a strange tribe and then induced to take part in all sorts of peculiar ceremonies. All her life, poor sad innocent creature that she is, she has been abused and roughly treated by men. When this man, Matshilobe, caught her by the arm, I will wager she was terrified by him, and prepared to say whatever he told her to say.'

'We are not interested in your wagers, Mr. Pulford,' said Mouncer-Philips, now rather enjoying himself. 'We are interested in your factual evidence.'

'Indeed, my Lord,' said Pulford smoothly, 'and factually I intend to prove my contention. Let me put it this way. In my opinion this case stands or falls on one point and one point alone. What were the exact words used by Edze Lupiniyari when she was first accosted by this man Matshilobe? His evidence is useless because he did not understand what she said. The evidence of Ali Hassim Khan is useless because he did not know what she said. The police evidence is useless because she had been so intimidated by the time she got to them she would have admitted to rape by the entire police post at Chapanda if so asked.'

'Mr. Pulford!' said Mouncer-Philips impatiently. 'I would ask you . . .'

But Pulford was in full cry. He raised his hand placatingly. 'One moment, Your Honour,' he said. 'If you will allow me now to cross-examine the witness, I think I shall be able to prove my point.'

'It seems to me you are balancing your entire case upon a very precarious point indeed,' said Mouncer-Philips. 'However, if you wish to take such risks, I am prepared to allow you to continue.'

'Thank you, m'lud. I would before I start, however, like to make matters as clear as possible for the jury. Many of them, I am sure, know that no word exists in the Chishona, Sindebele or Shangaan language for the word "love" in the romantic sense in which it is used in English. My contention is that Miss Lupiniyari almost certainly used the word current in her language "Ng'oniwe" to Matshilobe. She could have meant, "I have been raped", or "I have been seduced", or "I have been spoiled", or "I have just been loved". I am sure, ladies and gentlemen of the jury, that you can understand the quite fantastic importance that I attach to these words used by the witness and what the witness *meant* by the words she used. Now, Miss Lupiniyari has not understood a sentence of what I have said for the past few minutes because Mr. Medzedzi has not been translating. She is therefore completely neutral, completely unbiased, completely in the dark and should be able to answer my questions without prejudice or intimidation.'

He turned back to Lupin and again smiled at her encouragingly. To Field it seemed that the entire courtroom, including the judge himself, was holding its breath at Pulford's astounding histrionics.

Pulford said to Mr. Medzedzi, 'Make it clear to Miss Lupiniyari that I would like to ask her a few more questions and that she must not be afraid. Ask her if she understands that clearly.'

'Yes.'

'Tell her that she can say what she wants to in this courtroom and no one will be angry with her, and that she will suffer no retribution when she leaves this courtroom. Does she understand that quite clearly?'

'Yes.'

'Does she also understand that the reputation and character and the very life of this man, Inspector Field, depend upon her speaking the truth?'

'Yes.'

'Before the incident of which she complains, what did she think of Inspector Field?'

'I thought he was a good man.'

'So let us go back to the beginning of this matter. Now, you say that the defendant left a letter in the lounge and you took it after him?'

'Yes.'

'Why did you take it to him.'

'I thought it was perhaps important.'

Field knew exactly why Lupin had brought the letter. She would be bored in the house. Abdul would nag her. But she could walk across the police compound with her hips swaying and her head held high, quite certain that every prisoner in the compound and every African policeman within fifty yards would enjoy the spectacle. There she was, walking through the sunshine, bold and beautiful, and carrying in her hand an important letter to her master. It was much better than dusting silly old furniture.

'You could have left the letter at home and waited for him to come back?'

Lupin looked thoughtful. 'I thought it was better if I gave it to him.'

'So you saw him go into the storeroom and you went in after him. Did you close the door behind you?'

'Yes.'

'You went into the storeroom, therefore, and you went up close to the defendant and you gave him the letter?'

'Yes.'

'What did you say to him?'

'I said, "Nkosi, here is the letter you left behind".'

'And then he attacked you?' 'Yes.' 'Do you know why he attacked you?' 'No.'

'But you must have some idea! You came into the storeroom and closed the door behind you and you are a very pretty girl, and you stood very close to him. Why do you think he attacked you?'

Lupin looked puzzled. Her reply was low and the interpreter hesitated. 'Please tell the court what she said,' said Pulford sternly.

'It is the way with men.'

'I see.' Pulford now swung the point of his attack. 'Now, when Matshilobe followed you to the house he asked you various questions?'

'Yes.'

'Did you understand what he said?'

'Only very little.'

'Did he ask you what you had done?'

'Yes.'

'Tell me exactly what you replied. The exact words, please, in the dialect that you used?'

'I said, "Ng'oniwe".'

'Ah,' said Pulford, ' "Ng'oniwe".' He made no attempt to translate to the jury but said, 'After this man forced you, you lay next to him on the maize sacks, for how long?'

'I don't remember.'

'For a few seconds—a few minutes?'
'A few minutes.'
'You did not run out into the compound shouting that you had been attacked?'
'No.'
'You lay next to him until you were scared by seeing a face at the window?'
'Yes.'
'And you were frightened because you thought *you* had done wrong?'
'Yes.'
'You knew this man's wife was away and you thought you had done wrong?'
'Yes.'
'So when Matshilobe caught you in the house, you said "Ng'oniwe"?'
'Yes.'
'Did that mean that you had made love together?'
'Yes.'
'It means that you had lain with this man?'
'Yes.'
'He had not forced you—or if there was force it was a force you expected and submitted to gladly?'
Lupin hesitated for a second and then she said, 'Yes.'
'Matshilobe took the wrong meaning of what you said. You said you had been "loved" by this man and he took it that you had been raped by this man?'
'Yes.'
'So all the time the word "Ng'oniwe", which you used, meant love in the sense of love freely given, and not rape?'
'Yes.'
'It meant that the love between you was mutual and that the charge against him of raping you is false?'
Lupin raised her eyes defiantly to Pulford's, conscious of the noise of consternation in the court, and Field could not hear what she said. But Mr. Medzedzi's translation was quite clear and audible. 'I made love to this man because I wanted to,' she said. 'I loved him.'

In the interview room the events of the past ten minutes

seemed already remote. Mouncer-Philips had accepted the Prosecution's withdrawal of the charge graciously. He had thanked the jury for their attendance and the fact that they had been saved the onerous and indeed thankless task of having to listen through to the end of the case. He had complimented Pulford on his able—'I might even add dramatic'—handling of the case, and he had discharged the prisoner who had indeed committed a grave indiscretion but an indiscretion not answerable to in law . . .

Pulford, Cohen, Sarah and Field sat on the scrubbed table while Cohen opened the whisky and spread out four glasses and said, 'Christ, man, if I'd had notice I'd have got champagne. But there was no time to ice it, and hell, man, I thought you were going to get ten years . . .'

Sarah sat very close against Field and said nothing.

'When I commit my next crime, will you defend me, Mr. Pulford?' asked Cohen affably.

Pulford accepted the half tumbler of whisky. 'I'll consider it for a large fee,' he said. His eye caught Field's and he raised the glass. Field raised his in return.

'Professionalism wins out,' he said.

Pulford smiled. 'The crime didn't deserve the punishment it might have got. Besides, you had tried and condemned yourself before the case ever started.'

'It was pretty bloody clever of you all the same,' said Cohen filling his own glass half full.

Pulford sipped his whisky. 'No. The Crown were injudicious to pin their entire case upon that girl. It was quite obvious that she was acting under duress from the very beginning. In the end she was acting under *my* duress, and if the prosecution could have got her back in the witness-box she would probably have reversed her story all over again and sworn she was raped. With coaching she would make a very good actress.' He looked at Sarah and grinned. 'If Miss Van der Huizen will forgive the impertinence, ladies are like that.'

'I'm glad they are,' said Field gallantly.

There was a little laughter and, after a few more minutes and more whisky, Pulford said, 'You're taking a little holiday now, I expect?'

'Yes,' said Sarah shyly, 'we're going to a place I know in Beira. I've already rung up and made the booking.'

Field turned to her in amazement. 'You mean you've rung Sequiros?'

'Yes. Do you mind?'

'No,' said Field.

'All right,' intervened Cohen, 'I'm taking this brilliant advocate off now to fill him full of more whisky and extract all the secrets of his success.'

'You'll never let him get a word in edgeways,' laughed Field.

Cohen grinned. 'He's probably done all the talking he wants to anyway,' he said cheerfully. 'Besides, he'll be just as interested in the secrets of *my* success.'

He took Pulford by the elbow and steered him towards the door. The older man said affably, 'Don't forget to send us an invitation to the wedding.'

Cohen said, 'And don't think this is a happy ending. You're just lucky enough to have a happy beginning.'

When they had gone Field took her arm. 'We'd better leave,' he said. 'I don't quite know how to do it. I don't think it's quite the same as checking out of an hotel.'

She stood very close to him and he put his arms around her waist.

'You really *do* want to go to Beira, don't you?' she said.

'More than anything else I can think of.'

'Then we can talk about everything.'

'Discuss where we set up home, for example, and how I get a job.'

'Father wants us to take over the farm.'

He pulled her closer. 'Suppose I can't be any worse as a farmer than a policeman.'

She was silent for a second, then said timidly, 'He expects us to have lots and lots of children. I don't mind. Do you?'

There was something in her tone which puzzled him. He leant back to look at her, remembering Milly's bitter accusation. 'I'm not sure it's possible,' he began.

She leaned her head against his chest and sighed.

'Oh, yes it is,' she said softly. 'Everything seemed to start in Beira.'